Praise for #1
New York Times Bestselling Author

Sandra Brown

NOVELS BY SANDRA BROWN

Deadline
Low Pressure
Lethal
Mirror Image
Where There's Smoke
Charade
Exclusive
Envy
The Switch
The Crush
Fat Tuesday
Unspeakable
The Witness
The Alibi
Standoff
Best Kept Secrets
Breath of Scandal
French Silk

SANDRA BROWN

BREATH

of

SCANDAL

GRAND CENTRAL
PUBLISHING

NEW YORK   BOSTON

Grand Central Publishing
Hachette Book Group
1290 Avenue of the Americas
New York, NY 10104
www.HachetteBookGroup.com

Grand Central Publishing is a division of Hachette Book Group, Inc.
The Grand Central Publishing name and logo are trademarks of Hachette Book Group, Inc.

The Hachette Speakers Bureau provides a wide range of authors for speaking events. To find out more, go to www.hachettespeakersbureau.com or call (866) 376-6591.

The publisher is not responsible for websites (or their content) that are not owned by the publisher.

Printed in the United States of America

Originally published in hardcover by Hachette Book Group

First mass market edition: July 1991
Reissued: March 2015

10 9 8
OPM

Prologue

New York City, 1990

She was going back to Palmetto.

Standing at her office window, Jade Sperry adjusted the blinds and gazed down twenty stories at the snarled traffic around Lincoln Center. A cold wind whipped around the street corners with the impetus of the city buses that belched noxious fumes into the polluted air. Looking like frantic, yellow beetles, taxi cabs scurried from one congested traffic lane to another. Pedestrians never broke their stride, but continued to move, clutching their belongings.

It had been a struggle for Jade to adjust to such constant motion when she moved to New York. At first intersections proved hazardous. There was nothing quite as terrifying as standing on the curb of a busy avenue in downtown Manhattan, wondering which would mow her down first—a menacing taxi, a lumbering city bus, or the hoards of people pressing her from behind and growing impatient with the out-of-towner whose speech was as slow as her hesitant gait.

As with every challenge, Jade had ducked her head and tackled it. She didn't move as fast, or hear as quickly, or speak as rapidly as the natives, but she wasn't intimidated by them—just different. She hadn't been bred to bustle. Jade Sperry had been raised in an environment where the most industrious individual on a summer day might be a dragonfly skimming a tidal swamp.

By the time she reached New York, she had become accustomed to hard work and self-sacrifice. So she had acclimated and survived, because her South Carolinian stiff-necked pride was just as characteristic as her speech.

Today, it had all paid off. Thousands of hours of planning, plotting, and hard work had finally been rewarded. No one could guess how many years and tears she had invested in her return to her hometown.

She was going back to Palmetto.

There were those there who had much to atone for, and Jade would see to it that they did. The restitution she had dreamed of was within her grasp. She now had the power to make it happen.

She continued to gaze out the window, but little of the street scene below registered with her. Rather, she saw tall grass swaying in coastal marshes. She smelled pungent salt air and heady magnolias. She tasted low-country cooking. The skyscrapers were replaced by tall pines; the broad avenues became sluggishly flowing channels. She remembered how it felt to breathe air so heavy and thick that it didn't even stir the limp, gray Spanish moss that dripped from the branches of ancient live oaks.

She was going back to Palmetto.

And when she got there, all hell was going to break loose.

Chapter 1

———◆———

Palmetto, South Carolina, 1976

The hell you say!"

"Swear to God."

"You're a liar, Patchett."

"How 'bout it, Lamar? Am I lying, or not? Can't a good whore put a rubber on you using only her mouth?"

Lamar Griffith divided his quizzical look between his best friends, Hutch Jolly and Neal Patchett. "I don't know, Neal. Can she?"

"Why'd I bother asking you," Neal scoffed. "You've never been to a whore."

"And you have?" Hutch guffawed.

"Yeah, I have. Lots of times."

The three high school seniors occupied a booth at the local Dairy Barn. Hutch and Lamar shared one vinyl bench. Neal was sprawled along the other, across the pink Formica table.

"I don't believe a word of it," Hutch said.

"My old man took me to her."

Lamar grimaced at the thought. "Weren't you embarrassed?"

"Hell no."

Hutch looked at Lamar scornfully. "He's lying, you fool." Turning back to Neal, he asked, "Where is this whorehouse?"

Neal checked his reflection in the plate glass window at the end of the booth. His handsome face gazed back at him. Just the right amount of dark blond bangs dipped low over the brows above his sexy green eyes. His maroon and white high school letter jacket looked well used and hung jauntily off his shoulders.

"I didn't say he took me to a whorehouse. I said he took me to a whore."

Hutch Jolly wasn't as physically attractive as his friend Neal. He was a big, gawky boy with wide, bony shoulders and bright red hair. His ears poked straight out from the sides of his head. Leaning in closer, he licked his fleshy lips. His voice was soft and conspiratorial. "You mean to tell me there's a whore right here in town? Who is she? What's her name? Where does she live?"

Neal gave his friends a lazy smile. "You think I'm going to share a secret like that with you two? Next thing I'd know, you'd be beating down her door, making damn fools of yourselves. I'd be ashamed to claim I knew you."

He signaled the waitress and ordered another round of cherry Cokes. Once their fountain drinks had been delivered, Neal sneaked a silver flask from the inside pocket of his letter jacket and liberally laced his drink before offering it to the others. Hutch helped himself to the bourbon.

Lamar declined. "No, thanks. I've had enough."

"Chickenshit," Hutch said, gouging him in the gut with his elbow.

Neal slipped the flask back into his jacket pocket. "My old man says there are two things a man never gets enough of. Whiskey and women."

"Amen." Hutch agreed with anything Neal said.

"Don't you agree, Lamar?" Neal taunted.

The dark-haired boy shrugged. "Sure."

Frowning with displeasure, Neal flopped back against the booth. "You're getting downright serious on us, Lamar. If you can't keep up, we'll have to start leaving you behind."

Lamar's dark eyes filled with worry. "What do you mean 'keep up'?"

"I mean like raising hell. I mean like getting laid. I mean like getting drunk."

"His mama doesn't like for him to do those bad things." Hutch effeminately folded his large, ruddy hands beneath his chin and batted his eyelashes. Speaking in a falsetto voice, he looked and sounded ridiculous. Lamar took the jibe seriously.

"I puked my guts out the same as y'all last Friday night!" he exclaimed. "Didn't I steal those watermelons this summer like you told me to, Neal? Wasn't I the one who bought the spray paint when we wrote that graffiti on the post office wall?"

Hutch and Neal laughed at his vehemence. Neal reached across the table and slapped Lamar's cheek. "You've done real good, Lamar. Real good." Unable to keep a straight face, he burst into laughter again.

Hutch's bony shoulders were shaking with mirth. "You puked up more than the two of us put together, Lamar.

What'd your mama think of your hangover yesterday morning?"

"She didn't know I was feeling bad. I stayed in bed."

They were bored. Sunday nights were always boring. The bad girls were recuperating from Saturday night bacchanals and didn't want to be bothered. The good girls went to church. There were no sporting events scheduled on Sundays. They hadn't felt like crabbing or fishing that evening.

So Neal, always the leader and strategist, had rounded up the other two in his sports car and they had cruised the streets of Palmetto, looking for something to do to amuse themselves. But after cruising the main drag several times, they had failed to find any action in town.

"Want to go out to Walmart and look around?" Lamar had suggested.

The other two chorused, "No."

"I know," Neal said in a burst of inspiration, "let's go to one of the nigger churches. That's always a hoot."

"Un-uh," Hutch said, shaking his fiery head. "My daddy said he'd skin me if we did that again. Last time we went, it nearly started a race riot." Hutch's father, Fritz, was the county sheriff. Fritz Jolly had served as the boys' consciences on numerous occasions.

Their last resort had been to go to the Dairy Barn, hoping that some action would find them. As long as they kept placing orders and behaved themselves, the management wouldn't kick them out. Of course, there would be hell to pay if Neal was caught with the bottle of whiskey in his coat.

His father, Ivan, had told him before leaving the house not to take any beer with him. "How come?" Neal had asked.

"Because Fritz called me yesterday morning. He was good and pissed off. Said Hutch came home stinking drunk Friday night and that you had supplied the beer. He said the sheriff's son can't be driving around town drunk and raising hell. Dora Jolly was fit to be tied, too. I told him I'd look into it."

"Well?"

"Well, I'm looking into it," Ivan had thundered. "Lay off the beer tonight."

"Christ." Neal slammed out of the house. Once he got to his car, he chuckled and patted the inside pocket of his jacket, where he'd hidden the silver flask of expensive bourbon. Ivan would never miss it.

By now, however, the fun of having pulled one over on his old man had fizzled. Hutch was devouring his second hamburger. His table manners disgusted Neal. He ate each meal like it might be his last, taking huge bites, gulping noisily, not bothering to suspend conversation while he was chewing.

Lamar was always a gutless pain in the ass. He was a perennial worrier whose company Neal tolerated because of Lamar's culpability. It was amusing to have a sucker around to be the butt of practical jokes and a target for verbal abuse. Lamar was affable and above average-looking, but the only real purpose he served was to be Neal's punching bag.

Tonight, he was as sullen and nervous as ever. Every time anybody spoke to him, he jumped. Neal supposed Lamar's habitual jitters came from living with his mama. That old bat was enough to make anybody jumpy.

Myrajane Griffith thought she was hot snot because she was a former Cowan. At one time, the Cowans had been the largest producing cotton planters between Savannah and Charleston. But that had been long before folks nowadays could remember. The Cowans had fallen on hard times; most of them had died. The old plantation house near the coast was still standing, but it had long ago been foreclosed upon and condemned.

Still, Myrajane clung to her maiden name like a runt shoat to a hind teat. She was an employee of the Patchett Soybean Plant, like almost everybody else in the three neighboring counties. She rubbed elbows with coloreds and people she wouldn't have spit on in better days. She had browbeaten her husband until he died. When Ivan viewed Lamar's father's body in the casket, he had remarked that the poor bastard was smiling for the first time in years.

Jesus, Neal thought, *no wonder Lamar is nervous all the time, living with that harpy.*

Neal was glad his mother had died when he was a baby. A series of nannies, mostly colored women from around Palmetto, had reared him until he got too old to spank and started hitting back. His mother, Rebecca Flory Patchett, had been blond and pale and the worst lay Ivan had ever had, or so Ivan had told Neal when the boy had expressed curiosity about his mother's nature.

"Rebecca was a pretty little thing, but screwing her was like sticking it in an icepack. She gave me what I wanted, though." Here Ivan had socked him lightly on the jaw. "A son."

Neal thought that having one parent to answer to was bad enough, although Ivan was lenient and usually looked the other way whenever he got into trouble. Ivan paid for Neal's speeding tickets and covered the cost of the things he destroyed or shoplifted.

"For Chris' sake, do you know who my daddy is!" Neal had shouted to the hardware store clerk who had recently caught him stealing.

Sheriff Fritz Jolly had called Ivan to the scene to smooth things over. Neal had walked out of the store with the hunting knife he had pilfered, wearing a complacent smile that infuriated the frustrated sales clerk. The fellow later found his car with four slashed tires.

Neal wished he had something fun like that to do tonight.

"Church is out." Lamar's observation pulled Neal from his musings.

A group of young people filed into the Diary Barn. Neal immediately dismissed the boys as Jesus freaks and thereby unworthy of his attention. But he gave each girl a smoldering once-over. Just that did wonders for a girl's ego and made her dream good dreams at night.

Besides, it never hurt to prepare a field for future plowing. He might be desperate for company some night and need one of these girls. If and when he called, she would remember the lustful look he'd given her. He had once boasted that he could convert a church-choir soprano into a slut in five minutes flat. It wasn't an empty boast.

"Hi, Neal. Hi, Lamar. Hi, Hutch."

Donna Dee Monroe stopped at the end of their booth. Out of habit, Neal's eyes slid down her body, then back up. "Hi, Donna Dee. Did you get saved tonight?"

"I'm already saved. But I'm sure you're going to burn in hell, Neal Patchett."

He laughed. "Goddamn right. I look forward to every minute of getting there. Hi, Florene."

One of the girls with Donna Dee had been at the country

club Valentine's dance a few weeks ago. The pickings had been slim that night, so he'd flirted with her when ordinarily he wouldn't even have noticed her. He'd danced with her until she was melting—literally. When he got her outside and slipped his hand beneath her dress and between her thighs, his fingers had come away damp. Just as it was getting interesting, her daddy had come looking for her.

Now Neal lowered his eyelids and, in a sultry voice, asked, "Did you have any sins to confess tonight, Florene? Been entertaining any impure thoughts lately?"

The girl blushed to the roots of her hair, mumbled something unintelligible, and hurried to catch up with the group of churchgoers she had come in with.

Donna Dee lingered. She was a cheeky girl with dark, flashing eyes and a quick, sometimes ribald wit. Unfortunately, she wasn't too much in the looks department. Her hair was straight and thin. She wore it parted down the middle, not from choice but because that's all she could coax it to do. Her profile came to a point where her nostrils met her upper lip. Together with her uncorrected overbite and darting eyes, she resembled a friendly rat. She had a thing for Hutch, but, as usual, he ignored her.

"Look who's here," he said, drawing Neal's attention to the parking lot beyond the window. "Mr. Student Body President."

They watched Gary Parker pull his car into one of the spaces. His steady, Jade Sperry, was sitting in the front seat, close beside him.

"And he's got the best student body with him."

Neal shot Lamar a poisonous look, unable to tell whether Lamar was mocking him with that crack. Surely not. He had kept his interest in Jade Sperry a secret from everyone.

"That car of his is a piece of shit," Hutch commented to no one in particular.

Lamar said, "Doesn't seem to bother Jade."

"Of course not, you creep," Donna Dee said. "She's in love with him. It doesn't matter to her that he's as poor as Job's turkey. I'm gonna go say hi to them. See y'all later."

Neal glowered darkly through the window as he watched Gary and Jade. Gary must have said something amusing because Jade laughed and leaned into him, rubbing her temple against his chin.

"Damn, she's hot," Hutch groaned. "He's a frigging farmer. What attracts her?"

"His brain," Lamar said.

"Or maybe she's impressed by his big plow," Hutch joked.

Lamar laughed. Neal remained stonily silent. Motionless, his eyes unwavering, he watched Gary softly kiss Jade's lips before opening the car door and stepping out. It had been a chaste, tepid kiss. Neal wondered, not for the first time, if she had ever been kissed by somebody who meant business—somebody like him.

Jade was indisputably the best-looking girl in Palmetto High School. The best-looking girl was supposed to belong to Neal Patchett, just like the best clothes and the best car. His old man was the richest, most powerful man in the area. That alone entitled him to whatever he wanted. Apparently no one had informed Miss Jade Sperry of that.

No matter how high Gary's IQ was, Neal would never understand how she could prefer a piss-poor farmer

like Gary over him. Not only did she show a marked
lack of interest, but Neal got the impression that she felt
disgusted by him. With an inexplicable reverse snob-
bery, she regarded him as a lowlife. Oh, she was always
polite—Jade was courteous to everybody—but beneath
her polite veneer, Neal detected a scornful attitude that
ate at him.

Maybe she didn't know what she was missing. Maybe
she hadn't realized that she was settling for less than the
best. Maybe it was time she found out.

"Come on," he said suddenly, sliding out of the booth.
He tossed down enough money to cover the cost of their
drinks and Hutch's burgers, then sauntered to the door.

Outside, he headed for the window where customers
placed carry-out orders. He didn't have to ask Hutch and
Lamar if they cared to follow. They fell into step behind
him, as he had known they would.

Donna Dee opened the passenger-side door of Gary Parker's car and slid in beside Jade. "I didn't know you were
coming here," Jade said. "You could have ridden from
church with us."

"And been a fifth wheel? No, thanks."

There was no rancor in Donna Dee's voice. The two
girls had been inseparable since the first day of kinder-
garten. While it was obvious to anyone who saw them
together that Jade outshone the other girl, Donna Dee harbored no malice toward her more attractive, more accomplished friend.

"What'd you think of the sermon tonight?" Donna Dee
asked. "Did you feel God's breath on the back of your
neck every time the preacher said the word *fornication*?"

Jade had been uncomfortable with the subject of the sermon, but she replied evenly, "I've got nothing to be guilty about."

"Yet," Donna Dee said.

Jade sighed in consternation. "I knew I never should have confided in you that Gary and I had talked about it."

"Oh, for crying out loud," Donna Dee exclaimed. "Y'all have been going together for three years. Everybody thinks you've already done it a million times."

Jade bit her lower lip. "My mother included. We had an argument before Gary picked me up tonight."

"So?" Donna Dee borrowed a lipstick from Jade's purse and spread it on. "You're always having arguments with your mom. I hate to say it, Jade, but your mom's a real bitch."

"She doesn't understand that I love Gary."

"Sure she does. That's the problem. She doesn't want you to love him. She thinks you can do better than him."

"There is no one better."

"You know what I mean," Donna Dee said, still searching through Jade's purse. "She'd like to see you wind up with somebody rich and influential, you know— somebody like Neal."

Jade shuddered with disgust. "Fat chance."

"Do you think he really felt up Florene at the country club Valentine's dance? Or was she just bragging? She can be all mouth."

"I don't think being felt up by Neal Patchett is anything to brag about."

"Well, you're the exception."

"Thank heaven."

"Neal's good-looking," Donna Dee observed.

"I can't stand him. Look at him now. He thinks he's so cool."

The two girls watched Neal and his friends encircle Gary where he was waiting in line to place his take-out order. Neal punched Gary in the shoulder a couple of times, and when Gary told him to cut it out, he assumed a boxer's stance.

"He's so obnoxious," Jade said with distaste.

"Yeah. I wish Hutch didn't hang around with him so much."

It was no secret that Donna Dee was madly in love with Hutch Jolly. She wore her heart on her sleeve. Secretly, Jade thought Hutch looked and acted like a bumpkin, but, at the risk of hurting Donna Dee's feelings, she never voiced her opinion.

Nor had she ever told Donna Dee about all the times Hutch had called her asking for dates. She had declined his invitations because of Gary. But even if she hadn't had a steady boyfriend, she would never have dated Hutch because of Donna Dee.

"You don't like Hutch, do you, Jade?" Donna Dee asked her now.

"I like him fine." Truthfully, Hutch made her uncomfortable. They had trigonometry class together, and she often caught him staring at her. Whenever she did, he would blush beneath his freckles, then assume an arrogant air to cover his embarrassment.

"What's wrong with him?" There was a defensive edge to Donna Dee's voice.

"Nothing. Honestly. Nothing except the company he keeps."

"Do you think he'll invite me to the prom, Jade? I'll die if he doesn't."

"You won't die," Jade said wearily. Donna Dee looked so crestfallen at Jade's lack of empathy that she changed her tone. "I'm sorry, Donna Dee. I hope Hutch asks you. Really, I do."

Their senior prom, coming up in May, already seemed trivial and juvenile. To Jade it represented just one more delay in Gary and her getting on with their lives. She certainly didn't think it was anything to get in a big stew over, although maybe that was because she was guaranteed a date with Gary. Unlike Donna Dee, she didn't have to worry about the disgrace of not having an escort on that momentous night.

"I can't think of anybody else Hutch would ask, can you?" Donna Dee asked worriedly.

"No." Jade glanced at her wristwatch. "What's taking so long? I've got to be home by ten or my mother will start in again."

"And you've got to leave time to park, huh?" Donna Dee gazed at her friend and whispered, "When you and Gary make out, do you just want to die from being so turned on?"

"Yes," Jade admitted, shivering slightly. "And because we have to stop."

"You don't have to."

Jade's sleek, dark brows pulled together into a frown. "If Gary and I love each other, how can it be wrong, Donna Dee?"

"I never said it was."

"But the preacher does. And the Bible does. My mother does. Everybody does."

"Everybody says that fornication—"

"Don't use that word for it. It's such an ugly word."

"What would you call it then?"

"Making love."

Donna Dee shrugged. "Same difference. Anyway, everybody says that lovemaking outside of marriage is a sin, but does anybody really believe that?" Donna Dee shook her head of dark, straight hair. "I don't think so. I think everybody except us is sinning like crazy and having a damn good time. If I had a chance, I would."

"Would you?" Jade asked, wanting her friend's endorsement.

"If Hutch asked me, you bet your sweet ass I would."

Jade looked at Gary through the windshield and felt a warm rush of pleasure, coupled with anxiety. "Maybe it's not a sin. Maybe it's time Gary and I stopped listening to the preacher and followed our instincts. Oh, I just don't know," she moaned. "We've talked the subject to death and we only end up more frustrated than before."

"Oh, for pity's sake," Donna Dee grumbled. "I'm going back inside. See ya."

"Wait, Donna Dee," Jade said, catching her sleeve. "Are you mad?"

"No."

"You sound mad."

"Well gee, Jade, I wish I had your problems. I wish I had your naturally wavy black hair and flawless skin. I wish I had big blue eyes and eyelashes a mile long. I wish I had a boyfriend who panted after my body but also respected me. I wish I had a computer brain and a full scholarship to college."

"I haven't got the scholarship yet," Jade said, minimizing Donna Dee's backhanded compliments.

"Oh, but you will. It's only a matter of time. Everything always turns out right for you, Jade. That's why it's annoying as hell to listen to you whine. What have you got to complain about?

"You're gorgeous without even trying. You're smart. You're popular. You'll probably be valedictorian of our class, and if not you, then the boy who worships the ground you walk on and the air you breathe. If you want to screw yourselves into delirium, do it. If you don't, don't. But shut up about it, okay?"

After her outburst, Donna Dee swore beneath her breath. In a softer tone, she said, "You ought to pay me to be your best friend, Jade. It isn't an easy job, you know."

She snatched up her purse and stepped onto the pavement, closing the car door behind her.

"Hi, Gary." Neal's tone was deceptively friendly. Matching it, Lamar and Hutch repeated him.

"Hi, y'all." Gary's smile was open and guileless. "What's going on?"

"Nothing much," Neal replied. "You heard anything about your scholarship yet?"

"Not yet. Neither has Jade. Could be any day now, though."

"Do you want nuts on those sundaes, Gary?" the waitress in the window asked.

"Sure."

"Sure," Neal drawled. He looked toward the car where Jade was sitting. "Jade loves nuts. Big ones."

Hutch sputtered with laughter. Lamar snickered.

Gary's smile vanished. "Cut it out, Neal," he said crossly. He glanced over his shoulder toward the car.

Innocently, Neal raised his hands. "It was a joke. Can't you take a joke?" Playfully, he punched Gary's shoulder.

Gary flinched angrily. "Not where Jade's concerned."

"Here you go, Gary," the waitress said, sliding the two desserts through the window. "One butterscotch sundae and one chocolate. That'll be a dollar fifty."

"Thanks." Gary paid her, then pulled two paper napkins from the dispenser and took a sundae in each hand. He turned away from the window, but Neal blocked his path, flanked by Hutch and Lamar.

"Which one's Jade's?"

Missing the point of Neal's seemingly innocuous question, Gary shrugged. "The butterscotch."

Each sundae was crowned with a bright red cherry. Neal took the cherry by its stalk and plucked it off the mound of whipped cream. He sucked it into his mouth, then, with a dramatic gesture, pulled the stem out. He rolled the cherry in his mouth before catching it between his front teeth where it was visible. Looking directly at Jade, he suggestively sank his teeth into it, then chewed it with lascivious pleasure before swallowing it.

Facing Gary, he smirked. "Tell your girl friend I enjoyed eating her cherry."

"You sorry son of a bitch. Eat this."

Gary shoved one of the sundaes into Neal's smug face. Neal, taken completely off guard, staggered backward, choking on the goo that covered his face. Gary seized the advantage. Hooking his heel around Neal's, he yanked hard, pulling Neal off his feet. He went down backward onto the pavement.

Gary stood above him. "Keep your filthy mouth shut about Jade." He dumped the second sundae into Neal's lap, then strode to his car.

Neal leaped to his feet, sputtering threats. "I'll kill you

for that, Parker. Nobody fucks with me like that and gets away with it." He became aware of the comic spectacle he was making of himself and diverted his fury. "Jesus Christ!" he shouted to his two friends, who were immobilized with shock over seeing Neal outdone. "Are you gonna just stand there with your thumbs up your asses? Help me out here."

Hutch and Lamar sprang forward, offering handkerchiefs and paper napkins. As he wiped his face clean, Neal glared at Gary's retreating car. The farmer might think he had gotten the best of him, but he had another think coming.

Chapter 2

❖────◆────❖

I should have beaten him to within an inch of his life."

"You made your point, Gary." Jade laughed when she remembered Neal's flabbergasted expression as the soft frozen custard dripped off his nose.

"Why didn't I give him what he really had coming?"

"Because you're not a Neanderthal like him. A fistfight is beneath your dignity. Besides, you were outnumbered. You would have had to fight Hutch and Lamar, too."

"I'm not afraid of them!"

Jade thought that expending so much energy on machismo was ridiculous, but she did her best to stroke Gary's ego. "Please stop fretting about it. Neal's not worth it." After a short silence, she asked, "What did he say to make you so mad?"

"Something typical of him," he replied dismissively. "One of his sly innuendos. His mind is a septic tank. He insulted you." He slammed his fist into his opposite palm. "God, he's a son of a bitch. I don't care how rich he is, he's vermin."

"Knowing that, why are you letting him spoil our time together? I've got to be home soon."

Gary had soft brown hair and tender amber eyes. Gentleness was more at home on his face than anger. At Jade's mild rebuke, his face relaxed into its usual affable expression. He stroked her cheek with the backs of his fingers. "You're right. It would tickle Neal to know he had ruined our evening. It's just that I hate to hear your name coming out of his filthy mouth."

She combed her fingers up through his hair. "I love you, Gary Parker."

"I love you, too."

Kissing her with fervor and passion, he pressed his hand against the small of her back, bringing together as much of their bodies as was possible within the confines of the front seat of his car. He had parked in a remote spot on a road that bordered one of the tidal swamps.

Outside, the February evening was cool and damp. Inside the car, it was warm and getting warmer. Within minutes, the windows were fogged up. Jade and Gary were breathing heavily, their fine young bodies on fire with the kind of lust the preacher's sermon had condemned. Gary buried his fingers in her thick, inky-dark hair. He slipped his other hand beneath her sweater. "Jade?" She looked up at him, her eyes fluid with desire. "You know I love you, don't you?"

She took his hand and guided it to her breast. "I know you love me."

They had started dating in their sophomore year. Before that, Jade had been escorted to school dances and parties by boys whose parents served as chaperons. She had met boys at the movie theater on Friday nights, but

Donna Dee had always been with her. Beyond some hand-holding and an occasional, chaste good-night kiss, Jade hadn't had intimate contact with the opposite sex until she went out with Gary. She hadn't wanted to.

On their second date, he had parted her lips and French kissed her. Some girls claimed to love that; others said the very idea of it was revolting. After that night, Jade firmly believed that the latter group was comprised of those who had never been French kissed. Feeling Gary's tongue moving inside her mouth had been the most delicious sensation she had ever experienced.

For months, those deeply satisfying kisses were the extent of their necking. Their intimacy developed gradually, as their initial physical attraction matured into something stronger. She had yearned to feel his hand on her breast long before he had dared to place it there. From touching her through her clothing, he had advanced to reaching inside to caress bare skin. Now, her breast filled his gently kneading hand. They tempered the abandon with which they kissed so that they could fully experience the pleasure of their caresses. His lips whisked hers as she reached into his letter jacket and unbuttoned his shirt. Her hands moved over his smooth, hard chest. Reaching behind her, he unfastened her bra with a skill that he had developed from practice. He touched her nipples. They hardened beneath his stroking fingers.

Jade murmured her delight. When he pressed his open mouth over one nipple and applied his tongue to it, she gave a soft cry of longing. "Gary, I want to make love."

"I know. I know."

Her pantyhose fit tightly, but he worked his hand beneath them and into the dense curls that had been mashed flat. Only in the last few weeks had they allowed themselves to go this far. It was still new and strange and wonderful to feel Gary's fingers caressing the most secretive part of her body.

She bit her lower lip to hold back her moans of pleasure. Her breasts were raised to sensitive peaks that he gently sponged with his tongue. She wanted to weep from the joy of sharing her body with him. Tonight, she decided to return the pleasure he so unselfishly gave her. She loved his tall, solid, athlete's body and wanted to know it more intimately. Reaching between his thighs, she awkwardly pressed her palm against the fly of his pants.

Gary's head snapped back. He sucked in a sharp breath. His caressing hand fell still beneath her pantyhose.

"Jade?"

She was embarrassed, but resolutely kept her hand where it was instead of drawing it back. "Hmm?"

"You don't have to do that. What I mean is, I don't want you to think I expect it."

"I know. But I want to." Her palm applied more pressure.

Whispering her name repeatedly, he grappled with his belt buckle, a button, and his zipper, then tentatively guided her hand inside his trousers. Beneath his underwear his skin was hot. His shaft was hard. He folded her fingers around it. Jade was shocked by how big it was. She'd had indications, of course, but feeling an indistinct bulge against her belly through her clothes was far different from enclosing his fully extended sex with her hand.

While he kissed her fiercely, she bashfully explored his erection. Her hand made a sliding motion up and down that stopped his breath. He groaned her name and slipped his finger up between the fleshy lips of her sex.

The motion caused a friction unlike anything Jade had ever felt. She tilted her hips up, reaching for him, reaching for something that eluded her. Again he moved his finger. It was like being skimmed by Fourth of July sparklers. Her entire lower body tingled.

"Gary?" This was a marvelous discovery. She wanted to tell him about it, share it with him. "Gary?" Her hand closed tightly around his penis.

With a low, frustrated growl, Gary pulled away from her and sat up. He pushed her hand away from his lap. "Stop. If you don't, I'm going to make a mess."

"I don't care," she whispered.

"I do." Crossing his hands over the top of the steering wheel, he ground his forehead against his white knuckles. "Jade, I'm sick of this shit. I want to do it so bad."

The promising tingles that she had felt now blinked and went out. She regretted that. They had been stunning, breathtaking, almost scary, but she wished she could have found out what they led to. Was it an orgasm?

But her primary concern was for Gary, who she knew was far more frustrated than she. She moved closer to him and smoothed her hand over his head.

"I don't know which is worse," he said hoarsely, "not touching you at all, or touching you to this point, where I want you so much I hurt all over."

"I think not touching at all would be much worse. For me anyway."

"It would be hell for me, too. But we can't go on like this."

"Then let's not."

He raised his head and looked at her. For several moments, his brown eyes searched her face. Then he lowered his gaze and shook his head regretfully. "We can't, Jade. You're the best thing I've got going for me. I can't ruin it."

"Why would making love ruin it?"

"What if you got pregnant?"

"I wouldn't. Not if we take precautions."

"You still could. Then our chances for getting out of this place," he jutted his chin toward the windshield, "would be shot to hell. I'd have to grow soybeans for Ivan Patchett, and you'd have to go to work in his goddamn factory. Everybody would say I had no better sense than my daddy, and they'd be right."

Because of the ever-growing number of little Parkers, the joke around town was that Gary's father, Otis, didn't know when to quit. That was just one of the stigmas that Gary was determined to shrug off.

He drew Jade against his chest and propped his chin on the top of her head. "We can't gamble away our chance to make a better life."

"Making love now doesn't necessarily mean that our futures are doomed to misery."

"It scares me to tempt fate, though. The only time I really feel good is when I'm with you, Jade. The rest of the time I feel so alone. That sounds crazy, doesn't it? How could I feel alone with six younger brothers and sisters in the house? But it's true.

"Sometimes I think I must have been a foundling, that I don't really belong to my parents. My daddy is resigned to fields that flood and crops that rot and selling his produce in a feudalistic town like Palmetto. He hates being poor and ignorant but doesn't do anything to help himself. He takes whatever shit Ivan Patchett shovels him and is glad to get it.

"Well, I'm poor, but I'm not ignorant. I'm sure as hell not cowed by the Patchetts. I'm not going to be like my daddy, accepting things as they are just because that's the way they've always been. I'm going to make something of myself.

"I know I can, Jade, if I've got you pulling for me." He took her hand and pressed her palm to his lips, leaving it there while he spoke. "But in the meantime, I'm so afraid of letting you down."

"You could never let me down."

"One of these days, you might decide it's not worth the struggle. You might decide that you want a guy who hasn't got so far to go, who hasn't got anything to prove. A guy like Neal."

She pulled her hand away from his and blinked her eyes angrily. "Don't ever say anything like that to me again. It sounds like something my mother would say, and you know how angry it makes me when she starts planning my life for me."

"Maybe some of the things she says are right, Jade. A girl who looks like you deserves somebody with money and social status, somebody who could lay the world at your feet. That's what I want to do. What if you lose patience with me before I'm able to?"

"Listen to me, Gary Parker. I don't give a flip about social status. I don't pine after a life of luxury. I have ambitions of my own, which would be in place whether or not I loved you. Getting a scholarship is only the first step of many. Just like you, I've got my own family disgrace to live down. The only world I want at my feet is the one that I create for myself." She softened her tone and looped her arms around his neck. "The one that we create together."

"You're something, you know that?" He squeezed his eyes shut and whispered fervently, "God, I'm glad you chose me."

The house Jade shared with her mother had been built shortly after World War II to accommodate the influx of military personnel based around the shipping channels. In the thirty years since, the neighborhood of white frame tract houses had declined. Their pastel trims no longer looked cheerful and chic but tacky and cheap.

Unlike the others on the street, the Sperry house was kept neat. The house was small, having only two bedrooms and one bath. The living room was rectangular, with narrow windows that were heavily draped. It was the only room in the house that was carpeted. The furniture was inexpensive, but everything was kept spotlessly clean because Velta Sperry passionately hated any form of dirt. She wouldn't even allow plants in her house because they grew in open pots of soil. The only amenity in the living room was a color television set, which Velta had bought on credit from Sears.

She was sitting in an easy chair watching TV when Jade came in. Velta eyed her daughter critically, looking for telltale signs that she'd been misbehaving with that Parker boy. She couldn't detect anything amiss, but then, Jade was clever enough to cover the evidence.

By way of greeting, she said, "You barely made it by your curfew."

"But I did. It's just now ten."

"Church has been out for hours."

"We went to the Dairy Barn. Everybody was there."

"He probably speeded here to get you home in time." Velta disliked Jade's steady boyfriend and never referred to him by name if she could avoid it.

"He didn't speed. Gary's a very careful driver. You know that, Mama."

"Stop arguing with me," Velta said, raising her voice.

"Then stop criticizing Gary."

Velta resented Gary because, she claimed, Jade spent too much time with him—time that she and Jade could spend together. Actually, her dislike was based on Gary's origins. He was a soybean farmer's son. The Parkers had too many children already and continued, disgustingly, to turn out another baby every ten months or so.

Otis Parker was always in hock to the company credit union. Velta knew this because she worked in the credit office as a typist and file clerk. Velta didn't have much regard for anybody who didn't have money.

It would be just like that Parker boy to get Jade pregnant. She hoped Jade was too smart to let that happen, but, unfortunately, like her stunning good looks, the girl had inherited a romantic, passionate streak from her father.

Velta's eyes moved to the framed photograph on the end table. Ronald Sperry's laughing blue eyes—so like Jade's—stared back at her. The soldier's cap sat at a jaunty angle atop his dark curls. His Congressional Medal of Honor was suspended around his neck. Other medals were pinned to the breast pocket of his military uniform, attesting to his valor and courage during the Korean conflict.

Velta was sixteen when Palmetto's dashing war hero

had returned home. The low-country town had never had such a grand distinction. The entire population had turned out to welcome his train as it chugged into the depot. The red carpet had been rolled out for the town's favorite son, who was coming straight from Washington, D.C., where he had been wined and dined. He'd even shaken hands with the president.

Velta was introduced to him at a citywide dance held in his honor at the VFW hall. That very night, while they danced to tunes by Patti Page and Frank Sinatra, she made up her mind to marry Ronald Sperry.

For the next two years she pursued him shamelessly, not giving up until he popped the question. Lest something jinx it, Velta saw to it that they were married within a week of his proposal.

Unfortunately, there were no North Korean Communists in Palmetto. Years after his triumphant return home, Ronald was still at a loss as to what to do with the rest of his life. He had no grandiose ambitions. Though he was dashingly handsome, he had no desire to capitalize on the Medal of Honor the way Audie Murphy had. He didn't aspire to movie stardom.

Orphaned and penniless, he had joined the army only so he would have a place to sleep and food to eat. He had been an ideal soldier because there was always somebody telling him what to do and when to do it. His officers had ordered him to shoot straight and kill the gook commies and, because he was an excellent marksman, that's what he had done. On the afternoon that he wiped out twenty-two Koreans, it never occurred to him that his actions would merit a medal.

He was popular with people. He had a charisma and

magnetism that folks just naturally gravitated to. Everybody liked Ron Sperry. However, hanging out with the guys and telling amusing stories in the pool hall didn't produce revenue. He drifted from one meaningless, futureless job to another.

With each one he began, Velta's spirits rose. This would be the one that catapulted them to riches. The Medal of Honor gave them instant respectability, but never the riches and social acceptance Velta craved. Even a Medal of Honor didn't establish you with Southern society if you had no distinguished grandfather and lots of family money to go with it.

Velta had ranked fourth in a family of nine children. Her father had been a sharecropper until he dropped dead behind a plow mule, leaving destitute her mother and all the offspring who weren't already married. The family had to rely on the charity of others for food and shelter.

More than poverty and hunger, Velta feared scorn.

When the laurel wreath around Ron's head began to wilt, she surmised that people were laughing behind their backs. She berated him for squandering their one chance for fame and fortune. She threatened him and cajoled him, but he simply lacked the initiative to work for a living. She refused to let him reenlist in the army. That would be too demeaning, an admission of defeat, she had told him.

At her wits' end, she had already made up her mind to leave him when she got pregnant with Jade after six years of barrenness. Velta had then clung to the hope that a baby would prod her husband into doing something worthy of his previous success as a soldier. But after Jade's arrival it was Velta who had gone to work in Ivan Patchett's factory.

The last ten years of Ron's life had been studded with jobs acquired and jobs lost, big dreams that never came to fruition, promises that were diluted by ever-increasing amounts of liquor.

One day when Jade was at school and Velta was at work, he died while cleaning his rifle. Mercifully, Sheriff Jolly had ruled his death accidental. The local VFW had donated the money for Velta and Jade to travel to Arlington National Cemetery to give Ronald Sperry a hero's burial.

Looking at his photograph now, Velta didn't feel a whit of yearning for him. Ron had been handsome and sweet and ardent till the day he died, but what good had he done her?

Jade, on the other hand, missed him to this day. Velta resented the girl's fond attachment to his memory, just as she had been jealous of their mutual, blind admiration while he was alive.

He had often pulled Jade into his lap and said to her, "You'll do all right, little doll. You've got my looks and your mama's backbone. Don't ever be afraid and you'll do all right."

Jade was going to do better than all right. If Velta had anything to do with it, Jade was going to make a better marriage than she had.

"Neal Patchett called a while ago," she said, smiling for the first time since Jade had come in. "He's a charmer, that one."

"He's slime."

Velta was taken aback by Jade's vehemence. "That's an ugly thing to say."

"Neal is ugly."

"Ugly? Why, half the girls in the high school would give their right arms to have him calling them."

"Then half the girls can have him."

"I'm sure it's not too late for you to return his call."

Jade shook her head. "I've got to read a chapter in history before tomorrow."

"Jade," Velta called peremptorily when Jade headed for her bedroom. "It's rude not to return a telephone call, especially from someone like Neal."

"I don't want to talk to Neal, Mama."

"You spend hours on the phone with that Parker boy."

Jade rolled her lips inward and held them for several seconds before saying, "I've got to study. Good night."

Velta switched off the TV and followed Jade into her bedroom, catching the door before it closed. "You spend too much time studying. It's unnatural."

Jade removed her skirt and sweater and conscientiously hung them in her narrow closet. "I have to keep my grade point up if I want to get a scholarship."

"A scholarship," Velta hissed. "That's all you ever think about."

"Because that's the only way I can afford to go to college."

"Which in my opinion is a big waste of time for a pretty girl like you."

Jade turned away from her closet and faced her mother. "Mama, I don't want to have this argument again. I'm going to college, whether you approve of it or not."

"It's not a matter of approval. I just don't think it's necessary."

"It is if I want a career."

"You'll waste all that time and money and then wind up getting married anyway."

"Women nowadays can do both."

Velta crossed the room, pinched Jade's chin between her fingers, and angled her head back, exposing the faint red mark on Jade's neck and showing contempt for both the mark and her daughter. "What chance will you have of marrying somebody decent if you get pregnant by that Parker boy?"

"Gary isn't going to get me pregnant. And he's the most decent person I know. It's Gary I'm going to marry, Mama."

"Jade, boys talk girls into doing things they shouldn't by telling them they love them. If you give it to this boy, nobody worth having will want you."

Jade sank down on the edge of her bed and, looking up at her mother, shook her head sadly. "I haven't given 'it' to anybody, Mama. When I do, it'll be to Gary, and it'll be because we love each other."

Velta snorted. "You're too young to know what love is."

Jade's eyes turned a deeper blue, a sign of rising ire. "You wouldn't say that if I were claiming to be in love with Neal Patchett. You'd be urging me to trap him any way I could...even if it meant having sex with him."

"At least you would be somebody in this town if you married him."

"I *am* somebody!"

Velta clenched her fists at her sides. "You're just like your father—head in the clouds, idealistic."

"There's nothing wrong with having goals."

"Goals?" Velta scoffed. "A funny word to bring into a conversation about your father. He never met a single goal in his life. For all the years we were married, he never did one worthwhile thing."

"He loved me," Jade retorted. "Or don't you consider that worthwhile?"

Velta turned and walked stiffly to the door. Before leaving, she said, "When I was your age, I married the hero of the town. Right now, that's your Gary. He's good-looking, a star athlete, class president, everything a girl could want."

Velta sneered. "Take it from me, heroes are temporary, Jade. They fade like cheap curtains. The only thing that really counts is money. No matter how many awards that Parker boy wins, all he'll ever really be is old Otis Parker's firstborn. I want better than that for you."

"No, Mama," Jade argued softly. "You want better than that for *you*."

Velta slammed the door behind her.

Jade sat on a tall stool, nibbling a shortbread cookie. The heels of her shoes were hooked over the chrome rung that encircled the stool's legs. Her chemistry textbook lay open on her lap.

After school and half a day on Saturdays, Jade worked in Jones Brothers' General Store. During the week, she clocked in at four and worked until Velta picked her up on her way home from the factory, usually around six.

It wasn't a long shift, but it gave Pete, the last surviving of three brothers, a chance to sit with his ailing wife, who was in a nursing home, and it provided Jade with a little spending money.

The store was one of a diminishing breed. The planks of the hardwood floor were covered with a waxy-looking film from the lemon oil used on dustmops for countless decades. On the coldest of winter afternoons, old men gathered around the potbellied stove in the back room and discussed the state of the world between chaws of Redman and games of dominoes.

Pitchforks hung, tines down, from hooks screwed into the ceiling. A customer could outfit his horse or his newborn. He could purchase a deck of cards, a pair of dice, or a Bible. The variety of merchandise and customers made the job interesting.

Jade tried to concentrate on the material she was reading, but her mind wandered from chemistry to her personal problems, chiefly those with her mother, who refused to take seriously either Jade's love for Gary or her burning desire to have more out of life than the ordinary—husband, home, and children.

A family was important and Jade wanted one. But she wanted more. Most of the girls in her class had already resigned themselves to working for Ivan Patchett until they got married and started having babies, who would eventually work for Neal. Gary and she shared an ambition to break that dreary cycle.

Whether intentionally or not, Ron Sperry had imbued his daughter with the courage he had lacked, instilling in her a desire to make a better life for herself than her parents had had. At least on that, she and her mother agreed. It was their ultimate goals that differed . . . and their means of attaining them. Jade feared that those differences would never be reconciled, especially where Gary was concerned.

Gary was another source of worry that gloomy afternoon. Neither of them had heard from any of the scholarship boards to which they had applied. That, coupled with their escalating sexual frustration and the hell that Neal was giving them at school because of the incident at the Dairy Barn, had made them irritable and short-tempered with each other.

They needed a distraction. Perhaps if the weather was warm this weekend, they could have a cookout on the beach, or go for a long drive, something that would relax them and put things back into perspective.

She was still mulling it over when the bell over the entrance jangled. Jade looked up from her studies to see Donna Dee barreling through the door. Her cheeks were flushed and her chest was heaving as she gasped for air.

Jade jumped to her feet, and her chemistry book fell to the floor with a loud thud. "What in the world is the matter?"

Donna Dee fanned her hands in front of her face and drew several deep breaths. "I just came from school. Mr. Patterson asked if I'd stay and do some filing for him."

"And?"

"You got it. Your scholarship."

Jade's heart went straight to her throat. She didn't dare trust her ears, so she repeated, "I got it? A scholarship?"

Donna Dee bobbed her head quickly. "To South Carolina State."

"How do you know? Are you sure?"

"I saw the letter lying on Mr. Patterson's desk. It looked very official, you know, with gold seals and scrolls and stuff. I saw your name on it and kind of accidentally on purpose knocked it to the floor as I was reaching for a folder I was supposed to—"

"Donna Dee!"

"Okay. Anyway, I read the letter. The dean or someone

was congratulating our principal on producing two such fine students at Palmetto High School."

Jade's eyes widened. *"Two?"*

Donna Dee spread her arms out to her sides and squealed, "Gary got one, too."

They both started squealing then. Clasping arms, they hopped up and down until the glass jars of jelly beans on the counter began to rattle.

"Oh, Lord. Oh, I can't believe it! How much? Did it say how much?"

"It said 'full scholastic scholarships.' Doesn't that mean everything?"

"I don't know. I hope so. Oh, but I'm so grateful for whatever it is," Jade said breathlessly. "I've got to tell Gary. Was he still at school? Did you see him on the track?" The track team was preparing for its season by working out every day after school.

"No. I told Mr. Patterson I felt sick and had to leave. I ran to the stadium and looked for Gary. I was going to get him to come with me and tell you together."

"Maybe he was in the locker room."

Donna Dee shook her head. "I asked. Marvie Hibbs said he'd seen him leave."

Jade consulted the pendulum clock mounted on the wall. It was surrounded by cuckoo clocks, all about to strike five-thirty. "Sometimes Mr. Jones comes back before six. I'm sure he'll let me leave a few minutes early today."

"What for?"

"To go tell Gary."

"Why don't you just call?"

"I want to tell him in person. Will you drive me out to Gary's house? Please, Donna Dee?"

"He might already know," Donna Dee said. "I'm sure the dean sent letters to you, too. You've probably got one waiting for you at home."

"That's true. But the Parkers are on a rural postal route. Sometimes they get mail a day later. Besides, I've got to see him. Today. Now. Please, Donna Dee."

"Okay. But what about your mom? What'll happen when she shows up here to pick you up?"

"Mr. Jones will tell her where I went."

"She'll be pissed if you talk to Gary before you tell her."

"Then she'll just have to be pissed. He's got to be the first to know."

The elderly Mr. Jones didn't know what to make of it when he entered his store a few minutes later and Jade Sperry came flying at him with arms outstretched. She hugged him tight and kissed his wrinkled cheek.

"Mr. Jones, something very important has come up. I know it's early, but would you let me leave now? I'll make up the time another night. Please?" She spoke rapidly, the words running together.

"Well, seeing that you're about to bust, I reckon so."

"Thank you! Thank you!"

She kissed his cheek again and ducked into the back room to retrieve her school books, coat, and purse. She was too excited to be cold, so she bundled the coat against her chest, scooped her chemistry book off the floor, and dashed back to the front of the store. Donna Dee had been momentarily distracted by a new display of frosted eyeshadows. Jade herded her toward the door.

"See you tomorrow, Mr. Jones. When my mother stops for me, please tell her that I went with Donna Dee and will be home in about an hour. And tell her I've got some very good news."

"I'll do it."

"Thanks again. Bye-bye!"

"You girls be careful, hear?"

Stumbling over each other, Donna Dee and Jade rushed out the door and down the sidewalk to Donna Dee's car. Jade tossed her belongings into the backseat and got in while Donna Dee slid behind the wheel.

She negotiated the town's few traffic lights and within minutes they were speeding down the two-lane highway. It was a dreary, misty evening, but they kept the windows down, and the radio blaring.

The farther they got from the city limits, the less appealing the landscape became. They passed dwellings so ramshackle they couldn't even be called houses. Roofs and porches sagged. Windows were papered over and shutters gaped in disrepair. Ancient automobiles and unusable farm implements rusted in the front yards and housed flocks of scrawny fowl. It was like this all the way to the coast, a few miles away. Beyond the shore, the Atlantic was dappled with sea islands.

The isolated communities there didn't belong in the twentieth century. Poverty was rampant. Often there was no plumbing. Between the sea islands and the shore were tidal swamps that bred disease-carrying insects to further torment a suppressed element of Southern society. Diseases caused by malnutrition and poor hygiene, which had been obliterated in most Western countries, could still be found there.

Jade thought the economic climate in this part of the state was deplorable. It was no wonder that Gary often became despondent over the socioeconomic disparities that existed. The Parkers were poor by most standards, but they lived like kings compared to many others.

The industries that thrived in the Piedmont, in the northwestern part of South Carolina, were still struggling for a foothold in the low country. Tourism was a major industry along the coast, but often the developers of the resort areas resisted the idea of industry because of the pollutants that might spoil their playgrounds for the rich. Meanwhile, farmers like Otis Parker tried to scrape a living from exhausted and flood-ravaged land, and despots like Ivan Patchett got fat by sucking everyone else dry.

That trend had to be reversed. Perhaps she and Gary would be the forerunners, the first generation of a new South, the pioneers of—

"Oh, shit!"

The expletive yanked Jade from her noble daydream. "What's the matter?"

"We're out of gas."

"What?" She glanced at the gauge with disbelief.

"Did I stutter? We're out of gas."

Donna Dee let the car coast to the narrow shoulder of the road and roll to a standstill. Jade gaped at her friend incredulously. "How can you be out of gas?"

"In all the excitement, I forgot to check the gauge before we left town."

"What'll we do now?"

"Wait for somebody to come along, I guess."

"Oh, great!" Jade flopped back against the seat and pinched the bridge of her nose between two fingers.

After a brief silence, Donna Dee said, "Look, I made a mistake, okay? Everyone in the world except you is entitled to make a mistake now and then. I know you're eager to see Gary, and I understand why. I'm sorry."

Her apology made Jade feel ashamed. If it weren't for Donna Dee, she wouldn't even know about her scholarship yet.

"No, I'm the one who's sorry." She nudged Donna Dee's arm until the girl turned her head and looked at her. Jade smiled in apology. "I didn't mean to sound critical."

A grin tugged at Donna Dee's mouth, which was much too small for her teeth. "That's all right." Then the two began to laugh. "This is a hell of a fix!" Donna Dee exclaimed. Poking her head through the open window, she yelled theatrically, "Help, help! Two beautiful damsels are in distress!"

"You idiot, get your head back inside this car. Your hair's getting wet."

Donna Dee turned off the headlights so as not to run down the car's battery, and they settled down to wait for the first passerby. The sun had set before they left town. It was dark on the country road. After fifteen minutes without a single car coming by, Jade began to worry.

"It's not that cold, and it's stopped drizzling. Maybe we should walk back to town."

Donna Dee looked at her as though she'd lost her mind. "That's several miles."

"We can at least go to the nearest house that has a telephone."

Fearfully, Donna Dee glanced over her shoulder. "You want to go sashaying up to one of those nigger shacks? Un-uh. No way. We might never be seen again."

"Just because they're black doesn't mean they're dangerous. It's no more risky than hitching a ride. You don't know who'll stop."

"I'll take my chances."

They continued arguing about it until Donna Dee pointed down the road. "Headlights!" She shoved open her door and stepped out into the middle of the road, waving her arms above her head and shouting. "Whooo-eee! Hey! Stop!"

The sports-car driver accelerated deliberately. Donna Dee's feet straddled the center stripe of the highway and held their ground. The car skidded to a halt inches from her.

"Neal Patchett, you son of a bitch," she yelled. "You could've killed me."

Neal let his foot off the brake and the car rolled forward until the grille bumped into Donna Dee's skinny shins. She fell back a few steps, cursing him. Inside the car, Hutch and Lamar were howling with laughter.

Neal spotted Jade through the open windows of Donna Dee's car. "What're you two young ladies up to?"

"We were headed out to Gary's house, but my car ran out of gas," Donna Dee explained. "Have you got some gas?"

Hutch's belch was as loud as a cannon blast. "Not anymore."

Donna Dee shot him a withering glance. "Then can you give us a lift into town and drop us at the filling station? I'll call my daddy from there and he'll bring us back."

Hutch opened the passenger door and stepped out, unfolding his long body from the bucket seat. "Say 'pretty please,'" he taunted.

Lamar, riding in the back, as usual, leaned forward. "We don't give free rides, you know."

"You're all so cute," Donna Dee said with heavy sarcasm. "I can hardly contain myself."

Jade watched with dread as Neal got out of his car and swaggered around the front of Donna Dee's. Disregarding the mud that bordered the shoulder of the road, he moved to the passenger door and opened it.

"Get out."

"You smell like a brewery," she remarked as she alighted.

"We've tipped a few beers since school let out. Went fishing."

"Catch anything?"

"Not till now."

Jade didn't like the sound of that but chose to ignore it. Being careful not to touch him, she walked around him and picked her way toward the others. Ever since that night at the Dairy Barn, Neal had been provoking her more than usual, calling her house frequently and deliberately placing himself in her path in the hallways at school. She avoided him as much as possible. He made her skin crawl, and, after what had happened that Sunday night several weeks ago, she no longer attempted to hide her dislike.

Neal Patchett had been born with opportunities that he not only took for granted but squandered. Jade couldn't tolerate such gross wastefulness, especially since a conscientious boy like Gary had to scrape for every single advantage. Neal was lazy and disruptive at school, all but daring the teachers to flunk or discipline him. He knew they wouldn't. Most of them had spouses or relatives working in some capacity for Ivan.

Jade believed that more than the universal, adolescent penchant for hell-raising motivated Neal to misbehave. Some of his pranks went beyond mischief and bordered on cruelty. In everything he said and did there was a hint of inbred malevolence, a meanness of spirit. He was more dangerous than most people guessed, Jade thought. Part of the revulsion she felt toward him stemmed from a gut instinct of fear.

"How're we all going to crowd into there?" Donna Dee asked, dubiously regarding the interior of the sports car through the windshield.

"I've got it all figured out," Neal said. He pushed forward the driver's seat. "Climb back there with Lamar," he told Jade.

There was no backseat, merely a space beneath the sloping rear window. Jade hesitated. "Maybe I'd better stay with Donna Dee's car."

"Out here by yourself?" Donna Dee screeched.

"It shouldn't be that long," Jade said. "Thirty minutes at the most. I don't mind staying, really."

"Get in."

"Neal's right, Jade," Donna Dee argued. "You can't stay out here in the dark by yourself. Get in the back with Lamar. I'll ride in Hutch's lap." She sounded happy with the arrangement.

Jade didn't share her friend's enthusiasm. She felt distinctly uneasy, but then she figured she was being silly. Neal drove like a bat out of hell, but she would probably be safer staying with the group than stranded alone on a deserted highway on a rainy night.

She climbed over the seat and squeezed into the tiny space with Lamar, who did his best to make room for her. "Hi, Jade."

"Hi." She smiled at Lamar. He always seemed so apologetic and eager to please, and she felt sorry for him. It was a mystery to her why he hung around with Neal.

Neal slid behind the steering wheel and closed his door. "Hutch, get in."

Hutch obeyed on command.

Donna Dee moved around to the passenger side of the car. Before she could get in, Neal said to Hutch, "Shut the door."

Hutch shut the door and looked at Neal curiously. "What about Donna Dee?"

Neal revved the engine. "She stays."

Donna Dee grabbed the door handle, but Neal reached across Hutch's chest and pushed down the lock button.

"Let me in, you jerk!" Donna Dee pounded on the window.

Warily, Hutch said, "Neal, we shouldn't leave her—"

"Shut up!"

"Let her in!" Jade dived between the two bucket seats and leaned across Hutch's lap, reaching for the door handle. "Open the door, Donna Dee! Quick!" She flipped up the lock button, but before Donna Dee could open the door, Neal popped the clutch and the car lurched forward. "If she's not coming along, I'm not going either!" Jade shouted.

Now more intent on getting out of the car than letting Donna Dee in, she again reached for the door latch.

"Grab her hands, Hutch." Though he was executing a dangerous U-turn on the highway, which was slick with oil and drizzle, Neal didn't raise his voice. His icy calm terrified Jade.

"No!" She began to fight Hutch's attempts to hold her still. She flailed her arms, swatted at his hands, tried to wiggle between the bucket seats and at least get in a position to reach the door handle.

Her elbow caught Neal in the ear. "Jesus! Can't you hold her down, Lamar? I've got to drive, for Chris' sake."

Lamar grabbed her around the waist. Jade screamed and kicked her heel against the rear window. She lunged for the gear shift stick, but Neal gave her wrist a karate chop and her hand went numb. Jade saw Donna Dee momentarily spotlighted in the headlights. She was standing in the road, her eyes blinking rapidly.

"Donna Dee, help me!"

Hutch grabbed and held Jade's wrists. Lamar's arms locked around her waist. The car shot forward into the darkness.

"Let me out of here!"

"What are we doing, Neal?" Hutch asked.

"Just having a little fun." He shoved the car into fifth gear.

"This isn't fun, you jerk!" Jade shouted. "Take me back to Donna Dee. You can't leave her out there alone. She'll be scared."

"It is awfully dark out there, Neal," Lamar remarked uneasily.

"Do you want out?"

"No, I just—"

"Then shut up."

Neal's comrades obediently fell silent. Jade tried to regain her composure and quiet her fears. These boys weren't strangers—she'd known them all her life. Lamar and Hutch were stupid but basically likeable. Neal, however, could be vicious.

"We're not going in the direction of town, Neal," Hutch observed. "Where are you taking her?"

"She was on her way to see Gary, wasn't she?"

"So we're going out to Gary's house?" Lamar asked hesitantly.

"Hutch, will you please let go of my wrists?" Jade asked calmly. "You're hurting me."

"Sorry." He let her go. Likewise, Lamar released her.

"We're just giving you a ride out to Gary's place, Jade," he said with a short laugh. "Then he can drive you back to Donna Dee's car. His daddy probably has a gas can he uses on his tractor."

She looked at Lamar but didn't return his feeble smile. They lapsed into silence. If this were an ordinary ride, they would be ribbing one another, cracking jokes, discussing tomorrow's chemistry test. The taut silence made Jade even more uncomfortable. If Neal's two best buddies were uneasy, she had every reason to be afraid.

"The turn-off is coming up," Hutch said. Neal didn't downshift. "Fifty yards or so up there on your right, Neal."

The car sped past the narrow country road that came to a dead end at the Parkers' farm.

"What are you doing?" Jade demanded of Neal's handsome profile. "Let me out. I'll walk from the intersection."

"Neal, what the hell?" Hutch asked.

"I want to make a stop first."

Jade's heart began to pound in fear. An hour ago she had been celebrating the good news about her scholarship; now her palms were damp and cold with apprehension.

Neal turned left onto the next road, which wasn't much of a road. The dead stalks of tall weeds crowded twin ruts that were unpaved and very bumpy. The headlights rose and fell like the lights on a buoy in high seas.

"Are we going back to the channel?" Lamar asked.

"Yep."

"Why?"

"I forgot something," Neal said.

Mistrustfully, Hutch stared at his friend, but he said nothing. The ground beneath the wheels became marshy as they came closer to the water. Neal brought the car to a halt. He turned off the engine but left the headlights on. "Everybody out."

He opened his door and stepped to the muddy ground. Hutch hesitated before doing the same. Jade heard him ask, "What're we doing back here, Neal? What'd you forget?"

Lamar nudged her. "Better get out. When Neal gets something in his head, it's best to just go along. Otherwise, he gets mad."

"He can get as mad at me as he wants to. I don't care."

Neal moved to the rear of the car, unlocked the hatchback, and raised it. "I said, get out."

"Go to hell."

"Lamar, give me a hand."

Neal grabbed Jade's arm. She wasn't expecting the move and cried out in pain as he yanked her forward. Lamar gave her bottom a boost. If she hadn't placed her foot on the ground, she would have fallen face down into the mud.

She came upright and glared at Neal, wrenching her arm free. "Keep your hands off me."

"Or what? Your boyfriend will beat me up with two ice cream sundaes again?" He made a derisive sound, then turned his back on her and moved toward an ice chest, partially concealed in the dead grass. "Want a beer?"

"No."

"Hutch? Lamar?"

Neal opened the chest, took out three beers, and, without waiting for his friends to reply tossed a can to each of them. He popped the top off his and took a long draft. Like mimics, Hutch and Lamar did the same.

Jade leaned against the rear bumper of the car, studiously ignoring them and rubbing her arms against the damp chill. She hadn't thought to get her coat and books out of Donna Dee's car.

It was an extremely dark night. The low, moisture-laden clouds blocked out the moon. Nearby, she could hear the slow-moving water, but she couldn't see anything beyond the small patch of light the headlights gave off. The wind was light, but it was bone-chilling.

Neal finished his beer. Crumpling the can in his fist, he tossed it into the undergrowth on the bank of the narrow channel. The ground was littered with similar cans.

"Can we go now?" Jade tried to sound imperious despite her shivering.

Neal sauntered toward her. "Not yet."

"Why not?"

"Because before we go," he drawled, "the three of us are going to fuck you."

Chapter 3

———◆◆◆———

Donna Dee Monroe was in a quandary. It didn't feel right for her to be safe at home while Jade's whereabouts remained uncertain. Surely if Jade were home she would have called.

Donna Dee had waited inside her stranded car only five minutes before a farming family in a station wagon had stopped and offered her a lift into town. Her father had met her at the service station, filled a gas can, and returned her to her car. She was back in Palmetto less than twenty minutes after the three boys had disappeared with Jade.

The thought of being left behind still rankled. How dare they go off and leave her stranded like that? And why hadn't he let Jade out of the car when she made it obvious that she didn't want to go with them alone? Neal Patchett ought to be stood against a wall and shot right between the eyes.

As usual, Hutch had done Neal's bidding without a whimper of protest. It irked Donna Dee that Hutch cared so little for her that he would desert her on a lonely stretch of highway, prey to whatever kind of lowlife might have come along. Of course, the notion of being snatched up and carried off into the night by Hutch Jolly was madly romantic, and one fantasy she'd entertained many times. While it wouldn't be ideal to have Neal and Lamar tagging along when Hutch swept her away, Donna Dee envied Jade the adventure of being "kidnapped."

Now, alone in her bedroom, Donna Dee wondered what she should do about Jade. Had Neal tried to return Jade to the point where he had picked her up, or had he brought her back to town, or taken her straight to Gary's house? There was only one way to find out. Donna Dee reached for her telephone and began dialing the Parkers' number. But what if Jade wasn't there? In view of his recent fight with Neal at the Dairy Barn, Gary would go into a tailspin when he found out what Neal had done.

Donna Dee didn't want to get Jade into trouble with her mom or with Gary. She didn't want anybody mad at her, either. But she couldn't relax until she knew what was happening. Finally making up her mind, she placed a telephone call.

"Left?"

"That's right, Velta," Pete Jones said. "I got back from the nursing home a little before six. Jade and that Monroe girl were practically bouncing off the walls. When I agreed to let Jade leave early, they tore straight out of here. She said to tell you she'd be home in an hour with some good news."

Velta disliked surprises, even happy ones. She especially didn't welcome one this evening. She was tired. Her lower back ached from bending over her desk all day. She was hungry for dinner. She wanted to go home, eat, take a long bath, and go to bed.

Velta was barely forty, but she looked every day of it and then some, as now, when she pursed her narrow lips in vexation. "It's not like Jade to go off without asking my permission."

Pete Jones chuckled. "Something big was going on. Jade's feet were barely touching the ground."

"Did she say what her good news was?"

"Nope."

"Well, she'll turn up soon," she said with forced indifference. No sense in providing fodder for the gossip mill. "Thank you, Mr. Jones. Good night."

On the drive home, Velta scanned the streets for a sign of Donna Dee's car. This escapade was probably all her doing. Ever since Donna Dee's parents had given her that rattletrap automobile, the girls had had far too much independence. That's why Velta never let Jade take the car out unless she accounted for where she was going and how long she would be gone. People didn't think well of girls who had unlimited freedom.

By the time she arrived home, Velta was in a snit. The mailbox was full of mail that she was too tired and angry to sort through. She tossed it onto the kitchen table without even glancing through it. For dinner she heated up some soup. She had just finished her bath when the telephone rang. "Hello?"

"Hi, Mrs. Sperry. It's Donna Dee. May I speak with Jade, please?"

"Mr. Jones told me she was with you!"

"Uh, well, she was. She's not home yet?"

"Donna Dee, I want a full explanation, and I want it now. Jade left the store before six and it's almost nine. Where is she?"

"We were on our way to Gary's house and ran out of gas."

"Why were you going all the way out to the Parkers' place at that time of day?"

"She had something to tell Gary."

"Something that couldn't be told over the telephone?"

"Mrs. Sperry, don't press me on this, okay?" Donna Dee whined. "You need to hear it from Jade. Anyway, we ran out of gas about halfway there. Neal Patchett came by. He had Hutch and Lamar with him. They, uh, they took Jade with them."

"Took her where?"

"I don't know. They drove off and left me stranded. They meant it as a joke, I guess, but this is the lowest trick Neal has ever pulled."

"Are you at home now?"

"I have been for a while." She explained how she had returned to town. "I figured that Jade would have gotten home by now—you know, that either Neal or Gary would have brought her. The last I saw of them, they were headed in the direction of the Parker farm."

"Well, she isn't here. I haven't heard a word."

"Do you think Jade's all right?" Donna Dee asked uneasily.

"If Neal dropped her off at Gary's house, she's probably just lost track of time. I've had to get onto her lately for breaking her curfews."

"Why didn't she come back for me?"

"How long were you there alone?"

"Not long."

"You were probably already on your way back by the time she got there."

"I guess so, but maybe one of us ought to call Gary's house and make sure she's there. I didn't before, because there's bad blood between Gary and Neal. Gary wouldn't like knowing that Jade hitched a ride with Neal."

"Well, if she's at his place, he already knows, doesn't he?"

"That's true," Donna Dee said slowly as realization dawned. "Maybe he's mad and Jade's trying to smooth things over."

"Don't worry about it, Donna Dee. I'll call the Parkers myself. Good night."

Velta considered the advantages of calling the Parkers but decided against it. If Jade was with Gary, she was safe. If she was with Neal Patchett, why get Gary upset? What he didn't know wouldn't hurt him.

A smile tugged at the corners of Velta's lips and a rare sparkle appeared in her gray eyes. If Jade was with Neal, all the better. An evening in his company might change the girl's mind about a few things. She might come to realize how important it was to mingle with the right people, and how much more fun it would be to fall in love with a rich boy than a poor one.

All things considered, this might be the best thing that could have happened.

Had the choice been left solely to Jade, she probably would have lain on the marshy ground beside the channel until she died of hunger, thirst, or exposure. Her survival instinct was too powerful, however. She never knew how long she lay in the dark, curled into a defensive fetal position, numbed by the violation that had been inflicted on her.

The clouds wept for her. The mist that had been falling intermittently all day had turned into a miserable rain. Cold, mortified, and outraged, she finally uncoiled her body and managed to pull herself onto her hands and knees.

She crawled forward a few yards and found a shoe that she had, at some point during the attack, kicked off. She groped in the darkness for its mate but couldn't locate it. It didn't matter. Nothing mattered. She would just as soon die as live.

No, that wasn't entirely true. Because even more compelling than her will to survive was her determination to see that Hutch Jolly, Lamar Griffith, and Neal Patchett were punished for what they had done to her.

With that thought burning like a torch in her soul, she struggled to stand up and made feeble attempts to pull her blouse together. The buttons had been ripped off. The best she could do was to refasten her bra. Her breasts were sore.

The clouds overhead blotted out the moonlight. There was nothing to relieve the darkness. With her arms extended, she felt her way around the clearing like a blind person and only got her bearings when she stumbled over the deep tire tracks Neal's car had left in the muddy ground.

Dropping to her hands and knees again, she crawled along the tracks, knowing that if she followed them, they would eventually lead her back to the highway. A nocturnal creature slithered out of the undergrowth and crossed

her path. Snatching her hands back, she recoiled in fear
and held her breath, listening. Several minutes ticked by.
When she didn't hear anything except her own labored
heartbeat, or sense any movement in the tall grass that
lined the narrow road, she continued inching her way
along the tread tracks, concentrating only on placing
one palm on the cold, squishy ground, then the next. She
dragged her knees behind her until they were as sore
as the rest of her body. Rain trickled into her collar and
down her back and plastered her hair to her scalp.

Frequently she was tempted to give up. She wanted to
lie down and die, for in a matter of hours, her life had
turned ugly and bleak. She didn't want to acknowledge
what had happened to her or cope with the devastating
after-effects.

But if she gave up, her rapists might get off scot-free.

So she kept going. Hand, knee, hand, knee, hand,
knee...

After what seemed like hours, she reached the ditch
that ran alongside the highway. Crawling forward, she
reached out to touch the pavement. With a hoarse, glad cry,
she clambered forward and lay prostrate on the highway as
though she wanted to embrace it, like a pilgrim who has
finally reached a holy shrine. The road's surface was hard
beneath her cheek, but she lay face down on it to rest.

If she had made it this far, she could make it all the
way back to town, to the hospital, to the sheriff's office.
Thank God she had survived to report the crime. Hutch,
Lamar, and Neal wouldn't be hard to locate. Depending
on how long it took her to get back to town, they would be
locked behind bars within hours.

Long before she was sufficiently rested and ready to

stand up, she forced herself to her feet. Driven by the need to punish her violators, she staggered toward the center of the road. Following the broken white stripe would be less hazardous than groping her way along the uneven shoulder.

As she moved forward, she tried to calculate how long it would take her to reach Palmetto. Or should she try to go only as far as the first house she came to? From there she could call for help.

Her mother must be frantic with worry. Velta wanted to know where Jade was every single minute of the day. Surely Donna Dee had alerted someone to her abduction—unless Donna Dee had been raped, too.

"Oh, God, please no," she mumbled to herself.

She hopefully imagined volunteers looking for them already, combing the county in their search. Perhaps by the time she reached town, her three attackers would already be under arrest.

The car was almost upon her before she realized it was there. She had been so lost in thought that the weak headlights hadn't alerted her to its approach.

Neal! He had come back for her. He wasn't under arrest yet. He had returned to hurt her again, maybe kill her so she couldn't testify against him.

Jade stumbled across the highway and plunged into the ditch. There was knee-deep stagnant water in the bottom of it. It smelled foul. Cold slime oozed between her bare toes. Her fear, however, was stronger than her revulsion.

Panicked and whimpering, she thrashed her way through reeds and undergrowth that seemed to clutch at the hem of her skirt. When she reached the barbed-wire fence, she crouched down beside a fence post, hiding, trying to be invisible.

The car slowed down and crept along the shoulder. When its headlights fell on her, it stopped.

"No, no." She ducked her head against her shoulder and protected her middle with her crossed arms, which were bleeding from dozens of scratches left by the brambles in the ditch.

"Missy, missy, wha'chu doin' out heah this time o' evenin'?" The voice was black. So were the hands that were outstretched toward her. "Missy, you hurt?"

He touched her shoulder. She flinched. He quickly pulled back his hands. "I ain't gonna hurt you, missy. What's happened to you?"

Against the twin beams of the headlights, he was merely a silhouette, but Jade made out a pair of overalls and a slouchy felt hat. Again he extended his hands toward her. This time she didn't recoil. He placed his hands beneath her forearms and gingerly backed up, pulling her along with him, up out of the ditch.

Keeping one hand beneath her arm, the man opened the passenger side and helped her into his old pickup. The door closed with a loud clatter of rusty metal that jarred her. It was dry inside, but there was no heater. She began to shiver uncontrollably.

"Where you headed, missy?" he asked as he slid behind the wheel. "Do you stay 'round heah?"

"Would you take me to the hospital, please?" She didn't recognize her own voice. It was hoarse from screaming. Neal had slapped her for screaming. Hutch had covered her mouth with his large hand. Her screams had made Lamar anxious.

"The hospital? Sure thing, missy. You just rest now. Everythin's gonna be all right."

Jade did as the man suggested. She laid her head back against the seat and closed her eyes. She was safe. Warm tears seeped from her closed eyes and rolled down her cheeks. She cried silently as the ancient truck bounced along the highway.

Either she dozed or momentarily lost consciousness because, almost immediately it seemed, the truck slowed down and came to a halt. The man got out and went around to open the door for her.

"Thank you," she whispered as he helped her out. When she stepped to the ground, her lower body began to throb painfully. She swayed and had to grab a support pole. Closing her eyes, she rested her cheek against the cold metal surface until the dizziness subsided. "Thank you," she repeated.

She turned to the man who had kindly rescued her, but his truck was backing away. "No, wait." She shielded her eyes against the headlights, but couldn't make out what he or the truck looked like. There was no front license plate. When the pickup reached the main road, the forward gears were engaged and the truck lumbered off into the rainy darkness. Jade supposed that beating a hasty retreat was his only protection against those who would jump to conclusions about his involvement with a white rape victim. Unfortunately, there were still many in Palmetto who, given the situation, would act first and ask questions later.

She made hesitant progress toward the sliding glass doors where EMERGENCY was spelled out in red neon. The doors slid open. Beyond them, the blue-white fluorescent lighting was offensive. She dreaded being exposed to it, so she hovered just inside the door, waiting for someone

to notice her. Two nurses and a man who looked like a
janitor were chatting and laughing together at the desk.

Jade had thought she would welcome reporting the
attack, but now that it was imminent, she was filled with
dread. This was only the first of many difficult steps to
see that justice was done. In order to achieve her goal,
however, she was willing to bear whatever difficulties and
embarrassment she might encounter.

Leaving a trail of mud behind her, she worked up
her courage and shuffled toward the desk. "Excuse me."
Three pairs of eyes turned toward her. "Can you help me,
please?"

At the sight of her, their faces registered shock for
several seconds. Then the janitor stepped out of the way,
one of the nurses reached for the telephone, and the other
rounded the desk to lend Jade a supportive arm.

"What happened to you, honey? Were you in an
accident?"

"I was raped."

The nurse looked at her sharply. "Raped? Here in
Palmetto?"

"Beside a channel, just off the coastal highway."

"Sweet Jesus."

Jade was keenly aware of the janitor, who was taking
in every word and staring at her breasts through her gap-
ing blouse. The other nurse was speaking into the telephone. "Dr. Harvey, we need you in the ER. A girl just
came in. She says she was raped."

"I *was* raped." Jade's voice cracked. She was very near
tears. She wished the janitor would stop gawking at her.

"Come on, honey, let's put you in here to wait for the
doctor. Want me to call somebody for you?"

"Not until I've cleaned up."

The nurse led her into a small examination room. The curtain she pulled around the table was flimsy and billowy, like a yellow parachute. "Lordy, lordy, you're a mess. Get out of those clothes. Everything. The doctor'll have to do a pelvic, you know. Put this on." She handed Jade a blue-and-white striped cotton hospital gown.

"Can't you do it?" she asked tremulously.

"Do what, honey?" The nurse was laying out stainless steel tools. They looked repugnant and terrifying.

"The examination." She didn't want a man near her, touching her. She didn't think she could survive having to open her legs and expose herself to a man.

"I'm sorry, honey, no. Did he put those scratches on your arms?"

"They. There were three of them."

Horrified, the nurse whispered, "Blacks?"

"No, they're white."

She appeared relieved. "I'll call the sheriff's office. The doctor will be here in a jiffy."

The nurse went through the curtain, leaving Jade alone. Slowly, painfully, she removed her clothing. She piled her soggy, tattered blouse, skirt, and bra in a heap on the floor. Her underpants and pantyhose were gone, as were her shoes.

In the revealing light, she gazed down at her body, cramming her fist against her lips to keep from screaming. She was filthy. From the knees down, her legs were caked with mud. There were long, bleeding scratches on her arms. Her knees and the heels of her hands were raw and bloody beneath several layers of dirt.

Worst of all, her belly and the skin between her thighs

was smeared with a sticky substance, tinged pink by her own blood. She felt nastier than a spittoon. Hastily reaching for a stainless steel basin on the counter, she retched.

"Miss, uh, Sperry?"

The male voice came from just beyond the curtain. He cast a silhouette against the thin fabric. Jade choked on bile, coughed, and cleared her burning throat.

"I need to examine you now, Ms. Sperry."

"Just . . . just a minute." She fumbled with the gown and was finally able to pull it over her head. Its hem barely skimmed her upper thighs. She climbed onto the examination table and draped the cloth around her hips, covering as much of herself as she could. "Okay."

Her system received another unpleasant shock. The doctor was very young. He had a fresh face that looked like it rarely needed a shave. His eyes were bright and quizzical. She had hoped for someone who resembled the kindly, family physician in the famous Norman Rockwell paintings—a gray-haired, older gentleman with an endearing paunch and spectacles.

The doctor must have sensed her aversion to him. He did his best to look and sound compassionate, probably because he didn't want a hysterical girl on his hands. "The next few minutes are going to be uncomfortable, Ms. Sperry. I'm going to examine you, take some Polaroid pictures, ask you some questions. Some of the questions will be embarrassing, I'm afraid. Let's get them over with first, okay?"

Getting down to business, he opened the metal cover of a medical chart and whipped out a ballpoint pen from the breast pocket of his white lab coat.

"Full name?"

"Jade Elizabeth Sperry."

"Age?"

"Eighteen."

"Date of birth?"

He wrote the pertinent information in the spaces provided on the official form; then, as he had warned, the questions got more embarrassing. "Date of your last period?"

"I don't remember."

"I need to know. An approximation anyway."

Rubbing her temples, Jade thought back. She gave him a date that seemed feasible. He wrote it down.

"Any venereal diseases?"

The questions stunned her. "Pardon me?"

"Have you ever had a venereal disease or sexual contact with someone who has?"

Something inside her snapped and she lashed out in anger. "Until tonight I was a virgin!" In that instant, Jade knew that she had lost her innocence this night in more ways than one.

"I see. Okay." The doctor made a note of that on the chart. "Did the man—"

"Men. I already told the nurse that there were three of them. Didn't she tell you?"

"No, I'm sorry, she didn't. Three?"

"Three."

"Did all three achieve penetration?"

Her lower lip began to tremble. She caught it between her teeth. "Yes."

"You're certain?"

"Yes!"

"Did all three ejaculate?"

She was almost sick again. Swallowing another mouthful of bitter bile, she croaked, "Yes."

"Are you sure, Ms. Sperry?" he asked skeptically. "I mean, if you were a virgin, you might not be able to tell."

She glared at him but couldn't muster the energy to maintain the outrage for long. Her shoulders slumped forward in defeat. "They all three...did that."

He let the cover fall back over the chart and repocketed his pen. Poking his head around the curtain, he called for the nurse to assist him. She helped Jade to lie down, then guided her feet into frigid metal stirrups. The doctor worked his hands into a pair of rubber gloves, snapping them at his wrists. He sat down on a low stool at the end of the examination table and adjusted a blindingly bright light. He touched her bruised thighs and spread them wider. She made a small sound of protest.

"I warned you this would be uncomfortable, Ms. Sperry. I'll try not to hurt you."

She couldn't meet his eyes where he looked up at her from between her thighs. Instead she pinched her eyes shut as she felt him insert something hard, cold, and intrusive into her. She gripped the edges of the padded table.

"Try to relax. You did the right thing, you know. It's good that you didn't run home and shower before coming here."

She couldn't carry on a conversation, not while she was so thoroughly exposed to him and the nurse. Her skin was cold and clammy to the touch, but a red tide of embarrassment had heated her veins. Her head was pounding, and she could feel each heartbeat strike her eardrums.

"Do you think you can identify the men?"

"Oh, yes. I can identify them."

"Well, that's good, at least. They'll pay for it. That is, if you don't lose your nerve and drop the charges before the case comes to trial."

"I won't lose my nerve," she vowed, her jaw clenched and set.

"There, I'm finished. Except for the public hair. Not all of it is yours. I'll just collect some here. It'll go to the lab, too."

Jade cringed and kept her eyes tightly shut until she felt the nurse lowering her feet from the stirrups, helping her to sit up. The doctor cleaned beneath her fingernails with an orangewood stick, then peeled off his gloves and dropped them into a trash bin.

"Just stand there in front of the curtain," he said to Jade as he reached for a Polaroid camera. He instructed the nurse to help her adjust the gown.

For the next several minutes, she was photographed front and back. She was never completely naked, but she might as well have been. He took pictures of her face, her shoulders, breasts, belly, thighs, buttocks, any place where there was a scratch or a bruise. There weren't many. Neal had been careful about that.

"What about those scratches on your arms and knees?"

She shook her head. "I got those later, crawling along the highway."

"Okay. I'll fill out my report and get this stuff to the lab. There won't be anybody there at this time of night, but they can get on it first thing in the morning. The nurse will take you to a shower. We'll give you a set of OR scrubs to put on. Your clothes will go to the lab, too."

Jade nodded. "Thank you."

He bustled out, taking the laboratory evidence with him.

"Come with me, honey." The nurse pulled back the curtain and moved toward the door.

Jade hesitated, self-consciously tugging on the brief gown. "Like this? It barely covers my bottom."

"This is a hospital. Nobody notices."

Jade thought the janitor would notice. There didn't seem to be any choice, however. She followed the nurse out into the corridor and took tiny steps to keep the hem of the gown from flapping.

"You're lucky Doc Harvey came from a big city hospital. He knows what to do," the nurse remarked.

They went through a pair of swinging doors marked HOSPITAL PERSONNEL ONLY and entered a lounge area where several nurses were drinking coffee and eating snacks from the vending machines. They glanced up curiously as she crossed the room behind the nurse.

"Right in there," she said, holding open the door to a women's locker room. "Towels and everything else you'll need are in the closet next to the shower stall. There's a disposable douche in there, too."

Jade wished she would lower her voice. Everyone in the room was staring at her. "I've never douched," she whispered.

"Nothing to it. The instructions are printed on the box."

Jade slipped through the door. As the woman had said, she found everything she needed in the closet. She removed the hospital gown and stepped into the shower stall. Thankfully, the water was hot. Jade turned it on until it was scalding. She kept it as hot as she could stand it and welcomed its pounding sting. It was cleansing, purifying. She wanted to wash them and their hideous residue off her body. It amazed her that she had stood having it on her skin this long without losing her sanity.

After soaping three times, she propped one foot on the soap dish and washed the area between her thighs. It hurt so badly that it brought tears to her eyes, but she scrubbed and scrubbed until her skin was raw. Inexpertly, she used the douche and was glad that she did. Finally, she shampooed the mud out of her hair and rinsed her mouth out several times with hot water.

Afterward she felt better, although she knew she would never feel completely clean again. She had been sullied— mentally, physically, and emotionally. She could never again be what she had been. That thought left her feeling disconsolate and furious.

She dried off and then wrapped her wet hair in a coarse towel. There were several pairs of green scrubs folded on the top shelf of the closet. The second pair she held against her fit moderately well. The paper booties were meant to go over shoes, but she tied them onto her bare feet.

Timidly she opened the door and checked the lounge. The nurse was alone, sitting on a sofa watching a TV talk show. When she saw Jade, she stood up. "Would you like something? A Coke? Coffee?"

"No, thanks."

"They called from the desk. The sheriff's deputy is here to talk to you."

"I'm ready."

The booties whispered along the floor. The deputy was chewing the fat with the janitor and Dr. Harvey when she and the nurse approached the emergency-room desk. The law officer pushed his hat back on his head, assumed an authoritative stance, and regarded her suspiciously.

"Miss Sperry?"

"That's right."

"Please, sit down over here."

Gingerly, Jade sat on the edge of a lavender vinyl divan. He dropped into a chair facing her. Dr. Harvey remained standing at the end of the couch. The deputy, who wasn't any older than the doctor, took a small spiral notebook from the breast pocket of his uniform jacket.

"Dr. Harvey here says you claim you were raped tonight."

She divided her incredulous gaze between them. "Why does everybody keep saying I 'claimed' this or I 'said' that? I was raped. Do you think I'm lying?"

"Hold on. Nobody's accused you of lying. I'm just trying to find out what happened. Calm down, okay?"

Jade composed herself. It wasn't easy. She had to call upon all her reserves of self-discipline to keep from screaming. The janitor and the nurses were once again huddled together at the desk nearby. Jade didn't think she was being paranoid in assuming that they were whispering about her. Every once in a while one or all of them would glance in her direction, then quickly look away and resume their furtive conversation.

"What's your full name?" the deputy asked.

His image began to blur. She realized that her eyes were filling with tears. "I was raped," she stressed. "My rapists are running around free while I'm here being humiliated and insulted." She drew a ragged breath. "I've already given the doctor my full name, address, birthday, and so forth. Wouldn't you rather know what happened to me tonight and who committed the crime?"

"All in good time," he replied, unfazed by her tearful appeal. "I'm using standard police procedure in response to this complaint. If the case comes to trial, you don't want the perps to get off on a technicality, do you, little lady?"

"Why don't you just answer his questions, Miss Sperry?" the doctor suggested, speaking softly and courteously. "In the long run, it'll go faster. Can I get you something to drink?"

"No, thank you."

"I can give you a sedative if you want one."

Vigorously, she shook her head. Returning her attention to the deputy, she supplied unemotional responses to his routine questions.

"Now, about tonight," he said after clearing his throat, "you told Dr. Harvey that three men attacked and forcibly raped you."

"That's right."

"Were they armed?"

"No."

"No? They didn't hold you at gunpoint or anything like that?"

"They overpowered me and held me down on the ground."

"Hmm. Did they all achieve penetration?"

"That's in my report, Deputy," Dr. Harvey said helpfully.

"I'm doing the questioning, Doc, thanks. Answer the question, Miss Sperry."

"Yes," Jade said. "They all...penetrated and...and completed the act."

"Were you sodomized?"

"No, she wasn't." The doctor answered for her again when Jade appeared too stunned by the question to speak.

"Were you forced to have oral sex?"

She shook her head as she slowly bowed it. "No."

"Where did this alleged attack take place?"

Alleged? The word annoyed her, but she responded to his question. "Near a channel off the coastal highway. I don't believe the turnoff has a name. It's only a dirt track. I could lead you straight to it. Unless they took them, you could find articles of my clothing there."

"Can you provide the department with a description of the alleged assailants."

"I can do better than that, Deputy. I can name them."

"You know their names?"

"Oh yes."

"Well, hey, that's a real break for us. Shoot." His pencil was eagerly poised over the spiral notebook.

"Lamar Griffith."

The pencil lead scratched noisily against the paper. Then, cocking his head to one side in puzzlement, the deputy read the name he'd just written down. He looked up at Jade.

"Myrajane Griffith's kid?"

"Lamar Griffith," Jade repeated firmly. "Neal Patchett." The blood drained out of the deputy's face. Nervously, he wet his lips. "And Hutch Jolly."

For several moments he stared at her. Then, leaning forward, placing his nose inches from hers, he whispered, "You're shittin' me, right?"

She snatched the notebook and pencil from his hands and printed the three names on the ruled paper. Jabbing the bold message with the tip of the pencil, she cried, "Those are the names of the men who raped me. It's your duty to see that they're arrested and locked up in jail."

He swallowed visibly and glanced at the doctor, as though seeking help. "Miss, uh, uh—"

"Sperry," she shouted.

"Miss Sperry, you can't mean what you're saying."

"I mean every word of it."

"You got things mixed up."

"Neal, Hutch, and Lamar abducted me from my girl friend's car, took me to that remote spot, and all three of them raped me. After that, they left me there." She jumped to her feet. "Why are you just sitting there looking stupid? Find out about Donna Dee! Go after those boys! Put them in handcuffs! Take them to jail!"

"Miss Sperry." The doctor took her arm. He guided her back down to the sofa and signaled for the nurse. "Maybe you'd better bring her a Valium."

"I won't take it," Jade snapped, shaking off his arm. To the deputy she said, "If you're incapable of apprehending three criminals, call somebody who can."

"Shit, lady. You just named my boss's kid as a rapist."

"That's right. Hutch went second. He was the roughest. And the biggest. He nearly smothered me." She didn't realize she was clenching her hands so tightly, until they began to hurt. She glanced down at them and saw four half-moons gouged into her abraded palms.

"You'd better call the sheriff," the doctor told the deputy.

"Christ almighty," he said as he reluctantly stood up. He dragged his hand down his youthful, pudgy face. "I ain't looking forward to this, a'tall. The shit's going to hit the fan when I tell Sheriff Jolly that his and Ivan Patchett's boy have been accused of rape."

An hour later, Jade sat alone in the interrogation room. It smelled of stale tobacco smoke and anxious sweat.

The deputy had driven her straight from the hospital to the courthouse and deposited her in the cubicle as though washing his hands of the whole nasty affair.

Jade was certain that before it was over with, things were going to get nastier. The legal ramifications were overwhelming, but they were diminished by the personal affronts she would have to endure. How would she tell Gary?

She couldn't think about that now or she would go crazy. She had to deal with the here and now—Donna Dee, for instance. Jade was concerned for her safety. It was conceivable that after the boys left her, they had gone back and done the same thing to Donna Dee. Perhaps that had been Neal's plan—to separate them and render them virtually helpless. Donna Dee could be severely hurt, lying unconscious somewhere along the highway. Even dead.

Her anxious thoughts were interrupted when Sheriff Fritz Jolly entered the room. Instead of his uniform, he was wearing blue jeans and a flannel pajama top beneath a camouflage hunting vest. Obviously he had been roused from his bed. Rust-colored whiskers sprouted from his chin and cheeks.

"Evenin', Jade."

"Hello, Sheriff Jolly."

She frequently sold him chewing tobacco at the store. They were always friendly with each other. Now, he lowered his large, imposing frame into the chair across from hers and folded his hands on the scarred table between them. "I understand you got into some trouble tonight."

"I didn't get into trouble, Sheriff Jolly."

"Tell me about it."

"Can I wait until my mother gets here?" She didn't want to have to tell her story more than once. "The doctor at the hospital promised to call her and tell her to meet me here." The deputy hadn't given Jade time to place the call herself.

"Velta's already in the squad room, chomping at the bit," he said. "But I'd like to hear what you've got to say before we bring her in."

"Why was I put in this interrogation room?"

" 'Cause it's convenient and private."

She gazed at him mistrustfully. "I didn't do anything wrong."

"No one said you did. What happened?"

He won their staring contest. Jade glanced down at her tightly clasped hands and took a deep breath. "Neal, Lamar, and Hutch came up on Donna Dee and me where we had run out of gas. They took me away in Neal's car against my will. They drove to a place where they had been drinking beer and fishing earlier this afternoon and they..." She raised her head and met his eyes. "They took turns raping me."

He stared at her for several long moments but said nothing.

Jade added, "I'm afraid Donna Dee might have been hurt, too."

"The deputy told me you had asked about her. I called her house. She's at home. Unharmed."

She took a deep breath of relief. "Thank heaven."

His voice was low and confidence-inspiring when he spoke again. "That's a real serious charge to be making against those boys, Jade."

"Rape is a serious crime."

"It's hard for me to believe they would do something like that."

"It was hard for me to believe, too. This time yesterday, I would never have thought it possible."

"Well then," he said, "why don't you tell me what really happened?"

Chapter 4

———◆———

Neal's room was still dark when his father flung open the door and stormed in. Ivan moved straight to the bed, whipped back the covers, and brought his hand down hard on Neal's bare buttocks.

"You little shit!"

Neal rolled to the other side of the bed and leaped up. Father and son confronted each other across the rumpled bed. Neal was naked. Ivan was wearing boxer shorts and an old-fashioned white tank T-shirt. His iron-gray hair was standing on end at various points around his head. Even so, he didn't cut a comic figure. His scowl was fearsome.

"What the fuck got into you?" Neal demanded, settling his hands on his narrow hips. He looked tousled, drowsy, and sullen. His fine, hard body was a product of genetics rather than conditioning. It performed well in sports arenas, but Neal didn't exert it unless it was absolutely necessary. He took his lean, strong physique as his due.

"I just got a telephone call from Fritz," Ivan told him.

"So? It's the middle of the night. I'm going back to bed."

"Like hell you are."

Neal's head was halfway back to his pillow when Ivan caught him by the hair and pulled him up. He gave him a swift kick in the rear. Neal careened into the nearest wall. He spun around, fists raised, ready to do combat.

"Did you rape a girl last night?"

Neal immediately lowered his fists. "I don't know what the hell you're talking about."

"I'm talking about Jade Sperry, who's down at the courthouse accusing you of rape, that's what I'm talking about." Ivan pointed a stern index finger at the center of Neal's chest. "You'd better tell me the truth, boy." Ivan's roar would have awakened the dead.

Neal's eyes darted around the dim bedroom, lighting briefly on several items before finally coming to rest on Ivan's thunderous countenance. "If she claims it was rape, she's telling a goddamn lie."

"So you do know what I'm talking about, you lying little son of a bitch."

"I'm not lying!" Neal shouted. "Hutch, Lamar, and me picked her up and took her fishing with us. We drank some beer. Had some laughs. She got friendly—I mean *real* friendly, Daddy. She asked for it, and she got it."

Ivan glared at him, his shrewd eyes reflecting the breaking dawn light like shards of glass. "Bullshit. That Sperry girl ain't white trash. She's stuck like glue to that Parker boy. What would she want with you three stooges?"

Neal cursed beneath his breath and plowed a hand through his mussed hair. "I tell you, Daddy, she's been asking for it. She makes out like she's hot for Parker and nobody else, but every chance she gets, she wags her tail in my face. Then, when her boyfriend comes around, she goes back to being snooty and treating me like a pile of dogshit she's stepped in.

"You think I'm going to take that kind of crap from a girl? Hell no! Last night I decided to give her a taste of what a real man is like. If she wants to call it rape, that's her problem."

"The hell it is!" Ivan had listened to Neal's explanation with surprising patience. Now he ground his teeth. "It's not just her problem. She's made it the sheriff's problem. And now it's my problem."

Neal idly scratched his crotch. "What are you going to do?"

"Not a goddamn thing."

"Huh?" Neal's stance lost some of its swagger.

"I'm doing nothing until you level with me and tell me what happened. Did you force that girl?"

Neal's shoulders rose in a tense shrug. "Things got a little rough." Quickly he added, "But I know she wanted it."

"What about Hutch and Lamar?"

"They wanted a piece, too." He grinned. "I'm not selfish."

Ivan almost backhanded him for his insolence, then decided not to expend the energy and lowered his raised hand. "Hutch, I can see. But I can't imagine that titmouse of Myrajane's forcing himself between a girl's legs."

"Lamar needed some egging on, but he did all right."

There was a knock at the door. They turned to see their housekeeper, Eula, standing on the threshold. "Will y'all be wanting your mornin' coffee now, Mr. Patchett?"

"No!" Ivan barked. "I'll tell you when I want my coffee."

"Yessir. Just askin'."

She withdrew. Ivan stared at the empty doorway for a moment, then said to Neal, "Why didn't y'all go to nigger town and pick a gal who would keep her trap shut? Why'd you have to poke that Sperry girl?"

"She had it coming, that's why."

"Christ, what a mess."

Neal, seeming unconcerned, moved to the bed and stepped into the jeans he'd slung over the footboard the night before. "What're you going to do, Daddy?"

"I don't know yet. Let me think." Ivan paced the length of the bed. "They could lock you away for quite a spell on a rape conviction, you know."

"Why, that's crap," Neal stammered. "That's bullshit. They can't send a guy to prison for screwing a girl who damn well needed to be screwed."

Ivan said, "I know that and you know that. We just gotta make certain everybody else feels the way we do."

"Well, I'm not going to jail, that's for damn sure. In jail the niggers fuck white boys in the ass. You've got to do something, Daddy."

"Shut up and let me think!" Ivan shouted. Then suddenly he slapped Neal hard across the face. "You little bastard. You perfectly ruined my day."

Jade rested her head on her folded arms on the table in the interrogation room. The backs of her eyelids were hot and gritty. She had been kept at the courthouse all night. She had been allowed to go to the restroom only once, and then a deputy had escorted her there and back. It was as though she were under arrest, while, to her knowledge, nothing had been done to apprehend her attackers.

She had told Sheriff Jolly her story twice, keeping her

descriptions precise. During the second telling, she hadn't altered a single word from the first. Her remarkable memory had always served her well in school. Tonight, she had used it to give an accurate account of the gang rape. No matter how embarrassing the details, she hadn't glossed over them.

Without being abusive, the sheriff had tried to confound her. "Jade, Hutch was at home when I left a while ago."

"I don't know where he is now. I only know where he was and what he was doing about seven o'clock this evening."

"That's when you say it happened?"

"That *is* when it happened. Hutch wasn't at home then, was he?"

"He came in around nine and said he'd been out with Neal and Lamar."

"He had been. They raped me."

Fritz had dragged a large hand down his ruddy face, stretching the loose skin. "How do you account for the time between seven o'clock, when the alleged rape took place, and the time you arrived at the hospital, which was..." He consulted the deputy's spiral notebook. "You got to the hospital at eleven-thirty-four."

"For a long time after they left me, I lay there. Then I crawled to the highway. When the car came up behind me—"

"I thought you said it was a pickup."

"I did. It was a pickup. But at first I imagined it was Neal's car. I panicked and tried to hide in the ditch. The black man coaxed me out of the ditch and into his truck. He drove me to the hospital."

"He didn't give you his name?"

"No."

"And you can't describe him?"

"It was dark. All I know is that he had on a hat and overalls."

"That could be any man in the South. Wonder why, if he treated you so kindly, he didn't come into the hospital with you? Why'd he just vanish into thin air?"

"If you were a black man from around here and you were bringing a white girl, who had obviously been raped, to the emergency room, would you have stuck around, Sheriff Jolly?"

He had the grace to look chagrined. Then he said, "Some white women would rather die than be raped by a black man."

Jade came out of her chair, circled it, and gripped the top rung as she squared off with him across the table. "You think I got picked up by a black man, was raped by him, and want to make your son and his two friends the scapegoats? Is that your theory?"

"I have to cover all the angles, Jade. Especially when my own son is being accused of a felony."

"Well, rather than badgering me, why aren't you asking Hutch the questions?"

"I intend to."

Shortly after that conversation, he had allowed her mother to join her. Velta was always well groomed, so it was a shock to Jade to see her looking harried and disheveled. She rushed into the interrogation room, almost knocking aside Sheriff Jolly in her haste.

"Jade! What's happened? Nobody would tell me a thing. Where have you been?"

Right then, the last thing Jade needed was more questions. She needed to be held close and comforted. She needed unqualified acceptance. Instead, her mother demanded answers. In her place, Jade supposed she might have reacted the same way, but that didn't make her feel any better.

Velta's face didn't register a single emotion when Jade told her what had happened. After several seconds of blank staring, she dumbly repeated, "Raped?"

"Yes, Mama."

Awkwardly, she reached out to smooth back the strands of hair that had dried in unruly waves around Jade's face. "Who did it?"

When Jade told her, Velta pulled back her hand as though Jade's hair had given her an electric shock. "That's...that's crazy, Jade. You've known those boys all your life. They wouldn't do something like that."

"They did." Tears welled in her eyes. "Don't you believe me, Mama?"

"Of course, Jade. Of course I believe you."

Jade didn't think so, but lacked the energy and heart to try to make herself believed. At the sheriff's request, she related her story again for her mother. When she concluded, he left, saying he would be back.

Since being left alone, she and her mother had said nothing of substance to each other. Velta asked her if she was all right, and Jade, because of the absurdity of the question, simply replied yes. Not since stroking her hair had Velta touched her again.

At daybreak, a deputy appeared and offered Velta a cup of fresh coffee. Jade asked for a soda to moisten her sore throat. Swallowing was painful, partially because of the unshed tears that were dammed up inside her throat.

Suddenly the door to the interrogation room swung open. Jade raised her head, realizing that she must have drifted to sleep from sheer exhaustion. She uttered a small, fearful cry when the first person through the door was Neal Patchett.

Her breath became shallow and choppy, as though she'd been running. "What's he doing here?"

Ivan Patchett and Sheriff Jolly filed in behind Neal. "You're tossing around some serious words, young lady," Ivan said to her. "When Fritz called and told me what was going on, I demanded that you accuse my boy to his face. Hi, Velta."

Jade's mother reacted to Ivan's appearance in much the same manner as Jade had reacted to Neal's. "Hello, Ivan."

"These two young 'uns have created quite a ruckus this morning, haven't they?"

"Yes."

"I didn't create anything!" Jade objected to Ivan's making her mother his comrade against their misbehaving children. "This was done to me. I had nothing to do with it."

"Oh, come on, Jade," Neal said, speaking for the first time. "For Chris' sake, do you honestly expect anybody to believe you were raped?"

"Nobody has to take my word for it. They can look at the pictures of me they took at the hospital. The laboratory evidence will bear out what I'm saying."

He sat down on the corner of the table. "I'm not saying it didn't happen," he said smoothly. "I'm only saying that you're taking liberties with how it happened."

"I'm not!" She would have backed farther away from him if the back of her chair would have given way. As good-looking as he was, he was thoroughly repellant to her.

"Okay, let's all settle down," Sheriff Jolly said, taking command. "Neal, move over here, please." He indicated a place against the wall. "Ivan, you take that chair."

Ivan sat down. He glanced at Velta. "You'll get the day off with pay."

"Thank you."

Jade glared at her mother, furious at her for the deference she showed Ivan Patchett.

"Now, Jade," Fritz said, drawing her attention back to him. "Please tell your story again for Ivan and Neal's benefit."

That was a daunting request. She didn't know if she could speak aloud the intimate details of the rape with Neal and his father present. However, when the case came to trial, she would have an even larger audience.

Ivan was watching her indulgently, but she saw malevolence lurking behind the benign expression in his eyes. Neal was propped against the opposite wall, arms folded across his chest. He was smirking with complacence.

"Yeah, Jade. I'd like to hear all about how I raped you."

His scoffing tone spurred her on. He wasn't going to get away with what he'd done to her, not if she had to repeat the ugly truth a thousand times.

After taking a sip of the tepid soda the deputy had brought her earlier, she began with Donna Dee's car running out of gas and ended with her arrival at the hospital. "The rest of it," she finished quietly, "is now a matter of record."

"Have you found this mysterious nigger yet?" Ivan asked Fritz.

The sheriff shook his head. "She couldn't give us anything that would identify him."

"Hmm." A satisfied smile sat upon Ivan's lips.

"He was real," Jade insisted. "In the condition I was in, I couldn't have walked all the way back into town."

"That's Daddy's point," Neal said. "Your 'condition' wasn't nearly as bad as you're making it out to be. You had plenty of time to walk back to town, and that's what you did. On the way here, you got cold feet. You got to thinking about Parker and what he would think when he heard about our little party."

Jade jumped from her chair. "Don't you dare speak his name! You're not worthy to. I'd rather you rape me again than drag Gary into this."

"Jade, for heaven's sake, sit down." Velta grabbed her arm and pulled her back into her chair.

Ivan lit a cigar and negligently fanned out the match before tossing it to the floor.

Sheriff Jolly said, "Neal, you don't have to answer to any charges."

"I don't mind. She's lying."

"Ivan, are you sure you don't want to call your lawyer?"

"We waived that right, Fritz. Why bother him this early in the morning? We've got nothing to hide. Ask the boy any damn thing you please."

Fritz addressed Neal. "What happened when you came up on Donna Dee and Jade?"

"It's just like Jade said," he replied. "We offered her a ride. She got in my car of her own free will. She even had to climb over the seat to get in the back with Lamar."

"You didn't force her into the car?"

"Hell no."

"That's because I thought Donna Dee was coming too," Jade amended quickly. "When I saw that they intended to leave her, I tried to get out. They held me. They wouldn't let her in or me out."

Neal laughed. "It was all in fun. A fake kidnapping, you know? We were just messing around."

He picked up the story from there and told them about arriving at the spot near the channel. "Jade got out and sat there while we drank a beer."

"There wasn't anywhere else to go," she explained. "When you said what you did, and I realized what you intended to do, I ran. Tell them, Neal. You know it's the truth. I tried to run away from you."

"Neal, what did you say to her?" Fritz asked.

"I told her we were going to fuck her."

Velta laid her hand against her chest and crossed her legs. Ivan puffed on his cigar. Fritz rubbed his temple. "That corroborates Jade's story."

"That's when I turned and ran toward the road," she said. "I didn't get far. Neal grabbed me by the hair and pulled me down."

He gave a helpless little shrug. "She said something to the effect of, 'Like hell you are,' but she was laughing."

"I said nothing of the sort, and I certainly wasn't laughing. I was terrified."

"Of three friends?" Ivan snorted incredulously.

"She did start running," Neal said, "but not full out, not like she didn't want to be caught. I did grab her by the hair. We had a tussle. She put up token resistance—all for show."

"That's a lie," Jade whispered hoarsely, shaking her head in adamant denial. "That's a lie. He hurt me. He

ripped off my—" A thought struck her. She looked at
Neal's mud-stained jeans—they were the ones he'd been
wearing the night before. "He ripped off my pantyhose,
then my panties. He put them in the pocket of his jeans.
Check his pocket."

"Neal?" Fritz signaled with his head for the boy to
comply.

Ivan turned his head and looked over his shoulder at
Neal as he fished into his right pocket. He produced a pair
of yellow bikini panties. Velta, recognizing them, covered
her mouth to stifle a startled gasp.

Neal gazed at Jade, his eyes full of regret. Softly he
said, "You told me to keep them as a souvenir, honey.
Remember?"

"He's lying!" She shot from her chair and rounded the
table, her fingers curled into claws aimed at his sardonic
face. Fritz caught her around the waist and held her back.

The door opened and a deputy peered in. "Sheriff,
everything all right in here?"

"Everything's fine," he assured his deputy.

"Uh, sheriff, about those records at the lab."

"Yeah, I'd like to read the official report as soon as it's
available."

"That's just it, Sheriff Jolly." He shifted his weight nervously. "That's what I come to tell you. The smears and all
got throwed out by mistake. The whole kit on Miss Sperry
got burned up in the hospital incinerator this morning."

When she heard that, the fight went out of Jade. She
wilted over Fritz's arm and allowed him to direct her
back to her chair. With a tortured cry, she slumped forward. All the physical evidence of the rape had been
destroyed. Even if the emergency-room doctor testified

on her behalf, all he could actually attest to was that she had had sexual intercourse and that—seemingly—it had been rough. Under cross-examination, his testimony could be rendered useless. Besides, he couldn't identify her attackers.

Nothing that was said in this room would ever be permissible evidence in a court of law—not even Neal's confession that he'd had carnal knowledge of her. He could change his story entirely and deny that he had been involved in the incident at all. From now on, it would be Jade's word against theirs.

But out of the blanket of black despair that was about to suffocate her, there glimmered a ray of new hope. Suddenly she raised her head. "Donna Dee."

"What?" Sheriff Jolly turned to her.

"Call Donna Dee. She'll tell you that I resisted. She saw me struggling to get out of Neal's car. She'll verify that I didn't go with them voluntarily."

Fritz consulted his wristwatch, then said to the deputy, "Call Joe Monroe's house. Try and catch his girl before she leaves for school. Tell her I want her to stop by here, but don't tell her why."

The deputy doffed his hat and ducked out the door. They settled in to wait. Velta retrieved Jade's panties from the table and stuffed them into her purse. Ivan requested coffee, which was served to him by an obsequious female clerk. Neal left only long enough to get a Coke from the vending machine in the squad room. To keep from looking at him, Jade laid her head on her arms again and kept her eyes closed.

She longed for sleep. She wanted to take off the green operating-room scrubs and the ridiculous booties. She wanted to comb her hair and brush her teeth. She wanted privacy to weep for what was irretrievably lost—her virginity.

Gary, Gary, she silently groaned. He wouldn't blame her for the rape, but she wasn't so naïve as to believe that this wouldn't adversely affect their relationship. Thinking about to what extent was so heart-wrenching that she tried to concentrate on something else.

"How long have you been working for me, Velta?" she heard Ivan ask her mother. He was still puffing on his vile cigar. The smoke made Jade nauseated.

"A long time."

"Be a shame, wouldn't it, if we had to disassociate on account of this misunderstanding."

Jade looked up at him. "Don't try and intimidate her, Mr. Patchett. I hope my mother never works another day in your stinking factory. I don't want money she earns there paying for the food I eat and the clothes I wear."

Ordinarily Jade would never have spoken like that to an adult. But she had been the victim of a cruel and painful attack, and, like any injured animal, she was striking back.

Ivan flicked cigar ashes onto the floor. He frowned with stern disapproval. "You'd better put a muzzle on your girl there, Velta. She's got a real smart mouth."

Velta turned to Jade and whispered, "Hush! Why are you trying to make things worse?"

At that moment, Sheriff Jolly ushered in Donna Dee. Timidly, she hesitated before moving into the room. Her dark eyes bounced from one face to another. They finally landed on Jade. "What's going on? What happened? How come you're dressed like that?"

"Please step inside, Donna Dee." The sheriff nudged her forward and pulled up the only remaining chair for her. "Sit down. We want to ask you some questions."

"About what?" Her voice was quavering with fear of the unknown. "What's the matter? Did somebody get killed or something?"

"Nothing like that," Fritz said, trying to put the nervous girl at ease. "There was some trouble last night. You might be able to straighten out a few facts for us."

"Me? What kind of trouble?"

"Something happened after you ran out of gas late yesterday evening," he said.

"I made it home okay."

"But Jade didn't."

Donna Dee turned toward Jade. "What happened? You look terrible."

"I was raped."

Donna Dee sucked in a sharp gasp. Her small eyes popped wide. "Raped? Oh my God, Jade, for real? *Raped?*"

"So she says," Neal drawled.

Donna Dee's head snapped around toward him. "She was with you. How could she get raped?"

"He did it! He, Hutch, and Lamar raped me."

For the second time in the space of seconds, Donna Dee registered utter shock. "Hutch raped you?" she wheezed.

"She's a liar," Neal said.

"Shut up!" Sheriff Jolly's voice cracked like a whip. "All of you. This is my department. I'm in charge here. I'm asking the questions." He paused to make certain that Jade and Neal were properly quelled before addressing Donna Dee, who was looking at Jade, rapidly blinking her eyes.

Jade watched her friend's dark eyes move over her disarrayed hair, the scratches on her arms, her hospital scrubs.

"Raped?" She mouthed the word, but didn't utter a sound, either out of fear of the sheriff or profound disbelief. Emotion clogged Jade's throat. Forlornly, she nodded.

"Donna Dee?" The sheriff waited until she had turned her attention back to him. "Jade claims that the boys came along while y'all were stranded out there on the coastal highway. She said they talked her into Neal's car, then wouldn't let her out when it became obvious that they were going to leave you behind. Jade says she put up quite a fight to get out of the car. She said she was screaming and kicking against the rear window. Neal claims that it was all in fun. He says Jade was bound to know it was just a prank.

"Now, I know you can't testify to what took place after that, but I'd like to hear what you have to say about the mood everybody was in when the boys drove off with Jade in the car."

Ivan leaned across the table and placed his hand on Donna Dee's arm. "We're not denying that the boys had their fun with her, you understand." Donna Dee's gaze swung to Jade. She gave her a sharp, piercing look. "They all took a turn. Neal's admitted that. But now that Jade's had time to think about it, she's had a change of heart and is accusing these boys of taking her by force. Do you think that's fair?"

"Ivan," Fritz said sharply. "I'll take it from here."

With growing anxiety, Jade watched Donna Dee's expression gradually change. When she had first come into the room, she had been startled and puzzled. Then, upon hearing that Jade had been assaulted, Donna Dee had looked at her with compassion. Now, however, Donna Dee was regarding her with something akin to suspicion. Ivan Patchett had deliberately fed that suspicion by giving what had happened a sexual complexion and mitigating the violence. He, like everyone else, knew how Donna Dee felt about Hutch and had successfully kindled a fire of jealousy within her.

"Donna Dee, it wasn't my fault," Jade said earnestly, her voice cracking. "I didn't do anything to provoke them. I didn't even want to leave with them. You were there. You know that. They forced me."

"Donna Dee?"

She kept her eyes fastened on Jade's imploring face even as she turned her head toward the sheriff. Finally she looked at him. "They'd been drinking, I think."

"Neal has admitted that, too. Were they being abusive? Hostile? Threatening in any way?"

Donna Dee nervously licked her lips. "No. They were just being themselves. Acting smart-alecky. You know. Like always."

"Tell them about after I got into the car," Jade prompted. "You saw me fighting them, Donna Dee."

She shot Jade an impatient look before saying, "She's right."

Jade slumped with relief. She closed her eyes and pulled in the first deep, calming breath she had drawn for hours. At last, someone was taking her side and backing up her story.

"After Jade got into the car," Donna Dee said, "she started banging on the windows."

"That's right. I told you that, remember?"

"Would you say she was struggling to get out?" the sheriff asked, ignoring Jade.

"Uh-huh. Lamar was holding her in the back. She was trying to reach between the seats and grab the door handle or the gear shift. Neal was swatting at her hands. I think Hutch grabbed hold of her wrists."

"He did. Look." Jade thrust out her wrists, each of which had a ring of dark bruises around it.

When he saw her wrists, Sheriff Jolly frowned. He stared at the floor tiles between his boots while mercilessly gnawing on his lower lip. He glanced up at Ivan. "Then they did take her by force."

"Yes!" Jade cried.

"I didn't say that."

Following Jade's exultant exclamation, Donna Dee's words echoed dully.

"What?" Jade focused on Donna Dee with dismay.

"There was a struggle inside the car," the other girl hastened to say, "but the boys were just jacking around, you know? They were teasing with Jade the same way they were teasing me by leaving me behind."

Jade came out of her chair. "What are you saying, Donna Dee?"

"Sit down, Jade."

"Give it up, will you?" Neal remarked with a bored inflection.

"Jade, you're not behaving rationally," said Velta.

"She's not telling the truth and she knows it!" Jade, beside herself with distress, aimed an accusing finger at Donna Dee.

Since the physical evidence had been destroyed—and she was convinced that that was no accident—her only hope of getting a conviction was to have an eye-witness. Donna Dee hadn't witnessed the actual attack, but she could substantiate Jade's claim that she had been forced to remain in Neal's car. That, combined with the doctor's testimony, would provide any jury with reasonable doubt.

Jade slapped her abraded palms on the tabletop and bent over Donna Dee. "I know you're trying to protect Hutch, but he's a rapist. He raped me," she said, enunciating each harsh word.

"Hutch wouldn't do that."

"He did!"

Donna Dee recoiled from Jade and glanced warily at Sheriff Jolly. "That's all I know. Can I go now?"

"Donna Dee, don't do this," Jade pleaded as the sheriff moved her aside and assisted Donna Dee from her chair. She reached for the other girl's arm, but Donna Dee shook off her clutching hands. "Hutch doesn't deserve your protection," Jade screamed. "He violated me. For God's sake, Donna Dee, please tell them the truth."

Donna Dee spun around, her eyes flashing. "The truth? Okay, I'll tell them the truth." She addressed the others. "A few weeks ago, Jade said that she was tired of waiting on marriage to have sex. She said she wished she could talk Gary Parker into doing it." She turned a vicious gaze onto Jade. "I guess you got your chance last night, didn't you? Three times! Once with Neal. Once with Lamar. And once with...with Hutch."

Jade opened her mouth to speak but was too overwrought to utter a sound. Donna Dee gave her one last, hateful glare before opening the door and stamping out.

After she slammed the door behind her, the silence

was deafening. Neal was the first to speak. "I told you she was hot for it."

The sheriff shot him a dirty look, but Jade was too numb to notice. "Neal," Fritz said, "you're free to go. Ivan, wait for me outside. I want to talk to you before you leave."

As he stood, Ivan laid a consoling hand on Velta's shoulder. "Damn shame what our young 'uns put us through, isn't it?" He walked out behind Neal.

"You still have the option to file formal charges, Jade."

It took a moment for the sheriff's words to register. She was still numb from the blow of Donna Dee's betrayal. "What?"

"Do you want to formally charge the boys with rape?"

"Yes."

Fritz looked at Velta quickly, then back at Jade. "You'd better think about it long and hard before you sign the papers."

"I don't have to think about it," she said. "They raped me. They're going to suffer for this as much as I have." She was almost as hurt by Donna Dee's vilification as by the rape itself. In her heart, she included Donna Dee when she said, "They're going to pay for what they've done."

He sighed wearily and moved toward the door. "All right then. Get on home. I'll have the paperwork typed up and sent over later."

Chapter 5

———❖———

Sheriff Jolly wended his way through the squad room, which was busy now that the day shift had reported for work. Sensing the boss's ill temper, no one blocked his path. Indeed, everybody gave him wide berth and kept his eyes averted as he moved to his private office, where Ivan Patchett was waiting.

Fritz went in and closed the door. Ivan was devouring a doughnut. He dunked it into his coffee and bit off a third of it in one bite. "Damn good doughnuts, Fritz."

"Is that all that's on your mind this morning, Ivan? Doughnuts?"

Fritz dropped into his chair. Propping his elbows on his desk, he ran all ten fingers through his thick, wavy hair. In junior high school some smart-aleck had taunted Fritz by calling out, "Hey, Red!" He'd barely lived to tell about it. Nobody had ever dared try out the nickname on Fritz again.

Ivan Patchett wasn't intimidated either by Fritz's brawn or by the position he held in the community. On nothing more than a whim, Ivan could have Fritz voted into or out of office. Both were well aware of that.

From a physical standpoint, Ivan was far less prepossessing. His gray hair was thinning, but not drastically. He was of average height and weight. He wasn't particularly muscular, but he didn't look soft. His wardrobe was neither conservative or flamboyant, merely comfortable.

Ivan's mediocrity ended with his eyes. They reflected the arrogance of his knowing that he was indisputably the wealthiest, most influential individual in the tricounty area and that he could rule it like a principality if he pleased. His eyes glittered like ice, shot through with fire. That fire was a manifestation of the rapacious greed that governed him.

Ivan Patchett liked who and what he was and would do anything to protect the tyrannical control he wielded over his kingdom. He loved being feared more than he loved sex and gambling and even money. He had groomed his son to be exactly like him.

He sucked the sugar glaze off his ringless fingers. In Ivan's opinion, only fairies wore jewelry. "I don't mind telling you, Fritz, that I don't like what I'm seeing."

"What's that?"

"Your eyebrows are twitching. Whenever you get worried about something, your eyebrows twitch."

"Well, I'm damned sorry about that, Ivan," Fritz said testily, "But I tend to worry when my boy has been accused of raping a girl. That worries me something terrible."

"That charge won't stick for a minute."

"It might. She's just about made a believer out of me. Jade isn't some white-trash girl trying to get the goods on three prominent boys. Why would she make up a tale like that? She's pretty and smart and on her way to making something of herself. What's she got to gain by raising a stink if there's no truth to it?"

"How the hell do I know?" Ivan said, giving off the first signs of anger. "Attention, maybe. Or maybe she was pissed off at her boyfriend and saw a way to get back at him."

"You don't believe that any more than I do, Ivan. You know damn well there's more to this than some playfulness that got a little out of hand." Fritz eyed him closely. "Somebody over at the hospital owed you a favor, right? And this morning you called in the marker."

Ivan didn't even blink. "You sure you want to ask that, Sheriff? Are you sure you want to know?"

"I hate to think of police evidence being tampered with. It makes me want to puke."

Ivan leaned forward. His eyes shone. "Do you want Hutch's name linked to a rape charge?"

"Goddammit, of course not."

"Then relax," Ivan said. Putting his words into action, he leaned back in his chair and took another sip of his coffee. "It's taken care of. In a day or two it'll all blow over."

Fritz glanced worriedly toward the door. "That girl intends to formally charge them."

"She'll change her mind."

"What if she doesn't?"

"She will."

"What if she doesn't?" Fritz repeated, nearly shouting.

Ivan chuckled softly. "If she doesn't drop it, we'll make her out to be a whoring liar."

Nausea roiled in Fritz's stomach. "Who would believe that of Jade?"

"Before I get through with her," Ivan said with a dangerous leer, "men all over the county will be claiming she's sucked them off, and folks'll be itching to believe every sordid word of it."

Fritz felt ill. He had to get out in the fresh air. Standing, he said, "You'll have to excuse me, Ivan. I've been here since just after midnight. I'm going home to shower and eat something."

Ivan stood up, too. "You know what I find hardest to believe about all this? That that little shit Lamar could actually get it up. I'd've paid to see that." Laughing, he slapped Fritz on the back. It was all Fritz could do not to cringe and shake off his touch. "Neal said Hutch went at her like a rutting hog. What does your boy have to say for hisself?"

"I haven't talked to him yet. I called Dora and told her to keep him home from school. That's one reason I'm anxious to get home. I want Hutch to tell me that he didn't force that girl to do anything."

Ivan grabbed his arm and pulled him around, even though Fritz outsized him considerably. "You listen to me, *Sheriff*," he hissed. "I don't give a fuck what Hutch tells you or doesn't tell you, there'll be no public confessions— not on the witness stand, not at the altar of the Baptist church, not anywhere. You hear me? You got that down real good?"

"Ivan, if they're guilty—"

"Guilty my great-granny's ass. Guilty of what? Of getting laid? Since when is it a crime for horny young bucks to get laid? Afterward, the girl got a little scared."

He shrugged. "That's understandable, I guess. Our boys probably didn't use much finesse. But she's not hurt. She'll get over this. If our boys go to prison, their lives'll be ruined."

He pushed his face up very close to Fritz's. "My boy ain't going to do one frigging day in prison over a piece of tail. I don't care how bad Hutch's conscience hurts him, or how ethical you've convinced yourself you are, you bury this incident now, Fritz. *Now*."

Ivan released him and stepped back. He smoothed his hand over his hair, which was slick with grooming cream. He rolled his shoulders, forcing them to relax. Then, pasting on a hale and hearty grin, he opened the door and sauntered into the squad room.

Fritz watched Ivan leave, hating him for his cocksureness, despising him for his lack of morals, and admiring him for his unflagging audacity. Fritz barked a name. Within seconds the clerk appeared in front of him.

"Yes, sir?"

"Once you've typed up the complaint, take it over to the Sperrys' house and leave it with them." Wearing his most fearsome scowl, Fritz looked directly into the clerk's eyes. "Then forget about it. If it ever gets back to me that you breathed a word of what's going to be on that complaint, you'll sorely regret it—and I'm talking about for the rest of your life."

The clerk swallowed. "Yes, sir."

Fritz nodded, knowing he'd made himself implicitly understood. "If anybody asks, I'll be back in an hour."

It took only five minutes for Fritz to get home. He lived only a few blocks from Palmetto's downtown district, where the tallest skyscraper, the Citizens First National

Bank, was only six stories high. The town proper had a population of ten thousand, although ten times that many lived in the rural areas of the county.

The Jollys' neighborhood was old and comfortable. Fritz and Dora had bought the house as newlyweds in preparation for all the kids they planned to put in the many bedrooms. Unfortunately, Dora had developed an ovarian tumor shortly after Hutch was born and had to undergo a complete hysterectomy. She'd made a sewing room out of one of the spare bedrooms; Fritz and Hutch stored fishing and hunting gear in another.

Dora was in the kitchen washing dishes when Fritz came in through the back door and removed his vest. "Hi. Is the coffee still on?"

Dora Jolly was a tall, slender woman whose cheerful personality had given way to grim resignation over her untimely sterilization. She was an efficient homemaker, but no longer the loving, cheerful girl Fritz had married.

She wiped her wet hands on a dish towel. "What's going on, Fritz? How come you were called to the courthouse in the middle of the night? Why'd you have me keep Hutch home from school?"

Fritz poured his own coffee. "Where is he?"

"Upstairs in his bedroom. He's behaving as peculiar as you. I cooked his breakfast, but he ate next to nothing. There's something the matter with both of you. I want to know what it is."

"No, you don't, Dora. Believe me—you don't. Leave it at that."

Setting his unfinished coffee on the porcelain drainboard, he left the kitchen. The door to Hutch's second-story bedroom was closed. Fritz knocked once sharply, then opened it and went in.

Hutch was dressed but shoeless. He was sitting up in his unmade bed, propped against the headboard, staring sullenly into space. Beneath his freckles, his skin appeared more pale than usual. Last night he had said he got the long scratch on his cheek from a backlashing tree limb. Now that Fritz knew better, the sight of it turned his stomach.

Hutch regarded him warily as he approached the bed and sat down on the edge of it. "Your mother said you didn't eat breakfast."

"No, sir."

"Are you sick?"

He fidgeted with the fringe on the chenille bedspread and shrugged laconically. Fritz had questioned too many suspects not to recognize guilt when he saw it. His stomach churned harder.

"Well, boy, what's the matter with you?"

"Nothing."

"Why don't we stop dancing around the mulberry bush?" Fritz said tightly. "Tell me about it."

"Tell you about what?"

Fritz lost his patience. "I'm trying my damnedest to keep from knocking the hell out of you. Wise up and start talking. Spare yourself the beating that I'm scared shitless you deserve."

Hutch's own tenuous control snapped. He began swallowing convulsively. His torso heaved. His wide shoulders started to shake. He looked ready either to burst into tears or to vomit. Finally he was able to say, "You know about Jade, I guess."

"I know that she got to the hospital about eleven-thirty last night."

"Eleven-thirty!" Hutch exclaimed.

"She says an unidentified black man picked her up out of a ditch on the coastal highway and drove her there. She claims that you, Neal, and Lamar gang-raped her."

Raising his knees, Hutch planted his elbows on them while gouging his eyesockets with the heels of his hands. "I don't know what happened to me, Daddy. Swear to God, I didn't realize what I'd done till it was all over."

Fritz's chest suddenly felt as heavy as a sack of concrete mix. The last, vain glimmer of hope that the girl might be lying flickered out and died. Wearily, he rubbed his face. "You raped that girl?"

"I didn't mean to," Hutch sobbed. "Something came over me, over all of us. It was like I stood back and watched myself doing it. I couldn't believe I was doing it, but I couldn't stop myself either."

Fritz listened to his son's blubbering account of the incident. Each incriminating word was like a spike being driven into his head. Almost verbatim, Hutch's story matched Jade's.

"So you just left her there?" Fritz asked when Hutch finally stopped talking.

"What else could we do? Neal said—"

" 'Neal said,' " Fritz shouted. "Is that all you ever go by—what Neal said? Can't you think for yourself? Neal said, 'Let's rape Jade Sperry,' so you whip out your cock. If Neal had said, 'Now cut off your balls and eat them, Hutch,' would you have done that, too?"

"Well, it's no different with you and Ivan, is it?"

Fritz almost struck him across the face. He even raised his hand, but then drew it back. The bald truth of Hutch's words prevented him from delivering the blow. What was he striking out against? Did he want to punish Hutch, or himself and his guilty conscience? Dejectedly, he lowered his hand and hung his head.

After a moment Hutch said, "I'm sorry, Daddy. I didn't mean that."

"It's all right, son. This morning's no time to dodge the truth, no matter how ugly it is."

"Did you tell Mama about...Jade?" Fritz shook his head. "Am I going to go to prison?"

"Not if I can keep you out of it. I don't want another inmate to do to you what you and your friends did to that girl last night."

Hutch's large, masculine face crumpled like a baby's. He began to sob loudly and hoarsely. Awkwardly, Fritz embraced him and patted his back.

"I didn't mean to, Daddy. Swear to God. I'm sorry."

Fritz believed him. He even suspected that Hutch had a crush on the Sperry girl and that the last thing he would ever want to do was hurt her. His son didn't have an ounce of malice in his entire being. Left alone, he would never have committed an act of violence. But he had been with Neal. Neal had been the instigator. He always was. Fritz had seen a calamity like this coming for a long time. He just hadn't known what form it would take. Never in his wildest imaginings had he predicted that it would be so disastrous.

Neal's soul was twisted. Ivan had drummed into Neal's head that he was special, and the boy had come to believe it. There were no barriers between him and self-gratification. What he wanted, he took, and he had never had to account for his actions. Consequently Neal believed himself to be exempt from the laws that applied to other people.

It wasn't surprising to Fritz that Neal had selected Hutch and Lamar to be his best friends. Primarily, they were the only male classmates who could abide him. Secondly, they had malleable personalities. Never mutinous, they did whatever Neal wanted them to do. They feared him more than they feared any other authority figures, including their parents. Neal had slyly tapped into their egos and their insecurities to keep them blindly loyal and absolutely obedient to him.

Fritz knew Ivan could bury this incident. He had seen his dirty machinations succeed too many times to doubt his power. Even if the case came to trial—and it was highly unlikely it would get that far—the boys would never get convicted in Palmetto County. At least half the jury would be Patchett employees, and Ivan would bribe the other half. Jade Sperry's reputation would be publicly slaughtered.

No, Hutch wouldn't go to prison. But a mistake of this caliber didn't simply vanish in one clean swipe like chalk marks on a blackboard. Fritz had just enough religious conviction to fear Hell. He didn't particularly believe that it was a place one had to die in order to reach, either. A sinner could live it on earth.

"I reckon you'll be a whole lot sorrier before it's all over with, boy. I hate that for you."

Fritz knew that what he was doing was, in the long run, wrong for his boy and a grievous sin against that girl. His only alternative was to let Hutch's life be destroyed by one foolish mistake. Could anyone expect that of a parent? That was asking too much. The best Fritz could hope for was that he wouldn't live to see the day when Hutch would have to atone.

"Just keep your mouth shut," he told his son. "Don't talk to anybody about it. The fewer who know, the better. Ivan and me'll take care of it."

In spite of the weak sunshine filtering through high, thin clouds, it was dim and cool inside the house when Jade and Velta returned home. Jade turned up the thermostat. The warm air that began blowing through the ceiling vents smelled like scorched dust.

She moved down the hallway toward her bedroom. From the threshold, she gazed into the familiar room. In the twenty-four hours since she had left it, it had remained untouched. She, however, had been irrevocably changed.

The enormity of her loss crashed against her again like a tidal wave. These attacks of regret were becoming familiar, but they were still so fresh and new that each had tremendous impact. She would have to learn to brace herself for them and cope.

"Jade, would you like me to fix you something? Cocoa? Something to eat?"

She turned and looked at her mother. Velta's face was composed, but no one was home behind her eyes. She was extending kindness out of necessity. Jade longed for her father, who used to draw her onto his knee and rock her in the creaky old chair. *Don't ever be afraid, Jade.*

"No, thank you, Mama. I'll get something later, after I've bathed and dressed."

"I think we should talk."

"Do you?"

"Don't sass me, Jade," Velta snapped, indignantly pulling herself erect. "I'll be in the kitchen." She pivoted on her heel and stalked back down the hall.

Jade closed her bedroom door and stripped off the OR scrubs. She accidentally caught her reflection in the vanity table mirror. Wanting to hide her naked body from her own eyes, she took a robe from her closet and tightly wrapped herself in it.

In the bathroom, she filled the tub with hot water, sank into it up to her chin, then immersed her head. She wished she could take a deep breath, fill her lungs with the scalding water, and end her life.

But of course she couldn't. It wasn't courage she lacked to kill herself; it was peace. She wouldn't know peace again until she had gotten justice. Having come to that realization, her course of action became clear.

Velta's word was as good as a guarantee. When Jade emerged from her room, Velta was waiting for her in the kitchen. Seated at the small square table, she was stirring sugar into a cup of instant coffee. After pouring herself a glass of milk, Jade joined her.

"A deputy brought this to the door. He said for you to read it before going back to the courthouse."

Jade gazed at the long white envelope that lay on the table between them, but said nothing.

"I don't know how you could have gotten yourself in a fix like this, Jade," Velta began. "I truly don't."

Jade took a sip of her milk.

"But you shouldn't make a bad situation even worse by bringing formal charges against those boys." Velta plucked a paper napkin from the plastic dispenser in the center of the table and blotted up the coffee that had sloshed into her saucer.

Jade focused her concentration on the glass of milk in front of her and let her mother's words flow over her like rushing water over smooth stones. The only way she could survive this was to take herself out of the present and transport her mind to a point in the future when things were different.

"Can you imagine the effects a rape trial would have on us?" Velta rubbed her arms as though chilled by the thought. "You'll be remembered for that for the rest of your life. People will forget that your daddy won the Medal of Honor. Every time your name is mentioned, it'll be in connection with this unfortunate incident."

Her mother's belittling words shattered Jade's concentration. She closed her eyes and let her head fall back to rest on her neck. By an act of will, she withheld the bitter retorts that filled her breast and begged to be expressed.

"In many respects, the sheriff was right, Jade. I believe he had your best interests at heart. I truly do. Bringing this out into the open will mean trouble for everybody. Ivan will fire me for sure. He can't let me continue working for him if our children are on opposite sides of a courtroom battle. If I lose my job, what will we do?"

Velta paused to take a breath and another sip of coffee.

"Only the four of you know what really happened out there. Those boys will tell a completely different story, Jade. It will be their version against yours. Three against one. Who do you think folks will believe? People will say you asked for it by getting into Neal's car with them in the first place."

Velta tapped the tabletop with the nail of her index finger. "A rape victim always gets blamed for it. It might not be right, but that's the way it is. People will say that you're pretty and that you know it. They'll say you flaunted yourself at those boys until they lost control.

"People who have bragged on you for being an ideal student and a nice Christian girl will begin looking at you in a whole new light. Some might even start spreading lies about you just to make themselves important sources of gossip. Before too long, neither of us will be able to hold her head up in this town."

Velta sighed. "After this, you might as well kiss goodbye any hopes of marrying somebody important. I wish you'd thought of that before you went tattling."

Jade stood, went to the sink, and poured the remainder of her milk down the drain. Then she turned to confront her mother. "I've changed my mind, Mama. I'm not going to press charges."

Velta's lips fell open, then she came as close as she ever did to smiling. "Oh, Jade, I—"

"Wait, Mama, before you say anything, I want to make sure you know why I'm not going to. I didn't change my mind because of any advice I received from you or from Sheriff Jolly. And I don't care if Ivan Patchett fires you this afternoon. In fact, if you haven't got the guts to stand up to him and quit, I would just as soon he fire you. I loathe the idea of being dependent on him for anything.

"I also don't give a flip about what a trial might mean to your reputation or mine. I don't care what anybody thinks. Anyone who would believe such a vicious lie about me automatically sacrifices the value I would place on his opinion.

"The only reason I don't want a trial is Gary. Our relationship would be opened to public scrutiny. Strangers would discuss it over clotheslines. I couldn't bear knowing that something as pure and clean as the way we have loved each other was being turned into something ugly and shameful, something to snicker at.

"I love him too much to expose him to something this ugly. Can you imagine how he would feel, knowing that three boys had...had...emptied themselves into me?" Tears rolled down her cheeks. A crack seemed to open up in her chest like a fissure in the earth, and she uttered a moan. "No, Mama, you can't imagine what that would do to Gary, but I can. He would want to kill them. He might very well attempt it, and jeopardize his future in the process.

"A clever defense lawyer—and Ivan could afford to hire the best—might subpoena Gary to be a character witness against me. He would either have to discuss our intimacy in the open or perjure himself to keep from it. I won't let that happen." Resolute, she wiped the tears off her cheeks. "Finally, I realized that a trial would only postpone the inevitable."

"What do you mean?" Velta asked.

"*I* will be the one who has to see that they pay for this. Somehow, someday, I'll get restitution." Instantly her tears dried. "Why go through the legal motions when they're virtually guaranteed acquittal? Why put Gary through that misery? He'll be hurt enough when I break up with him. And in order to protect him, I'll have to break up with him," she added dully.

"By the way, Mama, we got our scholarships. The letter came yesterday. I was on my way to tell him the good news when Donna Dee's car ran out of gas." The unfairness of it was overwhelming and debilitating. She slumped against the drainboard.

Velta rose from her chair and briskly dusted her hands. "Well, whatever your reasons, I'm glad to hear that you plan to get on with your life. The best thing you could do is forget this ever happened."

Jade's head snapped up. Violent energy smoldered in the depths of her blue eyes. Though she stood very still, her body was taut and quivering. When she spoke, her voice was calm and chillingly controlled. "I'll never forget it."

By second period, there were sweat rings rimming the armholes of Lamar's shirt. He was nervous, upset, and confused.

Neal and Hutch were absent from school. That alone made him feel adrift. He had considered staying at home himself, but that would have required making up an excuse for his mother. Whenever possible, he avoided having any interaction with Myrajane, especially if it involved dissembling. She could spot a lie at fifty paces.

During homeroom, the principal, Mr. Patterson, had announced to the entire student body that seniors Gary Parker and Jade Sperry had received full college scholarships. Everybody had applauded.

"I know you'll want to extend these two outstanding students your congratulations," the principal had said over the PA system. "Unfortunately, Jade is absent today, but be sure to remember to congratulate her when she returns to school."

Upon hearing that Jade was absent, Lamar had really

begun to sweat. Between classes, he met Gary Parker in the hallway but pretended not to see him so he wouldn't have to speak. Could he ever face Gary again after what he'd done to his girl friend? Last night he had harbored a secret pride in his sexual accomplishment. In the cold light of day, however, he was reminded that his success had been at Jade's expense.

Seeing Gary graciously accepting congratulations from his classmates brought Lamar's guilt to the forefront. Swamped with shame and horror, he ducked into the nearest boys' restroom and threw up in the toilet.

He had fourth period with Donna Dee Monroe. When he entered the classroom, he was relieved to see her sitting at her desk, but his relief was short-lived. His stomach lurched threateningly when she made eye contact with him.

She knew.

He could tell from the searching look she gave him that she knew. Somehow she had found out what happened after they had deserted her on the highway. The stare she leveled on him made him feel worse than he did when his mother flew into a tirade over one of his many shortcomings. He felt naked and exposed. He wanted to crawl into a hole and hide. Instead, he had to endure fifty-five minutes of English class. The minutes ticked by with torturous slowness.

Who had told Donna Dee? Jade, he supposed. But when? How? The last time he had seen Jade, she had been lying on the ground with her knees drawn up to her chest. He remembered thinking that it might be best if she just died. Then there would be no one to testify to what he had done. His mother would never find out. Of course, he had buried the thought quickly, before the Lord had time to hear it and strike him down.

Apparently Jade hadn't been hurt as badly as she had looked. But how had she gotten back to town? Had she told anybody what had happened at the channel? Obviously so, because Donna Dee knew. Oh, Christ. If Donna Dee knew, then other people would find out, and eventually his mother would hear of it. There would be reprisals. No matter what Neal said, there had to be.

By now Sheriff Jolly probably knew. Even though his son was involved, he was a man of integrity. He would do what was right. Any minute now a burly deputy might come crashing through the door of the classroom brandishing a firearm and waving a warrant for Lamar Griffith's arrest.

Blood drained from his head so fast, he had to lay it on top of his desk to keep from fainting. His skin was clammy. He felt nauseated again.

Lamar thought seriously about running from the classroom, all the way downtown, and throwing himself on the mercy of the district attorney. Better to rat on his friends and turn state's evidence, better to have Ivan Patchett for a lifetime enemy, better to be locked up with thieves and pimps and serial killers, than to experience the wrath his mother would unleash.

As it turned out, Lamar missed his chance to make a mad dash for the door. While the pupils were supposed to be engrossed in reading Alexander Pope, Donna Dee approached the teacher's desk and whispered a request for a pass to the nurse's office.

"What's wrong?" the teacher asked.

"I don't feel well. You know." She gave the teacher that

look that women exchange to signal that they're having their period.

"Of course, dear. Go home and lie down with a heating pad."

Covertly, Lamar watched Donna Dee leave. As she closed the classroom door behind her, she looked directly at him, but he failed to interpret the meaning of her silent communiqué. It looked like she was telling him to keep his mouth shut.

By the time school was dismissed for the day, his unsteady knees barely supported him as he rushed to his car. Because he didn't know what else to do or where else to go for answers, he drove out to Neal's house.

It was situated on a piece of prime real estate. From the highway, a gravel road wound through thick woods. The cultivated lawn surrounding the house was as wide as a football field. Three ancient live oaks protected it with a dense canopy of branches. The roots snaked along the ground like lava tubes.

The two-story brick house was impressive, but Myrajane Griffith scorned it. "Old Rufus Patchett didn't have a lick of good taste. He designed that house so it would have eight columns across the veranda, when six would have done just as nicely. Rufus wanted to rile Daddy by building a house grander than ours. It's trashy to be so ostentatious," she'd often said.

But recently she had contradicted herself, saying, "It's disgraceful the way Ivan has let that lovely house go to rack and ruin. It needs a woman's touch. He should have remarried long ago. That Eula who works for him is a slovenly housekeeper. She's lazy and insolent."

Lamar had the good sense to keep his mouth shut and

not ask where his mother got her information. To his knowledge, she had never set foot in the Patchetts' house. She had dropped him off many times but had never been invited inside.

Ivan's father, Rufus, had made a fortune in cotton. The sweat of cotton pickers, sharecroppers, and gin workers had gone into the mortar that held the pastel bricks together. Rufus had been clever. While his contemporaries were haggling with brokers to squeeze one more penny out of a bale of cotton in a declining market, he'd switched to growing soybeans. Like Myrajane's family, most of the cotton planters had lost everything. They'd sold plots of acreage to Rufus for ten cents on the dollar just to keep from having to pay the taxes on soil they could no longer afford to cultivate.

Rufus had been land-hungry and gobbled up property right and left. Ignoring the derision of his peers, he had continued to plant soybeans. When it became feasible, he'd built the factory so he could manufacture the by-products himself. After Rufus died, Ivan had inherited all the land and the factory and the power that went with them. One day Neal would do the same. And his son after him.

Lamar, rather than feel envious of his friend, was relieved to know he didn't have that kind of responsibility ahead of him. He had been suckled on stiff-necked Cowan family pride and frankly thought it was destructive and stupid. What good had it done the Cowans? The only ones left were a distant cousin or two and Myrajane, who was stingy, grasping, and possessive. She'd made life hell for Lamar's late father, whom he still missed. Maybe if she had started out poor, they all would have been happier.

As Lamar approached the house, he saw that he wasn't Neal's only guest. Hutch's car was parked out front in the circular driveway.

Eula answered the door. Conscientiously, Lamar wiped his feet on the mat before stepping into the marble vestibule. "Hi, Eula. Is Neal here?"

"He's upstairs with Hutch, in his bedroom."

He jogged up the sweeping staircase and opened the second door on his left past the gallery. Neal was sitting on the floor, his back propped against the bed. Hutch was slouched in an easy chair. Remarkably, Neal looked the same as always. Hutch's freckles seemed to have turned darker overnight. Or was it that his skin beneath them was unnaturally pale? The scratch on his cheek stood out in stark contrast.

"Hi," Neal said. "Come in. Want a beer?"

"No, thanks."

Hutch said nothing. They made brief eye contact, but, because of the sinful secret they now shared, it was difficult for Lamar to look directly at his friends. Apparently Hutch felt the same.

Neal appeared unfazed. "How was school today, Lamar?"

"Okay, I guess."

"Anything momentous happen?" He took a swig of his beer.

"No." After a brief pause, he said, "Mr. Patterson announced that Gary and . . . and Jade got college scholarships." He shot Hutch a furtive glance. Hutch blanched paler than before.

"You don't say?" Neal drawled. "How 'bout that? Good for them."

Hutch bounded out of the easy chair and moved to the

window. In his wake, he left a string of curses. Regarding Hutch, Neal took another sip of his beer. "What's eating your ass? Aren't you glad about their scholarships?" Laughter lay just beneath his words.

Angrily Hutch spun around. "Aren't we even going to talk about it? Are we just going to pretend nothing happened?"

Now that Hutch had broached the subject, Lamar was relieved that he could finally talk about it with someone. "Jesus, I've been scared shitless all day."

"Scared? Of what?" Neal asked scoffingly.

"Of getting into trouble, what do you think?"

Neal sat up straighter, shaking his head as though puzzled by Lamar's concern. "Like I told you last night, we aren't going to get into trouble. Don't you listen to me when I tell you something, Lamar? We didn't do anything wrong."

Lamar glanced at Hutch. Hutch wasn't as complacent about the situation as Neal was, but he wouldn't speak up at the risk of appearing cowardly and getting on Neal's bad side. Lamar was on his own.

Lamar grabbed his diminishing bravery with both hands and held on. "Some people might see it different, Neal."

"What people?"

"People who hear about it."

"Who's gonna tell? Jade?" He snorted. "Hardly."

Hutch said, "She told my daddy."

"She told your daddy?" Lamar repeated in a high, squeaky voice. His knees gave out beneath him and he dropped to the floor with a thud. "What'd he do?"

"Not a goddamn thing!" Neal, obviously annoyed, stood up and tore another can of beer from the six-pack.

When he opened it, the foamy head bubbled over his hand. As he shook off the suds, he said, "You two really piss me off, you know? If you go around looking and acting guilty of something, everybody'll think you are."

"Maybe we are." Neal's eyes cut to Lamar. Lamar felt like an insect being pinned to a piece of Styrofoam, but he had to get this off his chest or burst. "No matter what you say, Neal, I don't think Jade wanted us to...you know."

"Are you nuts?" The words rushed from Hutch's mouth as though they'd been building up from internal pressure. "Of course she didn't want us to, you idiot. She fought like a hellcat. We raped her, pure and simple."

"Oh, Jesus." Lamar slumped to one side. His bowels felt watery. He feared he might mess himself. He thought he might vomit again. But if he disgraced himself, so what? He was going to die anyway the minute his mother got wind of the crime.

"Shut up!" Neal hissed. "Both of you, just shut up." His straight, white teeth were clenched and bared. "Listen, you dumb fucks, girls pull this bullshit all the time. She put up token resistance, sure. Do you think she wants us telling everybody that she was willingly gangbanged? Before we could advertise to all the other guys how easy she was, she had to pull this crap to make us look bad first. Don't you see that?"

Hutch looked desperate enough to grasp at any straw, no matter how flimsy. Lamar too wanted to believe Neal, but every time Neal began to sound logical, Lamar remembered the strength with which Jade had fought and how terrified she had looked when he and Hutch held her down for Neal.

Hutch wiped his perspiring forehead with the back of

his hand. His skin was the color of putty speckled with rusty paint. "We probably shouldn't have left her there."

"She made it back to town okay, didn't she?"

"How'd she get back?" Lamar asked.

Neal filled him in on what he knew and all that had transpired at the courthouse that morning. "I got the impression that Donna Dee knew," Lamar remarked when Neal was finished.

"Donna Dee vouched for us," Neal said. "She knew damn well that Jade knew what she was in for when she got into the car with three half-drunk randy bucks. Maybe we should have invited Donna Dee to our little party, too." He grinned and smacked his lips. "Although I can't see her being as good as her friend Jade. I've never had pussy that sweet before."

Lamar lowered his eyes to his hands, which lay limply in his lap. He had a compelling urge to wash them.

"Donna Dee was pissed at Jade for screwing you," Neal said to Hutch. "You could almost see the steam coming out of her ears. She's really got the hots for you. Why don't you be kind, Hutch? Give her a sampling of what you gave Jade."

Hutch's large hands balled into fists. His face regained its color. In fact, it turned beet red. Hutch's temper was reputably short around everybody except Neal, but there was a first time for everything. Lamar held his breath with fearful expectation.

Evidently Hutch thought better of antagonizing Neal any further. His hot color subsided and he relaxed his fists. "I'm going home now." He stomped across the room. Before he reached the door, Neal blocked his path.

"I'd be real disappointed if my two best friends turned

out to be squeamish chickenshits." He included Lamar in the warning look he gave Hutch. "Jade stirred up a hornets' nest this morning, but it's all over now. My old man called a while ago and said she had notified Fritz that she's decided against pressing charges. That's as good as an admission that she was asking for it." When neither responded, he said, "Well, isn't it?"

The two boys glanced at each other indecisively. Finally, Lamar mumbled, "Whatever you say, Neal."

"Okay then, relax, will you?"

Hutch said, "Daddy's put me on a curfew for the next couple of weeks. See y'all later."

After he left, Neal raised his hands high above his head and stretched, yawning expansively. "My old man yanked me out of bed before sunrise this morning. I've been lazy all day." he picked up his beer and drank the rest of it in one swallow. "You want to go shoot some baskets or something?"

"No, I've, uh, got to get home, too." Lamar rose to his feet. Awkwardly, he fidgeted with the zipper of his jacket, slid his hands into his pockets, took them out again. "Is my mother going to find out about this, Neal?"

"Why?" Neal smiled like an alligator. "Scared?"

"Damn right," Lamar admitted with a weak laugh.

Neal slapped him between the shoulder blades. "She won't find out. And even if she does, so what? You got laid. Big fucking deal. No pun intended."

Suddenly he grabbed a handful of Lamar's buttock and whispered softly, "You shot quite a load into her, my man. I was damned proud of you." He squeezed the flesh before releasing it, laughing in his characteristically careless way.

Lamar said goodbye and made his way to the staircase. The high ceilings of the house made him feel small and caged. He paused momentarily to draw a steadying breath. As he leaned against the balustrade, he realized that he was sweating profusely again. Perspiration had beaded on his upper lip. His palms were slick and cold with it.

He experienced another startling realization: his cock was hard. Very hard. Talking about his sexual prowess the night before had done it. He didn't know whether to gloat or to be sick again.

Chapter 6

———◆———

Gary Parker ambushed Donna Dee Monroe at her car in the student parking lot just after the three-thirty bell. His suspicion that she had been avoiding him was confirmed. When she saw him, she almost dropped her books.

"Gary! Wh-why aren't you running track?"

"I want to talk to you, Donna Dee."

"About what?" She tossed her books into the backseat and slid behind the wheel, eager to get away. Gary reached through the door and yanked out the ignition key.

"Hey, what—"

"I want to know what's going on with Jade."

"Jade?" she echoed.

"Jade. You know, Jade Sperry, your best friend."

"Yeah," she said, her expression suddenly hostile. "What about her?"

"Why has she been absent from school for so long? What's wrong with her? Every time I call, her mother tells me she's sick. Jade won't talk to me at all. Is she that sick? Have you seen her?"

"Not since last week," she replied curtly. "If her mother says she's sick, I guess she's sick."

"You haven't talked to Jade either?"

"No."

"I can't believe that, Donna Dee. You're her best friend."

"Well, you're her boyfriend. If she won't talk to you, what makes you think she'd talk to me? Please, give me my keys. I've got to get home." She extended her open palm; he ignored it.

"Are you saying you've tried to talk to Jade and she refused?"

Her small face was puckered with indecision and aggravation. "Listen, Gary, you'd just as well know that we had a falling out and are no longer speaking."

He regarded her with patent disbelief. "You've got to be kidding!"

"I'm not."

"What caused this falling out?"

"I'm not at liberty to say. Now please—" She reached for her keys, but he held them out of her reach. "Gary, give me my keys!"

"Not until you tell me what the hell is going on!"

Usually Gary was even-tempered. His current anger was a by-product of frustration and fear. For several days he had sensed that something was amiss. Classmates looked at him askance. Several whispered conversations had stopped the moment he had approached. Jade had a mysterious illness. Nothing had been normal since the day he had heard about his scholarship. Although he had nothing concrete to base it on, he had a strong premonition that his life had been tampered with.

"What's the matter with Jade?" he demanded.

"If you want to know about Jade, ask her." Donna Dee grabbed her keys before he had a chance to stop her.

He did, however, reach through the open window and grab her arm. "Does it have anything to do with Neal?"

Donna Dee's head came around so quickly, her neck made a cracking sound. "What makes you ask that?"

"Because he's being particularly obnoxious. All of a sudden he's treating me like a pal, except that he's so phony, he's transparent. It's like he's in on a joke that I don't know about yet."

Anxiously, Donna Dee wet her lips. Her eyes darted furtively. She looked trapped, which gave Gary a sick feeling deep in his gut that his guess was right.

"Does Neal's sudden friendliness toward me have anything to do with Jade?"

"I've gotta go."

"Donna Dee!"

"I've gotta go." She started her car and peeled out of the parking lot without looking back.

"Dammit!"

Gary ran to his car. He didn't make a conscious decision to skip track practice that afternoon. He simply reacted to the compulsion to see Jade immediately. If he had to beat down her door, he was going to see her.

Jade recognized the sound of his car. Moving to the living-room window, she watched him jog up the front walk and rap twice on the door. Involuntarily, she moaned with yearning before composing her features and pulling open the door.

"Jade!"

"Hello, Gary."

A wide grin broke across his face. It was obvious that he was overjoyed and relieved to see her. "Besides looking wan and thin, you look normal."

"What did you expect?"

"I don't know," he said with chagrin. "Open, oozing lesions, maybe."

He grasped her by the upper arms and pulled her into a fierce hug. He seemed not to notice that she didn't melt against him as she usually did.

"You had me worried sick," he whispered against her neck. "I'm glad to see that you're all right."

She was the one to end the embrace. Backing up over the threshold, she invited him inside. He glanced guiltily over his shoulder. "Are you sure it's okay, since your mother's not here?"

"It's okay." In light of the situation, breaking one of Velta's ironclad rules was the least of Jade's worries.

Once she had closed the door, Gary again drew her against him and gazed at her hungrily. "What's was wrong with you, Jade? You must've been real sick. Your mother said you were too sick to come to the telephone."

"That's what I told her to tell you." He looked at her quizzically. "Sit down, Gary."

Turning her back on him, she moved to a chair and sat down. When she looked up at him, it was apparent that he was at a loss over her lack of response. Jade was having difficulty dealing with it herself. Gary's tender touch reminded her of others that hadn't been tender. Although her brain knew that there was a vast difference, her body seemed unable to make the distinction between his caresses and the mauling it had received from her attackers. She should be grateful, she supposed. Without physical desire to contend with, what she had to do would be easier.

He came forward, knelt in front of her chair, and clasped her folded hands tightly between his. "Jade, I don't get it. What the hell is going on?"

"What don't you get?"

"Any of it. Why haven't you been at school? Why haven't you talked to me?"

"I've been sick."

"Too sick to come to the telephone and say hello?"

She made her voice cool. "There's something I've got to tell you, Gary."

"Oh, Jesus, no," he whispered huskily. He lunged forward and buried his face in her lap, clutching handfuls of her quilted robe and twisting it between his fingers. "Do you have a fatal disease? Are you going to die?"

Her heart broke. She couldn't resist sliding her fingers up through his wavy brown hair. As though it had a life of its own, it twined around her fingers. Tenderly she caressed his scalp. A sob issued from his throat; it was an echo of the one she held back.

Before she submitted to her heartache, she lifted his head. "It's nothing like that. I'm not going to die." He touched her face, skimming his fingertips over each feature. "It's just that..." She made several false starts, then said, "I've been emotionally sick."

He repeated the words as though they belonged to another language. "Over what?"

"I've been under too much pressure."

"From school?" He touched her hair, smoothing a strand away from her face. She resisted the impulse to rest her cheek in his palm. "That will let up now that we've got our scholarships. Hey! We haven't even seen each other since we were notified. Congratulations."

"To you, too."

"How are we going to celebrate?" His eyes turned smoky as his hand moved down her chest to her breast. "I know how I'd like to."

"No!" she cried shrilly as she shrank from his touch. He was so startled that he was easily pushed aside as she left her chair. Her motions were jerky and disjointed, as though she had only recently learned to walk.

"Jade?"

She spun around and confronted him. He was regarding her with perplexity. "Don't you understand what I'm trying to tell you? I've been under pressure about the scholarship, but other things, too. Primarily, us."

"What the hell are you talking about?"

Dragging it out was only making it worse, she realized. There wasn't a way to do this without inflicting wounds on him and herself. "You're a smart fellow," she said, deliberately giving her voice an impatient edge. "Can't you read between the lines? Do I have to spell it out? Can't you understand what I'm trying to tell you?"

Gary came to his feet. He settled his hands on his narrow hips and cocked his head to one side. "Are you trying to break up?"

"I...I think we need to take a break from each other, yes. Things were going too far, getting out of hand. We need to pull back."

Gary's arms fell to his sides. "I can't believe this. Jade?" He moved toward her and tried to take her into his arms. She staved him off.

"I can't take any more of this sexual pressure from you, Gary."

"Like you haven't been putting sexual pressure on me?" he shouted.

"Of course! I know I have. That's my point. It's not healthy for either of us to keep building bonfires we can't put out."

"Just a few weeks ago, you suggested that we start putting out the bonfires."

"I've changed my mind. We should wait, give ourselves plenty of time to make the correct decision." Hastily, she licked her lips. "But even that's not good enough. We need to date other people. We've gone steady ever since we were old enough to date. I want you to ... to start dating other girls."

For several moments he stared at her speechlessly. Then his eyes narrowed with suspicion. "This has something to do with Neal Patchett, doesn't it?"

A trapdoor seemed to open up beneath her. She felt herself falling through a black void. "No," she denied hoarsely.

Obviously he mistook her horror for guilt. "The hell it doesn't," he sneered. "He's been sucking up to me for more than a week. Ever since you got 'sick.' He's been acting like a man with a delicious secret that he's just dying to tell. Now I know what it is. He wanted to rub my nose in it. You went out with him, didn't you?"

"No."

"Don't lie to me. Donna Dee looked as guilty as sin when I mentioned his name, too. Is that what you quarreled with her about?"

"Donna Dee?" she said in a negative tone.

"I chased her down after school today. She's been avoiding me almost as diligently as you have."

"What did she say?"

"Don't worry. She didn't rat on you." He shook his head. "So, you finally fell for Neal's irresistible charm. That ought to make your mother happy."

Jade's dark hair whipped around her head as she vehemently shook her head. "No. I despise him. You know that, Gary."

"So you say." He rocked back and forth on the balls of his feet, barely containing his fury. "Maybe I'll ask him myself." He turned toward the door, but hadn't taken more than two steps before Jade launched herself against his back and clutched at him. "No, Gary, no. Stay away from him."

He turned and angrily pulled her against him. "If you had to cheat on me, why'd it have to be with Patchett?"

"You're wrong, Gary. Please don't think—"

"*Patchett,* for God's sake!" He released her so abruptly that she staggered backward. Gary yanked open the door and strode out.

"Gary!"

He didn't look back, although Jade knew he heard her calling his name until his car was halfway down the block. Jade stumbled back inside and slumped against the door. The tears that she had been holding in erupted in a torrent. She cried until she had no more tears left, and then she was seized by dry, racking sobs.

At first Gary considered driving straight to the Patchetts' estate and challenging Neal face to face. He could probably whip Neal in a fair fight, but he didn't want to give the bastard the satisfaction of knowing that he had provoked him. He would let him be smug and go around wearing that shit-eating grin if he wanted to. Gary Parker wasn't going to stoop to his level.

By the time he reached home, Gary's anger had given way to despair. The farmhouse looked uglier than ever as he drove into the yard. He hated the old house with its peeling paint and sagging porch. He hated the chickens that pecked about in the yard and the stink of the hog pen. He resented the laughter and chatter of his younger siblings as they ran to tackle him around his legs and impeded his progress across the dirt clearing.

"Gary, Mama said you have to help me with my arithmetic tonight."

"Gary, make Stevie stop following me."

"Gary, can you take me into town?"

"Shut up!"

Six pairs of astonished eyes looked up at him. He gazed around the circle of faces and hated their trusting, loving expressions. Who did they think he was, a saint?

He pushed them out of his path and, scattering chickens, ran across the yard to the barn. Inside, he found a dark corner where he dropped down into the hay and covered his head with his arms. Yearning and hate and love warred within him.

He yearned to get away from this place. He hated poverty, ugliness, dirt, and his lack of privacy. Yet he loved his family. In his recurring daydreams, he returned from college like a bountiful Santa Claus, handing out goodies to them. But the responsibility of making those dreams a reality was burdensome. Often, he considered simply disappearing.

He never would, of course. Not merely because his sense of responsibility was so deeply ingrained in him, but because of Jade. She made all the ugliness in his life bearable, because in her lay the promise that it wouldn't always be so. She was the nucleus of all his hopes.

"God," he groaned. How could he stand a life without her? *Jade,* he thought miserably, *what happened to you, to us, to our shared future?* They had planned to get their educations, then return to Palmetto and make the community more egalitarian. Now, it seemed, she had defected to the other side—to the Patchetts. *How could she?*

"Gary?"

His father entered through the wide barn door. Otis Parker wasn't yet fifty but he looked at least a decade older. He was thin and wiry, a slight man with perpetually stooped shoulders. His overalls hung loosely on his bony frame. He found his son sitting in the shadowed corner on a mound of sour-smelling hay.

"Gary? The kids said you was acting mean."

"Can't I have one moment's peace around here?"

"Something happen at school?"

"No! I'm just looking for some privacy." Gary felt like lashing out at something, and his father was a convenient target. "For once, can't you just leave me alone?" he shouted.

"All righty." Otis turned to go. "Don't forget to slop the hog."

Gary surged to his feet, his hands balled into fists. "Listen, old man, I've slopped that fucking hog for the last time. I'm sick to death of slopping the hog. I'm sick of being surrounded by screaming kids that you didn't have any better sense than to make. I'm sick of this place and the rotten stench of your failure. I'm sick of school and teachers and talk about scholarships when nobody really gives a shit about anything. Being the good boy sucks. It gets you nowhere. Nowhere."

His rage and energy spent, Gary fell to his knees in the dirty straw and began to cry. Several minutes elapsed before he felt his father's rough hand shaking his shoulder.

"Looks like you could use a swaller of this."

Otis was holding out to him a Mason jar of clear liquid. Gary reached for it hesitantly, uncapped it, and sniffed. Then he took a sip. The moonshine seared all the way down to his stomach. Coughing and wheezing, he passed the jar back to Otis, who took a big draft.

"Don't tell your mama 'bout this."

"Where'd you get it?"

"Reckon it's time you learned about Georgie. She's a nigger lady what's been making moonshine for years. She don't charge too much. It's all I can afford anyway. I keep it hid over yonder under that old saddle, if you ever need it when I ain't around." Otis carefully replaced the lid on the jar. "You got woman troubles?"

Gary shrugged noncommittally, though the reminder of Jade's betrayal burned his gut more than the moonshine did.

"They's 'bout the only thing in God's creation that can drive a man to go crazy and talk wild the way you was a-talkin'." Otis regarded him sternly. "I didn't like what you had to say about your little brothers and sisters 'cause it don't speak well of your mama."

"I'm sorry. I didn't mean it."

"Yeah, you did. But I want you to know that each one of our kids was conceived in love. We're proud of every single one." Otis's eyes grew misty. "We're 'specially proud of you. Can't figure out for the life of me where you come from, bein' so smart and all. I reckon you're ashamed of us."

"I'm not, Daddy."

Sighing, Otis said, "I ain't so dumb that I don't know why you never bring friends out here to the place, Gary. It's plain to see why. Listen, your mama and me, we don't want you to get educated so you can take care of us and our other children. We want you to get away from here for only one reason—'cause you want to so bad. You don't want to be a failure like me.

"All I've ever had to my name is this sorry piece of land, and it for damn sure ain't much. I wasn't even the one that acquired it, but my daddy. I've did the best I could to hold on to it."

Gary almost strangled on the remorse he felt for saying what he had. Otis sensed his guilt and forgivingly patted his son's knee, then used it as a prop when he stood up.

"You and Jade have a tiff?" Gary nodded. "Well, it'll blow over. A female's got to have her spells every now and again or she wouldn't be female. When they get on a tear, just leave 'em be for a while." Having dispensed that sage advice, he ambled toward the door. "Comin' up on suppertime. Best get your chores did."

Gary watched his father leave. His rolling, bowlegged gait carried him across the dismal yard, which was littered with broken, secondhand toys and chicken droppings. Gary covered his face with his hands, wishing that when he lowered them and opened his eyes he would be a million miles away, untethered from his obligations.

Everyone, including his family, expected too much of

him. He was doomed to failure before he began. No matter what mountains of achievement he scaled, he could never live up to everyone's expectations. He could never be good enough, rich enough. He could never be Neal Patchett.

For God's sake, did Jade have to run to him? So what if Neal was the richest boy in town? Jade knew how shallow he was. How could she stand to let him touch her? As Gary gazed at his derelict surroundings, the answer became instantly clear: Neal Patchett never went to school with chicken shit on his shoes.

Resentment gnawed at him like the raw liquor in his belly. She would be sorry. Before long she would come crawling back. She had a crush on Neal, that's all. It wouldn't last. It was him, Gary, she truly loved. What they had was too deep and abiding to throw away. Sooner or later Jade would regain her senses. In the meantime, he would...what?

His sense of responsibility reared its ugly head and drew him to his feet. He went out to slop the hog.

Chapter 7

———◆———

S ay, Jade."

Jade turned away from her locker, clutching her text-books to her chest. So few of her classmates spoke to her anymore that she was surprised and pleased that someone—anyone—had approached her.

The facts were murky, but the scuttlebutt around Palmetto High School was that Jade had been unfaithful to Gary Parker with Neal Patchett. It was said that as a result of Jade's two-timing, Gary had dumped her. In two and a half months, she had gone from being the most sought-after girl in the senior class to a social leper. While her classmates were caught up in the festive whirl preceding graduation, Jade was shunned.

The gossip wasn't contained within the walls of the high school. It had filtered into the community at large. When it reached Pete Jones's ears, he fired her from her part-time job with the thin excuse that he would prefer to have a young man working for him.

Things were no better at home. Velta complained that

she was getting the cold shoulder at work. "I heard my co-workers whispering about you. Didn't I tell you that you'd be blamed for what happened? You should have had that colored man bring you straight home. It was a big mistake to go to the hospital. Once you did that, you sealed your fate and mine."

Jade had no one to take her problems to. She would never forgive Donna Dee for betraying her. Apparently Donna Dee hadn't forgiven her, either, for inciting Hutch's libido. The chasm between them could never be bridged, but since there wasn't anyone to replace Donna Dee, losing her best friend and confidante was like losing a limb.

But it was for losing Gary that Jade wept bitterly every night. It was obvious from his attitude that he believed the lies being circulated about her. His anger and confusion were a fertile ground for ugly suspicions, which Neal Patchett had sown and cultivated. Working as subtly as the serpent in the Garden of Eden, Neal continued to torment Gary with innuendos. He tracked Jade like a bloodhound, his smoldering looks conveying that they shared a naughty secret. His suggestiveness made her sick to her stomach. But she hated Neal's gloating worse for Gary's sake. His self-confidence and pride had taken as brutal a beating as her body had.

"Hi, Patrice," she said to the girl who had the courage to buck the trend and speak to her.

Patrice Watley was plump, bleached, and wild. Jade didn't recall having a conversation with her since junior high, when the line between the good girls and the bad girls was distinctly drawn. Until recently, they had been on opposite sides of that line.

Patrice's mother had recently obtained her fourth

divorce and was in hot pursuit of husband number five. Her active love life had always kept her so busy that Patrice had been left to her own devices. As a result, she had packed a lot of living into eighteen years.

"I don't mean nothing by this, you understand," she whispered, moving closer to Jade. "But are you knocked up?"

Jade's knuckles turned white against the spines of her schoolbooks. "Of course not. What makes you ask a thing like that?"

Patrice smacked her lips with impatience and a trace of sympathy. "Say, look, Jade, I said I don't mean nothing by asking, but I know the signs, okay? I've been there twice myself."

Jade bowed her head, mindlessly poking her thumb into the silver coil of her spiral notebook. "I haven't been feeling well, that's all."

"How late are you?"

Jade felt herself crumbling on the inside. "Two months."

"Je-sus! And you're supposed to be smart. You ain't got much time, girl. You've got to do something fast."

Jade had refused to acknowledge what her late periods might signify. She hadn't even considered what she would do if the worst possibility became an actuality.

"You're gonna get rid of it, aren't you?"

"I . . . I hadn't thought—"

"Well, if you decide to, I can help," Patrice offered.

"Why would you?"

"Is it Neal Patchett's kid?"

Patrice had heard the rumors. Jade shrugged, indicating that she couldn't be sure whose child she might be carrying.

"Well, on the chance that it's Neal's, I want to help

you." Patrice took out a pack of cigarettes and lit one, although smoking wasn't permitted in the school building. She tilted back her head and sent a plume of smoke ceilingward.

"The son of a bitch did the same thing to me the summer after eighth grade. That was my first. My mama went positively apeshit. My stepdaddy at the time refused to pay for the abortion, so Mama went to Neal's old man for the money. Say, you want a cig? You're lookin' a little green around the gills."

Jade waved the cigarette smoke away from her face. "No, thanks."

"Where was I? Oh, yeah. So anyway, old Ivan gave us five hundred dollars. I went to Georgie over in nigger town. She only charges fifty, so we made money on the deal. Wouldn't you know it," she said, her irritation plain, "My old lady kept every frigging cent. Anyway, I'd be glad to speak to Georgie about you. She's kinda particular and doesn't like to take anybody who ain't referred, you know? And she's real secretive 'cause she doesn't want her other businesses to suffer."

"What other businesses?"

Patrice lowered her voice. "Besides abortions, she has another sideline, although she's supposed to be a seamstress. If you don't have much money and don't want anybody to find out, Georgie's the one to do it." She took another drag of her cigarette. "Look, I know this is a lot to take in. You can tell me to fuck off and I'll fuck off. It ain't no skin off my nose either way, see?"

"I appreciate your offer, Patrice, but I've got to think about it. I'm not even sure that I'm...that it'll be necessary."

Patrice glanced down at Jade's midsection and shrugged. "Sure. I understand, kiddo. The first time 'bout shivered my gizzard, too. But my old lady said no way in hell was she gonna have a squalling brat around the house. Besides, Neal Patchett is such a prick, who in her right mind would want to have his bastard?"

Jade's stomach rebelled at the thought. "I'll let you know what I decide, Patrice. Thanks." She rushed toward the nearest restroom. A few minutes later she left the stall. Weakly bending over the sink, she thrust her hands into cold water and splashed it on her face.

"It's not a baby," she whispered to her pale reflection in the mirror. "It's not anything. It's slime."

After that, each time Jade met Patrice in the hallway, Patrice raised one eyebrow in silent inquiry. Jade pretended not to notice, although Patrice had prompted her to admit that there had been another severe consequence of the rape.

She was pregnant.

She still refused to think of the fetus in terms of an individual, a *baby*. She'd wanted to postpone making a decision about it until after receiving her diploma, which was only a few weeks away. But the life inside her was developing.

She was very careful about the way she dressed. Nevertheless, if Patrice had guessed, it was only a matter of time before others would. Her worst fear was that someone would share his suspicions with Gary. He must never know. Pregnancy was irrefutable proof that she had been with someone other than him. Could she get through graduation without his finding out? Dare she try?

Despite everything, she had been named salutatorian of her class. Gary was valedictorian. She was so proud of him, although she didn't dare congratulate him personally. He was dating another girl, and when Jade happened to meet him in the hall, he always looked the other way.

The honor of being second in her class was a consolation prize in which she took pride. Years of study and hard work had gone into the achievement. With very little parental support, she had earned the honor. Damned if she was going to let Neal and his friends rob her of that, too.

When she stood at the microphone and addressed the audience at the commencement exercise, she wanted to look her attackers in the eye. They wouldn't see her cowed. They had raped her body and her reputation, but she was going to go out with her dignity intact.

But what if people snickered behind their engraved programs over the pregnancy she had tried unsuccessfully to conceal?

During prom week, while her classmates made big plans for that important weekend, Jade agonized over her problem. During a class change, one of the women counselors approached her.

"Who are you going to the prom with, Jade?"

"I'm not going, Mrs. Trenton."

"Not going? No one's asked you?"

"That's right." Neal had, but Jade had hung up on him without even honoring his tongue-in-cheek invitation with a reply. He'd even had the gall to suggest that they double date with Hutch and Donna Dee.

Mrs. Trenton looked her over carefully. "I'd like you to come by my office and see me one day this week, Jade. I believe we need to talk."

She knows.

As Jade moved down the school corridor, she realized that the choice to act now or to wait had been taken away from her. For that she was almost relieved. She wouldn't have to dwell on the dilemma any longer, or weigh her options. She merely had to act, go through the motions, and get it over with as soon as possible. When classes were dismissed for the day, she sought out Patrice Watley.

Jade had rarely gone into that part of town—and certainly never alone. To get there she had to cross the railroad tracks and drive past the deserted depot and the cotton gin, which was no longer in operation. Only then was she officially in "nigger town."

Several years earlier, Velta had hired a black woman to do their ironing. Whenever they went to the lady's house, Velta would order Jade to stay in the car and not to speak to anyone. After a few months, Velta had decided that having the ironing done was too expensive. "Besides," Jade overheard her telling a friend, "it scares me to death to go into that part of town. You never know what they're going to do."

A child, Jade hadn't understood what Velta feared would happen to them when they ventured across the tracks. No one had ever approached the car, spoken to them, or exhibited the merest interest or suggestion of threat. In fact, the ironing lady had always sent out several teacakes wrapped in a paper napkin for Jade. Flaky, buttery, golden, sugar-sprinkled disks—they had looked and smelled mouth-watering. She'd never had an opportunity to find out how they tasted, though. Velta had refused to let her eat them and threw them away the instant they returned home.

Jade parked her mother's car beneath a crepe myrtle tree a block away from the address Patrice had scribbled down for her. As she had pressed the slip of paper into Jade's hand, she whispered, "I'll call Georgie and tell her to be expecting you. Take cash."

The cash, which was most of what she had saved from working in Pete Jones's store, was inside the pocketbook she tucked beneath her arm as she went down the cracked and buckled sidewalk. Some of Velta's prejudicial paranoia had rubbed off on her, she was ashamed to realize. She kept her eyes lowered, looking neither right nor left as she passed the row of small houses that were packed wall-to-wall against each other on their narrow lots.

Georgie's house looked exactly like all the others. In spite of the cold fear in her gut and the serrated blade of her conscience that was sawing against her heart, Jade was curious about what went on there. The house was only two rooms wide, but deep, so that the back porch was almost even with the alley behind the house. It had been painted at one time, though now that white paint was a distant memory. The green tarpaper roof was patched and peeling. The metal chimney had rusted and left a brown stain bleeding down the exterior wall.

"Don't let appearances fool you," Patrice had told her. "Old Georgie's one rich nigger. She could blackmail half the population in the county if she saw fit."

From the outside, it appeared that no one was home. Heavy shades had been pulled over all the windows. Mustering her courage, Jade went up the front sidewalk, stepped onto the porch, and knocked on the frame of the screen door.

She felt dozens of eyes boring into her back from hiding places, but she reasoned that that was only her imagination. She didn't dare turn around either to nullify or to confirm her fears.

It suddenly struck her that there was no one else on the street—no cars passing by, no children playing in front yards, no young mothers pushing baby strollers along the sidewalks. Georgie's neighbors were as wary of white intruders as whites were of venturing into this neighborhood. That regrettable racial schism was one of the things that she and Gary had hoped to correct.

The front door was slowly pulled open, and Jade got her first look at Georgie through the screen. She was much younger than Jade had expected, or perhaps she only looked young because of her smooth, unlined face. Her full lips were enhanced with bright red lipstick. Her eyes were implacable disks of ebony. She was tall and so slender that her limbs looked almost spidery. Her hair had been cut close to form a tight cap around her head. She was dressed in a lilac cotton shirtwaist. Jade was relieved to see that she was immaculately clean.

She swallowed dryly. "My name is Jade. I believe Patrice called for me."

Georgie pushed open the screen door and Jade stepped inside. The house didn't smell unpleasant, as she had feared it might. She wondered what Georgie put in all the Mason jars. There were crates of them stacked in the hall.

The woman raised her hand and indicated that Jade should precede her. Moving toward the back of the house, Jade followed the hallway that divided the house into halves and formed a straight line from the front door to the back.

In the silence, a ticking wall clock sounded inordinately loud. From the kitchen came the high, thin, feeble whistle of a simmering teakettle.

Georgie indicated a room on their left. The only thing in it besides a table draped with a white rubber sheet was an old-fashioned, free-standing, enamel medicine cabinet. Jade hesitated on the threshold.

"Why did you come to me?"

She jumped at Georgie's whispery voice, even though she was much less frightened of the woman than she was of the table with the white rubber sheet and the medicine cabinet, which contained stainless steel implements capable of maiming or killing.

"I have something that needs taken care of," Jade answered huskily.

Georgie held out her hand. At first Jade was puzzled by the gesture. When she realized what it signified, she fumbled in her handbag for her wallet, took out five ten-dollar bills, and stacked them onto Georgie's pink palm. She was professional enough to get her money up front, but lady enough not to bluntly ask for it. It disappeared into the skirt pocket of her dress; she didn't thank Jade for it.

"Please remove your underpants and lie down on the table."

Jade's teeth began to chatter. Now that the time had come, she was overwhelmed with dread and fear. She clumsily laid her purse on the end of the table and reached beneath her skirt for her panties, which she pulled down and stepped out of. Stooping over to pick them up, she asked, "Shouldn't I undress completely?"

"Not until I've examined you. I might not do it."

"Why not?" Almost as much as Jade feared the abortion,

she feared being turned down as a candidate. "You've got to do it. You've already taken my money."

"Lie down. Please," the woman said, not unkindly. Jade lay down. Georgie raised her skirt, folding it back over her chest, exposing her from the waist down. Jade turned her head and stared at the blank wall.

"Some girls come to me too late," Georgie explained. She laid her hands on Jade's lower belly and began massaging it. "I can't help them if they wait too long."

"It's not too late for me. I asked Patrice."

"We'll see." Georgie continued kneading Jade's abdomen. Her eyes were closed. She let only her pressing hands guide her across the space between Jade's pelvic bones, working as high as her navel and as low as her pubic triangle. At last, satisfied, she gave Jade a hand up and lowered her skirt back into place.

Jade sat on the edge of the table, her legs awkwardly dangling over the side. The rubber sheet felt cold, clinical, and foreign beneath her bare bottom. She tried not to think about it. "Will you do it?"

"Is this the Patchett boy's child?"

"It's not a child," Jade protested. "It's a . . . a nothing."

"Did Neal Patchett put it there?"

"I can't be sure. There were three of them. Neal was one. The other two were his friends." Her eyes connected with Georgie's. "They raped me."

The woman held her stare for a long time. Then, quietly, she said, "I thought he only raped black girls. Get undressed. I'll help you."

Jade made slow progress down the sidewalk, taking small, careful steps. Her hands were cold and clammy, and she felt feverish. She alternately shivered and perspired. Georgie had urged her not to leave so soon, but she had insisted. Dusk was descending. She would have to think up a reasonable explanation for being late when she picked up Velta at the factory, but she didn't trouble herself with that now.

With trembling hands she unlocked the car door. For a long while she sat there, staring through the windshield at the fuchsia blossoms on the crepe myrtle, thinking. Eventually, when she felt a little better, she started the car and pulled out into the street, then drove fast until Georgie's house was far behind her.

She had to see Gary.

She told herself that the worst he could do was reject her, and he had already done that. But if she told him everything about that night, filled in the facts he didn't know, he might take her back.

The thought of his arms going around her with love and protection caused her to press heavily on the accelerator. Why, she asked herself, had she waited this long to tell him the truth? Gary knew her better than anyone in the world. If she poured out her heart, surely he would see that she had been victimized. She would explain that her reticence had been an attempt to protect him from public scorn. Since he was being scorned anyway, her silence was no longer effective or necessary.

Why let Neal, Hutch, and Lamar have that much control over their lives? Gary and she were strong, young, and intelligent. Together, safe and secure in each other's love, they could put this episode behind them, leave Palmetto forever, and build a future.

The thought of physical lovemaking was daunting. But

Gary was tender. He would be patient until all her fears and reluctance were abolished.

She nursed no illusions that life from now on would be easy. She would be asking a lot of Gary. He would have to be willing to accept the unacceptable. Which he would, if he loved her enough—and she had to believe that he did. He was dating someone else, but each time she had seen him, before he had a chance to slip on his mask of indifference, Jade had read in his brown eyes a painful yearning that matched her own. Focusing on that gave her courage as she sped through the twilight.

Lit from the inside, the windows of the Parker house made it look like a snaggle-toothed jack-o-lantern. Jade saw Mrs. Parker peer through the kitchen window when she heard the car pull up and stop. Since it was a warm, balmy evening, Gary's younger brothers and sisters were still outside, playing in the yard. Otis was driving a tractor toward the house from across a field.

Jade alighted, surprised to discover that her knees were weak. It was silly to get this nervous over seeing Gary. He had been as hurt as she by their breakup. She clung to the hope that he would be as eager to reconcile.

Mrs. Parker waved at her from behind the screened kitchen window. "Jade, where've you been keeping yourself? I haven't seen you in ages!"

"I know," she said, smiling for the first time in months and hugging Gary's little sisters. At least his family was willing to take her back. "I've missed all of you so much."

"Guess what, Jade? Joey finally learned to pee in the potty."

"How wonderful!"

"But he still has to wear diapers sometimes."

"I know how to skate now, Jade."

Jade reacted to each piece of good news, making much ado over the trivialities that were so important to them. "Where's your big brother?" His car was there, so she knew he was around somewhere.

"He's in the barn."

"Mama told him to slop the hog before supper."

"Well, I'd like to go see him now." Jade gently moved the children aside.

"Are you staying for supper?"

"I don't know. We'll see."

"Mama," one of the boys shouted toward the house, "can Jade stay for supper?"

Jade waved at Otis as she crossed the yard, being careful of where she stepped. Otis removed his hat and waved it high over his head in greeting. She was encouraged by the warm reception Gary's family had given her. Either they hadn't heard the rumors about her or had refused to believe them.

"Gary? Gary?" She stepped through the wide doors, her eyes trying to adjust to the darkness as they scanned the cavernous barn. The scent of hay was strong. "Gary, say something," she said, laughing nervously. "Where are you? What are you doing in here in the dark?"

He wasn't doing anything—except swinging at the end of the rope by which he had hanged himself from the rafters.

Chapter 8

———◆———

Atlanta, 1981

Dillon Burke, lying on the hotel bed wearing only his tuxedo trousers, idly plucked at his chest hair while gazing at the bathroom door, waiting for his bride to emerge. He was feeling more than a little drunk, although he had had only one glass of the champagne that had flowed so freely during the wedding reception that Debra's parents had held. The Newberrys were drinking Baptists. Because they contributed so generously to their church, the minister had looked the other way when the magnums were uncorked.

Dillon, however, was drunk on love and happiness. He smiled, recalling how Debra had sloshed champagne on his hand when they hooked arms and toasted each other. Unmindful of their audience, she had flirtatiously licked it off.

His grandma had always advised him to find himself a Baptist girl. "They're righteous girls for the most part," she had said, "but they're not burdened by guilt like the Catholic girls are."

In Debra's case, Granny Burke had been right. Debra's moral fiber was as durable as belted steel, but she was an extremely sensual creature. From her large, noisy family, she had learned to express affection openly, without shame or timidity.

Dillon was impatient for some of that unreserved, unselfish love now. Thinking about it had aroused him. The rented trousers had become uncomfortably tight. He left the bed and moved across the plush carpeting to the window, which afforded a panoramic view of downtown Atlanta. It was dusk; lights all over the city were twinkling on. He drew a contented breath that expanded his broad chest. God, life really could be grand. His was. He had had a rocky beginning, but good fortune was finally catching up with him.

Hearing the bathroom door open, he turned around and saw Debra standing in a pool of golden light. Her blond hair formed a translucent halo around her head. As she moved toward him, her breasts swayed with fluid enticement against the front of her ivory silk nightgown. With each step she took, the sexy fabric briefly molded to and delineated the delta between her thighs.

He drew her against him and kissed her with unchivalrous fervor, pressing his tongue between her parted lips— and tasted mouthwash.

"What?" Debra asked softly when she felt his smile against her lips.

"Did you gargle?"

"As a matter of fact, I did. After I brushed my teeth, which I did as soon as I got out of the bathtub."

"You bathed?" he asked, nuzzling her warm, fragrant neck.

"I think it's customary for brides to bathe before presenting themselves to their husbands."

"Do you want me to shower?"

"No." She sighed, tilting her head to one side so he would have better access to her throat. "I don't want you to do anything except what you're doing."

He chuckled. "Bet you do."

He lowered his hands to her breasts and slid his knuckles back and forth across the tips until they were distended. "See? I was right." Wrapping his arms around her, he pulled her against him and kissed her passionately. When he finally raised his head, he said, "I love you, Debra."

He had loved her almost from the moment he first saw her. They had met the first day of the fall semester at Georgia Tech. As seniors, they were enrolled in an advanced English course. Dillon was taking it as an elective. For Debra, a language major, the course on the origin of English was required.

After the first few words out of the effeminate professor's mouth, Dillon figured he would have to go through the hassle of getting a schedule change. He didn't think he could stomach three hours of the professor's nasal intonations each week for an entire semester.

Then Debra rushed in, five minutes late, blond hair windblown, cheeks rosy with embarrassment, apologetic for not being able to locate the classroom, and breathless from the exertion of running up two flights of stairs.

Dillon fell in love and lust instantly.

After class, he elbowed his way through the other

students in pursuit of the one who had changed his mind about a schedule change. "Hi," he said, falling into step beside Debra Newberry. He had memorized her name when she gave it to the professor, who had been peeved over her interruption.

She looked up at Dillon with eyes the color of the Caribbean. "Hi."

"Do you belong to anybody?"

They had reached the stairs. She stopped and turned to face him. "Excuse me?" Propelling her backward so they wouldn't cause a bottleneck, Dillon repeated his question. "I belong to myself," she replied in a manner that would have made Gloria Steinem proud.

"No steady boyfriend, husband, or significant other?"

"No. Although I can't see what business that is of yours."

"I was getting to that. Would you like to go to bed with me?"

"I don't know. Would I?"

She could have ignored him and simply marched downstairs. She could have gotten mad and slapped his face. She could have taken affront and given him a lecture on sexism. Instead, her reaction was just what he had hoped for—short of total capitulation, of course. She had turned the joke on him. He had asked the question with such an engaging grin that she couldn't possibly have taken offense.

With very few exceptions, women liked his looks. Dillon modestly acknowledged this because, after all, he had had nothing to do with his handsome face. Genetics was responsible. He had always taken his hazel eyes for granted, but women seemed to think that the gold flecks in them were unusual and intriguing. They claimed to envy his long black eyelashes and the way his brown hair got sun-streaked in the summer.

When Debra gave him a once-over, for the first time in recent memory Dillon really cared what a woman thought of his looks. Apparently she found them pleasing and worth flirting with. Instead of going to bed, they settled on having coffee together and were almost finished with their second cups before she got around to asking him his name. From the beginning, it hadn't mattered.

It was Thanksgiving Day before they went to bed together. They had been seeing each other exclusively, their dates usually ending with steamy necking and manual stimulation. With tremendous self-control, Dillon had restrained himself from even asking for more.

That afternoon, following an enormous Thanksgiving feast, they were in the Newberrys' kitchen cleaning up when Debra said, "Dillon, let's make love." He wasted no time in hustling her out of the house, which was crowded with kinfolk, and drove her to the nearest motel.

"You should have told me you were a virgin," he whispered afterward.

Seeing the uncertainty on his face, she nestled closer to him. "I didn't want you to think I was a freak."

"You know what this means, don't you?"

"That you won't respect me in the morning?" she asked impishly.

"No. It means we've got to get married."

"I was hoping you'd say that."

They postponed it for seven months, so that they could graduate first and because Debra had always dreamed of having a traditional June wedding. Besides, it took that long to make arrangements for a five-hundred-guests affair.

Now that the pomp of the ceremony was over, Dillon swept his bride into his arms and carried her to the bed, laying her down gently. "Don't you want me to take this off?" she asked, touching the front of her nightgown.

"Not yet. You probably paid a fortune for it. You should get to wear it longer than forty-five seconds. Besides," he added, "I like the way it feels."

He skimmed his hand over her belly as he kissed her receptive mouth. Beneath his large hands, she felt like a doll with movable parts that were always willing to be positioned just so. He never took advantage of her eagerness to please, and he was always careful not to hurt her. He was mindful not to press too hard now as his hands sandwiched her narrow ribcage and pulled her belly up against his face. He kissed it through the slithering fabric.

"Hmm," she moaned when he laid her back against the pillows. "Love me now, Dillon."

"I am." Though his erection was so full it was painful, he didn't want their first lovemaking as man and wife to be hasty and unremarkable. He had waited all his life to feel a oneness with another person. Debra was that person. The occasion must be solemnized properly.

Aligning his fingers with her ribs, he used his thumbs to stroke the undercurves of her breasts, then whisked their small centers. The silk layer between his flesh and hers only heightened the pleasure he derived from the caress and the degree of her response.

Reacting to her whispered appeal, he scooped one breast

from her loose neckline and took the nipple between his lips. He sucked it rhythmically, then worked erotic magic with his tongue.

"Dillon, please..."

His hand slid into the vee of her thighs. She angled her hips upward and rubbed her mound against the heel of his hand. He probably could have withstood that if she hadn't unfastened his trousers and freed his erection. "Christ," he hissed as she rolled the ball of her thumb over the sensitive tip.

As a result, the consummation of their marriage took place with him still in his tuxedo trousers and her in her negligee. It wasn't until afterward that they lay naked, entwined on the wide bed, their desire only momentarily sated.

"I have the most beautiful husband in the whole world." Debra was sprawled across his chest, caressing it with her open mouth and nuzzling her nose in the springy hair.

"Beautiful?" he said skeptically. "Hardly."

Stubbornly she shook her head. "Beautiful." She kissed one of his nipples and laughed when he grunted with pleasure.

"I've corrupted you. Before you met me, you were a nice girl," he teased.

"That was before I knew what I was missing."

Once she had accepted his marriage proposal, Dillon allowed himself to believe that she might truly love him, though she had professed it countless times. It was too good a fortune to befall him. He didn't deserve someone as beautiful and unspoiled as Debra Newberry. He hadn't earned the unqualified acceptance of her family. His distress over it had eventually sparked an argument.

In the middle of the quarrel, Debra had demanded, "What terrible secret are you afraid I'll discover that'll make me stop loving you?"

"I've got a record," he had blurted. "Do you think your parents will want a son-in-law who's done time?"

"I won't know what to think until you tell me about it, Dillon."

His parents had been killed when he was eight years old. "They were on their way to pick me up from summer camp. It was one of those freak highway accidents. A trailer truck jackknifed. Their car ran under it."

Because there was no one else to take him, he had been placed in the custody of his father's mother. "Granny Burke did her best, but I was an angry kid. Up till the time my mom and dad were killed, everything was okay. Dad was a good provider. Mom was attentive and loving. It didn't seem fair to them or to me that they should be killed.

"I started making trouble at school. My grades went to hell. I resented Granny for trying to take my parents' place, although, in hindsight, I realize what a tremendous burden I was to her at that time in her life. Eventually, I realized that this was the fate I'd drawn and that I had just as well make the best of it. For a few years, everything was fine.

"Then, when I was fourteen, Granny got sick. She had to go to the hospital. When I asked how serious her illness was, the doctors gave me a lot of bullshit about trusting in God's will. That's when I realized that my grandmother was going to die, too. To her credit, she told it to me straight. 'I'm sorry to leave you alone, Dillon,' she said, 'but it's out of my hands.'

"After she died I was placed in a foster home. I hated it. There were five kids besides me. I kept hearing about a war in a place called Vietnam, but it couldn't have been anything like the fighting that went on in that house, especially between the couple. I saw him hit her more than a few times.

"The day I turned sixteen, I split. I figured that living on my own would be better than staying in the foster home. There was supposed to be a trust fund waiting for me, but I was given the runaround about that until I figured that someone, probably the foster parents, had gotten hold of it. I considered that nothing more than a minor setback. I was certain I could make it on my own, but of course I couldn't—not without stealing to keep myself from starving.

"Eventually I got busted and was sent to a 'farm for troubled boys,' which is a euphemism for jail. From the day I got there, I devised plans to escape. I tried it twice. The second time, one of the guidance counselors beat the crap out of me."

"How dreadful," Debra murmured sympathetically.

Dillon gave her a grim, lopsided grin. "At first I thought so, too. Later, he explained that before anything he had to say could sink in, he had to get my undivided attention.

"He told me that I had been dealt a pretty shitty hand all right, but that how I played the cards was up to me. I could either continue getting into trouble until I ended up in prison for life, or I could turn things around and start making circumstances work in my favor."

"Obviously you took his advice."

"I earned my high school diploma in that place. When I got out, he arranged a job for me at the public utilities company, drafting schematics and such. It paid for my college tuition and lodging. You know the rest."

Debra gazed at him with mild annoyance. "That's it? That's the extent of your sordid, secretive past?"

"Isn't it enough?"

"Dillon, you were a child. You made a few mistakes."

He shook his head stubbornly. "I haven't been a child since I was eight years old and learned that my parents had been decapitated. Since then I've been accountable for everything I've done."

"Okay, so some of your mistakes were more serious than standard and the consequences of them more severe. Don't be so hard on yourself. You've risen above the errors of your youth. I'd like to meet that counselor and personally thank him for setting you straight."

"I wish you could meet him, too. Unfortunately, shortly after I left, another kid knifed him during a counseling session, then stood by and watched while he bled to death. So," he had summarized, "I don't have anybody to invite to this fancy wedding your mother is planning."

"You'll be there," Debra had said as she embraced him. "And since you make me so happy, that's all that matters to my family."

The Newberrys were old residents of an affluent community. Her parents came from large families. Debra had three brothers and two sisters. All but one of her sisters were married, so there was an army of aunts, uncles, and cousins at any family gathering.

Dillon had been welcomed into the fold by all of them. Initially, he had been aloof. It was a defense mechanism. He was afraid that if he acknowledged their acceptance, he would somehow jinx it, just as he had been afraid to accept Debra's unqualified love.

But now, as they lay together in the peaceful aftermath of marital lovemaking, Dillon granted himself the luxury of basking in his good fortune. He had earned the college degree that was going to open doors of opportunity for him. He was part of a large and loving family, which was something he had never had before. His bride was smart and sweet, funny and sexy.

He clasped handfuls of her hair and lifted her head off his chest, turning her face up to his. "You'd better stop that nibbling."

"Don't you like it?"

"I like it so much you might get more than you bargained for."

"Impossible." Smiling, she lowered her lips to his belly and kissed it. "Dillon?"

"Hmm?"

"Teach me how to, you know, uh, make love to you with my mouth."

His eyes, which had been drowsily half-closed, sprang open. Except for the time he had spent in the correctional institution, Dillon had always taken the availability of sex for granted. From the very first time, it had always come to him.

One morning during summer vacation from junior high school, Dillon had answered the knock on his grandmother's back door.

Mrs. Chandler, their next door neighbor, was young and vivacious. She had big eyes, big breasts, and long legs, which she often showed off by wearing short shorts that separated and defined her cleft and bottom. Her husband drove a truck for the Safeway chain and was away from home more often than not. Boredom kept her a frequent visitor of the Burkes.

"Hi, Dillon. Is your grandma home?"

She knew damned well that his grandmother wasn't at home because her car wasn't in the driveway. Dillon, with thirteen-year-old recalcitrance, was tempted to point that out. But that would have been rude, and his grandmother had taught him some manners. He said, "Granny went to the store."

"Oh, dear." Mrs. Chandler distressfully batted her eyelashes. "She told me to stop by and get those coupons she clipped for me. Do you know what she did with them?"

"They're on the hall table."

"Could I get them now, please? I was just about to go to the store myself when I remembered I didn't have them."

Dillon read through that lie, too. She wasn't dressed for grocery shopping. She was outfitted for seduction. Out of curiosity, he pushed open the screen door. She bounced in. He made no move toward the hall table.

Instead, he stood facing Mrs. Chandler. He was already taller than she. She commented on his height as she ran her hands up his bare arms and across his muscled but hairless chest. It wasn't fully developed, but it was showing tremendous promise.

"My, my, Dillon. I didn't realize how big you're getting."

His young body was bursting with male hormones; his head hummed with lust. "So are you. Big, I mean." His eyes moved down to her breasts. The large, dark areolas were distinct beneath her tight, white cotton blouse.

In seconds, even that was gone, and Mrs. Chandler was guiding his beardless face to her rosy nipples and poking them against his lips. Granny Burke pulled into the driveway just as the young, faithless wife from next door reached into Dillon's shorts to explore.

Two days later, Mrs. Chandler got desperate enough to risk getting caught. She sneaked through the back door while Dillon's grandmother was taking her afternoon nap. She held her index finger vertically against her pursed lips and signaled him into his bedroom. As they crept down the hall, they heard Granny's soft snores coming from her open bedroom door.

As soon as Dillon had shut the door to his room, Mrs. Chandler fell on him like a starving feline. Lacking the finesse that comes only from experience, Dillon was just as ravenous. When he drove into her, she was sticky and hot. He exploded with pleasure. When it was over, her only complaint was that he had come too soon.

Patting his hand, she said, "We'll work on that."

"How?" he asked, gazing at her with his serious, hazel eyes. "How do we work on it?" he whispered. "What should I have done? Show me."

His concern had been so unexpected, his interest so genuine, that she cried. She spent the remainder of the summer coaching him on how to please her and complaining that the "gorilla" she was married to didn't even know where "it" was or what it was for. "He just screws me until I'm too sore to walk and thinks he's proved that he's a terrific lover."

Dillon was a diligent student. He learned how to please, how to give what a woman needed and wanted. It was never far from his conscience that Mrs. Chandler was another man's wife. What they did together was immoral, he knew. He made repeated vows to himself that he would stop. But then she would come to him all excited and eager, and he couldn't resist her temptation or availability. Besides, he didn't feel he owed a truck driver any consideration. The driver of the rig that had killed his parents had walked away from the grisly scene unscathed.

A few days after Labor Day, Mrs. Chandler came to tell his grandmother that her husband was being transferred. "We're moving to Little Rock next weekend."

"Good riddance," Granny had muttered as she watched Mrs. Chandler pick her way through the rose bush hedge that separated their yards. Dillon had glanced sharply at his granny, wondering if she had known all summer long what was going on each afternoon in his bedroom while she was asleep in hers. They never talked about Mrs. Chandler again.

But Dillon never forgot her. He supposed men never forgot the first woman of whom they had carnal knowledge. He had used her body as an experimental laboratory, but he didn't feel guilty for that. She had pursued him and had derived as much satisfaction as he—and sometimes more.

He applied the lessons he'd learned with Mrs. Chandler to the easy girls at school—most of whom were older than he. Then one of his "stepsisters" in the foster home benefitted from his expertise. She was a heavy girl with foul breath and bad skin who was pathetically grateful for the tenderness he showed her each night. The girls he met on the streets were jaded, and his encounters with them had little emotional impact.

He was as randy as a billy goat by the time he was released from reform school and entered college. Again, nature was on his side. Both psychologically and physically, he was mature beyond his years. The potential that Mrs. Chandler had spotted in him at thirteen had become realized: he had a tall, strong, lean body, and he was personable and well liked. He had no difficulty making friends with other young men or wooing desirable coeds into his bed.

The first woman ever to have gone down on him was a whore, contracted by his fraternity as a party favor for the rushees. She had a routine: a wag of her tits; a quick blow job; that'll be ten bucks, please. There had been other times since then, but most women approached this specialized kind of lovemaking with dutiful resignation, as though it was something expected but unenjoyable. Never before had a woman gazed up at him with longing and love and asked to be taught the technique. He sifted Debra's hair through his fingers and said softly, "You don't have to."

She gave him a puzzled look. "I want to. Are you embarrassed?"

He laughed shortly, realizing that he was. "A little."

"I want to do it right."

"There's no right or wrong way."

"But I'll bet there's a difference between right and righter." She inched up his body and laid her lips against his, whispering, "Teach me the righter way."

Much later, Dillon gazed down at his bride while she slept peacefully beside him. She was so pretty that it made his throat ache with emotion. More than that, she was a beautiful person. Guile, in any of its various forms, was foreign to her.

He was the only man to have possessed her body, and that was a privilege he didn't take lightly. She had given him her heart and entrusted her love into his safekeeping. She was relying on him to keep her financially and emotionally secure for the rest of her life. The greatest challenge he would ever face was being all that Debra wanted and needed him to be.

In a fierce whisper that cut through the darkness of the still room, he told himself, "Don't fuck up."

Chapter 9

——◆◆——

"Mr. Burke, Pilot wants to see you right away."

Giving a mock salute, Dillon acknowledged the message that the passing secretary had called to him from the doorway of the cubicle office that he shared with three other draftsmen. He tossed down his pencil and covered his mouth with his fist. Behind it, he muttered curses while ignoring the covert glances of his co-workers.

He stood and yanked his jacket off the back of his chair. Without bothering to roll down his shirt sleeves, he shoved his arms into the sleeves of the jacket and strode from the office. It was one of hundreds that comprised the sprawling complex belonging to Pilot Engineering Industries of Tallahassee. The name of the company was misleading, as it had nothing to do with aviation. The construction engineering firm was named after its founder and CEO, Forrest G. Pilot. It was said that Forrest G. was a descendant of the notorious Pontius Pilate and that he had inherited his ancestor's penchant for crucifixion.

Today, it seemed, Dillon Burke was to be the one executed.

"He'll be with you presently, Mr. Burke. If you'll please be seated." Forrest G. Pilot's secretary nodded toward a chair in the reception area outside the inner sanctum.

Belligerently, Dillon threw himself into the chair. He was furious with himself for his behavior the day before. Apparently one of Pilot's spies had reported on Dillon's vocal criticism. Pilot didn't like discontent within his ranks. Ideally, his army of drones toiled in their assigned chambers and kept their opinions of his management to themselves. Until yesterday, Dillon had complied with that unwritten policy.

Initially he had felt lucky to be hired by Pilot Industries, which was well known throughout the Southeast. Neither he nor Debra had minded relocating. It had seemed like an extension of their honeymoon. His starting salary hadn't been terrific, but Dillon had been confident that he could quickly escalate it. He had reasoned that once his supervisors spotted his potential, they would want to keep him happy at the risk of losing him to a competitor. He had envisioned a meteoric rise straight to the top.

It hadn't worked out that way. The company hired dozens of young engineers fresh from college graduation. None was given an opportunity to advance. Dillon wasn't playing in the big league and he wasn't making big money. Debra claimed to be blissfully happy, although Dillon knew she must miss the luxuries her father had lavished on her. She deserved better than their cramped, one-bedroom apartment.

Time seemed to be standing still for him. Daily he grew more impatient. There was so much he wanted to do, and at Pilot Engineering Industries he wasn't getting to do any of it. He would have quit months earlier if the unemployment rate weren't so high. Until he had an excellent prospect, he couldn't afford to lose this job.

The buzzer on the secretary's desk sounded. "You can go in now, Mr. Burke," she said with chilly politeness.

Dillon adjusted his necktie as he approached the intimidating door. He grasped the brass knob aggressively and pushed it open.

Pilot set aside the drawing he had been studying and peered at Dillon over the silver frames of his reading glasses, nodding him into a chair on the other side of his desk. Dillon didn't let Pilot's stare intimidate him. He waited him out. Finally Pilot said, "I understand you're unhappy with us, Mr. Burke."

If he was going to get canned anyway, he had nothing to lose by being honest. Screw Forrest G. Pilot if he didn't like what he had to say. Debra, he knew, would be the first to back him up for speaking his mind. "That's right. I am."

"I like for my employees to be happy. It makes for a more congenial workplace."

"I didn't intend to be disruptive. I saw something I didn't like and expressed my viewpoint, that's all."

Pilot removed his glasses and ruminatively polished the lenses with a linen handkerchief. "Why should it upset you that Mr. Greyson was appointed supervising engineer for that medical-clinic project?"

"I wasn't upset. I was pissed off. I had submitted a formal request to my supervisor for that job. He assured me it would get to your desk."

"It did."

"Oh, I see. You passed over me in favor of Greyson."

"Mr. Greyson has been with the company for ten years. You were hired only last year, straight out of Georgia Tech. Your grades and the sample work you submitted when you applied were impressive enough for us to hire you, but you're still a rookie." He spread his hands wide. "Mr. Greyson has more experience."

"I've got more talent."

Dillon's immodest candor took the older man by surprise. He barked a short laugh. "And, it would appear, more balls."

"When I was hired," Dillon continued, "I was promised an opportunity to do some actual work. This medical clinic makes three times I've lost an on-site job to men who are no more qualified. Frankly, I feel they were less qualified. Your system of advancement stinks, Mr. Pilot. Hard work and talent should be rewarded, not compressed into those little glass boxes you call offices."

"Mr. Burke—"

"I'm an engineer. I want to build things. When other young boys were drawing cars and jet fighters, I was drawing buildings of the future and trying to figure out how to construct them."

Exasperated, he stood up and began pacing. "What I'm doing out there," he said, flinging his arm toward the door, "I was doing in my freshman engineering class at Tech."

"Some men consider a drafting job at Pilot Engineering a real plum."

"Sitting at a drafting table all day long, waiting for the five o'clock bell to ring, isn't my idea of challenging work. Anyway, in a few years computers will be doing the drafting. Draftsmen will become keyboard operators."

Pilot leaned back in his chair. "What *is* your idea of challenging work, Mr. Burke?"

"Working with the architect, hiring all the subs, overseeing the whole project. I want to be there from the time the first shovel of dirt is turned until the last light bulb is screwed in."

"Then I can't accommodate you."

Even though he had been expecting termination, when Dillon actually heard the words, they gave him a start. Jesus, what had he been thinking of to paint himself into such an inescapable corner? What was he going to do? How was he going to support himself and his bride?

"The first shovel of dirt has already been turned."

Dillon blinked Forrest G. Pilot back into focus. "Sir?"

"In fact, the ironwork was already up before the project was put on hold due to poor management."

"I don't understand."

"Sit down, Mr. Burke." When Dillon was reseated, he went on, "While you were getting pissed off at me for not assigning you the medical-clinic job, I was considering you for another."

Dillon swallowed hard, but prudently kept his mouth shut.

"Contrary to what you believe," Pilot said, "your work has not gone unnoticed. Nor have your leadership qualities. I pride myself on having a nose for sniffing out bright, ambitious young talent. As you said, some people are content with regimented work. Others are not. You're one of the latter.

"Unfortunately, having ambition and youth and talent isn't sufficient. To be really successful, one must also develop patience and self-discipline. What I should do is fire you on the spot for your insolence. But I'm not, chiefly because you're too valuable a talent to hand over to my competitors. And secondly, because the job I have in mind requires somebody who has the guts to be abrasive when it's called for.

"So, I think that now is the time for you to take your foot out of your mouth and tell me whether you're interested in the project I have in mind for you."

Dillon managed to maintain his dignity. "Naturally, I'm very interested."

"Before we go any further, I should tell you that there is one major drawback to this job."

There would be, Dillon thought dismally. The devil always got his due. Something good was always followed by something equally bad—that was Dillon Burke's version of Newton's law. It was the cosmic scorekeeper's system of checks and balances. However, nothing could be as bad as returning to that glass box and a drafting table. Motion was always preferable to stagnation.

"I'm willing to tackle just about anything, Mr. Pilot."

That night Dillon brought home a bouquet of flowers, a loaf of bakery-fresh bread, and a bottle of wine. "What's the occasion?" Debra gasped breathlessly after he released her from a searing hello kiss.

"What's for dinner?"

"Hamburgers. Why?"

"Good. Because I brought red wine."

"I think you drank a bottle on the way home," she said, sniffing his breath. "You're acting very strange. A husband bearing gifts in the first year of marriage is as suspect as the Trojan horse. Are you having an affair?"

"Absolutely." He lowered his hands to her bottom and pulled her against him. "With the sexiest broad ever to come out of Atlanta."

"Lil' ol' me?"

"None other, sugar pie. So," he drawled with a lecherous grin, "wanna fuck?"

"Uh-huh."

They raced each other to the bedroom, stripped off their clothes, and made love. Afterward, while Debra was catching her breath as she lay amid the rumpled sheets, Dillon slipped from the room and returned with the gifts he had brought home. He laid them out in front of her.

"What do these three items have in common?" he asked.

"They're all bribes."

"Cute. Try again."

"You must have had a terrific day at work. What's going on?"

"Will I have to find another girl to play with, or what?"

"Okay, okay. Flowers, wine, and bread," she mused. "Does it have anything to do with spores or mold, something like that?"

He shook his head. "It's not so much the flowers as the ribbon around them."

"Red, white and blue striped." She began to sing. " 'My country 'tis of Thee, sweet land—' "

"Another country whose colors are red, white, and blue."

"England."

"Another."

She picked up the bottle of wine and read the label. Then, lifting her quizzical gaze to Dillon, she said, "France?"

He broke into a wide grin. "Congratulations, young woman! You win first prize."

"Which is?"

"Two years, maybe more, in Paris!"

"Dillon?"

"Actually just outside Paris—Versailles, where the palace is located. I don't think you'll mind living in the suburbs, will you?"

Debra squealed, "Dillon, what are you talking about?"

He told her about the job Pilot had offered him. "It's for an international insurance firm. They were building a new office complex for their European headquarters. The contracting firm turned out to be incompetent, and the work was scrapped until a new one could be hired."

"Pilot bid on the project?"

"Right. Now Pilot needs a troubleshooting engineer to go over there and whip this mess into shape."

"And Forrest G. Pilot chose you."

He spread his arms away from his naked body and tried in vain to look humble. Debra launched herself against him. He toppled over backward, carrying her down with him and squashing the loaf of French bread.

"Can you believe that he thought living in France would be a drawback?" Dillon asked. "Little did he know that my wife's main ambition in life is to go to France and hone her skills in the language."

"Did you tell him that?"

"Hey, I ain't stupid. I appeared disgruntled over having to live abroad and said that if I accepted the job, I would have to have more money."

"What did he say?"

"A hundred dollars a week raise."

In an orgy of excitement, they made love again. The hamburgers Debra had planned to serve for dinner were substituted with the smashed loaf of bread and the tepid bottle of wine. After they had demolished the last crumb and drained the last drop, they lay together on top of the scattered, crushed flowers and drowsily discussed their sunny future.

The move was a nightmare. There were passports and visas to obtain, weepy relatives to bid goodbye, and a million loose ends to tie up. Those responsibilities generally fell to Debra while Dillon was busy familiarizing himself with the unfinished project he had taken on. He was eager to get under way. As it turned out, he went to France ahead of Debra to make living arrangements and met her at Charles de Gaulle Airport three weeks later.

Leaving customs, she rushed into his arms and they held each other close. As he escorted her through the busy international airport, he told her repeatedly how much he had missed her.

"You can't fool me, Burke," she teased as they entered the parking garage. "You've probably gone through a score of French mistresses in the last three weeks." Laughing, he ushered her toward a car. "Is this ours?" she asked incredulously.

" 'Fraid so."

"It's so tiny."

"That's the only way you can survive the traffic over here. You've got to be able to slither through or you're stuck for hours."

She gauged the small interior against the length of Dillon's legs. "Can you fit into that?"

"It's a tight squeeze. As a result, there's something I've got to tell you." Solemnly he said, "I can no longer father children."

Debra pressed her hand against his crotch. "As long as it still works, I don't care."

He was momentarily shocked by her public flirtation, but she reminded him that they were in France and that the French were famous for their tolerance of lovers.

He apologized to her for their apartment, which was on the third floor of a building with an elevator he didn't trust and that he ordered her never to use. It was a narrow, drafty building with four apartments on each floor. "It was the best I could do," Dillon said regretfully as he unlocked the door and swung it open. "Everything here is so expensive."

What he found antiquated and inconvenient, Debra dubbed quaint and charming. "We've got a balcony!" she exclaimed, rushing toward the window and pushing open the shutters.

"Not a very good view, though."

The balcony looked down over a sadly neglected courtyard. Within weeks, however, there were primroses blooming from the window boxes Debra had installed. She covered the cracks in the interior walls with colorful travel posters and made casual slipcovers out of bedsheets to hide the tackiness of the furniture, which had come with the apartment. It soon became a home that Dillon wouldn't have traded for the nearby Versailles Palace.

On weekends, native Parisians made an exodus to the country, leaving the city to tourists like the Burkes. They parked their car on the outskirts of the city and used the Metro. Soon they became expert at negotiating

its multilayered, underground stations. Like hungry gour-
mands at a feast, they consumed everything French.
They fell in love with the sights, smells, and sounds of
the City of Lights. They haunted the museums, parks, and
historically significant public buildings, and discovered
hideaway cafes where even Americans were charged fair
prices for exquisite meals.

Cathedrals with windows of stained glass were dark
sanctuaries where they sought privacy to kiss instead of
pray. American hotdogs paled in comparison to those sold
in Montmartre alongside original paintings.

To celebrate their first wedding anniversary, they spent
a long weekend in the wine country, sampling the local
vintages until they grew maudlin, and sleeping in small
hotels where the featherbeds were as thick and sumptuous
as the sauces served in the intimate dining rooms.

But there was a serpent in their paradise.

His name was Haskell Scanlan. Dillon's title was
supervising engineer in charge of construction. Haskell
handled business matters—payroll, purchasing, and bookkeeping. They had met briefly in Tallahassee. Dillon had
hoped that his first impression of the man would change
once they got to France. For Debra's sake he had hoped
they could be friends with Haskell and his wife.

Unfortunately, Haskell Scanlan turned out to be as big
a pain in the ass on foreign soil as on domestic. None of
the construction workers could stand him. An unmerci-
ful timekeeper, he docked their pay if they clocked in
thirty seconds late. When the foreman approached Dillon
about a pay increase, he took what he believed to be a fair
request to Haskell Scanlan. Haskell adamantly refused
even to consider it.

"For Chris' sake, give them the raise!" Dillon shouted after a half-hour of heated argument.

"Across the board?"

"Across the board."

"That'll only encourage them to ask for more later on."

"Hell, Haskell, they're only asking for what amounts to twenty cents an hour."

"Multiply it out. It adds up."

"Okay, so raise them ten cents an hour. That would demonstrate our goodwill and might give them enough incentive to stay with us. I lost two good carpenters last week because they could make more money working on that new sports arena that's under construction."

"The carpenters you lost were replaced."

"But it took several days out of my work schedule to interview and hire them. I don't like losing days. The building is scheduled for completion sometime next summer. I'd like to finish it by early spring."

"Why?"

"Because Debra's pregnant. Much as we love it here, I'd like my baby to be born at home."

"Personal interests shouldn't override the interests of the company."

"Fuck you."

Haskell had all but *tsk*ed him. "Resort to that kind of language if it makes you feel better. I assure you it's not going to change my mind."

Dillon resorted to that kind of language and a whole lot worse before the issue was settled. "I hate to jump the chain of command on him," he told Debra that night over dinner. "But the man's a penny-pinching prick who can't see anything except the bottom line. What he doesn't seem to understand is that the sooner we get the building up, the more money he'll save Pilot Industries."

"Maybe jumping the chain of command is warranted," Debra said. "You can't be effective if you're constantly quarreling with a man who's obviously jealous of you."

"Jealous?"

Haskell and his wife had come to dinner one evening at Debra's invitation, so she had had a chance to observe him. "Dillon, be realistic. You're everything he would love to be. You're handsome; he's not. You're tall and strong and manly, and he's a pale, puny weakling. Despite the language barriers, you get along well with the men, but they ridicule him. Didn't you tell me that they call him the French equivalent of 'asshole'? I don't even think his wife likes him."

He made a moue of grudging assent. "You may be right, but there's a big difference between determining the problem and solving it."

"Call Pilot. Lay it on the line."

"Issue an ultimatum—Haskell or me?" He shook his head. "I'm not ready to chance that. Haskell's been with the company longer and Pilot puts a lot of stock in seniority. If he chose Haskell, I wouldn't get to finish my building. Besides needing the job, I want to see my building finished for my own satisfaction."

Dillon lost two ironworkers the following week. He blew his top when Haskell refused to give him a budget with which to bargain.

"They're only trying to manipulate you."

"Go to hell." Dillon left quickly, so that he wouldn't slam his fist into Haskell's parsimonious puss. He decided he had no choice but to call Pilot.

Pilot wasn't pleased. "I certainly didn't think I'd have to worry about personality conflicts from two so-called professionals."

"I'm sorry I have to bother you with this, but if Haskell keeps his fist closed around the company purse, I'm going to lose qualified builders. I'll be forced to hire second-rate workers, and I don't think either of us wants that, do we, Mr. Pilot?"

Static crackled through the long-distance connection during the ensuing silence. At last Pilot said, "Tell him that I personally authorized a ten-cent-an-hour raise across the board."

"Fifteen?"

"Twelve, and that's it, Burke. Don't involve me in these squabbles again. I put you in charge of this project, so take charge."

Pilot hung up before Dillon had a chance to say thank you. He reasoned it was a good thing. Otherwise, it might look like Pilot was playing favorites instead of exercising sound business sense.

Haskell Scanlan didn't see it that way. "Did you go crying to Daddy?" he asked snidely when Dillon informed him of the conversation with Pilot.

"I told him what I thought was in the best interest of this project."

"Oh, sure," Haskell replied cattily. "Pilot looks at you and sees a younger reflection of himself. Beneath the gilt of his success, he's as brash and uncouth as you. He prides himself on being a self-made man. So don't make the mistake of believing that you won this quarrel on your own merit. You only won because you're the boss's ego trip."

Since he *had* ultimately won, Dillon didn't concern himself with Haskell's opinion. Beyond a few days of cold, miserable rain, things at the construction site ran smoothly through the autumn months. Dillon lost no more workers, because they knew he was responsible for their raise.

The workers seemed to appreciate his talent for remembering their names, his ability to tell a dirty joke like one of the boys, and his sense of knowing when to interfere in private disputes and when not to. He asked nothing of them that he didn't require of himself. He took risks, stayed overtime, ate a packed lunch alongside them, and earned their respect for mixing with them instead of setting himself apart.

Dillon preferred to know his building intimately— every rivet, every cable, every brick—rather than seal himself off in his trailer. He inspected every phase of the construction. His high standards caused his next altercation with Haskell Scanlan.

"What the hell is this?" Dillon was holding a strip of electrical conduit in his gloved hands. The unfortunate electrician whom Dillon had randomly selected to question glanced warily around the circle of onlookers and, seeing no one willing to leap to his rescue, began explaining in rapid French.

Dillon didn't understand a word of it. He shook the strip of wiring at the man's face. "This isn't what I ordered. Where'd you get it?"

One of the electricians spoke a smattering of English. He tapped Dillon's arm. Dillon angrily spun around. "What?" The man pointed toward the stacked spools of wiring. After a brief inspection, Dillon addressed the men now standing idle. "Don't install any more of this shit. Got that?" The man who had been serving as interpreter conveyed the message to the others.

Lifting one of the heavy spools onto his shoulder, Dillon used the service elevator to get to the ground floor, then barged through the door of the trailer. Haskell, seated at his computer terminal, jumped reflexively at the sudden interruption. When he saw Dillon, he frowned in disapproval of his barbaric behavior.

"I want to know what the hell this is." The reel of conduit landed on top of Haskell's desk with a solid thud. He sent his desk chair flying backward on its casters.

"What do you think you're doing?" he squealed. "Get that thing off my desk."

Dillon braced his hands on either side of the metal spool and leaned over it. "Listen to me, you little shit, I'm going to make you eat every foot of this worthless stuff if you don't come across with a full explanation of why you didn't buy what I wrote on the purchase order months ago. You've got ten seconds."

"The wiring you ordered was three times as expensive as this," Haskell said, having recovered some equanimity.

"The wiring I ordered is three times as *good* and three times as *safe*."

"This meets local building codes."

"It doesn't meet mine," Dillon said through clenched teeth.

"If I didn't know it was sufficient—"

"You don't know jackshit. This building is going to be filled with all types of sophisticated electronics. To avoid catastrophe, it's got to have the best possible wiring."

Dillon grabbed the telephone and dropped it into the

unsuspecting accountant's lap. "Now, get your skinny ass on the phone and place the order I originally sent in. I want the materials delivered no later than noon tomorrow, or I'm going to send every one of those electricians with nothing to do in here to jerk off on your desk."

The telephone clattered to the floor as Haskell shot to his feet. "You can't talk to me like that."

"I just have." Dillon nodded down at the telephone. "You're wasting time. Do it."

"I won't. It's my responsibility to see that we keep expenses down."

"I agree, as long as it doesn't compromise the integrity of the building. In this instance, it does."

"The wiring I ordered is sufficient and, according to the local government, safe."

"Well, according to Dillon Burke, it's crap. I won't install it in my building."

"*Your* building?" Haskell said with a supercilious smile.

"Just order the wiring I requested, Scanlan."

"No."

Dillon liked harmony as well as the next man, and he avoided confrontation whenever he could. But he wasn't about to lower his standards on his first project. Nor was he willing to go to Pilot again. Pilot had already told him to take charge.

"Either get on the telephone now," he said calmly, "or you're fired."

Haskell's pointed jaw fell open. "You can't fire me."

"The hell I can't."

"Oh yeah? We'll see what Mr. Pilot has to say about it."

"I'm sure we will. In the meantime, consider yourself

off this project. And, unless you want me to pound the crap out of your face, I suggest you stay away from me until you're gone for good."

Debra's adversary was boredom. Their first few months in France, she had occupied herself with decorating the apartment on a shoestring budget and had succeeded as far as the limitations of the building permitted.

They had discussed the possibility of her getting a job, but it wasn't feasible. There were no openings for teachers in the English-speaking schools, and shopkeepers preferred to hire their own rather than employ an American. So she wiled away the daytime hours by reading, strolling the narrow, quaint streets, and writing long letters to her many relatives. Although she tried to hide it from Dillon, she became homesick and listless. She had to forcibly stave off depression.

Her pregnancy rejuvenated her. She suffered no unpleasant side effects and swore she had never felt better. She was imbued with energy. Daily, she and Dillon marveled over the subtle changes in her body. This new kind of intimacy deepened their love for each other.

To help pass the time until the baby came, she enrolled in a cooking class that was held within walking distance of the apartment. There were four other women in the class and two men, all of retirement age. They, along with the grandmotherly chef, fussed over her like mother hens. Afterward her days were spent either in class or in her tiny apartment kitchen practicing what she had learned, or shopping in the neighborhood markets for the ingredients necessary to audition her culinary skills for Dillon. She would arrive home with her arms loaded with purchases and take them up by the creaky elevator that Dillon had forbidden her to use.

That particular afternoon she almost got caught, arriving home only moments before he did. Immediately he hugged her and planted a firm kiss on her cold lips. Then, grinning, he released her and said, "Let's go to Switzerland."

"Switzerland?"

"Yeah, you know, one of the countries that shares a border with France—goats and Heidi, Alps and snow, yo-do-la-dee-ho."

"Of course I know Switzerland. Remember our weekend in Geneva?"

"Was that where our room had the mirror on the ceiling?"

"So you do remember."

"How could I forget?" he growled, reaching for her again. Their mouths melded into a kiss.

"We don't need mirrors on the ceiling," she whispered when they finally pulled apart.

"But I need to get out of town and celebrate."

"Celebrate what?"

"I fired Haskell Scanlan today."

Debra's smiled faltered.

Dillon told her what had happened. "I hated like hell having to go to that extreme, but he left me no choice." He studied her worried expression. "You don't think I did the right thing?"

"I think you did exactly the right thing. Unfortunately, my opinion doesn't carry as much weight as Forrest G. Pilot's."

"That's why I want to leave for Switzerland tonight.

If he agrees with my decision, we'll have had a terrific weekend in the Alps. If he reverses it, I'll have to quit on principal, in which case we can no longer afford a trip to Switzerland. And if he fires me, the above is also true. So, while I'm still gainfully employed and feeling as good as I do, let's say to hell with everything else and go."

They took an express train to Lausanne and another to Zermatt. They joked with students, chatted with a grandmother from Montreux who was knitting a cap for her tenth grandchild, and snacked on the food Debra had had the foresight to bring along.

Dillon drank strong red wine from a bota one of the students offered him, but declined to take a toke of marijuana. When the couple sitting across from them began to neck, Dillon and Debra asked each other why not, and cuddled and kissed until they fell asleep.

In Zermatt, Dillon skied the expert slopes. Debra's pregnancy prohibited her from that, so she consoled herself by browsing in the glitzy shops and watching the endless parade of jetsetters. Together she and Dillon rode in a horse-drawn sleigh and watched skaters gliding on silver blades across a frozen pond. They gorged on cheese fondue, thick, dark bread, white wine, and Swiss chocolate.

During the train ride home, Dillon pulled her against him and tucked her head beneath his chin. "This was our real honeymoon."

"What was wrong with our trip to Bermuda?"

"Absolutely nothing. But then you were merely my bride. Now you're my wife." He slipped his hand into her coat and laid it on her swollen belly. "I love you."

While they were waiting to switch trains in Lausanne, she bought a tin of aspirin. "What's wrong?" he asked.

"My throat's getting sore."

She slept fitfully for the remainder of the trip to Paris and was frequently awakened by chills. "It hurts to swallow," she complained.

Dillon pressed his hand against her forehead. "You're burning up. Better take some more aspirin."

"I hate to without asking the doctor first. Aspirin might not be good for the baby."

By the time they reached Paris, Dillon was worried, although Debra assured him that her sore throat was simply the result of her exposure to mountain air. He fought Monday morning rush-hour traffic to get her to her obstetrician, and they reached his office just as it was opening. The nurse, with kindness and concern, guided Debra into an examination room and asked Dillon to wait outside. He didn't like it, but he waited. After several waiting patients averted their eyes, he realized he must look like a reprobate. He hadn't shaved during their trip and had spent a virtually sleepless night on the train.

Finally, he was ushered into the doctor's private office. "Madame Burke has a very nasty throat," he said in heavily accented English. "I—" He made a swabbing motion.

"He took a culture," Debra said with a grimace.

"Strep?" Dillon asked. "No offense, Dr. Gaultier, but if it's that serious, maybe you should recommend a specialist."

"I agree," he said, giving a brief nod. "Let us await the lab results. We should know by tomorrow."

"I'm sure it'll be all right," Debra assured her worried husband. "He prescribed an antibiotic. I'll stay in bed today and let you wait on me hand and foot."

Dillon tried to return her smile, but she looked so ill

that he couldn't find anything to smile about. He saw her into their apartment and got her into bed before running two blocks to the nearest pharmacy to have the prescription filled. She swallowed the capsule and drank a cup of tea before lapsing into a deep sleep.

Only then did Dillon remember to call the work site. He spoke to the foreman he had placed in temporary charge before leaving the previous Friday. The Frenchman convinced him that everything was all right and urged him to stay at home with his ailing wife. Throughout the long day, he sat at Debra's bedside, taking catnaps in the chair, waking her only when it was time for her medicine.

In spite of her fever and discomfort, she managed to quip jokes when he carried her into the bathroom to relieve herself. "Good thing this didn't happen in my ninth month. You wouldn't be able to lift me."

Dillon ate a sandwich for supper, but couldn't coax her to take any more than a cup of beef bouillon. "My throat's already feeling better, though," she told him. "I'm just very weak. A good night's sleep is all I need. You look like you could use one, too," she said, running her hand over his bearded chin.

After giving her her medicine, he undressed and got into bed with her. Exhausted, he fell asleep as soon as he lay down.

During the night he awakened. Squinting through the darkness, he consulted the clock on the nightstand. It was time to give Debra another capsule. He switched on the lamp.

And screamed.

Debra's lips were blue, and she lay very still.

"Oh, God! Oh, Jesus! Debra! Debra!" He threw his leg over her and straddled her thighs. He flattened his ear against her breasts. He sobbed with relief when he heard her heartbeat. But it was faint. She was barely breathing.

Dillon leaped from the bed and pulled on his clothes, fastening none of them. He crammed his bare feet into sneakers. Gathering Debra in his arms, blankets and all, he ran through the dark apartment and burst into the hallway. He descended the stairs at a treacherous pace. Should he summon an ambulance or drive her to the hospital himself? He finally opted for the latter, reasoning that by the time he located the number and, with his limited French, conveyed the urgency of the situation, it might be too late.

"God, no, no." A strong wind tore the words from his mouth as he raced from the building to his parked car. He deposited Debra in the front seat. She slumped to one side, and again his voice cracked on a rough prayer.

He knew approximately where the nearest hospital was located and sped off in that direction. The tires screeched on the pavement and echoed off silent buildings as the car careened around street corners. He steered with his left hand while massaging Debra's wrist with his right. He kept up a running chatter about how he would never forgive her if she died.

The emergency-room staff instantly discerned the seriousness of her condition and whisked her away on a gurney. Dillon had to run to catch up. At a door marked with words he couldn't read, he was barred entrance by people he couldn't understand. He fought them off and tried to lunge through the doors after the gurney. Eventually he was restrained and bodily removed to the waiting room, where an English-speaking nurse threatened him with expulsion from the hospital if he didn't calm down.

"Calm?" he cried hoarsely. "My wife looks like death, and you expect me to be calm? I want to be with her."

She remained firm and finally talked him through the various forms that had to be filled out for admittance to the hospital. Then, left alone, Dillon paced until he was too weary and distraught to take another step and dropped into a chair.

He hung his head, pressing his thumbs deeply into his eyesockets and praying to a god he wasn't convinced existed but paradoxically mistrusted. What else would this selfish deity claim from him? Hadn't he given up enough? Everyone he had ever loved had been taken away from him: his parents, his granny, the counselor at the reform school who had taken a special interest in him.

He was jinxed. *People, beware. If you love Dillon Burke, you die.*

"No, no," he groaned. "Not Debra. Please, not Debra. Don't take her, you stingy son of a bitch."

He bargained with the unseen power, vowing to sacrifice anything if Debra could be spared. He promised to live a good life, to feed the hungry and clothe the naked. He made an oath never to ask for anything ever again, if this one small favor could be granted—"Let her live."

"Monsieur Burke?"

Dillon's head snapped up. A doctor was standing a few feet from him. "Yes? My wife? Is she—"

"She is going to be all right."

"Oh, Christ," Dillon sobbed as his head fell back against the cold tiles of the waiting-room wall. "Oh, God."

"She had an allergic reaction to the antibiotic Dr.

Gaultier prescribed. It is no one's fault," he was quick to add. "We consulted Dr. Gaultier. There was nothing in her medical records sent from the United States to indicate that she had an allergy to this particular—"

"Look, I don't intend to sue anybody," Dillon interrupted him, coming to his feet. "Debra's alive and is going to be okay. That's all I care about."

Dillon was so relieved, his knees felt rubbery. It had all happened so fast. Life was precious. Life was fragile. Here one moment, gone the next. Every second should be milked for all it was worth because you never knew when the bottom was going to drop out. He would have to remember that. He would have to tell Debra about this revelation. They would make it their philosophy, live by it, hand it down to their—

His happy thoughts came to a sudden standstill.

"Doctor," he croaked. He knew before asking what the answer was going to be, but he had to ask. His lips were parched and his mouth was dry with dread. "Doctor, you haven't mentioned the baby. Is the baby all right?"

"I am sorry, Monsieur Burke. There was nothing we could do for the child. It was dead when Madame Burke arrived."

Dillon stared at the doctor without really seeing him. He had bargained for Debra's life, but had left the terms openended. Now he knew what the price had been.

Chapter 10

Morgantown, South Carolina, 1977

Dr. Mitchell R. Hearon, Dean of Student Affairs and Financial Aid at Dander College in Morgantown, South Carolina, opened Jade Sperry's application folder and passed her a slip of paper across his cluttered desk. "That's a voucher. Present it at the bursar's office on the day you register."

Her eyes moved from him to the stiff card he had handed her. Printed across the background etching of the college's administration building was a check made out to her. She tried to blink the figures into focus, but even that was beyond her.

"The amount will cover your tuition, books, and all fees," the dean said. "You'll be responsible for your living expenses, although the college will be happy to supply you with a list of available low-budget housing."

She could barely hear him over the clamor in her ears. "I...I don't know how to thank you, Dr. Hearon."

"You can thank me by doing your best. Study hard. Apply yourself. Make your goals realities."

"Yes, yes. I will." Relief and joy burst from her in the form of a laugh. She stood up abruptly, almost unbalancing herself. "Thank you! You won't be sorry. You—"

"You're very welcome, Miss Sperry. I think you'll be an asset to Dander College. We're small, but we have a sterling academic reputation. We pride ourselves on the diligence and integrity of our students."

Circumstances had forced Jade to forfeit the scholarship to South Carolina State. After working for more than a year in a large discount store in Savannah, she had begun applying to other universities and colleges for financial assistance. Again she glanced down at the check in her hand, barely allowing herself to believe that it was genuine.

To conclude the interview, Dr. Hearon stood and extended his hand. "I would appreciate a visit once you've been matriculated. I'll be interested to see what courses you choose for your first semester. The faculty takes a personal interest in each student."

"I'll come see you, I promise. Thank you again." Jade rushed to the door. After pulling it open, she glanced back at him over her shoulder. "Oh, and thank the other members of the scholarship committee, too."

"I will. Goodbye, Miss Sperry."

"Goodbye."

The long corridor beyond his office suite was empty and hushed. Jade wanted to shout her elation toward the Gothic arched ceiling but managed to contain herself. Nevertheless, she ran for the doors at the end of the corridor with far more abandon than the stateliness of the architecture ordained.

Once outside, she gave her exuberance free rein. She leaned against an imposing, fluted column and stared at the voucher before clutching it to her chest like a gleeful miser. Then, tucking it safely inside her handbag, she left the shade of the colonnaded porch of the administration building and walked into the late summer sunshine.

It seemed brighter and friendlier than when she had nervously entered the building. The flowers blooming along the landscaped sidewalks were brilliant. The sky was exceptionally blue, the clouds white and without blemish. She had never noticed how intensely green grass was, or was the grass on the campus of Dander College inordinately verdant?

It was as though she, like Dorothy in *The Wizard of Oz,* had suddenly been thrust from a world of black and white into one of vivid Technicolor. She had been through pure hell, but had emerged on the other side to discover that life might be worth the struggle after all.

The Westminster chimes in the campus chapel's bell tower struck the hour as she jogged past the library. She was imbued with a sense of peace and optimism that she hadn't experienced since before the rape. Today, she had been granted a new beginning.

Her car was reluctant to start and even more reluctant to go over thirty miles an hour without the heat indicator flashing on. It had barely survived the trip from Savannah. Since the drive took several hours, they had come the day before. After checking in to the Pine Haven Motor Court, Jade had used the remaining daylight hours to acquaint herself with the college community.

The campus formed the nucleus of the town, which Jade thought had charm and character. The only local industry was the college, and the domed administration building was the town's only skyscraper. Surrounding the campus were gracious neighborhoods comprised of stately homes that housed faculty members. Morgantown's commercial district was compact and sufficient to fulfill her needs.

Where would they live? Would they be able to find an inexpensive apartment close to campus so that she could walk to classes and keep the car free for Velta's use? The fall semester wouldn't begin for another month, but there was so much to do before that. Which should she look for first—a part-time job or a place to live?

She parked the car in front of cabin number 3 and, with a laugh of self-derision, chided herself for falling into her characteristic pattern of worrying. Today she would relax and celebrate. Being awarded this scholarship was the first positive step toward achieving her ultimate goal— seeing Gary's murderers punished.

As surely as Neal Patchett, Hutch Jolly, and Lamar Griffith had raped her, they were responsible for Gary's suicide. If her resolve to see justice done was ever shaken, she had only to recall the sight of Gary's body dangling at the end of that rope. With their violence and treachery and lies, Neal and his cronies had driven him to suicide.

Jade wouldn't rest until they had paid for their crimes. Revenge wouldn't come quickly. It would be a slow, painstaking process that might take years to fulfill, but she was prepared for that. Thanks to Dr. Hearon and his committee, she was on her way.

Expecting the cabin door to be locked, she was surprised when it swung open. "Mother? I got it!"

Jade stepped into the small, musty room. The air-conditioner in the window labored to put out cool air but to little avail. Her brain registered three things immediately. There was a packed suitcase at her mother's feet. A man Jade had come to loathe was standing on the other side of the suitcase. And Graham, her baby son, was crying in his portable crib.

Jade paused on the threshold and tried to puzzle through what the packed suitcase implied. Velta's stare was stony and defiant. The man's eyes were shifty and wouldn't meet Jade's. She wanted to demand an explanation, but maternal instincts won out. Dropping her handbag on the bed, she moved to the crib and lifted the crying baby into her arms.

She cuddled Graham against her chest. "Shh, darling. What's wrong? Mommy's here now. Everything's okay." She rocked him until he stopped crying, then addressed her mother. "What is he doing here?"

The man's name was Harvey something, or something Harvey. Jade couldn't remember. She had intentionally blocked it from her mind after ripping up his business card and hurling the pieces at his face. She had insisted that if he didn't leave the maternity ward voluntarily, she would have him evicted. Although he presented himself as the founder and director of a private adoption agency, Jade had a different interpretation of his career. He was to an adoption agency what a drug dealer is to a pharmacist.

Harvey had been Velta's find. She had told Jade that he was the answer to all their problems—namely, Jade's illegitimate child. Without consulting Jade, Velta had brought him to the hospital the day after Graham was born. Harvey had offered her several thousand dollars for her baby boy.

"A white, male newborn without any defects brings the highest price in the business," he had said.

That's when Jade had raised a hue and cry that had disturbed other patients and alerted the nursing staff.

Jade clutched Graham tighter now as she glared at her mother. "I told you long before Graham was born that I would never put him up for adoption. I repeated it after he was born. I meant it then, and I certainly mean it now. Ask your friend to leave, or I'll call the police."

"Harvey isn't here on account of you or your baby," Velta said.

Jade divided a wary glance between them. "Then what's he doing here? How did he know where to find us?"

"I called him last night and told him where we were."

"Why?"

Graham was beginning to wriggle within her tight embrace, but she didn't relax it. Despite what her mother had said, Jade was afraid she might snatch the child away from her. Unfortunately, their troubles hadn't drawn her and her mother any closer together. Over the last year, their tenuous relationship had steadily deteriorated. Jade's preoccupation with getting an education annoyed Velta. In her opinion, the solution to an illegitimate baby was a husband.

"Let's go back to Palmetto, Jade," she had suggested one day in early summer, when temperaments were as turbulent as the sultry weather. "At least there we would be outcasts in familiar surroundings. If you'd act halfway decent to them, I'm sure you could get one of those three boys to claim Graham and marry you."

Jade had almost struck her. "Preferably Neal Patchett?"

"Well, living in that fancy house of his would be a

world better than this dump!" Velta had cried, flinging her arms wide to encompass their shabby apartment in Savannah. "It wouldn't have happened in the first place if you'd been nicer to him."

Jade had picked up Graham, run outside, and hadn't come back until the thunderstorm broke. Velta never brought up returning to Palmetto again, so Jade assumed she had finally given up on the idea. Apparently she had, but had formed another plan that somehow involved Harvey.

"You still haven't told me what he's doing here," Jade said.

"Ever since that day at the hospital, Harvey and I have been seeing each other on a regular basis. Secretly, of course."

Jade hugged Graham even tighter. Had they cooked up a scheme to have Graham taken away from her? Would they try to have her declared an unfit mother? She would *not* let that happen. No one was ever going to take her child from her.

"Harvey had the decency to overlook your rudeness," Velta said. "Remembering the scene you caused in the hospital, I can't imagine why he's being so forgiving, except that he's got a good heart." Velta turned to the man and smiled. "Anyway, I could see when we got here yesterday that you fell in love with this place. Regardless of what I want, you're damned and determined to go to school here. So, last night when you went to get the hamburgers, I called Harvey in Savannah and accepted his proposal."

Shocked, Jade echoed, "His proposal? You mean a marriage proposal?"

"That's right," Velta replied defiantly. "We were waiting for you to get back so we could leave."

Jade gaped at them incredulously, then burst into laughter. "Mama, you can't be serious! You're actually eloping with this character? Tell me this is a joke."

"It's no joke, I assure you. Harvey cleared my things out of the apartment in Savannah and brought them with him. Whatever is left, you can have. Come on, Harvey. We've waited long enough."

Harvey, who hadn't said a word, picked up the suitcase and turned toward the door. Velta followed.

"Mama, wait!" Jade put Graham back in his crib and ran after her mother, catching up with her at the side of a gray sedan.

"Are you out of your mind?" Jade asked. "You can't just run off like this."

"I'm an adult. I can do whatever I want to."

Jade fell back a step. Velta was throwing up to her words she herself had recently spoken, and on more than one occasion, particularly when she had informed Velta that she had every intention of keeping the baby.

"Don't do this," Jade whispered urgently. "I know you're only doing it to spite me, Mama. I need you. Please don't go."

"You need me all right. But that's just too bad, Jade. You brought all your troubles on yourself. I'm not going to babysit while you trot off to college every day."

Jade took another tack. "Forget that I need you to help me with Graham. I'll make other arrangements," she added quickly. "But, Mama, please think about what this means to you."

"Is it hard for you to accept that a man finds me attractive?"

"Of course not. But maybe you want it so badly that you're seeing something that's not really there. Have you thought of that? At least give yourself time to get to know him better."

"No more time, Jade. It's long past time I did something for myself. I'm tired of paying for your mistakes. Because of you, I had to quit my job, sell my house, and completely relocate."

"It wasn't my fault," Jade protested in a hoarse, agonized voice.

"You got yourself raped, then insisted on keeping the baby when the best thing for everybody would have been to get rid of it."

"It wouldn't have been best for me, Mama. I wanted Graham. I love him."

"Well, Harvey loves me," Velta insisted. "After all I've been through, he wants to show me a good time."

Jade felt a responsibility toward her mother. It was her duty as a daughter to interfere in order to prevent a disaster, even if it meant offending her. Better her mother's feelings were hurt than her life ruined.

"He's unworthy of you, Mama," Jade said. She gave Harvey's oily hair and shiny suit a contemptuous glance. "He preys upon people's emotions for profit. He barters in human life. Is that the kind of man you want to marry? Daddy was awarded the Medal of Honor. He was a hero. How can you even think of—"

"Your hero father killed himself, Jade."

"That's not true!"

Velta's eyes narrowed maliciously. "We were fine until you came along. Then, Ron couldn't stand living with us, so he blew his brains to smithereens. So you've got two suicides marked up to you, Jade. In fact, you've given me nothing but trouble since the day you were conceived. I'm not going to live the rest of my life in your wake of destruction." Pushing Jade aside, she opened the passenger door and got in.

Harvey closed it soundly behind her, then went around to the driver's side and slid behind the steering wheel. Velta kept her head averted as they backed up and pulled away.

"Mama, no!" Jade charged after the car, but it sped off. "Mama!" she screamed. She watched until they were out of sight, then stood staring after them until Graham's cries penetrated her stunned disbelief.

Mindlessly, she trudged back into the tacky cabin. Graham was waving his chubby arms in a fit of pique. His mouth was wide open, showing his only two teeth. Jade cooed to him as she changed his diaper. Apparently, in her haste to pack and leave with Harvey, Velta hadn't bothered to change him the whole time Jade had been out.

She sat with her baby on the bed and rocked him while waiting for his bottle to warm. When it reached the desired temperature, she poked the nipple into his mouth. He attacked it eagerly. Because of his voracious appetite, she had weaned him from breast milk long before she was emotionally ready to stop nursing.

He clutched at her blouse, his stubby fingers digging into the material. As he sucked at the rubber nipple, she held him close so that she would get a sense of feeding him from her body.

It would forever remain a mystery to her how something so beautiful and sweet as he could have been spawned by something so ugly as the rape. She rarely associated

Graham's conception with the incident, because to do so would force her to speculate on whose seed had taken root in her body. She never wanted to know.

Divorcing Graham's origin from the rape had occurred that afternoon at Georgie's house. She had told Jade that she prided herself not only on her precision with medical instruments but on her instincts about people. On that afternoon, her instincts had prompted her to ask the young, frightened Jade if having her baby aborted was what she really wanted.

"You just don't seem the type o' girl what usually comes to me, Miss Sperry. That trashy Patrice Watley even said so. Are you sure you want to go through with this?"

And in that moment, Jade knew that she didn't. The fetus inside her, as if by a stroke of magic, had suddenly ceased to have any relevance to the rape. The child growing inside her was hers. She loved it instantly and completely.

The revelation delivered such an emotional impact that she had collapsed on Georgie's rubber-sheeted table. For half an hour she had sobbed uncontrollably, not from distress but from relief over being freed of the agonizing decision that had haunted her for weeks.

The outburst left her weak and tremulous. Eventually, she composed herself, tearfully thanked Georgie for her time, and left. Georgie had kept her fifty dollars, charging as much for talking an indecisive girl out of an abortion as she did to perform one.

"Ready to burp?" Jade tugged the nipple out of Graham's mouth. He put up a fuss, but it subsided when Jade patted his back until he belched expansively. "My goodness!" she exclaimed. "That was something!" He looked up at her and grinned. An infusion of love went through her body as potently as an intravenous narcotic. She ran her thumb across his lower lip, wiping off the marbleized mixture of milk and saliva. She sucked it off her thumb, then resettled him against her breast and gave him back his bottle.

Shaken and weak from expended emotion, she had left Georgie's house that day with renewed hope. If she explained everything to Gary, as she should have done the night of the rape, he would understand. As kind and loving as he was, he would agree with her decision to keep the baby. They would leave Palmetto, marry, and pursue their shared dreams. Gary would rear her baby as his own, and no one would ever know otherwise. With those plans set in her mind, she had sped toward Gary's house.

But that was where her memory always begged to take a detour. The road to Gary's farm always led straight to the barn and the grisly sight that had awaited her there.

"If only you had trusted in me a little while longer." She leaned over and whispered the words against Graham's velvety cheek. "Why'd you do it, Gary?" She knew why, of course. His faith in her had been destroyed. Those who had destroyed it were going about their lives unscathed—but not forever.

God had been merciful in one respect. Graham bore no resemblance to any of her three attackers. None of his features hinted at his paternity. He had dark, wavy hair, like hers. His eyes were going to remain blue and be tilted up slightly at the outer corners. The only face that emerged from his plump, baby prettiness was Ronald Sperry's, which was a masculine version of her own. It pleased her that he favored her father.

From the day it had happened, Jade had realized that the accidental ruling on her father's death was dubious. Nevertheless, hearing the truth from her mother had been a brutal blow. Velta had always vehemently denied that her husband's fatal, self-inflicted wound was intentional. For her to admit that it was, and to suggest that Jade was responsible, demonstrated to Jade the depth of her mother's antipathy.

Had she been so desperately unhappy living with her daughter that she would resort to running off with a slimy character like Harvey? It seemed so. Jade longed for one cherished memory of her mother that she could cling to. Unlike the treasured memories of her father, there were none of her mother.

After Graham finished feeding, she didn't return him to his crib but continued to hold him against her, as she often did when she needed the comfort of human contact. Now that the shock of Velta's desertion had lost some of its sting, the ramifications of how it affected her and Graham were beginning to sink in.

All Jade had with her was a change of clothing and about thirty dollars. That was barely enough money to get them back to Savannah. Once there, how could she possibly handle the move to Morgantown alone?

"What are we going to do, Graham?" She nuzzled her nose in his sweet-smelling neck. "What are we going to do?"

The easiest option would be to return to Savannah and resume her job, promising herself that as soon as she had saved enough money she would continue her education.

But saving money would be doubly difficult now that she would have the additional expense of child care. One postponement would pile onto another; the dream of seeking retribution would move farther from her grasp.

No, she couldn't let that happen.

There had to be a way. If a way wasn't provided, she would make one. She couldn't let this opportunity pass. She had already sacrificed one scholarship and wasn't going to sacrifice another.

Chapter 11

The doorbell echoed through the interior of the house. It was a dignified home, built in the Georgian style. The red brick was trimmed in white and accented with glossy black shutters on all the windows. It was set well away from the street, on a lawn that was meticulously manicured. The grass still glistened from its early morning watering by the automatic sprinkler system.

The obvious affluence made Jade feel self-conscious. She gave her skirt a critical glance, hoping the wrinkles didn't show too badly. She moistened her fingers with her tongue and wiped Graham's drooling mouth one final time, just as the front door was opened by a pretty, petite woman with ash-blond hair. Guessing, Jade placed her in her early fifties.

"Good morning." Her soft gray eyes were drawn immediately to Graham, then she graciously smiled at Jade. "May I help you?"

"Good morning. Are you Mrs. Hearon?"

She nodded. "That's right."

"My name is Jade Sperry. I apologize for calling on you so early, but I wanted to catch Dean Hearon before he left for his office." Taking Graham on campus with her had been a more discouraging prospect than bringing him to the dean's home. "Is he still here, by any chance?"

"He's having breakfast. Come in."

"I'd rather stay here on the porch," Jade said hesitantly. "What I have to see him about won't take long."

"Then there's no reason for you not to come in. Please. Is this your little boy? He's adorable."

Jade found herself being ushered through beautiful but homey rooms. They passed through a sunny kitchen where the tantalizing smell of bacon and eggs made her salivate. These days her diet consisted mainly of Rice Krispies and peanut-butter sandwiches. She didn't remember when she had last eaten a cooked meal.

They entered a glass-enclosed back porch that extended the width of the house. At a wrought-iron table with a glass top, Dean Hearon was finishing his breakfast. As on the day Jade had met him in his office, he was dressed in a brown suit and tie, but she could envision him wearing a sweater with suede elbow patches and baggy trousers with a shiny seat.

Grizzled hair encircled his balding head like a laurel wreath. Tufts of hair sprouted from his ears. He also had more than adequate nostril hair. Rather than repulsing, however, his hirsute features were endearing. His face was pleasant, his eyes friendly, his smile sweet. He glanced up curiously when his wife escorted Jade in. He removed the linen napkin he had tucked into his shirt collar and stood up.

"Well, Miss Sperry, isn't it? This is a pleasant surprise."

"Thank you." She shifted Graham to her left arm

and extended her right hand. After they shook hands, he motioned her into the chair across the table from him and invited her to sit down.

Jade felt flustered and gauche. The shoulder strap of her handbag was about to slide off her arm, and Graham was squirming and reaching for the drooping frond of a Boston fern hanging overhead.

"No, thank you, Dr. Hearon. I really can't stay. I apologize for interrupting your breakfast, but as I told Mrs. Hearon, I needed to see you before you left for campus."

"I've got time for one more cup of coffee. I'd love to have you join me. Cathy, please...Miss Sperry?" Again he gestured toward the chair. Jade dropped into it, not wanting to appear rude, but mainly because balancing Graham and holding on to her slipping handbag was a feat that would have challenged an expert juggler.

"Thank you. I'm sorry for dropping in like this. I should have called—No, Graham!" In the nick of time, she prevented her son from eating the leaves he had pulled off the fern. "I'm sorry. I hope he didn't damage the plant."

"That's the third time you've apologized since you came into the room, Miss Sperry. Such an overdose of contrition is making me nervous."

"Me too," Cathy Hearon said as she reentered, bearing a small tray. On it were a cup and saucer and a plate. On the plate were a wedge of honeydew melon wrapped in a paper-thin slice of prosciutto and a blueberry muffin.

"Oh, I didn't mean for you to—"

"Would you prefer tea over coffee?"

Jade didn't want to offend them by declining their hospitality. Besides, her stomach was growling. "Tea, please," she said quietly. "If it's not too much trouble."

"None at all. I've already got it brewed."

Cathy Hearon went for the tea. Jade smiled sickly at the Dean of Student Affairs. "Thank you for your hospitality."

"You're welcome. Butter?"

He passed her a Waterford crystal butter dish. As she smoothed butter onto the warm muffin, she handed Graham the teething ring she carried everywhere they went. For the time being, he seemed content to gnaw on it while she ate breakfast.

Mrs. Hearon poured her a cup of fragrant jasmine tea, then resumed her seat at the table.

"What's the baby's name?"

"Graham."

"Graham. I like that. Very unusual, isn't it, dear?"

"Uh-huh. Miss Sperry is the young woman from Palmetto whom I was telling you about."

"Oh, yes. You see, Miss Sperry, Mitch has distant relatives in Palmetto."

Jade swung her startled gaze to the dean. He hadn't said anything about Palmetto at their previous appointment. She didn't want them to ask, "Do you know . . ." The less said about Palmetto, the better, because she didn't want to lie to them about anything.

Thankfully, Graham provided a distraction. He banged his teething ring on the edge of the table, then threw it to the floor in favor of a shiny silver spoon. She picked up the teething ring, but he found the spoon tastier.

Cathy laughed as he wetly gummed the spoon. "He's not hurting that old spoon a bit. He can chew on it to his heart's content."

Dean Hearon was regarding Jade closely. "I don't

remember you mentioning that you were a mother when you came to see me a few weeks ago."

"No, sir, I didn't."

"Not that it's any of my business, of course. It wouldn't have made a difference to the scholarship committee, either."

Jade blotted her mouth with her linen napkin. "I'm afraid it is your business, Dr. Hearon. That's why I'm here this morning." She opened her handbag, removed the voucher, and slid it across the table toward him. "I must regretfully decline the scholarship."

Mrs. Hearon was the first to break a long, awkward silence. "Miss Sperry, I'm familiar with you because my husband told me about you. You made a favorable impression on him. But if it'll make you more comfortable, I'll leave you alone to discuss this matter privately."

Jade was touched by her sensitivity. "That won't be necessary, Mrs. Hearon. Anyway, there's nothing more to be said." She replaced the strap of her handbag on her shoulder, hoisted Graham off her lap, and stood up. "Thank you very much for the breakfast."

"Just a minute, Miss Sperry," Dean Hearon said. "Sit down, please." He waited until she complied. Folding his hands beneath his chin, he gave her a probing look. "Frankly, I'm stunned and disappointed. I've rarely seen a candidate for a full scholarship more deserving than you, or one as obviously delighted when it was granted. You fairly flew out of my office. What's happened since I last saw you?"

Jade considered a number of viable lies. However, looking into their eyes made lying impossible. They were curious, yes, but that distasteful human trait was allayed by something not so common—genuine concern.

"My mother eloped." Evidently her answer wasn't what they had expected, so she elaborated. "My mother took care of Graham while I worked. I had planned to continue working after classes and on weekends, but now I won't be able to afford child care in addition to our living expenses."

"Surely—"

Jade shook her head, cutting off the dean's interruption. "I've exhausted all options, believe me." At the expense of her job in Savannah, she had been making weekly runs to Morgantown in search of lodging, a job, and acceptable child-care facilities. Her search had been futile.

"Any child-care facility that I would consider—and I admit to being very particular—I can't afford, even if their hours of operation were compatible with my schedule. On top of that, with the influx of students beginning the fall semester, I haven't even been able to find a job. Since my mother is no longer available to help me, it's impossible for me to enroll this semester."

She lowered her eyes, unwilling for them to see her fear. Not only was her college career at stake, but their livelihood as well. Her supervisor in Savannah had lost patience with her for requesting so much time off and had fired her. Before her elopement, Velta had emptied their meager savings account, taking what was left from the sale of the house in Palmetto.

Jade was down to her last twenty dollars. Twelve of it had to pay for their room at the Pine Haven Motor Court tonight. Tomorrow she would run out of money. She supposed she would have to throw herself on the mercy of her former supervisor in Savannah and beg for her job back.

"Turning down this scholarship seems a rather dramatic and drastic step, Miss Sperry," Dean Hearon said.

"I agree, but at this time I have no alternative. It won't deter me from getting an education, Dr. Hearon. I promise you that. I have reasons for wanting to earn a diploma as quickly as possible."

"Those reasons being?"

"Personal."

Her terse answer caused him to frown. "Why did you apply for a scholarship at Dander College?"

"Truthfully?"

"You've been painfully candid thus far."

"It was one of the remaining few in a three-state area that I hadn't tried. I've been declined financial aid from scores of other colleges and universities. Since it's a church-related school, I relied on Dander's Christian benevolence."

"And if we had turned you down, what did you propose to do?"

"What I still plan to do—keep trying."

Dr. Hearon cleared his throat. "Am I correct in presuming that Graham's father—"

"Graham's father is dead." People would always want to know. That seemed the simplest answer. She doubted that they believed her, but they didn't pursue it.

"I know about a job," Cathy Hearon said suddenly. "Dear," she turned to her husband, "you know Dorothy Davis. She owns that shop where I buy most of my clothes." To Jade she said, "Just yesterday, Miss Dorothy told me she's looking for someone to handle her bookkeeping. She said her eyes have gotten so bad she can't read the invoices anymore."

"Doesn't surprise me. The old bat must be pushing eighty."

Cathy slapped the back of her husband's hand. "Don't listen to him, Jade. Miss Dorothy is rather crusty, but really a kind soul underneath. She's had to be tough in order to be a good businesswoman. Would you be interested?"

"I'm interested in anything, Mrs. Hearon. And business is my major. But a job alone won't help. I still haven't found a suitable daycare center or a place to live."

"Surely there's something available."

Jade thought of the twenty dollars in her purse. She couldn't even put down a deposit to move in. "I'm afraid not, Mrs. Hearon."

The Dean of Student Affairs consulted his watch and stood up. "I'm going to be late if I don't leave now. It's time to cut to the heart of the matter."

He lowered his bushy eyebrows in a vain attempt to make himself look stern. "Miss Sperry, I believe that what you are too proud to admit is that, through no fault of your own, you are destitute. I've never interviewed a young person more determined than you to get an education. Only the gravest set of circumstances could have dampened your enthusiasm and determination. I admire your pride.

"On the other hand," he said with an authoritative ring that had often roused dozing students, "too much pride can work against an individual. That's the time to step from behind your pride, expose your vulnerability, and give someone the honor of helping you.

"I'm sure that Cathy can maneuver you into the job Miss Davis has open, although I'd be reluctant to accept the position if I were you. She's a stingy, dried-up old stick of a woman who won't even gift wrap for free at Christmastime. If you can work for her, you deserve to be canonized.

"Finally, in case you haven't noticed, Cathy's eyes have grown misty every time she looks at Graham. Unfortunately, we never had children of our own. I've little doubt she'll spoil him rotten while you're with us."

"With you?" Jade cried. "Oh, but I—"

"Be quiet, Miss Sperry. I'm not finished, and time is of the essence. What you obviously didn't know is that Cathy and I have often taken a deserving student into our home for the term. We decided not to this year only because last spring semester we had a bad experience: the young man absconded with a pair of silver candlesticks. It wasn't the damned candlesticks I minded so much, but that my previously accurate gauge of human nature had failed me. You have restored it.

"So, unless you have designs on the silverware, you and your son are welcome to reside here for as long as you'd like. In any event, I'll take it as a personal affront if I don't see your name on the list of enrolling freshmen by the conclusion of registration today. Your transcript was damned near perfect, and it would be an abhorrent waste of intellect if you didn't further your education because of something so petty as shortage of money. Cathy, I have a hankering for fried oysters for dinner tonight."

With a brusque motion of his hand, he left.

Cathy Hearon patted Jade's arm. "He gets like that sometimes, but you'll get used to it."

Chapter 12

Columbia, South Carolina, 1978

Hey, Hutch! I thought you'd died or something. Come in, you ugly son of a bitch." Neal Patchett held open the door for his friend. Hutch stepped into the cluttered front room.

"Y'all busy?"

"Hell, no. I'm glad you stopped by. Lamar!" Neal shouted. "We've got company." Finding a spot between the posters of Loni Anderson and the Dallas Cowboys' Cheerleaders, Neal banged his fist on the wall. "Shovel out that chair, Hutch, and sit down. Want a beer?"

"Yeah, thanks."

"I thought you were in training, Mr. Jock." Neal socked him on the shoulder as he went to the kitchen for the beer.

"I am. Screw it." Hutch took the cold beer from Neal and chugged it, then belched loudly. "Ah, that's good. Hi, Lamar."

Lamar emerged from the hallway. He had a paisley

necktie draped around his neck, although he was wearing a pair of cut-offs and a tank top. In his hand was a tennis racquet. "Hi, Hutch. How's football practice going?"

"The team sucks this year. Don't count on any bowl games. Unpacking?"

Lamar set aside his tennis racquet and removed the tie from his neck. "I'm trying to get my bedroom organized."

"Why bother?" Hutch asked as he sprawled in the ratty easy chair. "This place'll be trashed within a week anyway. That's why I like it."

For the second year, Neal and Lamar were sharing digs off campus. The house was old and roomy and far enough away from neighbors so that the police weren't called until the parties got entirely out of hand. Their freshman year, Hutch hadn't been permitted to live with them because he was on the football team and was required to live in the athletes' dorm. He had envied them the freedom and relaxed atmosphere of the house.

"Last spring when Myrajane came up to pack for Lamar's return home, she took one look inside and nearly fainted clean away," Neal chuckled. "If my old man hadn't been there to catch her when she fell backward, we'd have had an outline of her body there on the front porch. You know, the way Wile E. Coyote leaves a hole shaped like himself when he falls to the desert floor?"

He took a joint from the drawer in the end table, lit it, and took two tokes. Hutch ruefully declined when Neal offered it to him. "Better not. Donna Dee can smell that stuff a mile off. I'll have another beer, though."

Neal passed the joint to Lamar, who puffed on it as he gave Hutch one of his nervous, tentative smiles. Neal returned from the kitchen and handed Hutch another beer.

"The little wife's got you on a short leash, huh?" Neal retrieved the joint and inhaled. "Damn fool bastard, why'd you have to get married right after we got to this pussy farm they call a university?"

"It's not so bad," Hutch grumbled.

Neal cupped his hand behind his ear. "What's that noise, Lamar?"

"What noise?"

"Don't you hear it? Sounds like the rattling of a ball and chain to me."

"Go to hell." Hutch drained his second beer and crumpled the aluminum can in one fist. "At least I can get off every night."

"So can I," Neal drawled, "but I don't marry 'em."

Hutch's first date with Donna Dee had been to their senior prom. In a way, he had felt obligated to ask her. It seemed as though she expected it—and both knew why, though they never discussed it. During the summer following graduation, whenever he wasn't with Neal and Lamar, he was with Donna Dee.

Hutch had always liked her well enough, but he began to like her a lot more. Neal's bland opinion of her carried less weight each time Hutch saw her. Though she sure was no beauty, she was funny and sweet and made it clear that she was devoted to him. She never missed church on Sunday, yet by their second date his hand was inside her brassiere fingering her nipples, and by the third she was giving him hand-jobs.

It had been her idea that they get into the backseat of his car after the citywide Fourth of July picnic and fireworks on the beach. "B-but I never thought...What I mean is, Donna Dee, I don't have a rubber with me."

"That's okay, Hutch. I want to love you so bad, I don't even care."

He reasoned that if she didn't care that she was about to lose her virginity, he shouldn't be a stickler for birth control. And hadn't Neal once told him that a virgin couldn't get pregnant? Besides, he was a little drunk and very horny, and Donna Dee was so damned compliant that lust had won out over common sense. From then on he always took along a supply of condoms just in case she got amorous again. As it turned out, he had needed one on every single date.

"Are you banging Donna Dee?" Neal had posed the question over the Labor Day weekend while they were water-skiing.

"No," Hutch had lied. "She's a nice girl. You know that."

Neal had looked at him with skepticism. "I'd hate to think my best friend was keeping secrets from me. If you're not getting in her pants, why spend so much time with her?"

"You sound jealous, Neal." Lamar had meant his comment as a joke. But Neal's face had turned dark with wrath. He packed up his belongings and went home. Since the motorboat and all the skiing gear belonged to him, Hutch and Lamar had no choice but to cut short their holiday, too.

When Donna Dee had gladly informed Hutch that she had squeaked through the entrance requirements to the university, he had greeted the news with mixed emotions. He wanted to see her at school and knew he would miss her if he didn't, but Neal had big plans for Lamar and him.

"We're gonna raise so much hell, it'll go down in the

annals of higher education," Neal had drunkenly promised. "We're gonna nail every coed that moves."

Their first semester in college, Hutch had managed to juggle his busy schedule between his guard position on the football team, keeping Donna Dee pacified, his classes, and Neal's expectations of him. On the gridiron, he did as he was told and left the game plans up to the backfield. Since he shared several freshmen classes with Donna Dee, she did all his written assignments. In return for this service, she expected love and affection, which he gladly dispensed when he wasn't too exhausted.

Following the Saturday games, and through Sunday night, he participated in the debauchery that went on at Neal's place. Grass, booze, and babes were always plentiful. It was one of these depraved weekends that caused the first serious quarrel between him and Donna Dee.

"I overheard three of them talking in the library about last weekend's orgy," she had told him as she sniffled into a Kleenex. "This blonde with a hickie on her neck was telling her friends that she had balled a redheaded football player, but she had been so stoned she couldn't remember his name. I know it was you, Hutch. You're the only junior varsity player with red hair. You told me you never did anything except drink a few beers when you went to Neal's place. Did you sleep with that blonde?"

He could almost hear Neal goading him to lie in order to get her off his back. Instead, a kernel of caring and integrity caused him to gaze miserably into her face and confess. "I guess I did, Donna Dee. Things get a little wild over there sometimes."

Donna Dee had collapsed in sobs, which startled Hutch and made him feel utterly helpless. Awkwardly he placed his arms around her. "I'm sorry, honey. It didn't mean anything. Being with another girl isn't the same as being with you. I . . . I love you."

He could hardly believe his own ears, but Donna Dee had heard him clearly. Her head popped up and she gazed at him through tearful eyes. "Do you, Hutch? Do you really?"

Hutch was bamboozled by what he'd said. Before he could sort it out, they were talking about an engagement ring for Valentine's Day and wedding bells in June. On a trip home to Palmetto to inform their parents of their plans, Fritz had privately expressed his concern.

"You're awfully young to be getting married, son," he'd said.

"I know, Daddy, but she really wants to."

"Do you?"

"Well, sure. I mean, I guess. I mean, yeah."

"Are you marrying her because you love her?"

"Sure. Why else would I?"

They exchanged an uncomfortable glance. Then Fritz sighed with resignation. "Well, if you're sure that's what you want."

The wedding took place on the second weekend in June. Three days before the wedding Donna Dee and Hutch were in the living room of her parents' house inspecting the gifts they had received. She laid aside the set of steak knives she had just opened and threaded the gift-wrap bow onto the coat hanger that was already filled with satin ribbons. "Hutch?"

"Hm-mm?" He was stuffing in a bologna sandwich that Mrs. Monroe had made for him.

"There's something I've got to ask you."

"Shoot."

Donna Dee took great care in tying the new bow onto the coat hanger, a practice which she had started with her first wedding shower. "Everything should be laid out in the open before two people get married, right?"

Hutch licked potato-chip salt off the tips of his fingers. "I guess."

"Well, it's about that night y'all took Jade to the channel."

Hutch froze, his fingers still at his lips. Slowly he lowered his hand and turned to Donna Dee, although his eyes fell short of connecting with hers. His prominent Adam's apple slid up and down as he swallowed. "What about it?"

"What she said wasn't true, was it? You didn't actually rape her." Donna Dee turned her pointed face up to his.

Hutch deliberated over whether to tell her the truth or what she wanted to hear. He had to admit either to rape or to lusting for her best friend. It was a no-win situation. "Course it wasn't rape," he mumbled. "She knew us. How could it be rape?"

"Did she try and stop you?"

His wide shoulders rose and fell in a heavy shrug. "She, uh...you know how some girls say they don't want it when they really do?"

Donna Dee looked away. "Did you want her, Hutch? I mean, you must have wanted to do that with her or you couldn't have gotten hard."

He shifted his big feet on the living-room carpet. "It wasn't like that, Donna Dee. Swear to God. It was...it was crazy. Hell, I don't know how else to explain it." In an impatient gesture, he spread his hands wide, palms up.

"It wasn't like I suddenly made up my mind to fuck Jade, okay?"

"Okay." Donna Dee took a tremulous breath and released it slowly. "I always thought she had lied about y'all forcing her. She just came on so strong, you couldn't help yourself, right? You're human. You're a man. A man can only take so much."

He disregarded her rapidly blinking eyes just as she disregarded the beads of perspiration on his upper lip. Neither was being honest, but, for their peace of mind, it was imperative that they continue deceiving each other and themselves.

At their wedding reception, Neal sidled up to Hutch and whispered, "I can highly recommend the maid of honor."

"That's Donna Dee's first cousin."

"I don't care whose cousin she is, she screws like a rabbit." Neal poked him in the ribs. "Think how much fun you can have at the family reunions."

"You're crazy," Hutch growled, shrugging off the companionable arm Neal had draped across his shoulders.

"Hey, my man. Is this marriage gonna cramp your style? I'd hate like hell to see that happen."

In that instant, Hutch decided to be faithful to his wife. No matter how they whitewashed it to make it acceptable to their consciences, Donna Dee had lied to get him out of a rape charge. Her jealousy of Jade was justified, though neither of them had ever acknowledged that, either. They were bound by a common sin that he didn't want to compound by being an unfaithful husband. Considering the hardship they had caused Jade, fidelity wasn't too high a price to pay.

Following their honeymoon trip to Hilton Head Island, Hutch had worked in his daddy's sheriff's department until it was time to report to team workouts. Donna Dee was eager to set up household in Columbia. In his opinion, her nesting instinct was overactive. Last night, while they were unpacking delicate china in a room with cinderblock walls, she had informed him of her plans to cut down on her class load.

"We'll save the money we'd spend on my tuition. Anyway, I'm no brain, Hutch. What will I do with humanities and biology? I know all I need to know about that, right?" She reached out and playfully squeezed his balls.

"You're still taking your pills, aren't you?"

"Sure. Why?"

He noticed that she didn't look him in the eye when she answered. "Because the last thing we need right now is a kid to take care of."

"I know that, silly."

"I promised my folks that I wouldn't drop out of school if we got married. The courses I've got to take this year are tough. The coach is on my ass for not digging in and hustling. I can't take on any more responsibilities right now."

She set aside what she was doing, put her arms around him, and kissed him slowly. "After all I've done for you, don't you know that your happiness always comes first with me?"

There it was again—that subtle reminder that she had stuck out her neck for him when he had desperately needed it. For the rest of their lives together, was that guilty secret going to serve as a rate of exchange? That dismal thought had plagued him through the night and brought him to

Neal's door this afternoon. Being with Neal and Lamar was like returning to the scene of the crime. It was also like probing a sore tooth. The more he did it, the more it bothered him. The problem was, he couldn't stop it.

"So, how is Donna Dee?" Lamar asked him now. "I haven't seen her since your wedding." The marijuana had mellowed Lamar. He was sprawled in a chair, one slender leg dangling over the padded armrest.

"She's fine. She said to tell y'all hi."

Neal took out an unopened bottle of Jack Daniels and twisted off the lid, then, he took a swig straight from the bottle. "You told Donna Dee you were coming here?"

"Sure."

"And she trusts you with us?" Neal crowed. "She's even dumber than I thought."

Hutch saw red. He shot to his feet. "She's not so dumb. She says that you're full of shit, and I believe she's right." He headed for the door.

Neal rolled out of his chair and stepped in front of Hutch, blocking his path. "Don't go away mad," he said soothingly. "I was just pricking you for the hell of it. Stick around. A few Delta Gammas have promised to come over and help us straighten up this place. And that ain't all they'll straighten up," he added with a leer. "They'll be more than Lamar and I can handle by ourselves."

"No, thanks," Hutch said testily. "I'm going home to my wife." He tried to sidestep Neal, but, despite the liquor and pot, Neal was still agile and in full command of his senses.

"Man, are you ever going to get out of her debt?"

Hutch fell still. "Debt?"

"Don't play stupid. I'm talking about repaying Donna Dee for what she did for us."

Hutch shot Lamar a quick, guilty glance, but Lamar had averted his eyes. "I don't know what you're talking about."

"The hell you don't," Neal said with a nasty laugh. "You're trying to repay Donna Dee for lying to save your ass from jail. First you fucked her. Then you married her. Now you're playing lap puppy."

"Shut up."

"She could really sink her claws into you if she knew how much you had enjoyed her best friend. Isn't that right, Lamar?" he asked, glancing at the other boy, who looked miserably uncomfortable. "You and I had a good time, but I believe ol' Hutch here thought Jade's box came gift-wrapped just for him."

Hutch thrust his homely face down to within inches of Neal's. "You're a sick son of a bitch, Neal. I don't want any more to do with you."

He knocked Neal aside and stormed through the door. Lamar called after him, "Hey, Hutch, Neal didn't mean anything by it. Don't go."

Hutch kept walking and didn't look back. "You'll be back," Neal shouted through the screen door. "You know who owns the candy store. When your sweet tooth starts acting up, you'll be back."

Shortly after Hutch stomped from the house, Lamar retreated to his bedroom, leaving Neal to rant and rave alone. Neal didn't lose his temper often, but when he did, Lamar was afraid of him. He couldn't say which frightened him more—Neal's temper tantrums or his sinister silences. When Neal grew still and quiet and his anger simmered inside him like brimstone in the depths of Hades, one could almost smell his fury.

Lamar hated living in that house, but he lacked the guts to tell Neal so and move out. During summer vacation he had stewed about it. He wished his mother would ask him to switch universities or suggest that he stay at home for a year before continuing his education. He wished for something—anything—that would prevent him from having to live under Neal's dominion for another year.

Nothing did, and he had never garnered the courage to tell Neal that he wanted to make other living arrangements. Meekly he had moved his stuff from Palmetto back into the old house they had leased for the second year. Boxes and suitcases were still piled around the walls of his bedroom, waiting to be unpacked. Lacking the initiative, he lay down on the bed and covered his eyes with his forearm. Now that Hutch had walked out, Lamar felt little hope that he could ever escape Neal. If he told Neal he wanted to move elsewhere, there was no telling what he might do. So, it seemed, he was stuck here.

It was a 'round-the-clock party. Neal surrounded himself with people who claimed to like him. Lamar suspected that they liked what Neal made available to them more than they liked Neal himself. He also figured that more than a few of them feared offending Neal, just as he did. They were intimidated into accepting his invitations.

The door to the house was always open to strangers on the lookout for sex, liquor, and soft drugs. The constant stream of pleasure-seeking students afforded Lamar very little privacy. Even when he retreated to his room and closed the door, someone was always stumbling in looking for a bathroom or an empty bed in which to copulate.

Just thinking about another nine months of incessant revelry made him weary. Neal was jealous of anything that diluted his tyranny over his friends. He demanded absolute loyalty and constant availability. That's why he had gotten on Hutch's case today. Neal was actually jealous of Donna Dee for taking up the majority of Hutch's time.

He had cut deep by bringing up the incident with Jade. The three of them had tried never to acknowledge that it had happened. Even when Gary Parker hanged himself and Jade and her mother left Palmetto, they avoided linking those incidents to what had taken place out by the channel that cold, dreary evening. Hard as they tried to keep it out of their conversations, however, it always found a way to pop in. Come to think of it, Neal was usually the one to bring it up.

Was Neal manipulating the incident as he had accused Donna Dee of doing? He triggered their memory of it whenever he wanted something. His reminders of it served to keep them in line. *For how long?* Lamar wondered. *For life?* The thought chilled him to the bone. The last thing he wanted was to be on the receiving end of Neal's ridicule. God forbid that Neal ever find out that he was in love.

Aside from his reluctance to live with Neal through another two years, he was miserable about leaving behind his newfound love, an eighth-grade English teacher at Palmetto Junior High. They had met by chance at the movies. Their first date had been nothing more romantic than going for coffee after the film, yet they had talked well into the night. For the remainder of the summer they saw each other almost every night. One evening after a drive along the seashore, Lamar had haltingly admitted, "I can't take you home. I live with my mother."

"I'd like to be alone with you, too."

They settled on a clandestine meeting in a motel. There, except for the rape of Jade Sperry, Lamar lost his virginity. Because his friends were under the misconception that he'd been having sex for years, he couldn't destroy the myth and confide in anyone about the greatest night of his life.

He had been meticulously discreet, which was no small feat when living with Myrajane. It didn't matter to her that Lamar had already lived away from home for a year; she wanted every minute of his time accounted for. A benevolent angel had prevented her from hearing about the incident involving Jade Sperry. Myrajane had been one of the first to condemn Jade when Gary committed suicide. Knowing the unfairness of that, Lamar had wrestled with his conscience over whether to set his mother straight on a few facts. He had put up only a token struggle, however, and had wisely kept his knowledge to himself.

To this day, he couldn't believe that he had had the good fortune to walk away from that unpleasantness unscathed. Feeling as though he were living on borrowed time, he took extra precautions to assure that his mother not find out about his love affair.

Now, he had two sins on his conscience. One never got off scot-free for his transgressions. Lamar was paying for his secret misdeeds by being condemned to another year under Neal's tyranny.

He forced himself to get up and prepare for the evening. He really should unpack before the Delta Gammas arrived. Otherwise, they would put things where he wouldn't know where to find them. Because Neal expected it, he would get a little stoned, a little drunk, and would probably bring one of the Delta Gammas into his bedroom and have sex.

His recently adopted philosophy of life was that, in order to survive in the cruel world, one did what one had to do, even if one didn't like it.

Chapter 13

———————

Morgantown, South Carolina, 1977–81

Boy! Was that exam a bitch or what?"

Jade smiled up at the fellow student who had fallen into step beside her as she left the science building. "That exam was definitely a bitch." The steeple chimes struck four o'clock. Trees cast long, slanted shadows across the campus lawn, and frisky autumn leaves tumbled in a brisk, cool wind.

"Biology's never been my bag. By the way, I'm Hank Arnett."

"Pleased to meet you, Hank. Jade Sperry."

"Hi, Jade." He smiled disarmingly. "So, do you think you passed the exam?"

"I'm on a scholarship. I have to do better than pass. I have to maintain at least a three-point grade average."

He whistled. "That's tough."

"If the sciences aren't your bag, what is?" she asked conversationally.

"Art. Give me a Monet over Madame Curie any day. Do you figure Picasso knew or even cared how paramecia procreate?"

Jade laughed. "I'm a business major."

"Hmm." He raised his eyebrows as though impressed. "With a face like yours, I would have guessed music. Literature, maybe."

"Nope, marketing and management."

"Jeez, my instincts were way off base. I sure as hell didn't have you pegged for a future tycoon."

She took that as a backhanded compliment. "Well, this is where I turn off." They stopped at the intersection of two paved sidewalks. "It was nice to meet you, Hank."

"Yeah, for me, too. Say, uh, I was going to grab a cup of coffee. How's that sound?"

"It sounds good, but I'm on my way to work."

"Where do you work?"

"I've really got to run, Hank. 'Bye." Before he could detain her, she turned and jogged to the parking lot.

Hank Arnett watched her until she disappeared from view. He had an even temperament, a tall, lanky physique, and a thick Southern drawl. His shoulders were wide and bony, and his thick, wavy, reddish brown hair was frequently pulled back in a pony tail. His affable face wasn't movie-star handsome, but the twinkle in his brown eyes was engaging. Most of his clothes were flea-market chic, and he wore them with panache without looking effeminate.

One of his virtues was tenacity. Possessing a good sense of humor, he found the foibles of life more amusing than irritating. During the course of her freshman year at Dander College, Jade would discover that. After their first meeting, Hank fell into the habit of walking her from their biology class to her car. Since it was her final class of the day before she had to report to work, she always had a good excuse for declining his invitations to have coffee. While she liked him very much, she discouraged his subtle overtures toward dating.

As Dean Mitch Hearon had predicted, Miss Dorothy Davis wasn't the easiest of employers. A maiden lady— and defensively proud of it—she was demanding and persnickety. Her store could outfit females from birth to burial. Miss Dorothy was personally acquainted with every scrap of merchandise in the store and could, by memory, provide a stock number for most of it. Her salespeople were terrified of her.

Jade's efficiency and diligence won Miss Dorothy's approval. She liked her for being a "sensible young person, not like most." Jade utilized her time at the store wisely, learning all she could about the manufacturing and marketing of clothing and other textile products and the day-to-day trials of running a business.

She had resolved that in order to irrevocably damage the Patchetts, she would have to attack them on an economic front. She wanted to strip the Patchetts of what was most important to them—money and the influence that accompanied it. She wanted to permanently cripple their power machine. Her ultimate goal was to create in Palmetto an economic upheaval that would benefit the community but overturn the Patchetts' monarchy. She nursed no delusions that it would be easy. She would have to be smart, savvy, and vested with more power than they before she could even attempt it. From now on, everything she did was in preparation of returning and bringing them down. She woke up every morning thinking about it, and fell asleep tasting the victory that was years away.

If it hadn't been for Neal, there would have been no rape. He and his father were her central targets. She didn't intend to let Hutch, Donna Dee, and Lamar off lightly, but they would topple as a consequence of the Patchetts' destruction.

Under an assumed name, she subscribed to the *Palmetto Post,* the daily newspaper, and had it mailed to a post-office box on campus. The newspaper kept her up to date on local news. During the summer she had read the announcement of Donna Dee's marriage to Hutch. Jade wondered if she had had three bridesmaids all dressed in pink as she had always wanted. She kept the newspapers away from the Hearons' house for fear that they would discover that she was persona non grata in her hometown. Mitch's relatives there must be "distant" indeed, because he had no contact with them—no calls or visits, not even birthday cards. The topic had never come up again, but it was months before Jade was able to let go of her fear of discovery. The couple had come to mean so much to her and Graham, and she didn't want anything to damage their relationship.

They charged her only fifty dollars a month for room and board, and that had been levied only to spare her pride. Miss Dorothy gave her a 10-percent discount on clothes for herself. But keeping Graham clothed when he was growing so swiftly was expensive, as were his pediatric checkups and inoculations. Every penny counted.

Because she couldn't allow anything to jeopardize her job, she wasn't too pleased when Hank Arnett unexpectedly appeared in Miss Dorothy's storeroom one afternoon.

Jade popped erect from the box of velour housecoats she was unpacking. "What are you doing here? Please leave. I'll lose my job."

"Have no fear, Jade. The old girl's not going to fire you. I told her I had an urgent message for you from your landlord."

"Dr. Hearon? What message?"

Hank's face creased in a dozen places when he smiled. "You live with Dean Hearon? Imagine that." He scratched his head. "I never thought to look into faculty housing. I combed all the dorms and sorority houses."

"Of all the dirty, rotten tricks!" She had always given evasive answers to his leading questions about where she lived. He had outsmarted her this time, but it was impossible to stay mad at Hank. "Now that you got what you came for, please go. I can't afford to lose this job."

"I'll go quietly under one condition."

"No conditions."

"Have it your way." He sat down on the corner of Miss Dorothy's desk and pilfered an apple from a basket of fruit, which Miss Dorothy ate religiously for its fiber content.

Jade cast a worried glance toward the storeroom door, half-expecting her employer to come storming through waving a dismissal slip. "What condition?" she whispered.

"Tomorrow, before biology class, you've got to have coffee with me. And don't say you've got another class because I've seen you studying in the library during that hour."

"Miss Sperry?"

The sound of Miss Dorothy's voice galvanized Jade into accepting his invitation and shooing him out with the apple tucked inside his jacket. He gave Miss Dorothy a crisp, military salute on his way out.

Her narrow nostrils quivered with indignation. "Who was that impertinent young man?"

Jade stammered a plausible explanation, but she was laughing on the inside and thinking just how impertinent Hank Arnett was.

They met for coffee the following day and fell into a habit of it. He asked her out on dates to dinner, the movies, and concerts, but, to his disappointment, she always declined. Other young men on campus pursued her too, but she stopped their advances cold. Only Hank had approached her in the friendly, nonthreatening, nonsexual way that she could tolerate.

On a sunny afternoon toward the end of the Christmas vacation, Jade was playing with Graham in the backyard when Cathy called to her. "You have company."

Hank loped across the yard and dropped down onto the grass beside her. "Hi. I'm a few days late saying this, but Merry Christmas and Happy New Year."

"Same to you."

"Was Santa good to you?"

"Too good," she said, reminded of the Hearons' embarrassing generosity, which she couldn't reciprocate. "You're back from Winston-Salem early."

He shrugged. "There wasn't much to do at home except eat. Mom said I looked thin and took it upon herself to remedy that. I reminded her that I've always been thin, but she stuffed me anyway. I may not eat again till Easter. Jade, who's the kid?"

His sentences ran together, but he stopped abruptly after posing the question. Cocking his head to one side, he looked at her curiously, rather like a puppy looks at his master when he speaks.

"This is my son. His name is Graham. Say hello to Hank, Graham." Graham toddled across the grass toward Hank and smacked him on the nose.

"Hey!" He raised both fists as though ready to box with the child, then socked him lightly in the tummy. Graham laughed.

"I'm not married and never have been, Hank."

"I didn't ask."

"But you wanted to."

"Is his father important to you?"

"As far as I'm concerned, Graham doesn't have a father."

Hank gave her a sweet smile and fell back into the grass, hauling the toddler down with him. Graham loved the rowdy game. His peals of laughter eventually brought Cathy to the back door to investigate. She invited Hank to stay for dinner.

"I'm going to miss you like hell." Hank stared dismally through the windshield of his car. It was raining—a heavy, ponderous spring rain. "If my mother wouldn't pitch a bitch, I'd stay here and go to summer school."

"You can't do that, Hank. Especially not on my account."

Jade was sitting in the passenger seat of his Volkswagen, which he had painted to look like a ladybug. He turned his head and gazed at her. "Jade, everything I do is on your account. Haven't you figured that out yet?"

She cast her eyes down. "I told you months ago that we were only going to be friends. That's all. I distinctly remember the conversation. It took place right after you returned from Christmas vacation. We were studying for that biology—"

"I remember, I remember," he said testily.

"Don't blame me if you're disappointed now. I was honest with you from the beginning." She reached for the door handle, but he caught her arm.

"You haven't been honest, Jade. You've told me that all you want is friendship, but you haven't told me why. I can only guess that your reason has something to do with Graham."

She shook her head adamantly.

"Listen, Jade, I'm crazy about that kid. I don't care who fathered him, I'd love to be his daddy."

"Please, Hank, don't," she groaned. "Don't say anything more. I can't return what you feel."

"How do you know?"

"I know."

"Why, Jade? Tell me. I know you like me."

"I like you very much."

"But...What?"

She looked away, refusing to answer.

"Jade." Hank cupped her face between his long, slender hands. "Some bastard hurt you. He broke your heart. Let me make up for that, okay? I love you so much, I can make up for any bad experience you suffered."

She clamped her teeth over her lower lip and shook her head as much as his bracketing hands would allow it to move.

"You're so beautiful, Jade. Jesus, I love you."

He lowered his head toward hers and, for the first time, kissed her. His lips were soft and gentle. They posed no threat, and yet Jade's heart began to drum. Shock and fear immobilized her. He kissed the features of her face, glancing his lips off her eyelids and cheekbones and murmuring about how beautiful and desirable she was, and how badly he wanted to make love to her.

Eventually he returned to her lips. Jade took several swift, short breaths, then ceased to breathe at all when his lips applied more pressure and tried to separate hers. Still petrified, she couldn't push him away. Mistakenly, he took that as an encouraging sign. He angled his head to one side and rubbed his lips against hers, parting them.

Jade's body stiffened. Hank removed his hands from either side of her head and set them on her shoulders, where his fingers tried to massage away her tension. Then he took one of her hands and pressed it against his chest. The other, he placed on his thigh.

His breathing grew rough and irregular. He made small, hungry sounds deep in his throat. Nevertheless, he exercised supreme self-discipline as he attempted to deepen their kiss and coax a response from her. Jade recoiled. Hank was gently persistent.

His tongue wasn't intrusive or imperious, but the moment it entered her mouth, Jade began to whimper with revulsion and fear. She didn't recall the ardent tenderness of Gary's kisses, only those which had been forced on her during the rape. She moved her hands to Hank's shoulders. Misreading her reaction, his arms went around her and hugged her tightly as he pressed her against the door and leaned over her.

"No!" Jade shoved him away, thrashing her head from

side to side and begging him to stop hurting her. She emitted dry, racking sobs. "Stop. Please don't. Oh, God!"

"Jade?" Mortified, Hank tried to take her into his arms, but she huddled against the car door. "Jade," he whispered, his voice mystified and anguished, "I'm sorry. I'm not going to hurt you. Jade?"

His fingers sifted through her hair until she quieted. Eventually, she raised her head and looked at him with wide, fearful eyes. "I told you. I can't."

"It's okay, Jade."

She was insistent that he comprehend what she was telling him. "I can't be with you like that. I can't be with any man. Ever. Don't expect it. Don't waste your time trying."

His eyes had lost their sparkle but not their kindness. He smiled lopsidedly and shrugged with self-deprecation. "It's my time. I'll waste it how I like."

He walked her to the front door and bade her a final goodbye, promising to write at least once a week through the summer. After letting herself in, Jade leaned against the door and closed her eyes.

"Jade, would you and Hank like some cake and coffee?"

Cathy had entered the vestibule from the rear of the house, and drew up short when she saw Jade's bleak expression. "Hank's not with me, Cathy. He said to tell you both goodbye and that he would look forward to seeing you in the fall."

"Oh, I thought he would come in for a while."

"No. How's Graham? Did he go to bed without a fuss? I'd better go up and check on him."

As Jade moved past her, Cathy reached out and caught

her hand. "What's wrong, Jade? Are you upset about Hank leaving for the summer? Or did you two have a spat?"

Jade slumped down onto the third step of the staircase and covered her face with her hands, laughing mirthlessly behind them. "Oh Lord, I wish it were that simple."

Cathy sat down on the step beneath her, removed Jade's hands from her face, and regarded her with maternal concern. "What's the matter, Jade? Can you talk about it?"

"Where's Hank? What's going on?" Mitch asked as he joined them. He had on a summer-weight robe over his pajamas. Cathy, Jade noticed for the first time, was also dressed for bed and had a few curlers in the top of her hair. They had been waiting up for her.

The Hearons had been more like parents to her than her own. Ronald Sperry was little more than a medal in a box, a photograph, a warm but distant memory. Jade had made several attempts to locate her mother, but with no success. Velta had covered her tracks well—or Harvey had covered them for her. Evidently she had washed her hands of Jade and Graham. The severance with her mother nearly broke Jade's heart, but she had come to accept it and hoped that Velta had found some happiness.

Jade certainly had. From the day the Hearons had insisted that she and Graham move in with them, they had treated her as their own daughter, although they insisted that she call them by their first names. Graham's version of "Cathy" was something like "Caff." He called Mitch "Poppy."

The days had fallen into weeks and the weeks into months, and before long Jade couldn't imagine life without Cathy and Mitch. She and Graham shared a large, comfortable bedroom suite on the second floor of their house. Cathy prepared sumptuous meals for them. The lovely house, initially their refuge, became their home.

Cathy carried pictures of Graham in her wallet and boasted about each of his accomplishments like a grand-mother. They honored Jade's privacy and never questioned her about his father, although she was certain they won-dered about it. Any awkwardness that arose from introduc-ing Jade and Graham to their friends was either patently ignored or handled with Cathy Hearon's characteristic tact-fulness. Jade owed them a debt of gratitude she could never repay, but she hoped that she and Graham had returned some of the joy they had received. Without the Hearons' generosity, her life would have taken a vastly different turn. Not only would she have missed college, but, more impor-tant, their affection, acceptance, and compassion.

Now, taking a seat in the small chair beside the foyer table, Mitch said, "Are you ladies going to tell me what's going on?"

"Something happened between Hank and Jade tonight."

Jade smiled wanly. "No, Cathy. Nothing happened between us tonight. Nothing ever will. That's the prob-lem." She took a deep breath. "Unfortunately, Hank has fallen in love with me."

"You don't return his feelings?" Cathy probed gently.

"I love him dearly as a friend."

"Being considered a friend is a tough blow for a boy in love," Mitch said.

"I know," Jade said miserably. "I tried to tell him months ago that it was hopeless. I encouraged him to date other girls. I knew he would get hurt if he kept seeing me, but he wouldn't listen. Now the worst has happened, and it breaks my heart."

"Are you so sure that you won't eventually come to love him?" Cathy asked hopefully. "He's such an easygoing young man, and utterly captivated by you. Perhaps after the separation this summer..."

Jade was already shaking her head. "I won't fall in love with him—with anyone."

Their troubled faces conveyed their concern. It would have been a tremendous relief to unburden herself and tell them the whole truth. But she didn't want anyone to know about the rape. She'd learned that assault victims were victims for life. Even if they were entirely innocent, as she was, they were forever regarded with curiosity and suspicion, as though they had been branded. She lived in fear of the Hearons finding out about her. They probably would consider her the sinned against rather than the sinner, but she was unwilling to take the chance. Each time she was tempted to confide in them, she had only to remind herself that her classmates, her best friend, even her own mother had doubted her.

"I'm tired," Jade said, rising. "Good night." She hugged them in turn before going upstairs, trusting them to respect her privacy. They asked no further questions.

Even while taking a summer curriculum, Jade was able to work longer hours in the store until she was as familiar with the stock and the accounts as was Miss Dorothy herself. By the end of the summer, Jade had become so indispensable to her that she fired her accountant and turned all the bookkeeping over to Jade.

"I'll need more money," Jade had told her softly but firmly. "At least fifty dollars a week."

They settled on a forty-dollar raise. Jade saved most

of it. If there was ever another crisis in her life, she was determined to have more than twenty dollars on which to survive.

The Hearons and she managed to endure Graham's Terrible Twos. Cathy merely moved everything breakable out of his reach. In the afternoons when Mitch returned home from the campus, he expended some of Graham's excess energy by taking him for long walks. No matter what the weather, hand in hand they strolled down the sidewalks of the neighborhood. Mitch discussed with him the marvels of the universe, and, as though he understood, Graham listened. Their excursions usually produced something interesting—acorns, caterpillars, a bouquet of dandelions for the dining-room table.

Hank returned in the fall. Jade was surprised at how glad she was to see him. As promised, he had written at least once each week. His letters were newsy and anecdotal, and he always included an original drawing for Graham. After seeing each other daily for almost a month, Jade reopened the topic of their relationship. "Hank, you haven't forgotten what I told you last spring, have you?"

"No," he replied. "Have you forgotten what I told you?"

She gazed at him forlornly. "But I feel guilty. You should be going out and having fun. You should be developing other relationships that would be much more... fulfilling."

He folded his long arms across his chest. "What you're waltzing around is that I should be getting laid, right?"

"Right."

"When I want to, I will, okay? Right now, the only woman I'm interested in making love with is having some problems. Until she works them out, I'm willing to make do."

"Please don't, Hank. I'll never work these problems out. I don't want to be responsible for your unhappiness."

"I'm not unhappy. I'd rather be with you, not screwing, than be with someone else screwing and wishing it were you. Does that make sense?"

"Absolutely none."

He laughed, but his eyes turned serious. "There is something you can do for me, though."

"What?"

"Get some professional help."

"You mean a psychiatrist?"

"Or psychologist, or counselor." He gnawed on his lower lip a moment before saying, "Jade, I'm not fishing to know, you understand, but I feel something traumatic happened that turned you off men. Am I warm?"

"Not men. I like men."

"Then it's sexual intimacy you're afraid of. You weren't repulsed when I tried to make love to you. You were scared."

She neither disagreed nor conceded, but kept her eyes averted.

"Maybe if you talked it over with somebody, he or she could help you overcome it."

"Don't base any hopes on it."

"It wouldn't hurt to try."

They didn't discuss it again, but he had planted a seed in Jade's mind. She carefully weighed the benefits and drawbacks. One deterrent was the expense. She begrudged having to invest money on professional counseling when she held out very little hope for a return on that investment. Another drawback was Hank himself. If she began seeing a psychologist, he might expect an instant recovery and start pressing her for more than she could give. Besides, the main purpose in her life now wasn't to have a successful relationship with a man, but to avenge Gary's death. Dealing with her phobia might splinter her focus.

The benefit, of course, was obvious. She might return to "normal."

It wasn't until a year after the subject came up that she scheduled her first appointment. For several weeks she kept her decision to herself. When she finally informed Hank, he grabbed her by the shoulders, squeezed them hard, and exclaimed, "Great! Terrific!"

The immediate outcome of the sessions was neither great nor terrific. Discussing the rape with the female psychologist opened up wounds that Jade had hoped were cauterized by time and distance. She came away from each session feeling as though she had been violated again. After months of therapy, however, she gained confidence that one day she might be able to put her fears aside. If that ever happened, she would be as glad as Hank.

On a chilly, blustery afternoon in early March of her junior year, she jogged up the sidewalk to the house and let herself in. "Cathy? Mitch? Graham? Mommy's home," she called. "Where is everybody?"

Graham barreled into the foyer and tackled her around the knees. It seemed that he grew an inch every day. He now moved with the impetus of a locomotive.

She bent down to give him a hug. "Where's Cathy?"

"Store."

"So you're here with Poppy?" she asked as she slipped off her coat.

"Poppy's 'sleep."

"Asleep?" She headed toward his study, calling his name with increasing alarm when he didn't answer. "Mitch?"

Jade drew up short on the threshold of the bookshelf-lined room. Even though she knew he couldn't hear her, she softly repeated, "Mitch?" He was sitting behind his desk with an open book in his lap, his head slumped to one side, obviously dead.

That evening, Jade and Cathy quietly grieved together in the room in which he had died, surrounded by the books he had loved. Cathy was so immersed in shock and bereavement that it fell to Jade to handle the business of the burial.

She notified the chancellor of the college, wrote and issued a press release to the local media, and drove Cathy to the funeral home to pick out a casket. Later, when Cathy retreated to her bedroom, Jade received friends who came by to offer condolences and leave food.

The wife of a young history professor volunteered to keep Graham until after the funeral. Jade gladly accepted her offer, knowing that he would be constantly underfoot and confused by the comings and goings of so many strangers in the house. Besides, every time he asked where Poppy was, it was like a knife wound to Cathy and her.

Hank remained close at hand. He ran errands when needed and did all the tasks that no one else could manage. The morning of the funeral, he arrived early. Jade, wearing a black turtleneck sweater-dress and a single strand of faux pearls, greeted him at the door. Her hair was sleekly pulled into a ponytail at her nape and tied with a black velvet bow. The faint shadows of sadness and fatigue beneath her eyes only heightened their deep blue color.

She led Hank into the kitchen, where she had already brewed a pot of coffee. Handing him a cup, she said, "Cathy's still upstairs dressing. I suppose I'd better go hurry her along. She can't find anything. She's absent-minded. They'd been married for thirty-three years, so she feels adrift. They had such a perfect marriage. He was always so..."

Her voice cracked, her shoulders sagged, and she permitted Hank to pull her into his arms. It felt good to be held. His hands smoothed up and down her back as he whispered words of comfort and solace into her ear. He was warm. The fragrance he wore was alluring and familiar. She liked the scratchy feel of his wool jacket beneath her cheek.

And before either realized it was happening, the embrace changed personality. As the psychologist had counseled her to do, Jade concentrated on everything that was sensually pleasing, giving no thought to anything except what was favorable and good. To her dismay, she found it all to be.

Raising her head, she gazed up at him with perplexity. He smiled at her gently, seemingly reading her thoughts. One of his hands slowly moved up to her cheek, and he stroked it with the back of his knuckle. His thumb made two light passes across her lips before he softly kissed her.

Jade's heart was tripping madly, but it wasn't from fear. She didn't freeze up, nor did she turn away or flinch. Hank raised his head and paused, giving her time to object.

When she didn't, he released a long sigh that spread across her lips before he caressed them again.

"Hank?"

"Don't tell me to stop," he pleaded.

"I wasn't going to." She took a step closer.

Moaning, Hank placed his arms around her and drew her closer. His lips nudged hers apart. He raked her teeth with the tip of his tongue. "Jade?" he murmured. "Jade?"

The doorbell rang. Jade stirred. Hank released her and stepped back. "Goddammit."

She gave him a nervous, breathless smile. "Excuse me." On her way through the house, she reflexively moistened her lips and tasted his kiss. It hadn't been bad at all. In fact, it had been quite delicious. It was wicked to think such a thing on the day she was burying Mitch, but she couldn't wait until she and Hank were alone again.

But when she pulled open the front door, her smile congealed. She stood face to face with one of her rapists.

Chapter 14

——•◆•——

Myrajane Cowan Griffith couldn't have looked more affronted if she had been hit in the face with a bucket of cold water. "You're that Sperry girl," she said, making it sound like an accusation. "What in the world are you doing here?"

Jade reflexively gripped the brass doorknob, her eyes fixed on Lamar. The changes in him over the last four years were negligible. He was wearing his hair longer. His body had filled out so that he now looked more man than boy. But his dark eyes were still wary, still nervous, and, as he gazed with astonishment at Jade, still apologetic.

"May we come in?" Myrajane asked snidely.

Jade tore her eyes away from Lamar and looked at his mother. Myrajane hadn't aged gracefully. The nastier aspects of her personality were evident in her face, which was lined and drawn. With an amateur hand, she had tried to camouflage the erosion with cosmetics. The results were pathetic. Her garish blue eyeshadow had collected in the creases of her eyelids, and her lipstick had bled into the cracks radiating from her mouth.

Jade stepped aside and nodded them into the foyer. With her inexpertly painted lips twitching with disapproval, Myrajane gave her a critical once-over. "You haven't told me why you're answering the door to my cousin's house."

"I live here," Jade replied.

"Jade?" Feeling wooden, she turned as Hank approached from the back of the house. Myrajane gaped at his ponytail with palpable horror. "I'm Hank Arnett," he said, extending his hand to Lamar. "Were you friends of Dr. Hearon?"

"Mitchell was my second cousin," Myrajane declared icily. "Where is his widow?"

Her tone of voice implied that the situation was being handled poorly by people unsuitable to handle it at all. "I'll let Cathy know you're here," Jade said, heading toward the staircase. "Hank, if you will..."

Her voice trailed off as she vaguely gestured toward the living room. Hank was looking at her strangely. Apparently he noticed that something was amiss, but his worst guess wouldn't have come close to describing what she had felt when she opened the door and saw Lamar.

Turning quickly, she ran upstairs. On the landing, she pressed her back flat against the wall and crammed her fists against her lips. She pinched her eyes shut, but patches of color burst against her eyelids from the inside. There was a roaring sound in her ears.

Four years. The impact should have been dulled in four years. But when she came face to face with Lamar, rage had bubbled within her so hotly that she had wanted to claw at his face and pummel his body. She had wanted to hurt him as badly as she had been hurt. Miraculously, she had contained herself, but the thought of being under the same roof with him made her shudder with revulsion. She wanted to wash herself, take a scalding bath, scrub herself as she had done following the rape.

She had no choice, however, except to bear up. For Cathy's sake she couldn't make a spectacle of herself. Cathy needed her today. Moving mechanically, she walked to the master-bedroom door and knocked.

"Cathy, you have guests downstairs."

"Come in, please."

Cathy was having difficulty fastening the high collar of her black dress. Jade moved behind her and did it for her. Cathy looked at herself in the mirror.

"Mitch hated me in black. He said it was too dramatic a color for me." Inquisitively, she tilted her head to one side. "Do you think he meant that as a compliment?"

Jade rested her chin on the other woman's shoulder and pressed the side of her head against Cathy, looking in the mirror at the two of them. "Of course he did. He thought you were ravishing."

Cathy smiled tremulously. "Sometimes I forget that he's gone, Jade. I turn to say something to him, and then I suddenly remember and experience the pain all over again. It's like a fresh wound, you know?"

How well she knew. That's exactly how she had felt when she opened the door to Lamar Griffith a few minutes earlier. "Myrajane Griffith from Palmetto just arrived. She's waiting downstairs for you."

Cathy was fiddling with the articles on her dresser. "Where's my handkerchief? I wanted to carry the one Mitch bought me that summer we went to Austria."

The embroidered handkerchief was in plain sight. Jade

picked it up and handed it to Cathy. "She said she was Mitch's cousin."

"You must mean Myrajane Cowan."

"Griffith is her married name."

"I'd forgotten. I don't know her very well. Mitch couldn't stand her. Her mother and Mitch's mother were first cousins, I believe. We hadn't seen her for years, but she's the type who would have felt slighted if she hadn't been personally notified. I called her the night Mitch died."

"Mrs. Griffith and...and her son, Lamar, were almost as shocked to see me here as I was to see them."

Cathy ceased looking for her wristwatch among the scattered items on the dresser. Even in her bereavement, she discerned the hollowness in Jade's voice.

"I didn't leave Palmetto under ideal circumstances, Cathy. There was a...a scandal. I wanted you to hear it from me first in case they say something to you about it."

Cathy's eyes blinked angrily. "They'd better not."

"And I don't want them to know about Graham. No one in Palmetto knows about him, and I have reasons for wanting to keep it that way."

"Reasons you can't share with me?"

Jade looked away and shook her head.

"Jade," Cathy said, reaching for her hand, "Mitch loved you. I love you. Nothing can change that. If I'd known that Myrajane conjured up bad memories for you, I wouldn't have phoned her."

The two women embraced. "Thank you," Jade whispered.

Arm in arm they went downstairs and entered the living room. Myrajane was sitting on the edge of the sofa, her posture rigid. Lamar was occupying a chair, looking tense and uncomfortable. Hank was pacing in front of the windows. He looked relieved when Cathy and Jade appeared.

"Someone else is pulling up at the curb," he said. "I'll get the door."

Cathy retained hold of Jade's arm as she moved across the room to welcome Myrajane. "Thank you for coming, Myrajane. Hello, Lamar. Mitch would have been pleased that you came. I believe you already know Jade."

"We certainly do," Myrajane said, giving Jade a censorious look, which Cathy ignored.

"Jade has lived with us for more than three years," Cathy said. "Mitch regarded her as the daughter we never had. He adored her, and so do I. Jade, would you please bring in a tray of coffee so our guests can help themselves? Please excuse me, Myrajane. I need to say hello to the new arrivals."

As usual, Cathy had adroitly avoided an awkward situation. The Griffiths soon became absorbed with the other guests who arrived to pay their respects before the funeral. Jade was kept busy greeting people at the door and keeping carafes filled with coffee.

During the funeral service in the campus chapel, she almost forgot the unheralded appearance of Lamar and his mother. Seated next to Cathy, at Cathy's request, she remained transfixed on the flower-banked coffin. Memories of Mitch drifted through her mind while he was eulogized by faculty members. He had been a respected academician, a devoted husband, a kind and loving surrogate father for her and grandfather for Graham. Their lives would not have been the same without his influence. They would miss him terribly.

At the grave site, people commended her for being strong for Cathy's sake. Because her eyes remained dry, no one guessed how much she wept on the inside. The day seemed to drag on interminably. A steady stream of Mitch's friends and colleagues came to the house to pay their respects to his widow. The crowd didn't begin to thin out until dusk. By nightfall, only a few guests remained. When they departed, Cathy and Jade finally found themselves alone.

"I suppose I should go pick up Graham," Jade said.

"Why don't you let him spend another night? They offered. You know he's being well taken care of. And you've been on your feet all day. I know you're tired."

"I'm exhausted," Jade admitted, sinking down on the sofa beside Cathy and slipping off her black suede heels. "But no more than you, I'm sure."

"Actually, I enjoyed talking about Mitch. He meant so much to so many people."

Jade reached for Cathy's hand and held it between her own. "He certainly did."

They were quiet for a while before Cathy said, "I failed to notice when Hank left, and didn't get to thank him for all he's done the last couple of days."

"I sent him away with that elderly couple from Birmingham. They hadn't gotten a motel room yet and seemed bewildered as to how to go about it. You were with someone else, so Hank couldn't say goodbye."

"He's a dear boy."

"Yes, he is. Very dear." They were quiet for another few moments, then Jade said, "Thank you for handling the situation with Mrs. Griffith and Lamar. I stayed as far from them as possible until they left."

"The spiteful witch managed to intercept me as I was coming out of the bathroom. She gripped my arm and asked if I was aware of the scandal that had driven you out of Palmetto. I told her that if she had anything negative to say about you, she wasn't welcome in my house."

Cathy's smooth brow wrinkled with concern. "Jade, is it this 'scandal' in Palmetto that's prevented you from having a romantic relationship with Hank?"

Jade pulled the black ribbon from her hair and shook it free. She studied the black velvet as she threaded it through her fingers. Quietly she said, "When I was a senior in high school, I was raped by three boys. Lamar Griffith was one of them."

Although she hadn't planned on it, the moment suddenly seemed right to tell Cathy. "Myrajane doesn't know that, of course. All she's heard is that I was responsible for my boyfriend's suicide."

Once the floodgate had been lifted, the words couldn't be contained. For almost half an hour they poured out of her. She told the story unemotionally, almost by rote because she had recited it to herself whenever her determination to seek revenge waned. Once her initial shock had worn off, Cathy cried quietly into her handkerchief.

"Oh, Jade," she sobbed when Jade was done. "I'm very glad you told me. You shouldn't have had to bear this alone. This explains so much. How could your mother desert you and Graham?"

"She doubted my innocence and resented me for not staying in Palmetto and forcing one of the boys to claim Graham and marry me."

"My God! How could she even suggest such a thing?"

Jade leaned forward and hugged Cathy. "You're the

first person who has ever wholeheartedly taken my word for what happened. I know Mitch would have, too. I was tempted to tell you many times. Now I'm glad I didn't, since Mitch was related to Lamar."

"I'm rather glad that Mitch wasn't here to hear your story, too. He would have—" She broke off and raised her hand to her chest. "Oh, but I wish he were here, Jade. How can I stand never to see him again, hear his voice, touch him?"

"I shouldn't have bothered you with my problems. Not tonight."

"No, Mitch would have urged you to. It's drawn us closer together, and he would have wanted that."

Jade held her until Cathy's tears subsided. "I'm going upstairs now, Jade," she whispered hoarsely as she stood. "Good night."

"Will you be all right?"

Cathy smiled wanly. "No. But I need to be alone... with him... to say my final goodbyes."

After she went upstairs, the house seemed inordinately quiet. As Jade went through the rooms collecting napkins and glasses, she thought how glad she would be to have Graham back, generating noise, creating his little whirlwinds of activity. That might alleviate the emptiness that Mitch had left behind.

She wasn't sure she could ever go into his study again without envisioning him there, slumped over in his chair. That would never do, she thought with self-admonishment. She must force herself to picture him perusing one of the books he loved, or walking down the sidewalk hand in hand with Graham, or telling one of his wonderful stories.

The doorbell intruded on her thoughts. She gave her reflection in the hall mirror a cursory glance before pulling open the door.

"Jade—"

She tried to slam the door, but Lamar's hand shot out and caught it.

"Please, Jade. Let me talk to you for a minute."

She glared at him, her breasts rising and falling with each agitated breath. "Go away."

"Please, Jade. I tried all day to find the right time to speak to you."

"There will never be a right time. Certainly not today."

Again she tried to close the door, but he insinuated himself between it and the frame. "Jesus, Jade, do you think it was easy for me to come here?"

"I wouldn't know, you see, because I've never raped anyone. I wouldn't know how difficult or easy it is to face a victim afterward, although you and your friends didn't seem to have any trouble seeing me at school every day. Which is why I can't fathom why you found it so difficult to come here tonight."

He looked miserable. "Whatever you say to me isn't as bad as what I deserve, Jade. I can't undo what we did, God knows. But please let me talk to you—for just a few minutes. That's all I ask."

She let him inside—perhaps because he acknowledged that what had taken place beside the channel had been against her will. When she thought about it later, that was the only reason she could provide for having let him in.

He quietly closed the door after stepping inside. "Where's Mrs. Hearon?"

"Upstairs."

"Can we sit down somewhere?"

"No." In a subconsciously defensive gesture, Jade folded her arms across her middle. "Say what you came to say, Lamar."

He was better-looking than he had been during high school, but no more self-assertive. He didn't argue with her. "Jade, what we did to you—"

"You forced me down into the mud, held my arms and legs, and took turns raping me. That's what you did, Lamar."

"Oh, Jesus," he groaned.

"Apparently your recollections of that night are cloudy. Mine are not. Neal slapped me several times while telling me to shut up. Hutch was the roughest. He hurt me the most."

Lamar's skin took on a greenish cast beneath the hall chandelier.

"You were hesitant, but you did it just the same."

"Because I had no choice, Jade."

"No choice? What choice did *I* have?"

"If I had wanted to stop it, what could I have done? Beaten up Neal and Hutch?" He gave a short, barking laugh. "Sure. I can see it now. Don't you understand?"

"No," she retorted, her eyes blazing. "Because even if you couldn't stop it, you didn't have to participate. You could have stayed behind to help me. You could have come forward and backed up my account of what happened."

"Neal would have killed me."

"You stood by and let my reputation be trampled. You said nothing when Neal taunted Gary and finally drove him to suicide."

"I couldn't say anything, Jade. I had to go along with Neal. I'm sorry." Tears shimmered his eyes. "You're strong.

You've always been strong. People look up to you. You don't know what it's like to have only two friends."

"I know what it's like to have none!" Those last, lonely months of her senior year, she had been snubbed by everyone except Patrice Watley.

Lamar was earnestly stammering his excuses. "You can't imagine what it's like to be under Neal's thumb. It wasn't until this year that I finally got away from him, and it pissed him off royally. We'd been living together in this old house—"

"I'm not interested."

"Well, anyway, I moved out before the semester was over last spring, and he didn't speak to me for weeks afterward. He acted the same way when Hutch got married. By the way, did you know that he married Donna Dee Monroe?"

"They deserve each other."

"Hutch played football for a couple of years. Neal was even jealous of the team. After our sophomore year, Hutch surprised everybody by joining the navy. Neal said he just wanted to get away from Donna Dee because she kept hounding him to make a baby. They live in Hawaii now, but I hear they're about to come back stateside. Hutch still isn't a daddy."

He might be. The thought made Jade shudder. "Is that why you came here, Lamar? To give me an update on my rapists?"

"Jade, I nearly fainted when you opened that door this morning. I was speechless with fear."

"Fear?" she asked with a bitter laugh. "Were you afraid that I might kill you?"

"No, worse. I was afraid you might point an accusing finger and start screaming rape."

"I tried that once, and it didn't do any good."

"Your contempt is justified."

"Why, thank you, Lamar. I'm glad I have your approval."

"I didn't mean that the way it sounded." He lowered his head and stared at the floor, expelling a deep breath.

"I think you'd better go."

"I still haven't said what I came to say." She gave him a level stare that demanded he not postpone it any longer. "I want you to understand why . . . why I had to go along with them that night. At that time in our lives, Hutch would do anything Neal told him to. Besides, I think Hutch had a crush on you."

"How dare you dignify rape as being something romantic." She lowered her arms to her sides, her hands forming fists. "The only difference between what you did to me and murder is that I'm still alive. And if Neal had told you and Hutch to kill me, I'd probably be dead."

His eyes begged her for tolerance. "Everything you've said is true, Jade. It was a crime, a violent act of retribution aimed at Gary for besting Neal in that fight at the Dairy Barn. At least to Neal it was. And he was always mouthing about how high and mighty you acted around him. I think he resented that you preferred Gary over him. To Hutch . . ." He shrugged. "I have my theories, but only Hutch knows why he went along."

He paused and took a deep breath. "For me, it was a test of manhood. I had to prove to them and to myself that I was a man. Unfortunately, it didn't work."

Jade glanced at him sharply. He raised his head and looked directly into her eyes. "I'm a homosexual, Jade."

He gave a scoffing laugh. "I believe I am a classic case

study—weak father, domineering mother. My suspicions about myself weren't confirmed until after my morally depraved freshman year of college, when I fucked plenty, but didn't enjoy it very much.

"The following summer I met a man in Palmetto. He taught at the junior high until he was discovered fondling one of his students in the boys' restroom. My mother couldn't have guessed how shattered I was when she called to catch me up on local gossip and told me the whole sordid story about my lover. I guess he got his kicks initiating young converts like me. Anyway, he went back east somewhere. My first love affair ended in tragedy."

"So did mine."

"Yeah," he said quietly, looking away. "I attracted new friends and lovers at school. One became jealous of my sexual activities with women during Neal's bacchanals. I participated because I didn't want Neal to find out about me. God forbid that my mother ever does. She'd probably sic the Klan on me. Can you imagine what her reaction would be to learning that the Cowan family tree will die because her son is a queer?"

Graham might be a Cowan, but Myrajane would never know it.

"I haven't come out of the closet yet," Lamar confessed. "But, after seeing you today, I wanted you to know. I thought it might help explain why I did what I did."

For several moments Jade regarded him with smoldering contempt. "You didn't come here to explain anything for *my* benefit, Lamar. You confessed your dark sin because you want me to absolve you. Well, you're out of luck. Your sexual preference doesn't justify rape.

"You didn't just violate me, you caused Gary's death.

Even if I could forgive you for the first offense, I sure as hell won't pardon you for the second. No, Lamar, as long as I live, I'll hold a grudge.

"Until I saw you this morning, I was under the misconception that time had anesthetized me. Then there you were, and it all came rushing back, as horrendously vivid as ever. I was on my back in the cold mud again, begging the three of you not to do it." Her eyes narrowed dangerously. "I'll never forget it, and as long as I remember it, you will remain unforgiven."

He stared at a spot beyond her shoulder. The handsome features of his face were drawn with sadness and resignation. Finally his eyes swung back to her. "That's what I figured you would say. I thought—hoped—it was worth a try." He turned toward the door, but paused and came back around. "I don't suppose it would do any good to add that I'm sorry."

"No."

Dejectedly, he nodded his head and went out, pulling the door closed behind him. Jade rushed to the door and quickly locked it. She pressed her forehead against the hard wood until it hurt. Their taunting words echoed inside her head. Neal had held her arms and goaded Lamar into taking his turn. Hutch, panting from his recent exertion, called Lamar a faggot for being squeamish. Covering her ears, Jade turned her back to the door and slid down its cool surface until her bottom touched the floor. She bent her head over her raised knees and, just as she had that night, she moaned plaintively, "No, please don't."

But Lamar had done it anyway and had seemed extremely proud of himself afterward. How dare he come to her now, airing his guilty conscience, revealing his tormenting secret, and asking her forgiveness?

To him it must appear that she had survived the incident and was doing well. He didn't know that, even after months of therapy, she was incapable of accepting or returning a man's affection. That night had been imprinted on her soul as indelibly as a birthmark. She would never be rid of it. It was a life sentence that she couldn't ask anyone else to share, especially not someone as precious to her as Hank.

Because of the circumstances, she had been able to avoid him today. But tomorrow she would tell him that she would never be able to express her love physically. It was impossible for her to be what he wanted her to be, what he deserved to have. This time, she must make him believe and accept it.

The darkness in her heart matched the night. The silence of the house closed in around her. She mourned for Graham, who wouldn't have Poppy in his life anymore. Her heart was broken for Cathy, who had lost her husband and best friend. She grieved for Hank and the heartache she must inflict on him.

In the bleak hours of the night, she almost envied Mitch his newfound peace.

Jade graduated from Dander College at the top of her class. In her speech at the commencement exercise, she publicly thanked the late dean, Dr. Mitchell Hearon, for having shown faith in her. Cathy took dozens of pictures of her in her cap and gown and held a reception in her honor.

The day Jade left Miss Dorothy Davis's store for the

last time, the old woman's back was as straight as ever, but there were tears in her eyes. "It's just as well that I've got the store up for sale," she sniffed. "It would take me weeks to find someone to replace you."

What she was really saying was that she could never replace Jade, and they both knew it. For the last year of her employment there, Jade had supervised the entire operation of the store. The other employees answered to her. Miss Dorothy had merely been a figurehead.

"I want you to have this," she said, handing Jade a white envelope. Inside it was the first check Miss Dorothy had made out in years.

"Five thousand dollars!" Jade exclaimed when she read the spidery handwriting.

"You've earned it. If I left it to you in my will, the damned attorneys would end up with it," she said cantankerously.

"I don't know what to say."

"Say goodbye. You're leaving, aren't you?"

For fear that she would break Miss Dorothy's brittle bones, Jade didn't hug her as tightly as she wanted to. She would miss the store and its eccentric owner, but not nearly as much as she would miss Cathy. Leaving Cathy would be much worse than her separation from her mother.

When she reached home, she sat in the driveway looking at the house and remembering that morning she had audaciously carried Graham up the front steps. He came sprinting through that same door now. He was a sturdy boy with Irish blue eyes and the hint of a vertical cleft in his chin. He wasn't even winded when he reached the car.

"Cathy wants to know why you're sitting out here in the car."

Because I dread going inside and imparting my news, she thought. To him she said, "I was waiting for my best boy to come out here and get me."

"Me?"

"None other. What did you do today?"

As they walked toward the house, he chattered about *Sesame Street* and a trip to the "place with lots of flowers."

"The nursery," Cathy said, having overheard the tail end of their conversation. The three of them gravitated to the kitchen, where Jade usually visited with Cathy while she prepared dinner. "I bought some impatiens for the pots on the front porch."

"They'll be pretty there. What color?"

Jade tried to keep the conversation lively, but, when it flagged, she realized that it was her fault, not Cathy's. She couldn't delay the inevitable any longer.

"Cathy, I've got something to tell you."

"I was wondering when you were going to get around to it. I could tell you have something on your mind."

She sat down across the table from Jade. Graham was coloring in a large book, his tongue securely anchored in one corner of his lips.

"I don't know how else to tell you, except to come right out and say it." Jade took a deep breath. "I've accepted a job with a clothing manufacturing firm in Charlotte."

"North Carolina?"

"Yes. I had hoped to find something closer to Morgantown, but, as you know, the college is the only industry here. This is a good job with a respectable starting salary. I'll be working directly with the vice president in charge of purchasing." She looked at Cathy with a silent appeal for understanding. "Even though it means that Graham and I have to move, it's too good an opportunity for me to pass up."

Jade was prepared to catch her, should Cathy collapse in tearful distress. Instead, the older woman's face lit up like a Christmas tree. "I love the idea of a change. When do we leave?"

Chapter 15

———◆———

Tallahassee, Florida, 1983

Nearly everyone on the transatlantic flight had fallen asleep midway through the inane movie. Dillon couldn't sleep. The coach seat hadn't been designed for a man his size. The best he could do was rest his head against the back of the seat and close his eyes.

Hearing Debra stir, he turned to check on her. She adjusted the blanket over their sleeping son, then looked up at Dillon and smiled. "He's a good traveler," she whispered. "No one would guess that this is his first flight."

Six-month-old Charlie was lying on his back in a padded carrier. When he snuffled in his sleep, his adoring parents gazed at each other again and smiled. "Try to get some sleep," Dillon said softly. He reached across the seat that separated them to stroke her hair. "Your family won't give us a minute's peace once we get to Atlanta."

"Are you kidding? They'll be so dazzled by Charlie, we'll be completely ignored." She blew him a kiss, then nestled more comfortably beneath the airline blanket and closed her eyes.

Dillon continued to watch her, his heart expanding with emotion when he recalled how close he had come to losing her a year and a half earlier. For months following the illness that had resulted in the loss of their child, Debra had been severely depressed. Her parents came to France and helped nurse her through her physical ordeal. The Newberrys stayed as long as they could, then entrusted her to Dillon, who felt ill-equipped to deal with her despondency.

She had no interest in resuming her previous activities, including the cooking class. She no longer kept the apartment tidy. When Dillon returned home from work in the evenings, he did the housework. Laundry piled up until he found time for it. Debra slept the days away. That seemed to be the only way she could deal with her grief.

Dillon grieved for their lost child by pushing himself to the limit at work. Physical exertion was his panacea. Exhaustion provided a temporary haven of forgetfulness. Debra had found no such relief from her misery. She even refused to discuss the issue with Dillon whenever he broached the subject, believing that talking about it might be cathartic. He consulted with her obstetrician and was advised to give her time.

"Madame Burke has suffered severe emotional distress. You must have patience with her."

Dillon was the epitome of patience with Debra. What he lacked was patience with the platitudes of so-called professionals. When weeks passed and he saw no improvement, he considered sending her home for a while. He thought that perhaps being with her large family might boost her spirits and restore her optimism.

However, he never could bring himself even to suggest it. It bothered him to see her staring listlessly into space, but it would have been worse not to see her at all. Having no other choice, he exercised the patience that the doctor recommended.

During that time, sex was Debra's only obsession. As soon as her body had healed, she urged him to make love with her, although the frantic coupling they engaged in wasn't what Dillon would call making love. The act wasn't prompted by passion or desire but desperation. Pleasure was neither's goal. He wanted to pierce through her self-imposed isolation. She wanted to get pregnant again as quickly as possible.

No time was given to foreplay. Every night they sweatily clutched each other, rocking their bed in a frenzy of mating. Afterward, Dillon felt empty and joyless, but he continued doing it because those few minutes were the only ones throughout the day when Debra showed signs of life.

At times when Dillon wanted to pull out his hair in frustration, he could comfort himself by saying, "At least I don't have Haskell Scanlan to contend with." Forrest G. Pilot had countermanded Dillon's dismissal of the accountant but had reassigned him to a position in the States. That was satisfactory to Dillon. He didn't care what Scanlan was doing or where he was, so long as he was out of his life. Scanlan's replacement was a much more amenable Frenchman who spoke flawless English.

Debra underwent a 180-degree reversal the day she confirmed that she was pregnant. When Dillon arrived home, she flew into his arms the moment he cleared the door. Such exuberance was so unexpected that he toppled over backward. She landed on top of him, laughing as she had before the disastrous trip to Zermatt.

"I'm pregnant, Dillon. I'm pregnant."

Before he had time to recover from his surprise, she was tearing open his shirt and ravenously kissing his chest and throat. They made love on the floor, and it was as before—with fervor tempered by love and caring.

"Jesus, it's good to have you back," he whispered fiercely as he held her hips between his hands and thrust himself into her.

As though an opaque curtain had been lifted, their life was sunny again. Life was good, but Dillon's nemesis— his pessimism—plagued him during Debra's pregnancy. What if tragedy struck again? Debra might suffer another bout of depression that neither would have the stamina to withstand. As she approached her second trimester, the period during which she had lost the first baby, Dillon's anxiety escalated to a frantic pitch. One evening he abruptly announced, "I'm sending you home to have the baby, and I don't want any arguments."

"I am home."

"You know what I mean. To Georgia. To your mama. She'll see that you take it easy like you're supposed to. Anyway, I want our baby to be born on American soil."

She looked at him shrewdly. "You finally got one, didn't you?"

"Got one what?"

"A mistress. According to our neighbor downstairs, all Frenchmen have at least one. She warned me that it was only a matter of time before you adopted that custom, especially since my figure is no longer svelte and seductive."

"You're seductive as hell," he snarled, laying his hands on the mound of her abdomen. He pushed up her top and kissed the taut skin. His lips worked their way up to her braless breasts. "You've adapted a few French customs yourself," he murmured as he flicked his tongue over one dark nipple.

"All my bras are too small now." She cupped her breasts and offered them to him. His mouth caressed her until their mingled sighs proved the neighbor downstairs wrong.

Later, as they lay with her back to his chest, his hand protectively resting on her belly, she asked sleepily, "When did you plan to pack me off to Mother?"

"Forget it," he sighed, kissing her ear. "You're not going anywhere."

It wasn't until he held his squirming, squalling newborn son in his arms that Dillon relaxed his vigilance over capricious fate. In his father's eyes, Charles Dillon Burke was a miracle. From the first moment Dillon saw him, he was besotted with his child and fatherhood in general.

His luck at work continued to hold. The insurance building had been completed to everyone's satisfaction. Forrest G. Pilot himself had come from Florida to inspect it personally. He had aged considerably, Dillon thought, and appeared to be under a strain, yet he commended Dillon on his fine work and demonstrated his appreciation in the form of a cash bonus.

"Take six weeks off with pay. That should give you plenty of time to make the move before reporting back to work."

Before going on to Tallahassee, they planned to spend at least two weeks with the Newberrys in Atlanta and let them get well acquainted with their newest grandson. Dillon was confident that Forrest G. had big plans for him. He had more than fulfilled the older man's expectations.

Resting his head on the hard seat cushion, Dillon closed his eyes contentedly. Over the roar of the jet engines he could hear Debra's steady breathing and the sweet, guttural baby sounds that Charlie made in his sleep.

"What the hell is all this about?" Dillon roared. "Where's Forrest G.? What are you doing behind that desk?"

Haskell Scanlan leaned back in the sumptuous leather desk chair and smugly regarded Dillon. "It's my privilege to inform you that Mr. Pilot no longer works here."

It took every ounce of Dillon's self-control not to hurdle the desk, grab Scanlan by his scrawny neck, and wring the life out of him. This was a hell of a shock to receive on his first day back.

When he noticed the unfamiliar sign in the parking lot, he had hoped that it meant only a new name and logo for the original company. But as soon as he entered what had formerly been Forrest G.'s executive office, he was met with an unpleasant surprise. Pilot Engineering Industries was under new ownership and management—and at its helm was Haskell Scanlan.

Dillon glared down at his old enemy. "What happened to Forrest G.?"

Scanlan's long fingers slid back and forth along the edge of his glossy desk. "Your mentor has retired."

Dillon scoffed. "He wouldn't vacate that chair without putting up a fight."

"There was some nastiness," Scanlan admitted with an insincere moue. "I'm surprised you didn't read about it in the newspapers."

"I've been busy getting my family settled. What happened?"

"With the assets that were available, the company you now work for decided it could do more than Mr. Pilot was doing."

"In other words, it was a hostile takeover. A conglomerate came in and muscled out Forrest G." Dillon's eyes narrowed on Scanlan. "I wonder who supplied their inside information."

Scanlan's grin was as obnoxious as fingernails on a chalkboard. "I did what I could to assist the new ownership."

"I'm sure you did," Dillon sneered. "I'm sure you kissed ass until your lips were raw."

Scanlan shot from his chair, his eyes batting furiously, his cheeks puffing out like those of an adder. Dillon leaned across the desk. "Go ahead, Scanlan, hit me. Please. Give me a good reason to beat the hell out of you."

Scanlan took a step back. "If you value your job, you'd better watch the way you address me, Mr. Burke. We haven't dismissed a single employee since we seized control, but it's inevitable. I wouldn't mind you being the first to go."

Dillon was tempted to tell Scanlan to go fuck himself and then storm out. But where would that leave him? He wasn't short of cash, thanks to the bonus Forrest G. had given him. However, he had incurred a lot of expenses during the move. There wouldn't be that many jobs available in Tallahassee, and he couldn't very well ask Debra and Charlie to move again after just getting settled.

They had decided not to buy a house until they were more familiar with the city. Instead, they had leased a house in a neat, respectable neighborhood. The yard was smaller than Dillon wanted and had only one tree. But Debra seemed pleased with it.

For the time being, it would be stupid to bite the hand that was feeding them. "What have you got for me?" he grumbled.

Scanlan pinched up the creases of his slacks as he sat back down. He reached for a folder, opened it, and ran his index finger down a column of figures. "Ah, there's a cubicle on the second floor that's available. Number 1120. You can move your supplies in there today and begin tomorrow."

"You're putting me back on a drawing board?" Dillon shouted. "What the hell are you trying to pull?"

"That's the only job I currently have available. Take it or leave it."

Dillon muttered a string of French obscenities.

"It goes without saying," Scanlan added, "that the job of draftsman doesn't pay as much as field work, so your salary will be scaled down until it's commensurate with the position."

"You must really be enjoying this," Dillon said.

Scanlan smiled pleasantly. "Enormously."

"I can't go back to drawing. There's got to be something else."

Scanlan assessed him for a moment, then swiveled his chair around and pulled a folder from the built-in filing cabinet behind him. "Actually, I just remembered something. We recently acquired a property in Mississippi that needs massive renovation before it can be utilized productively and profitably. Are you interested?"

Dillon summed up his explanation to Debra. "So it's either take the job in Mississippi or start drafting again."

He socked his fist against his opposite palm. "I don't know why I didn't bust the little bastard and walk out."

"Yes, you do. You're not a street fighter any longer. You're a family man, a professional, who isn't going to let slimy characters like Scanlan defeat you."

"Well, right now this slimy character is holding the aces, and he damn well knows it. After I left him, I tried to set up job interviews. I must have made two dozen phone calls. The answer was always the same. Nobody has any work. Nobody is hiring."

"Short of separating Scanlan's body from his head, what do you want to do?"

"I don't know, Debra." He dropped onto the sofa and tiredly rubbed his eyes. "I sure as hell don't want to go back to drafting."

"Then you'll take the other job, and we'll move to Mississippi."

Dillon plucked Charlie off Debra's lap and settled him in the crook of his elbow. The baby tightly clutched his father's index finger. "I've got an alternative. It's not great, but keep in mind that it's only temporary."

After he had laid out his alternate plan, she asked, "Where would you live?"

"In the trailer at the site. I could make do with a cot, a small refrigerator, and a hotplate."

"What about a bathroom?"

"I'll use the Port-o-lets. And the building I'll be working on has a shower room. Scanlan gave me the plans to study before I make my decision."

Her expression relayed her lack of enthusiasm. "You'd come home every weekend?"

"Without fail. I swear."

"I don't see why we can't all move to Mississippi."

"Because Scanlan would likely pull me off the job the minute we got settled. He could keep us hopscotching indefinitely."

"But this is indefinite, too," she said plaintively. "He could keep you there forever."

Dillon stubbornly shook his head. "I won't have the emotional attachment to this job the way I did to the building in Versailles. I'll leave it flat the minute I hear of anything opening up. I've left applications all over town. Something's bound to come through before too long.

"Scanlan has never forgiven me for pulling rank on him in France. He got his revenge on Forrest G., and now he's given me a choice between a shit detail and moving back into one of those damned glass boxes. He expects me to take that because it's easier. I don't want to give the bastard the satisfaction."

Keeping Charlie cradled in one arm, he drew his wife close and kissed her temple. "Trust me, Debra. This is the best way. The weeks will speed by so fast, you won't even have time to miss me."

Unfortunately, the commuting arrangement wasn't as temporary or as easy as Dillon had hoped. His accommodations in Mississippi were squalid, but he didn't tell Debra that because she was doing her best to keep a positive attitude.

There was no end in sight. An exceptionally rainy fall had caused construction sites all over the South to stand deserted. There were heavy layoffs. No one wanted to hire a construction engineer, no matter how bright, ambitious, or doggedly determined.

Dillon had bought a new car while they were in

Atlanta. He left that with Debra and traveled the long trip to and from Mississippi on a used motorcycle. He arrived home late each Friday night and had to leave early on Sunday afternoons. That barely gave him time to rest up from his exhausting weekend before Monday morning came around.

The work itself was uninspiring. Most of it involved interior refurbishing. He replaced collapsing walls, rebuilt falling ceilings, resurfaced floors. The building was old and ugly and when he was finished it would still be old and ugly. Nevertheless, he operated under the same rigid standards as he would have had the building been new. He ran a tight ship and insisted that the workers give 100 percent to the job. It was a matter of pride. Besides, he wasn't going to give Scanlan an inch of advantage over him. He might demote or dismiss him out of pique, but never for doing substandard work.

The situation put a strain on Dillon's family. Because they crowded so much togetherness into their weekends, they had to work at it, and that took away some of the enjoyment. Household chores that Debra couldn't do fell to Dillon. Ordinarily he wouldn't have minded doing them, but he spent precious hours every Saturday morning doing menial tasks when all he wanted to do was sleep, make love to his wife, and marvel over the rapid development of his son.

Although they were surrounded by young families like themselves, they had no social life. That began to tell on Debra. She spent all week, every week, alone with a baby less than a year old. She doted on Charlie and was an excellent mother, but she had no outlet for self-expression and seemed disinclined to get involved in any neighborhood activities. Dillon began to notice signs of increasing depression, and it frightened him.

One Sunday evening as he was preparing to leave for the long trip to Mississippi, he drew her into his arms. "I'll take next Friday off and come home a day early. Do you think you could stand that?"

Her smile was tremulous but brilliant. "Oh, Dillon, would you? That would be wonderful."

"I didn't get to all the chores on your list this weekend. I'll have plenty of time to do everything next week and still be lazy. Get a babysitter for Saturday night. We'll dress up and go out. Dinner. Dancing. A movie. Whatever you want."

"I love you," she said, burying her nose in the collar of his shirt. They held each other and kissed some more, until he either had to make love to her again or leave. Regrettably, he picked up his crash helmet. Debra followed him to the door, carrying Charlie, who, out of practice, had learned to wave bye-bye.

Dillon didn't dare formally request the day off from Scanlan, so he bribed one of the subcontractors to oversee things while he was away. It only cost him a case of beer.

On Thursday afternoon, he called Debra. "This isn't to say you're not coming, is it?" she asked anxiously.

"Oh, ye of little faith. Of course I'm coming." He lowered his voice and added in a Groucho Marx accent, "I plan on coming a lot this weekend." She giggled. "What are you doing?"

"Putting together a few surprises for you."

"Hmm. I can't wait. Is that my son I hear in the background?"

"He's squealing because he knows I'm talking to you."

"Tell him I'll be there in a few hours."

"Be careful, Dillon. The weather here is terrible."

"I'll be there before you know it."

The inclement weather couldn't have stopped him from making the trip, but it certainly slowed him down. The Florida panhandle was experiencing the coldest weather on record. Rainfall was heavy. Sometimes pellets of sleet would strike the visor of his helmet. Inside his leather gloves, his fingers froze in their grip around the handlebars. When he finally arrived, Tallahassee had never looked so good.

The moment he opened the front door of his house, he was greeted with tantalizing aromas wafting from the kitchen. In the center of the dining table were a vase of fresh flowers and a chocolate cake with his name spelled out in the icing. A pot roast was simmering in the oven.

"Debra?" He dropped his helmet and gloves in a chair and moved toward the back of the house, where the bedrooms were. "Are you in the tub?" He checked Charlie's room, but the crib was empty. "What are you two up to? Is this part of the surprise?"

Dillon opened the door to the master bedroom and paused to gaze at his wife and son as they slumbered peacefully on the bed. Charlie was tucked into the curve of Debra's arm. Her golden hair looked beautiful spread out across the pillow. Dillon's heart ached with love. She had worn herself out to make this a special weekend for him. He moved toward the bed, sat down on the edge, and stroked her flawless cheek.

That's when he realized they weren't sleeping.

Haskell Scanlan often worked late in his pursuit of success, but on one particular evening he stayed even later than usual. It was after dark before he left the building. His car was the only one remaining in the parking lot.

A tall, shadowed figure appeared and blocked his path. Even before Scanlan could exclaim his astonishment, a fist with the impetus of a pile driver slammed into his mouth, breaking off all his front teeth at the gum line and snapping his head back with such impact that he was in traction for two months. Before he slumped to the ground, he was caught by the collar and struck again. The second blow fractured his jaw. A final blow was delivered to his midsection; it ruptured his spleen.

He had been in the hospital for a week, wavering in semiconsciousness, before he could communicate to the police whom he suspected of the brutal and seemingly unprovoked attack.

The police squad car rolled to a stop at the address he'd given them. No one answered the doorbell. The two officers questioned the next-door neighbor.

"After the funerals," she told them, "he only stuck around for a few days."

"Funerals?"

"His wife and son died three weeks ago of suffocation. Remember when we had that freak ice storm? Before Mrs. Burke lay down to take a nap, she turned on the furnace for the first time of the season. It wasn't ventilating properly, so they died in their sleep. Mr. Burke found them when he got home."

"You don't know where he is?"

"I haven't seen him for more than a week. I assumed he went back to work."

The officers got a search warrant and went into the house. As far as they could tell, nothing had been disturbed since the day of the fatal accident. There was a bouquet of dead flowers standing in a vase of smelly, stagnant water on the dining table. Beside it was the remains of a chocolate cake that ants had gotten to.

No one at the construction site in Mississippi had seen Mr. Burke since the Thursday night he left for home. His co-workers expressed sorrow over the deaths of his family. "He was crazy about that kid," one said. "Talked about him all the time."

"How'd he feel about his wife?"

"Her picture's still here in the trailer where he left it. He didn't screw around on her, if that's what you're asking."

Assault charges were never filed for the attack on Haskell Scanlan. The only viable suspect had vanished. It seemed as though he had simply walked away from everything.

Chapter 16

———◆◆◆———

Palmetto, South Carolina, 1987

A freaking faggot! Can you believe it?" Neal Patchett shook his head in disbelief and took another sip of his bourbon and water.

Hutch Jolly was as shocked as Neal by the news about Lamar. Hutch just wasn't as outspoken. "I hadn't been around Lamar very much for the last few years," he remarked. "Not near as much as you."

"What the hell's that supposed to mean?" Neal asked defensively.

"Hell. It's not supposed to mean a damn thing except that I hadn't been around him much. Did you notice any changes in him over the years?"

"No, and that can only mean one thing."

"What's that?"

"He was queer all along," Neal said. "All those years he stuck to us like glue, he was a fairy. It gives me the willies to think about it. I lived with the guy! Jesus!"

Until now Donna Dee had refrained from entering the conversation. "The way y'all are bad-mouthing somebody who just died is pitiful. I don't care if Lamar was gay, he was still a human being. He was our friend. I feel sorry for him."

Neal snickered. "You ought to have a talk with your old lady, Hutch. Set her straight on a few things. Feeling sorry for queers the way she does, maybe she should have moved out to San Francisco like Lamar did.

"You know," he continued, "that should have been my first clue. First he moves out of the house we shared, then he got all fired up about going to California as soon as we graduated. Who in their right mind would want to live among all those freaks unless you were one of them? I should have known then he was a faggot."

Donna Dee opened her mouth to speak, but Hutch shot her a warning glance and asked, "Is there any of that clam dip left, honey?"

Resentfully she flounced from the room and went into the kitchen. She was frequently short-tempered. Lately she'd been on a tear about moving to a larger house. They had bought this one after returning from Hutch's stint in Hawaii. It wasn't much better than the one they'd had on base, but it was all they could afford.

Besides, Donna Dee only used the house—among a number of other things—as an excuse for her bad moods. Hutch ignored the racket of clattering dishes and banging cabinet doors coming from the kitchen and freshened his guest's drink.

Neal was still on the subject of Lamar Griffith's recent demise. "You know that disease he died of—what's it called?"

"AIDS," Donna Dee said as she rejoined them, bearing a tray of dip and chips.

"My daddy says that only queers can get it. It comes from fucking each other in the ass. How's that for a way to go?"

Hutch dug into the dip. Most of his football muscle had turned to flab and collected around his middle, but he continued to feed his athlete's appetite. "The paper said he died of pneumonia," he mumbled around a mouthful.

"That's what Myrajane wants everybody to believe," Neal said. "She didn't even have Lamar buried here in the Cowan plot she's so damned proud of. He was cremated out in California. The pile of ashes probably wasn't this high," he said, indicating a space of about two inches with his hands. "I heard he didn't weigh a hundred pounds at the end."

He laughed. "Christ, can you imagine what the funeral was like? It must have been a sideshow—a bunch of fairies sitting around sniveling. "Oh, dear me, I don't know what I'll do without my precious Lamar,'" Neal said in a singsong falsetto.

Donna Dee shot to her feet. "You are, and always have been, a prick, Neal Patchett. Excuse me." She left the room again. Seconds later, they heard the bedroom door slam.

Neal rolled his tongue in one cheek. "Your old lady's a barrel of laughs, Hutch."

Hutch glanced in the direction of Donna Dee's angry exit. "I've been having to work some overtime, and she doesn't enjoy being alone at night."

The only job Hutch could find when he mustered out of the navy was at the soybean plant. Donna Dee resented his working for the Patchetts, although he didn't want to tell Neal that. Going back to college had never been considered. Even if he had the money, he lacked the initiative.

Donna Dee was working as a receptionist in a gynecologist's office. One of the benefits was that she got free treatment and advice. They'd been married almost ten years, yet she had still failed to conceive. She fought her barrenness with a fanaticism that bewildered Hutch.

Over the years he had tried to reason with her about it. "You don't understand!" she would scream at him. "If we don't have a baby, then there's no reason for us to be together." He failed to see the logic in that, but didn't pursue the argument because it always resulted in a fight that left him feeling rotten. He figured it was a female hormonal thing that men weren't equipped to understand. His own mother had suffered from the same malady because she had wanted more kids.

At least once a week, Donna Dee came home from work with an article about a new reproductive technique for infertile couples. Invariably, the revolutionary method of fertilization would involve him in some demeaning and embarrassing way.

Either they would screw until his balls ached, or he'd have to jack off in a plastic bag, or she would walk around with a thermometer in her mouth, and when the time was right, she would say, "Now," and he'd have to perform whether it was the middle of the night or during Sunday lunch. Once she had even caught him while he was taking a crap and had knocked on the bathroom door, saying, "Don't bother pulling your pants back on. It's time." He thought her tactics hardly romantic.

Hutch supposed he shouldn't be judgmental of her

obsession. He wasn't the one who was malfunctioning. His sperm count was fine. Every doctor they had consulted had said the same thing: Donna Dee couldn't make a baby. But Donna Dee was damned and determined to make one. It was as though she had to prove to the world, to him, and to herself that she could. What he feared was that her baby mania had something to do with the Jade Sperry incident. He didn't want to know for certain that guilt was Donna Dee's propellant, so he had never suggested it.

Neal drained his glass of bourbon and set it on the edge of the coffee table. "You married too early, Hutch. Didn't I tell you so? But you wouldn't listen. Now you're stuck at home with a wife who's got a burr up her ass, and I'm still out catting around." He smacked his lips with satisfaction. "A different pussy every night." Leaning forward, he lowered his voice. "Come along with me tonight. We'll raise some hell, just like old times. I can't think of a more befitting send-off for our pal Lamar."

"No, thanks. I promised Donna Dee we'd go to the picture show."

"Too bad." With a sigh, Neal got up and sauntered to the door. Hutch ambled after him. "By the way," Neal said, "my old man told me to ask after your mama. How's she doing?"

"As well as can be expected. She finally sold the house and got her a smaller place. She does a lot of work at the church, filling time, you know, since she doesn't have Daddy to take care of."

A year earlier, Sheriff Fritz Jolly had been investigating a burned-out building when a beam collapsed. The fall had broken his hip. He was hospitalized for months.

Even after returning home, he never regained his original strength and developed one complication after another until he died of an infection.

"Tell her my daddy said that if she needs anything to holler."

"Thanks, Neal. I'll give her the message. She'll appreciate it."

"Looking after her is the least he can do. Your daddy did a lot of favors for mine. You know . . ." He reached out and tapped the pocket of Hutch's shirt. "It never hurts to have an open-minded man in the sheriff's department. How well do you like working in the factory?"

"It stinks like shit."

Neal chuckled and lightly socked Hutch on the shoulder. "Let me see what I can do."

Hutch grabbed Neal's sleeve as he tried to leave. "What do you mean?"

Neal removed Hutch's hand. "Better go see to your old lady. Apologize for your prick of a friend. I've never run across a woman yet who didn't cream over an apology."

Hutch shook his large, rusty head like an irritated dog. "Tell me what you meant about my job at the plant."

Neal frowned as though he were reluctant to impart a secret. Lowering his voice, he said, "It's time somebody did some creative thinking for you, Hutch. The sheriff who took office after your daddy died is so tight-assed, he squeaks when he walks. My daddy thinks the department needs some new blood. Now do you see what I'm getting at?"

"Me?" Hutch said, lowering his voice to match Neal's conspiratorial tone.

Neal smiled broadly. "Think how tickled your grieving mama would be if you followed in your daddy's footsteps."

"I applied for a deputy's position when I left the navy. They weren't hiring."

Neal placed his hands on his hips and shook his head as though annoyed with a dim-witted child. "Your problem is that you've got no faith, Hutch. Have the Patchetts ever failed to do something we wanted to do? A word here, a word there—we can make things happen."

"Having a better job would sure make things here at home a lot easier." Hutch glanced toward the back of the house, where Donna Dee was sulking. "I'd do just about anything to get into the sheriff's department."

Neal gave him a sly smile and slapped him lightly on the cheek. "That's what we're counting on, Hutch. That's what we're counting on."

Ivan was relaxing in his den with a glass of Jack Daniels when Neal got home. He strolled in and headed straight for the liquor cabinet. Maintaining the suspense, he fixed himself a drink.

Ivan, having enough of it, tossed aside his newspaper and asked, "Well, did he go for it?"

"Daddy, he swallowed the bait like a starving catfish."

Ivan's palm struck the armrest of the leather sofa. "Damn! That's good news. I can't wait to personally boot out the bastard that's in there now. We'll have to take it slow, of course. Hutch'll start out as a deputy and work his way up. Let's say a year, eighteen months at most, and we ought to be sitting pretty as far as local law enforcement goes."

Neal saluted his father with his glass. "You might be old, but you've still got a few tricks up your sleeve."

"Old, hell," Ivan bellowed. "I can still outmaneuver, outdrink, and outfornicate men twenty years younger than me."

"Maybe *some* men twenty years younger than you," Neal smirked.

Ivan glared at him. "Listen to me, boy. As far as the drinking and whoring go, you seem to be doing all right. But don't forget the maneuvering. You don't spend enough time working. You've got to put work before whiskey and women, or you're sunk before you even venture into the water."

"I work," Neal said sullenly. "I went to the plant three days this week."

"And spent the other four wearing out the tread on the tires of that new car I bought you."

"What good does it do me to put in an appearance at the factory? You're still the boss. And you shoot down every idea I come up with."

Looking disgruntled, Ivan thrust out his empty glass. "Get me another whiskey." Neal did as he was told, but he didn't do it graciously.

Ivan sipped his fresh drink. "For the time being, I see no need to spend money on improving or expanding the business. But I have been giving our future a lot of thought lately and have decided it's time you got married."

Neal was caught raising his highball glass to his mouth. He froze, leveling his eyes on his father. "You decided *what*?"

"It's time you got married."

"Go screw yourself."

"I won't have that sass from you," Ivan thundered, pounding the armrest with his fist. "Right now all you're fit for is driving fast, drinking hard, and running with loose women." Ivan aimed his blunt index finger at his son. "If you want to be respected and feared, the first step is to get married."

"What makes you think I want a whining wife hanging around my neck? That kind of life is for dumb sons of bitches like Hutch. I like my life the way it is."

"Then I guess you're not bothered by the gossip about Lamar and you."

Neal's reaction was prickly and swift. "What gossip?"

Now that he was assured of Neal's attention, Ivan leaned back against the sofa cushions in a more relaxed posture. "Y'all ran around together ever since you were kids. Folks are going to find it hard to believe that you didn't know he was queer." Ivan peered at his son from beneath his brows. "I'm kinda wondering about that myself."

"Get on with it, old man," Neal said in a dangerous tone.

"Y'all did live together, alone. Now that Lamar's perversion has become public knowledge, it's just a matter of time before folks start speculating about you."

Neal's anger was evident only through his eyes, which had narrowed to slits. "Anybody who would think me queer has to be crazy. There are at least a hundred women within the city limits of this town alone who know damn good and well I'm straight. You're just blowing smoke so I'll bend to your will."

Ivan's voice remained calm. "You told me yourself that Lamar had women while y'all were at college. Folks might assume your philandering is just a cover-up, too." He took a sip of his drink, but his calculating eyes never strayed from Neal.

"That boy of Myrajane's was more fucked up than Hogan's goat. I don't want folks to say the same about my boy." He nodded sagely. "A wife would nip the gossip in the bud. It'd be even better if a baby came along nine months after the wedding." Drawing a deep, contented breath, he gazed around the room. "I'm gonna hate like hell to die, boy. I don't want to give up a single thing that belongs to me." His shrewd eyes swung back to his son. "I could go a lot more gracefully if I knew that I was leaving behind a dynasty."

He turned the full force of his malevolence onto his son. "The only thing that's standing between me and a guarantee of immortality is you. The very least you can do is go to work on making a son and heir."

"God knows I've had plenty of experience."

Ivan took Neal's droll comment as concession. He picked up the society section of *The Post and Courier* from Charleston, which he'd been reading when Neal came in. He thrust it at Neal. The first page was covered with photos of young ladies in frilly white dresses.

"This season's crop of debutantes," Ivan said tersely. "Choose one."

Marla Sue Pickens was perfect: blond, blue-eyed, and Baptist. Her mother's pedigree was impeccable. Her daddy and his business partner had stockpiled a fortune by making pipe from scrap metal. Ivan liked the blend of gentility and crass commercialism in her background.

Marla Sue was the third child and only daughter. Her elder brother was heir apparent to the metal-pipe business. The other brother was a physician, practicing in Charleston.

As for Marla Sue herself, she was an even-tempered young woman who took for granted her family's affluence and her natural prettiness. She was currently enrolled in Bryn Mawr, but she had no ambitions beyond making a good marriage, being a gracious hostess, and breeding another generation of South Carolinians as flawless as herself.

This blueprint for her future was derived not so much from vanity as naïveté, because, for all her pseudo-sophistication, Marla Sue wasn't very bright. Ivan regarded this, too, as an asset. He heartily approved Neal's choice, which had been based solely upon physical appearance. Marla Sue unwittingly cooperated by falling in love with Neal the night they met.

A socially prominent acquaintance in Charleston owed Ivan a favor. "I'll consider the debt canceled if you can finagle an invitation for me and my boy to one of those debutante shindigs."

For the first half of the evening the Patchetts observed from the sidelines. Marla Sue wasn't difficult to pick out. She shone like the strand of diamonds around her slender, aristocratic neck. Feeling high on champagne and optimism, Ivan clapped Neal on the back as they watched Marla Sue waltz past with her current partner. "Well, boy, what do you think?"

Neal gave the girl the heavy-lidded once-over that had melted scruples previously frozen solid. "She's got zero tits."

"Hell, boy! As soon as she says, 'I do,' you can buy her a set of big ones."

Neal asked Marla Sue to dance and exercised the charm he was famous for. She fell for every calculated syllable of flattery. She simpered and blushed and believed him whole-heartedly when he humbly said, "I'd love to call you sometime, but I know you're probably too busy to talk to a hick from Palmetto like me."

"Oh, no, I'm not!" she declared with breathless sincerity. Then, lowering her eyes and softening her voice until it was scarcely audible, she added, "I mean, if you want to, I'd love to hear from you sometime, Neal."

"I'm too old for you."

"Oh, I don't think so. Not at all. Ten years is nothing."

The next day she received two dozen white roses, followed up by a telephone call. They made a date for lunch. After the lunch date, he didn't call her for a week. "All a part of the program," he reassured Ivan, who was impatient over the calculated delay.

Neal's strategy proved effective. Marla Sue was tearfully glad finally to hear from him and invited him to have Sunday dinner in Charleston with her family. Neal was on his best behavior, responding deferentially to her father's questions. He flattered Marla Sue's mother and sisters-in-law until they were putty in his hands.

It was all he could do to keep a straight face. His old man was right—there was nothing quite as satisfying as manipulating people. Except possibly sex, and he was getting none of that from Marla Sue.

Ivan had ordered him not to lay an improper hand on her. "That girl's got her cherry sure as hell. You leave it alone until the wedding night."

"Do you think I'm dense?" Neal asked resentfully. "She believes I respect her too much to bed her before we're married. It makes her giddy to think she exercises that kind of control over me."

To relieve the tension the courtship was placing on his sex life, he turned to a woman in Palmetto who had an insatiable sexual appetite and a husband whose job required him to travel.

Neal saw Marla Sue as much as her schooling allowed. His long-distance telephone bill was atrocious, and he spent a fortune on flowers. The investments paid off, however. He was invited to spend a whole weekend in Charleston with her. Armed with a three-carat diamond and an unassuming demeanor, he asked her to honor him by becoming his wife. As expected, she said yes immediately.

The wedding was predicted to be the social event of the year. One thing Neal couldn't manipulate was the mother of the bride, who wanted to do everything according to Emily Post. By the time the wedding weekend arrived, he was ready to be done with the whole affair and get on with his life.

He and Ivan moved to a Charleston hotel for the duration of the nuptial festivities, which commenced on Friday at a luncheon given in honor of the bride and groom at the home of the bride's maternal grandparents.

"Just think," Marla Sue whispered in his ear, "tomorrow night it'll just be us. Alone."

Neal groaned and embraced her. "Don't talk about it, darling, or I'll get a hard-on right here in your grandma's parlor." Despite her conservative upbringing, she loved it when he talked that way.

He pulled her into his arms and hugged her close. It was then that he caught sight of the other young woman standing across the room. She was giving him a cool, bold look that he instantly recognized as an invitation. As he watched, she dipped her finger into her wine cooler, then poked it into her mouth and drew it out slowly. He got hard.

"Neal!" Marla Sue softly squealed, blushing prettily. "Behave yourself."

"Then stop tempting me," he said, letting her believe she was responsible for his erection.

A few minutes later, the other young woman approached them. "When do I get to meet the groom, Marla Sue?"

"Oh, Neal, this is my lifelong friend. She's my maid of honor."

He didn't quite catch her name—which was insignificant, anyway. He had caught the suggestive message in her eyes. "So pleased to meet you at last," she drawled. They shook hands. As their hands slid apart, the pad of her middle finger caressed his palm.

At dusk that Friday evening, everyone in the wedding party convened for a rehearsal in the sanctuary of the big Baptist church, where baskets of flowers and candelabras were already being arranged by a harried decorator. Each time Neal's eyes wandered toward the maid of honor, he was further convinced that the title was a misnomer. If she was a maiden, he could fly; and the looks she was transmitting sure as hell weren't honorable. Her daddy, he had learned, was Mr. Pickens's business partner. He had to admire a girl with the gall to flirt so openly and still be clever enough not to get caught.

From the church, a caravan of cars traveled a few blocks to the restaurant where Ivan was hosting the rehearsal dinner. He had spared no expense. It was a lavish affair. He rose to the occasion, deporting himself as the perfect host. With a glass of champagne held aloft, he got misty-eyed when he said, "If only Neal's mama could be here tonight to celebrate this happy occasion, it would be perfect. Son, I hope you and your precious bride, Marla Sue, will be a fraction as happy together as me and Rebecca were."

While Neal decorously sipped from his wine goblet in acknowledgment of the sentimental toast, the maid of honor was fondling his balls beneath the napkin in his lap.

When the dinner formally concluded, everybody got down to having a good time. Among the guests was the newly elected sheriff of Palmetto County, Hutch Jolly, who was Neal's best man. He and his wife danced to the music of the three-piece ensemble.

Marla Sue opened wedding gifts, squealing with delight as one treasure after another was unwrapped. The maid of honor made a point of brushing past Neal as she left the room. "Excuse me," she breathed seductively.

Neal waited about sixty seconds before bending toward his bride and excusing himself. "I've got something to do."

"What?"

He cupped her face between his hands. "Brides shouldn't ask nosy questions unless they want wedding surprises to be spoiled."

Her blue eyes twinkled. "I love you so much."

"I love you, too."

He gave her a soft kiss before wending his way through the crowd. He had almost made it to the door when he was waylaid by Hutch and Donna Dee. "She seems to be a nice girl," Donna Dee said. "Far better than you deserve."

"You know, Donna Dee, with that two-edged tongue

of yours," Neal said, "it's a wonder you haven't sliced Hutch's cock to ribbons."

"Eat shit and die, Neal."

Hutch tried to be the peacemaker. "Looks like you're really marrying into a fine family, Neal. Her folks seem crazy about you."

Somewhere in the building, a young woman with the hots for him was waiting. The danger of getting caught added spice. The intrigue was irresistible. He was in a fit of impatience to join her. "Y'all make yourselves at home, hear? Daddy spent a mint on this party. Drink up."

Before they could detain him, he stepped through the door. The private dining room where the party was being held was adjacent to a foyer. To the right was a short hallway. Neal almost went past it before the door to the powder room opened. The maid of honor smiled at him invitingly.

"What took you so long? I was beginning to think you weren't coming."

He slipped into the powder room and locked the door behind him. The dim room was reminiscent of an expensive bordello, full of floral chintz and gilt-framed mirrors. He barely had time to take in the room's appointments before the bridesmaid embraced him. Their open mouths ground together in a rapacious kiss.

"You're crazy," he mumbled as he devoured her neck. "You must really hate Marla Sue."

"I adore Marla Sue." She squirmed against him, tearing at the buttons on his shirt and caressing his smooth chest with sharp fingernails and a wet, wicked tongue. "This is a hobby of mine, that's all. Some girls collect music boxes or antique bottles. I collect grooms."

When he hiked up her skirt and gripped her derriere, he discovered that she was wearing a garter belt and stockings but no panties. He pulled her high and hard against his straining fly.

Since his hands were occupied, she opened the bodice of her silk dress and shimmied her braless breasts against his starched shirt. The abrasion made her nipples hard. Neal ducked his head to take one into his mouth. She unbuttoned his fly and worked down his underwear until his stiff organ was fully exposed.

"Mmm," she moaned as she stroked it.

"You want it, baby?" he grunted. "You got it."

He placed his hands on her shoulders and pushed her to her knees in front of him. She was game, promptly taking him into her mouth. He plowed his fingers through her hair and thrust his hips forward. Throwing his head back, he rolled it from side to side against the door, becoming lost in the sensations of her mouth.

She managed to wrest her head out of his grip. "Sorry. No way am I going to get the short shrift." She backed up to an upholstered chaise and lay down, raising her knees. Neal stumbled forward and fell on her. He buried his face between her breasts, kneaded them roughly, and slammed his body into hers. The harder he pumped, the better she seemed to like it. They came together explosively. He bit one of her breasts to keep from crying out.

For several moments afterward, they lay panting against each other. When Neal finally pulled away from her, she sat up, shoved her hair out of her eyes, and investigated the teeth marks on her breast. "You son of a bitch."

Chuckling, he restored his clothing, moved to the sink and washed his hands, then smoothed back his hair. At the door, he looked back at her. She was still sprawled on the chaise in disarray. "You'd better wash before going back to the party," he said, nodding toward her pelvic region. "You reek to high heaven of come."

When he unlocked the door and opened it, he was met with an unpleasant shock. Ivan was standing on the threshold, his expression murderous.

"You stupid little cocksucker!" Ivan thundered.

Ever since they'd left the rehearsal dinner, Ivan had been berating Neal for his indiscretion. It had been a wild and crazy thing to do, but it had also been a hell of a lot of fun. He was a groom, but he wasn't dead. No red-blooded man under the age of ninety-five could have resisted such freely given snatch.

No one other than Ivan had discovered them. Nobody else had even missed him. Neal had returned to the party and taken his bride in his arms and kissed her while her friends and family smiled indulgently. The maid of honor wasn't going to tell. What harm had been done? His old man's anger was unwarranted, and the temper tantrum was beginning to grate on Neal's nerves.

"Actually, Daddy, she was the cocksucker," he said blandly.

Ivan let go of the car's steering wheel and backhanded him across the mouth. The blow caught Neal completely off guard. "What the hell!" he shouted. "Don't ever do that again."

"Don't *you* ever do anything that stupid again. Banging the bridesmaid while the bride and her family are in the next room," he muttered. "What the hell were you thinking of? You could have blown this whole thing wide open by pulling that damn fool stunt."

"But I didn't," Neal shouted. "So just shut up about it."

"I've hired three whores for your bachelor party. You couldn't have waited an hour longer for one of them?"

"I intend for you to get your money's worth, but I'll bet nothing your hired whores do is as exciting as fucking your bride's maid of honor the night before the wedding."

Ivan looked like he might strike him again. Instead, he gripped the steering wheel and pressed down hard on the accelerator. They were headed to the hotel where Neal's groomsmen had been invited to meet them and celebrate his last night as a single man.

"I didn't decide for you to get married on a whim, you know," Ivan growled. "If all I wanted was a breeder for grandkids, we could have found you a decent enough girl in Palmetto. We picked this girl 'cause her daddy's pockets are lined with hundred-dollar bills. She's due to come into a lot of money when she turns twenty-five, and most of it will come your way. But if you go screwing her friends in bathrooms, do you think she'll entrust you with a nickel?"

"Wait a minute, wait a minute," Neal said heatedly. "You don't expect me to change my lifestyle just because I get married, do you? If you do, you've got another think coming."

Ivan cut his eyes toward his son, though he didn't decrease his speed. "I don't care if you diddle every belle from Charleston to Miami and back again. Just exercise some good sense. Treat your wife like a piece of bone china you only use on special occasions. Bring her little presents now and then. Give her babies to keep her occupied. Then you can screw whoever you want to, and she won't raise a stink about it. But for God's sake don't flaunt your infidelities in her face."

Neal resented the lecture. If he knew about anything, he knew about women. "Listen, old man, I know how to treat a woman, okay?"

"You don't know near as much as you think you do."

"I don't need you telling me—*Daddy!*"

But Ivan didn't have a chance. He never saw the freight train.

Chapter 17

———◆———

Los Angeles, 1991

Graham? It's me."

"Hi, Mom! Have you seen any movie stars yet?"

Jade, sitting with her feet tucked beneath her, grinned into the telephone receiver. She could envision Graham's fourteen-year-old face. A shock of wavy, dark hair would be dipping over his brows. Beneath them, his blue eyes would be sparkling.

"None so far, but I bought you a souvenir today." She glanced at the Los Angeles Rams sweatshirt she had purchased earlier.

"What is it?"

"You'll have to wait and see."

"Is it cool? Will I like it?"

"It's supercool and you'll love it."

She inquired about things at home. He assured her that there had been no glitches in their well-oiled schedule. Cathy Hearon was a born organizer.

"Is it still raining in New York?"

"Yeah," Graham said dismally. "Cats and dogs."

"Too bad. It's gorgeous and sunny here."

"Have you gone swimming?"

"I've been too busy."

"Mom? Do we have to move to that place in South Carolina?"

Jade's smile evaporated. Her son's lack of enthusiasm for relocating bothered her tremendously. "You know the answer to that, Graham. Why do you keep asking me?"

"I won't know anybody," he mumbled dejectedly. "I'll have to leave all my friends."

The closer they came to making the move from New York, the more frequently they had this conversation. Graham knew that the project was important to her from a career standpoint. He didn't know its personal implications—no one did.

He had taken their previous moves in stride. Now that he was a teenager, friendships had become more meaningful. He was resistant to the idea of leaving them.

"You'll make new friends, Graham."

"There's nothing to do there."

"That's not true. Palmetto's near the ocean. You'll be able to go to the beach whenever you want. We'll go fishing and crabbing."

"I don't even like crab."

She let that pass. "Palmetto schools have soccer teams now—I've already checked. You'll be able to continue playing."

"But it won't be the same."

"No. It won't be the same. It's very different from the city."

"It's hicksville."

Dead end. There was no argument to that. Compared to the Big Apple, Palmetto was definitely hicksville. After an ensuing silence, Jade said with excitement, "Tomorrow I'm interviewing the contractor I came all this way to see. Wish me luck."

"Good luck. I hope you can hire him. And, Mom, be careful. There are some real weirdos in California."

"And none in New York?"

"At least here you can easily spot them."

"I'm always careful," she promised. "I hope I can conclude my business in a couple more days and come home. We'll go out together and do something special. Deal?"

"Deal."

She was consumed by homesickness for him as she hung up the phone. There were days when he was ornery, but generally he was an ideal son. As he grew older, he assumed a proprietary and protective air toward her, which Jade found both amusing and touching.

He was already taller than she. That had taken some getting used to. He was strong, athletic, and boundlessly energetic. Jade took secret pride in his physical attractiveness, but whenever someone remarked on it, she stressed her pride in his intelligence and character. He had a keen sense of humor and a sensitivity that she found personally gratifying.

She didn't lightly dismiss his reluctance to leave his friends and school and move to another state—another world. The move for him was still months away, as he wouldn't leave school until the current semester was over. She hoped that when the time came, he would be psychologically prepared for it, although he had already had more than a year to get accustomed to the idea.

Jade vividly recalled that winter day last year when the project in Palmetto had been approved. Her presentation before GSS's board of directors had been flawless. The topic had been so thoroughly researched that she had stockpiled an arsenal of statistics to support her arguments. The incisive questions put to her by the board members had been answered articulately and with enough elaboration to gain their trust without sounding ingratiating. She hadn't given them the hard sell, but had let the facts and figures speak for themselves.

George Stein, the CEO, was the last surviving founder of GSS. Although he was nearly eighty, he was still at the helm of the conglomerate that had been founded when Charlie Chaplin was the number one box-office star. It had started with one steel mill and had, through the decades, continued to expand. Now GSS provided an umbrella for companies all over the world, encompassing myriad enterprises, both commercial and technical.

It was common for GSS to buy struggling companies and either dissolve them or reorganize their operations to make them profitable. Initially Jade had been hired to analyze three textile plants that GSS had acquired. Her extensive evaluation had resulted in a career-making meeting.

Her recommendation to the board had been to close the three existing plants and build a new, larger, more technically advanced one. Several board members had muttered assent. Mr. Stein, whose yellowish hands and bald head were speckled with age spots, had stared at Jade for a considerably long time. The rest of his body was ravaged by time, but his eyes were as keen as those of a twenty-year-old.

"You seem uncompromising in your position, Ms. Sperry."

"I am. I'm certain that's the only way GSS will make any money in the textile business. And Palmetto, South Carolina, is the perfect location for a plant like this because of its proximity to the shipping channel. What better way to utilize our own shipping interests and reach the foreign markets?"

"What about the management personnel of these plants? Do we simply unload them, too?"

"Not at all. I suggest we offer to relocate them in Palmetto, or, if they decline the offer, to give them six months severance pay when we shut down."

At the conclusion of the discussion, Stein called for a vote. Jade's plan was unanimously approved. "Very well, Ms. Sperry," Stein had said after counting the show of hands, "the project is yours. Textile, is it?"

"Yes," she had said, trying to camouflage her swelling elation behind a professional demeanor. "I'd like to call it TexTile."

TexTile had now been in the developing stages for more than a year. GSS attorneys had quietly purchased land. By a narrow margin, the zoning had been approved by Palmetto's City Council. Working jointly with David Seffrin, a developer under the auspices of GSS, Jade had retained the architect and already had the blueprints.

She was in Los Angeles to hire a general contractor. Once that vital job had been awarded, everything would be in place. She would move to Palmetto—which would undoubtedly come as a shock to the townfolk, who had no reason to link her to the vast land acquisition—and excavation would begin in preparation of building. She would start making arrangements to relocate the management personnel who had chosen that alternative.

A flurry of unrest had gone through the executive ranks of GSS when Jade had joined the company. Few men, and even fewer women, were hired as vice presidents. It took a while before her business acumen convinced others in similar positions that her youth and attractiveness didn't nullify her competence. At first her male counterparts had given her a wide berth, circling warily, sniffing suspiciously, trying to determine how far her ambitions extended and whether she posed a threat to their individual aspirations.

They'd sniffed for other reasons, too.

Her legs had been chauvinistically discussed over drinks and in the men's locker room at the company gym. Several among them, single and married, had expressed an interest in exploring her long, slender thighs all the way to the top. Unfortunately, none who had dared to test the waters had been granted even the privilege of wading.

Throughout her career in the business world, Jade had ignored petty gossip and sexual innuendoes directed at her. She kept her personal life just that. She avoided the inevitable inner-office politics. She didn't invite confidences and shared none. She treated everyone in a friendly but detached manner. Her focus had always been on her work, not on her colleagues.

Within a very short time, she had proved her mettle at GSS and had been richly rewarded by being placed in charge of the TexTile plant. However, no one—not George Stein, not anybody—knew how vitally important this move was to her. She wanted to do a good job, and yes, she wanted to make the new TexTile plant a state-of-the-art, commercial success. But none had guessed that her obsession with returning to Palmetto with GSS's clout behind her was more personal than professional.

"Soon," she murmured as she left the lounge chair she had relaxed in while talking to Graham.

She moved to the window across the room. Her accommodations for this trip hadn't been randomly selected. She had chosen to stay at this hotel because it was located across the street from a busy construction site. Other hotel guests might have viewed that as a disadvantage, but the unsightly view was exactly what Jade had requested when she placed her reservation.

Since her arrival in Los Angeles three days earlier, she had been spying on the construction site, jotting down details and impressions. Jade didn't regard this as trickery, merely a sound business practice. If she wanted to succeed in wreaking havoc on Palmetto's unjust economy, she could leave nothing to chance.

Finding the right contracting outfit for TexTile was essential. The contractor couldn't be someone who would decide he didn't like Palmetto and pull out midway through the job, or—what she feared most, because it had happened before—that he wouldn't like working for a woman. And because Jade fully intended to oversee every facet of the TexTile plant she needed to have only the strongest allies in her corner. She had placed stringent demands on herself to be the smartest and toughest she could be. The people around her could be no less—especially the builder. For a long while, he and she would be GSS's only representatives in Palmetto.

Before leaving New York, she had packed a pair of hightech binoculars. She used them now to assess the work in progress across the street. She wanted to learn how the contractor ran his daily operation. Were safety precautions enforced? Were materials wasted? Were his crews diligent or lackadaisical?

Aimed directly across the street at the corresponding floor of her sixteenth-story room, the automatic focusing mechanism instantly brought the construction workers to within touching distance. It was lunchtime. The laborers were idly joking among themselves as they uncapped Thermoses and unwrapped sandwiches. By all appearances, it was a convivial crew, which was a good sign and a tribute to the contractor. Movement just beyond her field of vision caught her eye and she moved the binoculars a fraction.

It was he.

This one man had attracted her attention the first time she had raised the binoculars and pointed them at the unfinished building. For three days he had continued to arouse her curiosity. Unlike the others, he wasn't taking a lunch break. It seemed he never rested or associated with co-workers. He worked incessantly and independently, keeping his helmeted head down, his concentration focused on the business at hand.

Now, while he was hunkered down consulting a set of blueprints, a sudden gust of wind blew a corn-chip bag against his leg. She saw his lips move as he kicked the bag back toward the circle of workers. One picked up the cellophane bag and hastily stuffed it into his lunchbox.

Good for you, she thought. Keeping the work site clean was one of her prerequisites.

She had seen all she needed to see, but she was irrationally reluctant to lower the binoculars. His separatism intrigued her. His bearded face never smiled. She'd never seen him without his opaque sunglasses. He was wearing clothes similar to those he had worn yesterday and the day before—old Levi's, a faded red tank top, boots, and work gloves. His arms were sleek and well muscled, the skin baked to a dark bronze. The temperature was mild, typical of Southern California, yet through the powerful binoculars she was able to see that sweat had dampened his dense chest hair and had formed a triangle in the cloth of his top.

As she continued to watch, he removed his hard hat only long enough to rake back a mane of sun-streaked brown hair that almost reached his shoulders. Then, just as he was about to replace his hat, he turned his head and looked toward the hotel. As though she had beckoned him, he seemed to be looking straight at her window. It sent a jolt through her.

Guiltily, she dropped the binoculars and jumped away from the window, even though the glass was tinted and mirrored from the outside. He couldn't possibly have seen her, yet she was shaken. If his stare behind the dark sunglasses was as intense as his stance, he was a man who wouldn't appreciate being spied on.

Her palms were damp. She wiped them on her skirt. Her tummy felt weightless. She quickly poured herself a glass of water and drank it. She couldn't imagine what had come over her. For years, the sexes had been homogenized in her mind. Her attempt to have a romantic relationship with Hank had ended in heartache for both of them. Professional counseling hadn't helped.

After months of therapy, the female psychologist had said, "We know what caused your condition. How you deal with it is up to you. In order for healing to take place, Miss Sperry, you must participate in the process."

Jade's candid reply had been, "I can't. I tried, and only ended up hurting someone I care about a great deal."

"Then I'm afraid we're at an impasse. It's going to take courage on your part to establish another sexual relationship."

Jade didn't lack courage, but rather the selfishness to break another person's heart. Because there were no guarantees that she would ever be "cured," she refused to take chances at another's expense. That's why her very real physical reaction to the man in the binoculars stunned her. She sat down at the small writing desk and made another notation in her notebook. Her energy was generated by something much stronger than a potent sex drive. Robbed of the privilege of ever completely loving a man, or of accepting a man's love, she was more determined than ever to seek restitution. No one in Palmetto would have to endure the injustices the Patchetts had chosen to perpetrate. After all these years, she was very close to achieving her goals.

The days in L.A. had been well spent. After observing and analyzing for three days, she was convinced that Dave Seffrin had found the contractor for TexTile. Tomorrow she would come out from behind the binoculars and introduce herself.

Standing before the mirror on the door of her hotel room, Jade analyzed her image. She had observed her thirtieth birthday two years before. Time's ravages had been slight. She had maintained a youthful slenderness without compromising any feminine curves. There was still a natural rosiness in her cheeks. Her hair was glossy and dark, with no signs of graying yet. Her eyes, as blue as ever, were still her most arresting feature.

Her favorite wardrobe color was black. She wore it frequently. The smart, two-piece suit she had chosen to wear today was black, but lightweight enough to feel comfortable in the Southern California climate.

As she left the hotel, Jade recalled all the years since her graduation from Dander College that had led her to this point. She had stayed at the job in Charlotte, North Carolina, until a better one in Birmingham, Alabama, had come along. Her duties had been in purchasing, but she was hired in a middle-management position. There followed a series of other jobs, although she stayed within the area of textile and clothing manufacturing, taking with her the knowledge she had gained under Miss Dorothy Davis's tutelage.

She, Graham, and Cathy, who became a member of the family, relocated several times. Intuitively, Jade knew when she had acquired all that her current position could offer and it was time to progress. Her employers always regretted seeing her leave. The only exception was one whom she was forced to threaten with a charge of sexual harassment. Because he was her superior and didn't take her threats seriously, she left after only six months.

Most of her experiences had been rewarding. Along the way, she had learned the technical aspects of the business, marketing strategy, and how to maximize production efficiency. Her ultimate goal, however, exceeded the boundaries of these comparatively small industries. Her scope was much broader. When the right opportunity came along, she would be prepared for it.

She studied. She faithfully perused business magazines, so she was well acquainted with GSS long before she read *The Wall Street Journal* article that would have such a pivotal effect on her future. She already knew that GSS was one of the largest and ever-growing conglomerates in the world. The focus of the article was on GSS's recent acquisition of three textile plants, which, according to the vice president being interviewed for the article, were currently albatrosses.

After reading the article several times, a plan began to form in Jade's mind. At the time, she was working for a company headquartered in Atlanta, but she knew where she wanted to go next. That evening, she had placed a long-distance call to New York City.

"Hank? Hi. It's Jade."

"Hey, what's up? How are you? How's Graham?"

"Growing like a weed. One of these days he'll be as tall as you."

"Is Cathy okay?"

"She's fine. As invaluable to me as ever."

Following Jade's encounter with Lamar Griffith at Mitch's funeral, she had had a solemn and frank talk with Hank. She told him that, in spite of the psychotherapy she had undergone, she could not engage in a physical relationship. At the risk of sacrificing his friendship, she wanted him fully to understand that it would remain platonic.

Encouraged by the kiss they had shared that morning, he was initially dismayed, then angry, over Jade's sudden reversal. He stormed out; Jade didn't see him for months. Then one evening he unexpectedly showed up at the house as though nothing had happened. Their friendship resumed where it had left off. By way of explanation, he had simply said, "I'd rather be your friend than nothing."

As she moved from city to city and job to job, she and Hank stayed in close contact, writing and calling each other frequently. Consequently, he wasn't surprised to hear from her when she called him in New York, where he had moved as soon as he'd received his degree in art and design.

Once they had caught up on personal news, she asked, "Didn't you do some work for GSS at one time?"

"Last year. There was an article about them in the *Journal* today."

"That's what sparked my memory."

"I was commissioned to redesign their corporate offices," he told her. "I figured they needed a hefty tax writeoff. The bid I submitted was so capitalistically inspired that even I was ashamed to ask that much."

"I doubt that."

He laughed. "Anyway, they went for it."

Hank had done very well for himself. After working with a commercial decorating firm for a few years he had gone out on his own, taking most of his clients with him. Their references had provided him with a solid and lucrative client base. Now, he designed interiors for new commercial buildings or existing ones under renovation. By delegating most of the dirty work to his two apprentices, he enjoyed creative leisure time, most of which he spent painting.

"As a company, how is GSS to work for?"

"Old man Stein—George is his first name—runs the place with an iron fist. Everybody is scared to death of him."

"Did you meet him personally?"

"Naturally. We consulted on my designs to see if they were compatible with his idea of a productive work environment. Later, he became a real fan of my art. Forgive my immodesty."

Jade wrestled with indecision. She hesitated to ask Hank for this particular favor. So far she hadn't involved anyone else in her quest for retribution. Even Cathy, who knew about the rape and its appalling consequences, thought that Jade's orchestrated career advancements were simply that. She didn't know Jade's ulterior motive.

Hank would grant any favor she asked, but she hated to exploit him. On the other hand, he wouldn't be affected by the outcome. Rather than using a friend, she was simply taking advantage of a unique opportunity.

"Hank, could you get me an introduction?"

"To George Stein?" he asked, obviously surprised.

"If he's the one everybody's scared of, he's the one I need to talk to."

"Can I ask why?"

"I want to work for them."

"You mean here in New York? God, I'd love having y'all up here, but I'd better warn you, they sure talk fast. You can't find a fried catfish that's fit to eat anywhere in this town, and, compared to George Stein, Leona Helmsley is Miss Congeniality."

"I'm fully aware of the drawbacks, but it's time I started playing hardball with the big boys."

"GSS has a personnel department for each of its companies. Why not go through normal channels?"

"How many people apply for a job every day? My resumé looks good, but it could be months before it's even reviewed. Besides, I want to go in at the top, not middle management."

Hank whistled through his teeth. "Couldn't you have started out with a smaller favor, something like asking me to scale the Empire State Building naked at high noon?"

"I know it's asking a lot, Hank. If you can't arrange it, I'll understand."

"Did I say I couldn't? It's just that George is a crotchety old man who has to be stroked just right or you've blown it. Give me a couple of days to think of an angle."

"I'd rather meet him in a friendly, relaxed environment, somewhere away from his phalanx of subordinates. Can you swing that?"

Hank came through for her. He invited Mr. Stein to his studio to see a painting he had just completed. He baited the elderly man by telling him that the contemporary piece would look fantastic behind his desk.

Jade was waiting at Hank's Soho loft when Stein's chauffeur dropped him there. She was introduced as an out-of-town friend. Stein fell in love with the painting, haggled with Hank over a price, and purchased it for his office, which left him in a favorable mood.

Over drinks, Stein politely asked, "Are you also an artist, Ms. Sperry?"

If Jade had scripted it, she couldn't have come up with a better opening line. "No, I work in the manufacturing and marketing of textiles."

"She's a vice president for an outfit in Atlanta that makes a line of workclothes," Hank supplied.

"I read that GSS has recently acquired the three Kelso plants," Jade remarked.

"That's right." Stein smelled a rat. He was frowning.

"Hmm." Jade appeared unimpressed. She took a sip of her wine. "Hank, you really should water that plant in the corner. It—"

George Stein interrupted, "Are you familiar with the Kelso plants, Ms. Sperry?"

"Only by reputation."

"Which is?"

She demurred. "I hope GSS can make them profitable, but—"

"But?" the old man prompted.

"But it will no doubt require a vast reorganization of the entire operation from management on down. Modernizing three plants will be expensive." She shrugged, leaving him to draw his own conclusions.

"Will they be worth all that expense?"

"Coming up with an answer to that question would take months of evaluation, Mr. Stein. I'm hardly in a position to offer an opinion."

"I asked for one, didn't I?"

Hank stifled a laugh behind the cocktail olive he popped into his mouth. Jade said, "I know the business from the looms to the invoices, Mr. Stein. I know a well-run plant when I see one. I recognize problems that should be corrected, and I'm confident in my ability to solve those problems. However, I don't offer opinions with nothing except industry gossip to base them on. Isn't there someone within your organization who could provide you a more educated opinion?" She knew before asking that there wasn't. Otherwise Stein wouldn't be soliciting hers.

Before leaving Hank's loft, he asked her to send him her resumé. "I assume you'd be interested in working for us."

"If the offer is attractive enough, Mr. Stein."

Jade, recalling that bizarre interview, now smiled to herself as she left the hotel. The Los Angeles haze was even thicker due to the dust from the construction site across the street. The racket was deafening, but Jade didn't mind it. It was only a two-block walk to the contractor's trailer. She decided to walk.

Memories of her first meeting with George Stein conjured up memories that had nothing to do with business.

"You're as good as hired," Hank had said after Stein left. "Let's party."

He uncorked another bottle of chilled white wine. While they sat on the pile of cushions that served as furniture, he reached for her hand and stroked the back of it with his thumb. "I've met someone, Jade," he began.

"You mean a woman?"

"Uh-huh. I met her in the Macy's home interiors department. She was trying to sell the ugliest sofa I've ever seen to an equally ugly broad. We made eye contact as she pointed out the finer points of this upholstered atrocity. By the time the broad produced her charge card, I couldn't stop laughing."

Jade leaned forward, eager to know more. "What's her name?"

"Deidre. She's got a degree in interior design and only took the job at Macy's until she could get something better."

"So you've got a lot in common."

"She comes from a small town in Nebraska, has a freckled nose, a cute ass, and an infectious giggle."

"And you like her a lot."

He probed Jade's eyes, as though looking for something. "Yeah. What's even more amazing, she likes me."

"I don't find that at all amazing. Do you have good sex?"

He gave a lazy grin. "Apparently they shuck more than corn in Nebraska."

"I'm glad, Hank," Jade said, pressing his hands between her own. "Very glad."

"I'm thinking of marrying her." He gave her a hesitant glance, then looked meaningfully into her eyes. "What do you think, Jade? Should I?"

He hadn't been asking advice. He had been asking if he should give up his hopes for her and make plans with someone else. "Marry her, Hank," she said huskily. "That would make me very happy."

Before leaving for this business trip to L.A., Jade had dropped in on Hank and Deidre to see their twin daughters. They had just turned six weeks old. Hank was still her best friend. She had hired him as the designer for the offices at the TexTile plant in Palmetto.

Jade blinked the present into focus and realized that she had reached her destination. She experienced the rush of adrenaline that accompanies any professional undertaking, especially a surprise attack. David Seffrin had arranged for her to meet the contractor under consideration, but, at her request, he had kept the exact day and time of the appointment open.

"I'll see what my schedule is and contact him myself once I get to L.A.," she had told the developer.

She wanted to see things as they actually were, not as the prospective builder for TexTile would have them appear.

Boldly, she entered the trailer without knocking. Inside were two desks. At one, a secretary was typing on a computer keyboard. A man was speaking into a telephone at the other desk. He had his back to Jade.

The secretary lifted her magenta fingernails off the keys. "Can I help you?"

"I'm here to see Mr. Matthias."

The secretary directed a glance to the opposite end of the trailer. "Do you have an appointment?"

"No, but Mr. Seffrin has spoken to Mr. Matthias on my behalf. If you'll please tell him that Ms. Sperry from GSS in New York is here to see—"

"Ms. Sperry?"

The casters on his chair squealed as he spun it around. Jade turned slowly, keeping her expression cool. "Mr. Matthias? I'm Jade Sperry. How do you do?"

Flustered, he kept his eyes on Jade as he spoke briefly into the telephone before hanging up. Standing, he buttoned his suit jacket and moved down the length of the trailer, his hand extended. "I didn't know we had an appointment today." He shot his secretary an impatient look.

"We don't. I wasn't sure what my schedule would be while I was here in L.A. As it turns out, I'm free today. On the outside chance that you had no plans for lunch, I thought I'd stop by."

"Lunch? Today? Well, say, sure."

"What about Mr. Hemphill?" the secretary asked.

"Cancel," her boss snapped discourteously. "Say, when would you like to go?" he asked Jade.

"Now."

"Oh. I, uh, thought you might want to look around first."

"I've already looked around, Mr. Matthias."

"Okay, well, that's good. Say, do you have transportation? If not, we can take my car." He rushed forward and held the trailer door open for her.

Once they were settled in the leather interior of his

Jaguar and had agreed on a restaurant, she asked, "Have you read the information Mr. Seffrin sent you?"

"Sure have. Cover to cover. I'm your man for that project in South Carolina, all right."

"What makes you think so, Mr. Matthias?"

Jade listened while he, after a token display of modesty, enumerated his outstanding qualifications. One could count on a good business lunch lasting at least two hours. Even fighting L.A. traffic, Jade and Mr. Matthias returned to the trailer well under that amount of time.

She declined his invitation to continue their discussion inside. "Thank you for your time, Mr. Matthias."

She turned to go. He stepped around her, blocking her path on the sidewalk. "Say, wait. When will I hear from you?"

"Mr. Seffrin and I have several other contractors to interview," she lied.

Throughout lunch, she had tried to keep an open mind, but every word out of his mouth confirmed her negative first impression. She thought that he must have written his own press releases and recommendations because he certainly seemed to have an elevated opinion of himself.

The more he boasted, the less impressed Jade became. As badly as she wanted to commence work on the project, she faced the dismal fact that this trip had been pointless and she was still without a general contractor.

"It could be weeks or even months before we make a final decision," she told Matthias evasively.

"Say, listen, you aren't steamed because of what happened back there at the restaurant, are you?"

"You mean when you invited me to go to your apartment for dessert?" she asked coldly, dropping all vestiges of professionalism. "No, Mr. Matthias, I'm not steamed. I'm repulsed."

"Say, you're a classy-looking lady. It was worth a try," he quipped, flashing her a stupid grin. "You can't blame a guy for making a pass at you."

"Oh yes I can, Mr. Matthias."

"Then you're one of those women's libbers with penis envy. Ball busters, I call you. I believe you had your mind made up about me before we ever left for lunch."

"You're right, I did." Since he hadn't spared any words, she saw no reason to keep her impressions to herself. "Your office is a mess. I'm not talking about the clutter that hard work generates, I'm talking about overflowing ashtrays, empty soda cans, and a muddy floor.

"Secondly, I arrived without an appointment just to see how you would handle the situation. Your previous luncheon engagement deserved a personal call from you to explain the postponement. Furthermore, I couldn't spend months working with an individual who begins almost every sentence with 'say.' And finally, I knew you weren't right for this job the moment I saw your hands."

"What's wrong with my hands?"

"They're soft, and your nails are manicured."

"Say, lady, where do you get off—?"

The siren of an approaching LAPD squad car silenced Matthias. The car rolled to a stop just yards from where Jade and he were standing.

"What the hell is going on?" Forgetting Jade, Matthias marched forward and grabbed one of the policemen by the sleeve. "What are you doing here?"

"Who are you?"

"Wayne Matthias. I'm the boss here."

"We got a complaint call. Apparently one of your workers went berserk and attacked another one. Somewhere up there," the policeman added, tilting his head back and scanning the top stories of the unfinished building.

"Shit. This is all I need," Matthias muttered, loosening the knot of his necktie. A crowd of pedestrians was collecting, curious to know what was going on. "You'd better keep these people back. I don't want a lawsuit on my hands if somebody gets hurt."

Jade was herded back along with the other onlookers, but she felt compelled to stay and see what difficulty had warranted a call to the police. She and the others stood in expectant silence as they watched the service elevator slowly descend. When it reached the ground, the clanging metal door was slid open and a man was thrust forward into the arresting arms of the uniformed policeman.

"You!" Matthias sneered with disgust. "I might have known it would be you."

It was the man Jade had been watching through the binoculars.

Chapter 18

The policeman elbowed Matthias aside and confronted the man, whose hands had been secured behind him with someone's leather belt. Two other workers stepped off the elevator behind him, through they kept their distance.

He hadn't given up without a struggle, Jade noticed. He was bleeding from a cut above his brow, but the other men's faces had sustained worse damage. He regarded those standing around him with contempt, especially Matthias.

One of the policemen asked, "Okay, what happened up there?"

"He could have killed us all," a worker blurted out. "Nearly did before we wrestled him down and got his hands tied."

The policeman nodded to his partner. "Get that belt off and put him in cuffs." He asked the speaker, "Who are you?"

"I'm the foreman. We were up there working on the air ducts, and he started bitching about the lousy quality of the materials. I told him the materials were none of his goddamn business and to get back to work. He refused and demanded to see Mr. Matthias here. I told him that the boss didn't give a rat's ass about his opinion of things and to get back to work or I'd fire his ass. That's when he threw a punch at me." He touched a swelling bruise on his chin.

"Is that right?" The cop turned to a Latino worker who had come down in the elevator with them.

"*Sí.* He start hitting everybody."

"He was yelling and calling Mr. Matthias here dirty names."

"Me?" Matthias asked, stepping forward. "What'd I do? I wasn't even up there."

"You ordered that shit." The low, vibrating voice of the accused man, speaking for the first time, stunned everyone else into silence. "Your building will burn like paper if it ever gets so much as a strong fart in those air ducts."

Matthias cursed beneath his breath. "He's fucked in the head. I've thought so ever since I hired him, but I felt sorry for him, you know," he said, speaking in a wheedling tone to the policeman. "He's been a pain in the ass ever since he got here, but so long as he put in a full day's—" His breath whooshed out of his body when the man's flying fist slammed into his gut, bending him double.

The policeman had barely taken the belt from around the worker's hands before he launched his attack on Matthias. The astonished officer tried to subdue him again but was angrily shoved aside. The worker grabbed Matthias by his collar and threw him against the chain-link fence. The two policemen converged on them and wrestled the man away from the gasping Matthias. It took both of them to get handcuffs on him. He was read his rights as he was led to the patrol car and stuffed into the backseat.

"I'll nail your ass for this," Matthias screamed, shaking his pale, soft fist at the man. "I'll have you charged with assault, you son of a bitch."

"Better than being a murderer," the man shouted through the backseat window of the patrol car.

"You'll have to come down to the station to file the complaint," the policeman told Matthias. "You, too," he said to the workers. "We'll have to get statements from all of you."

They shook their heads and muttered among themselves as the patrolman joined his partner in the car and drove away.

The crowd dispersed, but Jade hung around, unseen, for almost two hours before Matthias roared away in his Jaguar. The secretary was still at the computer terminal typing when Jade entered the trailer unannounced for the second time that day. "What do you want?" the secretary asked ungraciously.

"Some information, please."

"Mr. Matthias has left for the day."

"I'm sure you can help me."

"With what?"

"I want to know about the man who was arrested this afternoon."

Her face lost some of its hostility. "You think he's cute, too, huh?"

"I'm sorry?"

"He's a hunk. Don't you think so?"

"Can you help me or not?" Jade asked pleasantly.

The secretary shrugged, then turned her swivel chair

back to the computer terminal and called up a file. "I positively creamed the day he came in here asking to fill out an application."

"What's his name?"

"Dillon Burke. Beards have always been a real turn-on for me. I've got this girl friend—she calls beards womb sweepers. Isn't that *terrible?*" She giggled. "They make a man so mysterious, you know?"

"Actually, I'm more interested in his background."

The secretary scanned the data on the screen. "He started working for Matthias on April twenty-eighth last year."

"Before that?"

"Doesn't say. See for yourself. That's all we've got on him. Not even a mailing address."

She turned the screen toward Jade, who checked the scanty information, then ripped a sheet of paper off a note pad and jotted down the man's name and social security number. "Exactly what does he do?"

"Everything. To look at him you'd never guess it, but he's smart and knows what he's doing. Matthias asks Mr. Burke's advice all the time, but he'd never admit it."

Jade assimilated that. "So his allegations were true?"

"Allegations? Oh, you mean what he said about Matthias using crappy materials?"

"Is it true?"

"Look, I don't see that that's any of your business. I've already told you more—"

"He flirted with me." Jade had a hunch, and she played on it. "While we were at lunch, Matthias slid his hand under my skirt and asked me to join him in his apartment for the rest of the afternoon."

The secretary's eyes narrowed to slits. The purplish fingernails curled toward her palms like claws. "Why, that two-timing, slimy, horny little shit!"

Jade watched Dillon Burke as he was escorted through a door and led to a desk where he signed a receipt for his belongings. As he strapped on his wristwatch, the desk sergeant said something to him that brought his head around. He looked at Jade with that disturbing intensity she had first noticed through the binoculars.

Beneath dense brows, his hazel eyes regarded her suspiciously. They moved from the top of her head to the toes of her black eel pumps and back up again. It took all her willpower not to squirm.

"Are you sure?" she heard him ask the police sergeant when he turned back around.

"Don't look a gift horse in the mouth, buddy. Go on, get out of here before we change our minds."

Jade stood up, surprised to discover that her knees were unsteady. She didn't like police stations. They were too reminiscent of the night she had spent in the interrogation room at the Palmetto County courthouse. She hadn't been surprised to read that Hutch now occupied the office once held by his father.

"Mr. Burke?" she said as she approached him. "Will you come with me, please?"

When he quizzically tilted his head to one side, his long hair brushed his shoulder. "What for? Who the hell are you?"

"My name is Jade Sperry. Please?" She gestured toward the door. Her blue eyes didn't flinch from his hard stare, though it was disconcerting. "As the sergeant said, they might change their minds and decide to keep you overnight. This way."

She moved toward the entrance, giving the false impression that she was confident he would follow her. For all she knew, as soon as they cleared the door, he would bolt and she would never see him again. To her relief, he fell into step beside her.

She led him to the limousine parked at the curb. The chauffeur hastened to open the back door for them. She offered to let Burke precede her. He hesitated only a few seconds before getting into the plush backseat. The limo was an extravagance, she knew. But she wanted him flabbergasted and humbled by the good fortune that had miraculously befallen him. She wanted him to say yes to her proposition.

Jade reached for the electric button that raised the glass partition between the chauffeur and the backseat. Saying nothing, Burke followed her motions with watchful eyes.

The limo pulled into traffic and glided through it as soundlessly as a silver snake. Jade crossed her legs, then wished she hadn't. Her stockings made a silky-scratchy sound in the silence. Burke looked down at her legs, then raised an inquisitive gaze to her face.

To cover her nervousness, Jade opened her purse and took out a pack of cigarettes and a new lighter. "Cigarette?"

"I don't smoke."

"Oh." She laughed with self-derision as she set the cigarettes and lighter on the small built-in bar of the limo. "I've seen too many movies, I guess."

"Movies?"

"Whenever a prisoner is brought out, the first thing

he's offered is a cigarette. I bought some, thinking... this is the first time I've gotten anybody out of jail."

With a cynical eye, he gazed around the lush interior of the limo. "This is a first for me, too."

"You've never been in jail before?"

He turned to her abruptly, startling her with the unexpected movement. "Have you?"

He seemed very large and very close, and suddenly she doubted the wisdom of her impulsiveness. She recalled how quickly he had attacked Matthias when the belt was removed from his hands. His sheer physicality frightened her, but she didn't recoil, for she supposed that's what he wanted her to do. He was trying to intimidate her, probably because he felt intimidated himself.

"I've never been incarcerated, no," she answered evenly.

He subjected her to another slow, thorough once-over. "Somehow I didn't think so."

"Does the cut over your eye hurt?" It was no longer bleeding, but the wound still looked fresh.

"I'll live." He slouched in the seat, setting his eyes forward again toward the tinted pane of glass that separated them from the driver. "Where are we going?"

"I thought you might be hungry. Will you join me for dinner?"

"Dinner?" he asked with a mirthless smile. He looked down at his workclothes and boots. "I'm not exactly dressed for any place fancy."

"Will that bother you?"

"Hell no. Will it bother you?"

"Not in the least."

They rode in silence for several minutes before his curiosity got the best of him again. "When are you going to tell me what the hell is going on? If Matthias sent you as a bribe or something, then—"

"I assure you, he didn't. You'll get a full explanation after dinner, Mr. Burke. Besides, we've arrived."

The limo rolled to a stop at a steak house. Jade had consulted with the hotel concierge before deciding on this restaurant and giving the address to the limo driver. The family-owned establishment advertised wholesome food at reasonable prices. The location wasn't elitist, and the interior looked like the set of a Gene Autry movie. The large dining room was dim, relieved only by pools of golden light cast by lanterns suspended from the ceiling.

Jade was pleased with her selection as they were escorted to a corner table by a hostess wearing a fringed leather skirt and western boots. Mr. Burke would feel less conspicuous here than in a more expensive restaurant.

He ordered a draft beer from the cocktail waitress. Jade asked for a soda and lime. He spoke a terse thanks when the drinks arrived. As he sipped his beer, Jade covertly watched him, wondering what he would look like without the beard. He neatly whisked specks of the beer's head off his mustache, which covered his upper lip and rode nicely above the fuller lower one.

His hands, she noticed, weren't soft. They were working hands with callused knuckles. The nails were clipped and clean, but they hadn't been buffed to a high gloss. Work gloves had left faint tan lines around his wrists. The strong arms that had impressed her through the binoculars appeared even stronger up close. Today he was wearing a plaid flannel shirt over his tank top. It had been left unbuttoned. The sleeves had been ripped out. His exposed chest had certainly impressed the cocktail waitress.

"When you're finished, do I get my turn?"

Jade lifted her eyes from his chest to his face. "Pardon?"

"Do I get my turn to scope you over as thoroughly as you're looking at me? It might get sloppy if we tried to ogle each other at the same time."

The arrival of the waitress kept Jade from having to reply. Briskly she placed their order. "My guest will have your largest steak cooked medium rare, french fries, and salad. I'll have the small filet mignon. We'll order dessert later." She slapped the menus into the waitress's hand, then faced her companion.

He was gripping the beer mug so tightly that his knuckles had turned white. His voice vibrated with anger. "I'm a big boy, Miss whoever-the-hell-you-are. I can read a menu and order for myself."

She hadn't been scoping him out, at least not in the way he imagined, and his remark about her ogling him had made her mad. "I apologize for the rudeness. I sometimes do that without thinking. It's a bad habit of mine."

"Are you going to tell me what I'm doing here with you?"

"After dinner."

He muttered a word that wasn't in keeping with civilized dinner conversation. "In the meantime, may I have another beer?"

"Of course." By the time he was finished with his second beer, their food arrived. He fell on it ravenously, leaving Jade to wonder when he had last eaten a good cut of beef. He used his utensils correctly, but quickly.

"Would you like another steak?" she inquired gently, leaning across the table toward him. The instant she adopted that compassionate tone of voice, she realized she had blundered.

He regarded her coldly. "No."

He was refusing more out of pride than because his hunger was appeased, but Jade let it drop. Their plates were removed. He curtly declined dessert and merely shrugged when she suggested coffee. "Two coffees," Jade told their waitress. Once they had been served, she began her explanation.

"I was at the construction site this afternoon when you were arrested, Mr. Burke." She watched his eyes for signs of reaction, but there were none. They remained steadily on her, registering nothing. A flicker of surprise or interest would have been expected. The lack of one was disturbing.

"I was impressed with several things. For one, you weren't afraid to speak out and hold your ground even though your opinion was unwelcome and unpopular. That demonstrates conviction and courage, which are attributes I'm looking for. I need someone tough."

A laugh originated as a low rumble deep in his chest. "Well, I'll be damned. You sure went to a lot of trouble."

"Yes, I did."

Resting his forearms on the table, he leaned forward and spoke to her softly over two cups of forgotten, cooling coffee. "Now I get it. You're looking for adventure because your rich, successful husband is a workaholic who's too busy making a buck to pay attention to you. Or maybe you found out that he's banging a girl in the typing pool and you're out to get him back.

"You happened by today when all that excitement was going on and got wet over a hard-hat fantasy. So you had your chauffeur drive you down to city hall, and—being the rich, powerful, and bossy bitch you are—pulled a few strings that got me out of jail. Is that it?"

Complacently, he eased back in his chair. "Okay, fine. I'd hate for you to be out that trouble for nothing. For a thousand dollars, I'll fuck you all night long."

Chapter 19

Asmall shudder passed through Jade. "How dare you?"

Reaching across the table, he lightly encircled her wrist in his large hand. "Okay, five hundred. I lost my job today. I'm in no position to bargain."

Jade yanked her arm free. Her first impulse was to dress him down as soundly as she had Matthias earlier in the day for sexist transgressions that had been far less offensive than Burke's. When compared to the man seated across the table from her, even the sleazy Matthias came out ahead—at least on the surface.

But Jade had a gut instinct that there was more to Dillon Burke than met the eye. The untrimmed beard, long hair, and rudeness were affectations. She didn't know how she knew this. She just *knew.* Rather than leaving him with a scathing reproof, she stayed, unwilling to give up on him. *Why?* she wondered. What quirk of coincidence had placed her at the site at the time of his arrest? For days she had been watching him through binoculars from her hotel window. It was as though fate had pointed him out to her.

He was still observing her with his guarded, hooded gaze. In his place, wouldn't she have been confused? In any event, the TexTile plant was worth giving him the benefit of the doubt.

She signaled their waitress. "Are you sure you won't have dessert, Mr. Burke?"

He stared at her with misgiving, then said brusquely, "Apple pie."

"Two," Jade told the waitress. "And we'll need fresh cups of coffee. Keep them coming. We'll probably be here for a while."

After the waitress withdrew, Jade stared into Dillon's unwavering hazel eyes. "I want something so badly that I taste it at night in my sleep. You can help me get it, but it has nothing to do with sex. Knowing that, are you still interested in hearing my proposition?"

His eyes remained on Jade even when he leaned back to give the waitress room to serve their pie and fresh coffees. Picking up his dessert fork, he said, "You've got from now until I finish my pie to interest me."

"Your allegations were right. Matthias was using substandard materials and bribing a city inspector to approve them."

"Son of a bitch," he whispered beneath his breath. "I knew it! I saw things I couldn't believe were getting past, but with every inspection, Matthias got the city's stamp of approval."

"He was charging his client the price of quality materials and skimming off the difference."

"I don't give a shit about the money. The goddamn building could have fallen down, especially if there was a quake. How'd you find out?"

"Through his secretary. She had a lot to say about him

when I told her he had flirted with me during our luncheon meeting."

"Oh, great," he muttered. "That puts me in a league with Matthias."

"Hardly, Mr. Burke."

"So who are you, an investigator? Did you do all this so I would testify against Matthias in court?"

"No. I'm no longer interested in what happens to Matthias. I made photocopies of his purchase orders and other incriminating documents, then called him on his cellular phone. I threatened to take my findings to the D.A. unless he declined to press charges against you."

"You didn't have to personally escort me out of jail."

"Yes, I did."

"Why?"

"Because I'm about to offer you the job I had intended for Matthias. You're finished with your pie. Shall I keep talking?"

He didn't verbally encourage her to continue, but he scooted aside the empty dessert plate and picked up his coffee cup.

After allowing herself a smile, Jade told him who she represented. He was only vaguely familiar with GSS. "For almost thirteen months, our legal department has been quietly acquiring property in Palmetto, South Carolina. We're going to build a plant there."

"What kind of plant?"

"Textile. But in addition to the cloth being woven there, we'll manufacture moderately priced clothing. The economic climate in that area of the state is poor. Until the last decade or so, the developers of resorts along the coast discouraged industrial development."

"Because of the pollutants."

"Exactly. But after the formation of a pollution-control board, that's no longer an issue. The lobbyists have lost their muscle. The State Development Board wholeheartedly approves us because GSS is dedicated to protecting the environment."

"I'll bet they're also dedicated to making a buck," he said cynically.

"For everybody. We're bringing in some management and middle management, but the plant will employ hundreds of local people in as many specialized jobs. It will completely change the complexion of the economy."

"I've never heard of Palmetto."

"It's located near the coastline between Savannah and Charleston. The population of the town proper is just over ten thousand, but thousands more live in a tri-county area. The entire region will benefit when GSS moves in."

"What role do you play?"

"I'm the project supervisor."

He arched one of his eyebrows. "You're the head honcho?"

"In a manner of speaking."

"And you came all the way to Southern California to hire construction workers?" he asked skeptically.

"I came to hire a general contractor."

"A developer usually does that."

"GSS has a development company. A man named David Seffrin is in charge of TexTile. He sent me out to meet Matthias, who had come highly recommended, although I now doubt the authenticity of his references."

"If this Seffrin is the developer, why are you hiring?"

"The contractor awarded this job must meet with my

approval. This plant is my baby, Mr. Burke. It has been from its inception. I'll be working closely with the contractor for a long time, so it's essential that I feel he's right for the project." Leaning forward slightly, she said, "I believe you are the man I need."

His sharp barking laugh drew glances from other restaurant patrons. "Yeah, right." He looked himself over, fingering a ragged hole in the knee of his jeans. "I look like the boss man, all right. You could pick me out of any lineup."

"I couldn't care less what you look like."

He shook his head adamantly. "I'm not your man. Sorry to disappoint you."

"You're from the South, Mr. Burke." He gave her a sharp, inquisitive look. "One Southern accent recognizes another," she said. "And you were familiar with the issue of industry versus tourism."

"So you'd hire me on the basis of my Southern accent alone?"

"No, I'd hire you on the basis of your qualifications."

"I'm not qualified."

"Don't bullshit me." Again, his eyebrow arched in surprise. "You can decline my offer, but don't lie to me. I'm sure you have a good reason to hide behind your beard and that monstrous chip on your shoulder, but you're qualified for this job.

"The secretary didn't only talk about Matthias, she told me a lot about you. Things were in a mess when you happened along. Soon after you were hired, you began spotting problems and giving Matthias advice until he didn't make a move without consulting you first. He doesn't hire any subcontractors without getting your opinion. Isn't that right?"

He merely stared at her stonily.

"She said you seemed to be an expert on everything, from reading blueprints to ironwork to installing electrical conduit. She said Matthias resented you for quarreling with him over inferior materials, but that he didn't dare fire you because you had made yourself indispensable. Is this true?"

He pulled the corner of his mustache through his teeth.

"I have your social security number," she added quietly. "I'll check on you. So don't bother lying to me."

He muttered a string of curses, then said, "Maybe at one time I was qualified, but I haven't done anything more than menial labor in seven years. I haven't wanted to. I *don't* want to. I just want to be left the hell alone."

"Why?"

"None of your goddamn business."

Once again his raised, angry voice attracted the attention of nearby diners. "I think it's time we left," Jade suggested. "Ready?"

"Past ready."

"Where can we drop you?" she asked, once they were ensconced in the backseat of the limo.

"At the site. My pickup is parked there. At least I hope to God it's still there."

Jade gave the address to the chauffeur, then sat back against the seat. "In spite of the fact he needs you, Matthias won't welcome you back. So what will you do tomorrow, Mr. Burke?"

"Sleep late, I guess."

"And then?"

"Go looking for a job."

"Just any job?"

"That's right. Just any job. Just anywhere. It doesn't really matter."

"I think it does." He whipped his head around and glared at her for contradicting him. "I think it matters a lot more than you'll admit to yourself." She reached for the attaché case on the floorboard and opened it. "This is the prospectus Mr. Seffrin prepared for the TexTile plant. I'd like you to keep it and look it over." She handed him the proposal, which was bound in a clear plastic folder. "I'm going back to New York tomorrow. Is there a number where I can reach you in a few days?"

"No. And looking over this prospectus won't change my mind."

"The salary is five thousand dollars a month, effective upon signing a contract. A twenty-five-thousand-dollar bonus will be payable upon completion to my satisfaction." There was no mention of a bonus in the prospectus. George Stein would blow a gasket, but she needed all the perks she could devise.

"I don't give a damn about money."

"Oh, really? You were going to charge a thousand dollars to spend the night with me," she reminded him.

"I was trying to insult you."

"It worked."

He ran his hand through his long, unkempt hair. "Thanks for getting me out of jail, but you've wasted your time."

"I don't think so." The limousine slid to the curb at the dark, deserted work site. "You know where to contact me when you've reached a decision, Mr. Burke."

"You don't listen, do you? I've already reached a decision. My answer is no." The chauffeur came around and opened the door for him. He set one foot on the pavement, but turned back and asked, "What did you say your first name is?"

"Jade."

"Thanks for dinner, Jade, but I like my steaks well done." Moving suddenly, he cupped the back of her head and hauled her against him. His mouth covered hers in a hard kiss. He thrust his tongue between her lips, spearing deeply but briefly, before immediately releasing her. "I apologize for the rudeness. I sometimes do that without thinking. It's a bad habit of mine."

He got out, leaving her speechless, her lips damp and throbbing.

Standing in the doorway of her office, Dillon felt gawky, out of place, and too large for his clothes. After years of working outdoors, being inside an office building made him feel claustrophobic.

Jade Sperry was sitting behind her desk, speaking into the telephone. Her back was to the door. Her dark hair had been pulled into a low ponytail and secured with a gold clasp, but she was idly twining one stray curl around her index finger.

"Another thing, Cathy, please call Graham's school and make an appointment with the principal. I want to see him before I leave...Uh-huh...No, I won't forget. Thanks for reminding me. I'll be home around six. Bye."

She hung up the phone and spun around in her chair, drawing a quick little breath when she saw him standing there. "I'm sorry. Can I help you?"

"How soon they forget."

Astonishment altered her features, making her eyes larger and brighter and her mouth softer. "Mr. Burke?"

He shrugged self-consciously.

Quickly she stood up and rounded her desk. She was

wearing a white blouse, a straight black skirt, and the same black high heels she had been wearing in L.A. two weeks earlier. Her legs were as good as he remembered.

"I didn't recognize you without your beard," she said. "And you hair's shorter, isn't it?"

"That's a polite way of saying that I finally got a hair-cut. I even dressed up." Self-derisively he spread his arms at his sides. He had worn his best pair of jeans and a new shirt. As an afterthought, he had even bought a necktie at the K-Mart where he had purchased the shirt. It had been so long since he had tied a necktie, it had taken him three tries and countless cuss words to get it right.

Studying his new image in the YMCA mirror, he decided that he had done the best he could, and that if he wasn't good enough for her, that was just too damn bad. Who needed this anyway?

He did.

Dillon had come to that conclusion after days of soul-searching anguish. Damn her! Jade Sperry had succeeded in getting him excited over something for the first time in seven years. The lady was nuts to entrust a project of this magnitude to a burned-out, bummed-out drifter like him, but—God!—the challenge was irresistible.

"I'm sorry for staring," she said, recovering her composure. "You look so different. Sit down, please."

He took the chair she indicated. "I probably should have called first." Actually he hadn't dared. He was afraid she would tell him that the position had already been filled. It was going to be a crushing disappointment if it had been. The prospect made his voice husky. "I hope I'm not catching you at a bad time."

"Not at all." She resumed her place behind her desk.

He surveyed her office with interest. Everything in it was sleek and contemporary, yet it was warm, with pots of African violets blooming on the windowsill and framed art renderings, drawn by an amateur hand, decorating the walls. Each crayon picture was signed, "Graham Sperry."

"My son," she remarked, following his gaze. "He's fourteen now. It embarrasses him that I keep his grade-school drawings."

"Fourteen," Dillon murmured. Charlie would have been eight his next birthday. He smoothed his hand over his heavy mustache, which he had decided to keep when he shaved off his beard.

"Can I get you a coffee or something cold?"

"No, thanks."

"When did you leave L.A.?"

"A week ago. I drove."

"Oh, I see. That must have been quite an experience."

"It was okay," he replied laconically. Was she stalling, unwilling to tell him she'd found somebody with a better attitude?

"Is this your first time in New York?"

"Yes."

"What do you think?"

"It's all right."

After a short silence, she said, "I hope you have good news for me."

"Is the job still open?"

"Yes."

"Not anymore."

Her eyes lit up, but she kept her voice calm. "I'm very pleased to hear that, Mr. Burke."

"Why? You found me in jail. You don't know how I work. I don't have my own business."

"I decided while I was in California that I didn't want a company. An individual is less intimidating than a large company."

"I still don't get it," Dillon said.

"We want TexTile to belong to the community of Palmetto. Using local construction workers and regionally based subcontractors would be a move in the right direction. I shared this idea with Mr. Seffrin, and he agrees. The fact that you don't have your own labor force is actually a plus. And," she added, emphasizing her Southern drawl, "you speak their language. You don't sound like an interloper, and we're trying to avoid appearing as such."

"And this Seffrin fellow—"

"Trusts my instincts, although I must tell you that during this interim, we've been looking elsewhere. You're still my first choice, so I'm very pleased to see you here. Now, tell me how you work." She clasped her hands on top of her desk and assumed a listening expression.

"Essentially, I've done a little bit of everything relating to building, but what I like most is putting the whole thing together."

"Before I knew he was an outright crook, the first thing that turned me off Matthias was his hands," she said. "They were soft. He manages from behind a desk. I need someone who supervises every aspect of the construction, who works one to one with the subs and the laborers."

"No problem there. That's the way I like to do it."

"Good. This job also requires someone who is committed to the project. From the time we break ground until completion, you can count on it taking at least two years."

"I've got nothing better to do."

"Relocating in Palmetto won't be a problem for you?"

"Absolutely none. As you guessed, I grew up in the South and got my degree from Georgia Tech."

"Is there anything else you'd like to discuss before I have the contracts department draw up our work agreement?"

"What about the subs?"

"What about them?"

"I'll get no fewer than three bids for every job," he said. "Am I obligated to award the job to the lowest bidder?"

"Not if you don't feel comfortable about it."

"Sometimes the lowest bid turns out to be the most expensive in the long run—if the work has to be redone."

"I think we understand each other, Mr. Burke. Now, if I can see your references, we'll be all set."

He shifted uncomfortably in his chair. He had been dreading this part. "I can't provide you with references."

"Oh? Why not?"

"For the last several years, I've moved around a lot. Burned bridges. I'd get in a fight, or get drunk, or get fed up with the boss's incompetence and never go back." He shrugged. "References weren't a priority. Anyway, I don't have any."

"How do I know that you won't get in a fight, get drunk, and walk out on me?"

"You don't. You'll just have to take my word for it."

Dillon held his breath. Since he had come this far, he wasn't certain he could bear the disappointment if she rejected him now. He wanted this job. It was essential to him. It meant the difference between starting to live again and merely continuing to exist.

She stood up again and moved around the desk. "You'll

need to be in Palmetto by May first. I've scheduled a town meeting during which I will announce our plans, and you should be there."

"You mean I'm hired?"

"You're hired. Between now and May first, almost every minute of your workday will revolve around meetings with Seffrin, the architect, the designer, and me. You've got your work cut out for you, Mr. Burke. I'll try and scare up an empty office for you to use."

He was hired! He was too stunned to react.

She extended her hand. "Do we have a deal?"

Dillon stood up and enclosed her hand. There was a vast difference between shaking hands with Jade Sperry and shaking hands with another man. Her hand was small, for one thing, and cool and dry and soft. It didn't seem to fit into such a masculine gesture, yet the feel of it left an impression long after he had released it.

"Excuse me. I won't be long."

She left him alone in her office. He moved to the window and gazed out over the city. It was still hard for him to believe that this was happening. The night she had taken him to dinner, he had thrown up a dozen barriers to her and her proposal. Afterward, however, he couldn't stop thinking about it.

Finally he had relented and picked up the prospectus she had left with him. After he'd read it a dozen times, GSS's TexTile plant became as much an obsession as his grief was.

For seven years he had been outrunning his guilt. The coroner's report stated that Debra and Charlie had died accidentally, but Dillon knew he was responsible. After the ambulances had taken away their bodies, while he was raging through the house, demented with grief, he had discovered the list of chores he hadn't got around to the preceding weekend. The last item on the list was, "Check furnace."

After leaving Tallahassee, he had aimlessly wandered about, with his guilt in tow. He had taken it with him to the frozen frontiers of Alaska and into the teeming jungles of Central America. He had tried to drown it in gallons of whiskey, abuse it with meaningless sex, and kill it by taking unnecessary risks. Yet, he couldn't shake it off. It was like regenerative living tissue, a part of him as distinguishable as a fingerprint.

After days of contemplating Jade Sperry's proposal, it occurred to him that perhaps he could merge his two obsessions. If he accepted this job and performed it well enough, it might atone for his failure that had brought about the deaths of his wife and son.

"Everything is set."

Dillon jumped reflexively when Jade reentered the room, bringing with her a three-page contract. He studied it carefully, filled in the missing details, then signed his name.

She said, "As soon as you have a permanent address in Palmetto, please call it in for the records."

"If it's all the same to you, I'd like to live on the premises."

"At the construction site?"

"I'd like to lease a trailer large enough to serve as an office and living quarters."

"Suit yourself." Jade stood and moved toward the door. Dillon followed.

"I've notified Mr. Seffrin. His office is in another building, but he's on his way over.

"Mr. Stein heard that you were in the building and asked to meet you, too. Beforehand, there's another matter I feel we should clear up."

She lowered her eyes. From his angle, her black, curly eyelashes looked like they had been painted onto her fair cheeks with a fine brush. "You shouldn't have kissed me that night in L.A. Nothing like that can happen again. If you have a problem working under a woman's supervision, I need to know."

He deliberately waited to respond until she lifted her eyes back to his. "I would have to be a blind eunuch not to notice that you're a woman. You're a beautiful woman. But it wouldn't matter if you had a mustache as thick as mine. I want this job.

"You've also left no doubt in my mind that I answer to you. That's cool. I don't have any sexist hang-ups. Finally, you're safe from me. When I want a woman, I'll find one, but it'll be for the night only. I don't want one I have to look at or talk to the morning after."

Her deep swallow was audible. "I understand."

"No, you don't understand, but that's immaterial. Just rest assured that I haven't made a practice of romancing the people I work for."

"Then why did you kiss me?"

He smiled wryly, tilting up one half of his mustache. "Because you pissed me off."

"How?"

"I wasn't having a very good day to begin with," he said sarcastically. "Then you came along, a real cool customer dressed fit to kill and flashing a Gold Card. I'm a grown-up. I don't appreciate being ordered around any more than you like being condescended to because you wear perfume and pantyhose. I don't know a man alive who likes being patronized by a woman."

"And vice versa."

"Then you should have slapped me when I kissed you."

"You didn't give me a chance."

The conversation had lasted ten times longer than the kiss, and he was ready to drop the subject. It made him uncomfortable. He didn't know what had motivated him to kiss her. The only thing he was sure of was that he didn't *want* to know. Nevertheless, he couldn't let the matter drop without asking one more question of her.

"If that kiss bothered you so much, why'd you hire me?"

"Because I've dedicated my life to the success of this project, Mr. Burke. Measured against that, one kiss is hardly important." Her eyes turned a darker hue and, not for the first time, Dillon wondered what motivated her. "However, it mustn't happen again."

"As I explained, it wasn't sexually motivated."

"Good." Her smile indicated that she was as relieved as he that the topic was closed. "Before we go see Mr. Stein, is there anything else on your mind?"

"Yeah. Who is Mr. Stein?"

Chapter 20

------◆------

Palmetto, May 1991

The civic auditorium was packed to capacity that balmy first day of May. Jade was seated in a row of chairs that had been set up on the stage at the front of the room. It was rapidly filling up with a noisy, curious crowd.

Gradually word had gotten around that a large parcel of land had been purchased and rezoned for industrial use. Dillon had been in Palmetto for several weeks, obtaining the necessary building permits and arranging for public utilities to be accessible at the site, but he had kept as low a profile as possible and certainly had made no public announcement.

Gossip was rampant. Rumors circulated that everything from a theme park to a nuclear reactor was being built in Palmetto. Jade had requested that the city council—the members of which weren't even certain what GSS planned—call this town meeting to allay fears and to enthuse and involve the community.

Her speech had been thoroughly prepared, but there were butterflies in her tummy. To calm them, she thought about the house she had leased for as long as she, Cathy, and Graham would be living in Palmetto. It was an older house that had spacious rooms, hardwood floors, and ceiling fans. The owners had completely refurbished and modernized it before deciding to tackle another renovation project in Charleston. Jade, working through a realtor in New York, had signed a lease as soon as the house became available.

Cathy would love the sunny kitchen and screened back porch, which would undoubtedly remind her of her house in Morgantown. The deep, tree-shaded backyard was encircled with azalea bushes. Jade had designated one of the upstairs bedrooms as Graham's. He would like the built-in shelves where he could arrange his stereo system.

Enthusiastically, she had described the room to him via long-distance. "It's got three large windows that overlook the front yard and a walk-in closet with so much more space than you've got now. You're going to love it."

He was still feeling some uncertainty and reluctance. "It sounds okay, I guess. How far is it from where you're building the plant?"

"Several miles. Why?"

"Just wondering. Dillon said maybe I could come out there sometime."

Dillon had been introduced to Graham in New York when he dropped in at the office one afternoon after school. They had met only one other time, but Graham frequently mentioned the man. Hank was the only adult male Graham was close to. Jade reasoned that his idol worship of Dillon was harmless, as long as it went no further. Although Dillon Burke was exactly what she needed to build TexTile, she wasn't certain that he was a suitable role model for her impressionable son, especially since Dillon might be looking to replace the son he had lost.

She knew more about Dillon than he suspected. Besides herself, the contractor would be the most important individual on the project. During the two-week interval between their meeting in Los Angeles and his appearance in New York, Jade had utilized GSS's wealth of resources to delve into his background, hoping to prove that her instincts about him were right.

She now knew about his troubled childhood, the time he had spent in a detention center, and his college career. She knew about Pilot Engineering Enterprises and his difficulties with the new management after it was acquired. The tragic deaths of his wife and child explained his cynicism. She had learned from former employers who remembered him that he was an exceptional but wasted talent.

When she had asked him for references, it had been to test his integrity. His truthfulness had convinced her that she had made the right choice. He had personal reasons for wanting to tackle this project. They weren't as strong as hers, but they were powerful in their own right. If he hadn't shown up in New York, she would have returned to L.A. and sought him out.

It was decided that Graham and Cathy would stay in New York until Graham completed the school term. If the prospect of seeing Dillon again made him more agreeable to relocating, fine. However, Jade didn't want him to regard Dillon as a playmate. She was confident that once

Graham started school in Palmetto next fall, he would make new friends and adjust quickly.

Although he had grown up with two women, he was a well-adjusted boy, without any ambiguities regarding his sexuality. He was four when he had first asked, "Mom, where's my dad?" They had just moved from Morgantown to Charlotte, and Jade had enrolled him in a preschool. He was bright and inquisitive, so it wasn't surprising that, after his first few weeks in the school, he had noticed that his family lacked what all others seemed to have.

"You don't have a dad," she had gently explained. "You don't need one. You've got Cathy and me, and before he died, you had Poppy. You're very lucky to have this many people who love you so much."

He was temporarily pacified, but the topic came up again after a visit from Hank. "Is Hank my dad?"

"No, darling. He's just a dear friend who loves you."

Graham's stubborn streak had grown in proportion to the rest of him. The twin bars of his eyebrows drew closer together over the bridge of his nose, and his blue eyes darkened mutinously. "Then who was my dad? I had to have one."

"You had one, but he isn't important."

On the contrary, having a father was extremely important to a seven-year-old. Unlike before, the topic wasn't so easily dismissed. "Are you divorced from him?" he asked.

"No."

"Can he come to see me sometime?"

"No."

"Didn't he like me when I got borned?"

"He wasn't there. Just me. And I loved you enough for ten people. A hundred." By then he had reached an age where hugs were unwelcome, but he had let her hold him in her arms for a long time that night.

There had come a time when he dealt with the problem in his own way, sometimes deviously. It got back to Jade that Graham was spinning tales about a father who died while saving a baby from a burning building.

"Why did you say that, Graham?" She posed the question gently, not as a reprimand.

He shrugged. He was pouty, but his eyes were shimmering with tears he was too manly to shed, having just turned ten.

"Do the kids at school tease you about not having a father?"

"Sometimes."

Her hopes that Graham wouldn't feel short-changed had been unrealistic. Having only one parent made a difference. Much of her youth had been spent in a single-parent home, but during her formative childhood years her father had been there. After his death, she had photographs and memories of him to sustain her. She had never forgotten their quiet talks together, his warm, encompassing hugs, his goodnight kisses, or his whispering to her, "Don't ever be afraid, Jade."

Telling Graham the truth wasn't an option she considered. If he knew that he was the result of a rape, he would likely blame himself for living. She refused to lay that kind of guilt on her child, recalling the cruel responsibility Velta had placed on her the last time she'd seen her.

Cathy disagreed. Every time Graham raised the topic of his father, she urged Jade to tell him, but to no avail. The stigma of not having a father was bad enough, without his knowing the rest. To help ease his conflict, she had given him permission to lie. "I hate lies, Graham. You know that. Sometimes, though, I think they're okay, if they're told to protect someone else and not oneself.

"So, when your friends ask you about your father, you can protect them from being embarrassed by simply saying that he died. I give you my permission to say just that—he died before you were born. Okay?"

Evidently it had been okay, because Graham had never broached the subject again. He had reached a level of maturity where he could work it out for himself. Thinking about how quickly the years were passing made Jade's heart wrench with homesickness for him. She couldn't wait till June, when he would join her in Palmetto.

"You've drawn quite a crowd."

Jade snapped out of her reverie and turned her head in response to the low voice near her ear. Dillon sat down in the vacant chair beside hers. "Good morning, Dillon. You look very handsome."

"Thanks," he replied self-consciously.

He was wearing a new suit for the occasion, and his hair had been trimmed.

She had dressed with utmost care herself. There would be old-timers in the crowd who remembered the scandal she had created when she left. Most were merely curious about Palmetto's new industry. Either way, she was going to be the focal point of everyone's attention today. She wanted to dazzle them.

"I drove out to your trailer last night, but you weren't there," she told Dillon.

"Sorry I missed you."

"It looked as though you're settled in."

"There wasn't much to settle. I'm ready to get to work."

"I didn't know you had a dog."

"Dog?"

"There was a dog lying on the top step of the trailer."

"Oh, him," he said, frowning. "He showed up a few days ago, and I made the mistake of feeding him a few table scraps."

Tilting her head, she smiled teasingly. "And now he's adopted you?"

"Not for long. I'm going to take him to the pound the first chance I get."

"After his leg heals, you mean. That looked like a home-made bandage," she said, her goading grin still in place.

Dillon's scowl deepened. "He'd been in a fight, had a bad scratch. I poured peroxide into it and patched it up. That's all."

"I don't know, Dillon," she said breezily. "I think you've got a pet for life."

He switched subjects by nodding out over the crowd. "Did you expect this?"

"Yes. For the first time, my name appeared in the local newspaper yesterday evening."

His gaze swung back to her. "Any reason why your name should spark so much local interest?"

"There might be. I grew up here."

He reacted to that as to an electric shock. His hazel eyes focused on her sharply. "Funny how you failed to mention that."

Before she had an opportunity to reply, Palmetto's mayor approached her. "Ms. Sperry, let's give these folks another five minutes or so to find a seat, then you can make your presentation. How long d'y'all figure it'll take?"

"Approximately ten minutes. Then I'll open the floor for questions."

"Mighty fine. Take all the time you want, little lady. This is a landmark day. I still can't get over it."

Cutting short his sexist effusiveness, she introduced Dillon to him. As the two men were shaking hands, Jade chanced to glance between them and spotted a woman seated in the crowd.

Reflexively her lips formed the name. "Donna Dee."

Her former friend had never had her overbite corrected; her small face still came to a point above her upper lip. She was wearing her hair in a short bob now, but it was still unrelentingly straight.

Nevertheless, there were marked changes in her appearance. She no longer looked comically animated, but harsh. Her eyes seemed to have receded into her skull, making her look more furtive than ever. She resembled a mistrustful animal peering at the world from inside its lair.

Her gaze now was uncharacteristically still, fixed on Jade. Time had etched distinct lines on each side of her protruding mouth. Jade and Donna Dee were the same age, yet Donna Dee looked at least a decade older.

Jade felt a sharp twinge of remorse that she couldn't remember with fondness all the nights they had slept over at each other's house, giggling and planning their futures, which invariably revolved around the men whom they would marry—Gary and Hutch. At least one of them had gotten her wish. Jade's thoughts must have manifested themselves in her expression because Donna Dee was the first to break their stare. She lowered her eyes to her lap.

It was odd that Hutch wasn't in attendance. There were a number of deputies helping to control the crowd, but

Hutch wasn't among them. Hutch had always been big and strong, but basically a coward. No doubt he was trying to avoid their first confrontation in fifteen years.

There were several faces in the crowd that were vaguely familiar to Jade. She could put names with others. She hadn't spotted Myrajane Griffith, but then Myrajane wouldn't be one to fraternize with the general public, believing most to be riffraff. And, of course, Lamar wasn't there. Jade had heard from him only once after seeing him in Morgantown. As before, he had pleaded for her understanding. She regretted that his death had been so tragic, but her resolve hadn't diminished—he had died unforgiven.

The mayor approached her again. He checked his wristwatch and importantly tugged on the hem of his coat. "Well, whenever you're ready, Ms. Sperry, I reckon we can start."

Feeling a rush of energy, she said, "I'm ready."

The mayor waxed poetic at the microphone until everyone in the audience was either torpid with boredom or fidgeting restlessly. At last, he introduced Jade.

The applause from the audience was polite but reserved.

"Ladies and gentlemen, thank you for coming this morning. Your number indicates to me that GSS has made an excellent choice for the site of their TexTile plant. Palmetto was chosen for several reasons. Among them were its availability of raw building materials and its accessibility to the shipyards, which will make the transportation of goods feasible and relatively inexpensive to domestic and foreign markets.

"The overwhelming reason for the selection of this location, however, was the duality of the benefit to be derived from this enterprise. The TexTile plant will provide hundreds of jobs. It will resuscitate a flagging economy. And TexTile will prosper because of a strong, willing, and resourceful labor force—in other words, you."

Jade held her breath. As she had hoped, there was a smattering of applause, then a groundswell of it, until it was deafening in the crowded room. She smiled inwardly, knowing that she had them. Strategically, she hadn't begun by trying to impress them with the wealth and might of GSS. That would have spawned only resentment. Rather, she had flattered the region and its people.

The mood shift was palpable. The crowd assumed a more cordial personality. Her audience was no longer suspicious of the Yankee company that was going to muscle its way in and inundate their county with outsiders. She talked them through the plant's procedure, from the time the ginned cotton arrived until it left in the form of ready-made garments, destined for any number of world markets.

"This plant will belong to the community," Jade stressed. "The more you put into it, the greater the payoffs will be. It will generate thousands of dollars each year in local taxes alone, which can be channeled into making much-needed improvements for the community. On an individual basis, it will mean better job opportunities for workers in numerous and diverse fields of endeavor."

"What kind of jobs?" someone shouted from the back of the room.

"Assembly line, shipping and freight, maintenance and engineering, clerical. The list of opportunities is virtually endless. To begin with, we'll need construction workers.

At this time, I'd like to introduce Mr. Dillon Burke. He's our general contractor."

She turned to Dillon and motioned him forward. He approached the lectern. His appearance was daunting, if for no other reason than his exceptional physique. That, coupled with his thick, curving mustache and compelling eyes, caused a silence to fall over the murmuring crowd. Jade gave him an encouraging smile as she relinquished the microphone to him.

After a brief speech, he excused himself, returning moments later carrying an architectural drawing of the completed plant. A gasp went up from the audience when they saw it.

"This is what the facility will look like when we're finished," Dillon explained. "As you can see, it will be a state-of-the-art operation that will take years to build. I'll be encouraging the subcontractors to hire regional workers."

He propped the drawing against the lectern and promptly returned to his seat. "Thank you, Mr. Burke." Jade addressed the crowd again. "I'm willing to take questions from the—"

The back door of the room was flung open with such force that it crashed against the inside wall. Every head turned to see what the commotion was about. An expectant hush fell over the room as two men entered.

Looking neither right nor left, they came down the center aisle between the rows of folding chairs until they reached the edge of the stage. Jade's heart was in her throat, but she ignored the rude interruption. "I'll take your questions now." Several hands were raised, but she wasn't given a chance to acknowledge them.

"I have a question for you, Ms. Sperry," a voice from her past announced. "Where in hell did you get the nerve to show your face in this town?"

Jade retained her composure, although her expression turned glacial as she lowered her gaze to the man in front of the lectern.

Ivan Patchett glared up at her from his wheelchair.

Chapter 21

———◆———

The flustered mayor intervened. He didn't want to risk having the town's number-one citizen offended. He didn't want Jade to be insulted, either. No matter how one looked at it, it was an explosive situation. The only way to avoid catastrophe was to call the meeting to an abrupt conclusion.

Over the din, Jade spoke into the microphone, promising that any further questions would be answered in a series of newspaper articles.

"What the hell is going on?" Dillon demanded when he reached her side. "Who is that old geezer?"

"I'll tell you about it later. Right now I just want to get away from here."

"You haven't answered my question yet!"

Ivan hadn't been deterred by the noisy confusion. Although the meeting had been adjourned, the crowd was slow to disperse. Most were holding back to see what was going to happen next. They sensed that the fireworks were about to begin, and, as was customary, Ivan milked his audience.

Jade would have chosen another time and place for her first encounter with the Patchetts, but Ivan was forcing her hand, and she wasn't about to back down. She stepped off the platform and confronted him.

"I have every right to be in this town or any other place I choose to go. The free enterprise system is still operative in America."

"Not in *my* town."

"Well, well. Jade Sperry. So you're the mystery person behind all this. Who'd have thought it?"

Neal was standing behind Ivan's wheelchair. Mistakenly, Jade had thought she was immune to his effect on her. She wasn't. Rage and hatred surged through her, almost obscuring his smiling face. *Patience,* she told herself. He wouldn't be wearing that smug smile much longer.

Since she had continued to receive the Palmetto newspaper all these years, she knew about their accident at the railroad crossing in Charleston. Both of Ivan's legs had been severed above the knees. Neal had suffered a crushed pelvis, broken bones, contusions, and other serious injuries that had kept him hospitalized for months. His wedding to Marla Sue Pickens had never taken place. The reasons for it being called off were nebulous.

Neal's appearance hadn't suffered any ill-effects either from aging or the accident. He was as handsome and arrogant as ever. "I thought this whole thing stunk to high heaven the first time those rezoning requests showed up on the city-council agenda. Naturally, I voted against them. Tried to sway the others, but some had stars in their eyes and don't know what's good for this town." He grinned slyly. "Got to tell you, Jade, I admire the sneaky way you went about this."

"Don't compliment her." Snarling, Ivan pointed a finger up at Jade. "I'm royally pissed off at you, young lady. You might think you've been real clever. You might think that since I'm confined to this goddamn chair I'm weak and incompetent."

He rolled the chair forward until his stumps were almost touching her knees. She held her ground, though the sight of him repulsed her and the thought of his touching her was revolting.

"You listen here, girly," he hissed. "I'm stronger than ever. That frigging train didn't damage my brain, you know." His eyes narrowed to malicious slits. "You can count on this—that goddamn plant of yours will never be built in my territory."

A cane was lying across his lap. He picked it up and thrashed it across the architectural drawing that was still propped against the lectern. It fell face down on the floor. From the corner of her eye, Jade saw Dillon lunge forward. She extended her arm, halting him in the center of his chest.

Her voice was amazingly calm. "I'll grant that at one time you were fearsome, Mr. Patchett." Her eyes roved over him unemotionally. "Now, you're merely pathetic."

She sidestepped his wheelchair and brushed past Neal without acknowledging him or anything he had said. Outside, people were still milling about. All looked at her expectantly as she emerged from the building. Obviously they were waiting to see how she had fared against Ivan.

With a confident stride, she moved down the sidewalk toward her new Jeep Cherokee and unlocked the driver's door. She tossed her briefcase inside and was about to slide behind the steering wheel when her arm was grabbed from behind.

Dillon had put on a pair of opaque sunglasses, but even with his eyes obscured by the dark lenses she could tell that he was furious. Out of deference to curious passersby, he kept his voice low and taut.

"What the hell was that all about?"

"This isn't the time or place to discuss it."

He lowered his face closer to hers. "The hell it's not. Before I turn a single spade of dirt, I want to know if I've got shotguns aimed at my back. Who was that old bastard in the wheelchair?"

"His name is Ivan Patchett, and he hasn't always been in a wheelchair." She raised her hand to brush back a strand of loose hair. Her hand was shaking. She hoped Dillon wouldn't notice. "However, he has always been a bastard."

"Patchett? The soybean guy?"

"That's right. Now, please let go of my arm. I've been on public display enough for one morning. I don't want to engage in a wrestling match with you here on Main Street."

He glanced down at his hand, which had shackled her upper arm. Apparently he hadn't realized until then that he was touching her. He released her immediately. "The other guy was his son?"

"Neal."

"What's your beef with them?"

"That's my business." She tried to get into the car, but he trapped her arm again as quickly as a snare.

"You made it my business when you got me out of that L.A. jail." As he strained each rough word through his teeth, his mustache barely moved. "You led me to believe that everything was going to be peachy keen down here in Dixie, that all the townsfolk were behind this thing one hundred percent, and that I'd have people lining up to work for me. Obviously that isn't quite the way it is. I want to know what I'm up against."

"What you're up against at the moment, Mr. Burke, is me." Despite the stragglers still ambling along the sidewalk, she wrenched her arm from his grasp. "Your responsibilities do not extend to public relations. That's my department. From here on, I'll thank you not to try and second-guess my motives. And I'll fire you if you dare try to interfere."

She ducked into the car and slammed the door. She didn't look back as she pulled out of the parking space and drove away.

Jade knew Dillon had every right to be concerned about public support because it could radically affect his work schedule. Her dealings with the Patchetts, however, were none of his business and never would be. Besides, she didn't think he would welcome knowing that he was playing even a small role in a revenge plot. In any case, she wasn't going to tell him more than he needed to know.

As she entered her house, her recently installed telephone was ringing. "Hello?"

"Is the meeting over yet?"

"Mr. Stein!" she exclaimed. "Yes, it just now concluded."

"Why didn't you call me? I told you to call me."

"I was about to. I'm barely inside the door."

"Well? How did it go?"

"Splendidly. We couldn't have asked for a better response." She briefly filled him in on what had transpired, omitting any mention of the Patchetts.

"So, you're still sold on the commercial potential of this area."

"Without qualification."

"Good. Then let me tell you about a few ideas I've been toying with."

Jade sat down to listen.

"Are you still here? Can't you take a hint?"

With the toe of his new shoe, Dillon nudged the stray dog aside as he unlocked the trailer door. "Beat it!" The mongrel looked up at him with woebegone eyes, lay back down on the step, and rested his head on his forepaws. "Suit yourself," Dillon grumbled. "But don't expect me to keep feeding you."

He slammed the trailer door so hard that the structure shook. Taking a soda from the refrigerator in the narrow kitchen, he stood in the wedge of cool air and drank half the soda in one swallow. He rolled the cold can against his forehead. "Dammit."

He didn't welcome anything in his life that made him think or feel. Seven years ago, he had officially stopped feeling. More than his wife and son had been interred in those graves. He had buried his sentience, too. Nothing except his body had continued to exist. On the inside, he was hollow and empty. He liked it that way. He planned to keep it that way.

He had walked away from the house where Debra and Charlie had died, leaving everything behind. From that day on, he had kept himself detached from the world. He owned no property except for the few essentials that he could carry with him in his pickup. He remained indifferent to other people. He hadn't stayed anywhere long enough to cultivate friendships. He hadn't wanted any.

He had learned the hard way that no matter how well you did what was expected of you, no matter how good a person you tried to be, you still got your teeth kicked in. You were punished for wrongdoings you weren't even aware of. Debts were always collected, and the tariff was the lives of the people you loved.

From this cruel lesson, Dillon had developed a logical philosophy: Don't love.

His life was a safe, painless void, and that's the way he wanted it to stay. He didn't need a sap of a dog forming an attachment to him. He didn't want to care about this job to the extent of being protective and possessive and to thinking of it as "his plant." He sure as hell didn't need a woman getting under his skin.

Cursing, he slammed the refrigerator door. Such was life. There was a dumb mutt curled up on his front step, licking his hand every time he went through the door. He was already as protective as a mama bear toward the Tex-Tile plant, and ground hadn't even been broken yet. And he was angry at Jade Sperry. Anger was an emotion. He didn't want to feel any emotion where she was concerned.

After weeks of conferences and meetings in New York with men in Burberry suits, men who had never had blisters on their hands, he couldn't wait for the actual construction to get under way. Now, it seemed that, just when he had allowed himself to get emotionally involved in his work for the first time in years, the project might be scrapped.

A fool could have predicted that Patchett wouldn't roll over and play dead when another industry came to town, placing his business in a distant second place. Jade Sperry was no fool. She had known beforehand that she would make an enemy out of Patchett. After the words they had exchanged at the town meeting, Dillon believed that she had been enemies with him for a long time—with his son, too.

Old man Patchett had said, "Where in hell did you get the nerve to show your face in this town?" That suggested a scandal. Had Jade left Palmetto in disgrace?

Dillon drained his soda and crumpled the can in his fist. He couldn't imagine the competent, calm, cool, and collected Ms. Sperry being involved in a scandal, especially one of a licentious nature. He didn't want to imagine her in any context, but she frequently figured into his thoughts.

That was natural, he assured himself. She was his boss. He would be thinking about his boss if his boss were a man. If his boss were a man, however, he wouldn't be having the same thoughts as those he often entertained about Jade.

He had been physically faithful to Debra for almost a year following her death. Then, one cold, lonely night in one of the plains states—Montana? Idaho?—he had picked up a woman in a bar and taken her to a motel room. Afterward, he was disgusted with himself and more lonely than before. He cried for Debra in dry, racking sobs. In spite of his emotional disability, his physical appetites recovered and grew to be strong and healthy again. The second time he took a woman to bed, he had less difficulty dealing with it. The third time, it was almost easy. By then he had developed the ability to disassociate the physical act from his conscience. His body could be stimulated without arousing his guilt. He could achieve pleasurable release without involving his heart and mind.

His aloof manner had made him even more appealing to

women than before. They found his latent hostility exciting. His wounded demeanor beckoned to their maternal
instincts. None, however, had appeased anything except
his sex drive. He was just as haunted when he left them
as before. Names and faces were never recorded in his
memory.

A name and a face were now recurring with frequency
in his thoughts. That bothered him considerably.

The mutt outside began to bark. "Shut up," Dillon hollered through the door. Then he heard a car motor and
pulled the door open. Jade Sperry alighted from a shiny
new pickup truck with the TexTile logo stenciled on the
door.

"Does he bite?" she asked, nodding toward the dog.

"I don't know. He's not mine."

"I don't think he knows that. He's already guard-
ing you."

Bending at the waist, she beckoned the dog forward
by making kissing noises with her mouth. "Come here,
pooch." The dog stopped barking, whimpered a few
times, then crept down the steps toward her. She let him
smell her hand. He licked it. She scratched him behind
the ears.

"Some watchdog," Dillon remarked drolly.

Straightening up, Jade tossed him a set of keys to the
truck. "I hope you like it." He snatched the keys out of the
air with one fist. "It's yours to drive for as long as you're
on the job."

"I've already got a truck."

She glanced at his battered pickup. "That's for personal use. Anytime you're representing TexTile, use the
company truck, please."

"Yes, ma'am. Anything else?"

She climbed the steps to the trailer. The dog trailed behind her, wagging his tail. She took a gasoline credit card from her purse and handed it to Dillon. "Use this, too."

"Thanks."

"The bills will be sent directly to me."

"They sure as hell better be."

He was being rude and obnoxious, but it bothered him to take gifts from a woman. It reminded him of being tutored by Mrs. Chandler on how to make love. Do this, do that. Not so hard. Harder. Slower. Faster. Dillon had been a quick learner and, before long, had mastered his own technique. He liked it much better when he had the upper hand.

It was an untimely and unpopular attitude, he knew, but he couldn't help it. He was perversely glad that he was on the step above Jade and she had to tilt her head back in order to speak to him face to face. She might be the boss lady and have the means to buy new trucks, but she wasn't going to bash his masculinity.

"You'll have to drive me home."

"Sure."

"I'd like to see the office you've set up first." He didn't budge. She smiled up at him with feigned sweetness. "If this is a convenient time, Mr. Burke."

He locked eyes with her, sensing that there was an undeclared war of wills going on. Eventually, he stepped aside and waved her into the trailer. To keep the dog from coming inside, he closed the door, then wished he hadn't. The trailer was too small for two people—at least it seemed that way now that he was alone in it with Jade.

He had never seen her dressed in anything except suitable office attire. She had changed since the town meeting and was now wearing a pair of jeans and a white pullover. If he hadn't known better, he would never have guessed she had carried a child for nine months. Her thighs and ass were firm and slender. Her belly was flat. Her breasts...

He cleared his throat. "The phone lines will be installed tomorrow."

"Good," she said, turning away from her inspection of the desk he had installed. The living area of the trailer had been converted into a compact office. The only items not used for business were a radio and a small portable TV set. "This doesn't leave you much room to live in."

"I don't need much room."

"Are you sure you won't reconsider my hiring a secretary for you?"

He shook his head. "If I decide later on that I need one, I'll let you know." Her eyes roved beyond him, toward the kitchen and bedroom. "Did you want to check out my bed, too?"

Her eyes sprang quickly to his. He would have bet his next paycheck that a scathing comment was on the tip of her tongue, but that she thought better of speaking it. She said crisply, "The only thing that interests me is where you'll be conducting company business."

There was a limit to Ms. Sperry's toughness, he decided. It didn't extend to interplay between the sexes. That's where her sophistication collapsed like an umbrella. He had observed her interaction with the men at GSS headquarters in New York. She was uncomfortable with double entendres and innuendos. The lady wasn't a flirt. With her, it was all business, or it was zilch.

He had concluded that she wasn't married. She had never mentioned an ex, either. One of the young executives at GSS had sidled up to him at the office coffee machine and asked, "Are you screwing Jade?"

Dillon had never approved of locker room braggadocio, especially between strangers. "What possible business is that of yours?"

"I've got fifty bucks riding on a bet."

Dillon calmly took a sip of his steaming coffee while dangerously squinting at the other man. "Tell you what, if you want to talk sex, why don't you go fuck yourself, then come and tell me how it was."

Apparently Jade had left a few of her male counterparts frustrated enough to generate speculation about her sexuality. Dillon was rather curious himself about her kid's father but had refrained from broaching the subject.

"Perhaps we should get another trailer," she said now in her brisk, businesslike fashion.

"What for?"

"I need an office, too. It would be more convenient to have it here at the site than downtown. Besides, you should have a facility where you can confer with subs, and so on. What do you think? Something large enough to accommodate my desk and a sitting area."

"It's your money."

"I'll look into it tomorrow."

"Fine."

"Well, I guess that's everything."

She was at the door, her hand already on the latch, when he stepped around her and blocked her path. "Not quite everything, Jade."

Reflexively, she took a hasty step back. His sudden

movement seemed to have startled her, inordinately so, he thought. She looked almost afraid of him.

"What do you want?"

He couldn't account for her breathlessness, either. She had all the control. What did she have to fear from him? For the time being, he tabled personal curiosity and addressed the practical matters. "Tell me about Ivan Patchett."

"What about him?"

"I can understand why he's upset over the TexTile plant. It will usurp some of his power. Palmetto has been his kingdom, and he's ruled it for a long time."

"I suppose you could look at it that way," she said.

"I think *you* looked at it that way."

"Meaning?"

"Knowing that the plant would adversely effect Patchett— is that why you decided to build it here?"

"You've read the prospectus. You know that Palmetto is the perfect location."

"I also know that you could have picked a dozen or more towns along the Southeastern seaboard that would have been equally as perfect. Why Palmetto?"

"I was familiar with it."

"Which brings me to my second question. Why did Patchett think it nervy of you to show your face around here?"

She tossed her head, rearranging the cloud of loose, dark curls lying against her shoulders. "I didn't leave Palmetto under ideal circumstances."

"And these 'circumstances' somehow involved the Patchetts?"

"Among others."

"Especially the younger Patchett."

"Why do you say that?"

He studied her face for a moment, then took his best shot. "Who is your son's father, Jade?"

"Graham doesn't have a father."

"Wrong. That hasn't happened since Bethlehem. You were pregnant when you left Palmetto, weren't you?"

She merely regarded him with frosty blue eyes.

"Did Neal Patchett get you pregnant, then refuse to marry you? Is that it?"

"Absolutely not. I despise Neal Patchett and always have." Pushing him out of her way, she yanked the door open and stepped outside. The dog bounded to his feet and vigorously wagged his tail, eager for another kind word. Jade ignored the dog and marched down the steps, turning on the lowest one to address Dillon again.

"Look, I know I got a little high-handed with you this morning in town, and I'm sorry. I should have reassured you that I've got the situation under control and let it go at that."

"*Do* you have the situation under control?"

"Absolutely. I can handle whatever difficulties might arise, and, as I'm sure you realize, there will be many before we're finished. You should concern yourself only with those relating to the actual construction.

"And please keep your speculations about my son and me to yourself. Better yet, don't speculate on us at all. Once the excavation begins, you should be so busy that you don't have time to think about anything except the business at hand."

Dillon was more intrigued than ever. Her volatile reaction to his questions only reinforced his curiosity. This was a small town. People talked. Sooner or later he would know more about her murky past. Judiciously, he chose not to pursue it any further now.

He locked the trailer and followed her to the new pickup, where she was already sitting on the passenger side. He climbed behind the wheel and started the motor. "Pretty fancy," he remarked as he surveyed the interior.

"GSS is a first-class corporation," she said stiffly.

He guided the truck along the rutted path leading to the highway. "You'll have to give me directions to your house." He knew the place she had rented, but he didn't want her to know that.

Following her terse directions, he drove through town. Shortly, he realized that she wasn't leading him to her leased house. "I'm surprised you wanted to live this far out," he commented conversationally as they left the city limits.

"We're not going directly to my house. I want your opinion on something."

He shot her a puzzled glance, but she didn't elaborate. He continued driving on the two-lane highway, which, he knew, eventually led to the Atlantic coast.

"Turn right at the next crossroads." As instructed, he took a sharp turn onto a narrow gravel road. "You can pull up anywhere along here." As soon as he brought the truck to a stop, she alighted. "I'd like you to come with me."

Dillon got out and followed her to a barbed-wire fence. A rusty NO TRESPASSING sign was nailed to one of the posts. Ignoring it, she asked him to hold apart two of the wires, wide enough for her to climb through.

He said, "You know this is private property."

"Yes, I know." When she had safely climbed through, she placed her foot on the bottom wire, stretching it down and raising the next one as high as she could. "Come on. I don't think we'll get caught."

Because of his height, Dillon had to exercise more caution than she when he squeezed between the two strands of barbed wire. Once he was inside the fence, he placed is hands on his hips and looked down at her "Now what? What can we see on this side that we couldn't see from the road?"

They were standing in a fallow field. If it was a nice walk in the country she had in mind, he wished she had told him to change his clothes. He had left his tie and jacket behind, but he was still in the dress slacks and shoes he had worn to the town meeting.

"I only want to take a look around." She struck off across the field on foot. "I didn't want to come alone."

"Coming alone can be a real drag, all right," he joked. As anticipated, she wasn't amused.

For half an hour they tramped across the uncultivated ground. She walked along the fence, then asked him to pace off yardage, which he did without understanding the reason behind her odd request. She took a spiral notebook from her handbag and made several notations.

The wind picked up, but she didn't notice, not even when it whipped her hair across her face and mouth. Dark clouds moved in, scuttling low. Dillon heard distant thunder. They continued to walk and pace for no reason apparent to him.

Finally, she gathered her windblown hair into her fist and held it secure at her nape, as she tilted her head back to look up at him. "What do you think?"

In that stance, with her feet widely spaced, her hand behind her head, and her wind-plastered top clearly defining the shape, size, and substance of her breasts, all his thoughts were carnally governed.

"What do I think?" he repeated gruffly. "I think we might get wet."

She glanced at the sky with eyes that were a darker blue than the stormclouds. "I believe you're right. But what do you think about this property?"

Impatiently, he shoved his hand through his own wind-blown hair. "Is that why we've been stamping around here for the last half-hour—so you could hear my opinion of this miserable piece of land? I could have told you my opinion without having to get mud on my new shoes."

"You don't think it's valuable?"

"Valuable?" he shouted above the wind. "I think it's worthless. Probably half of it is in flood plain."

"I'm thinking about buying it for GSS."

Having said that, she did an about-face and picked her way over the uneven ground back toward the fence. Befuddled, Dillon followed her. "What the hell for?"

"Future expansion. Please pay close attention to those wires, Dillon."

They got through the fence without mishap and walked back to the truck. He slammed the passenger door behind her and jogged around the hood. He had barely ducked inside when fat raindrops began spattering the windshield.

He cursed the mess on the bottom of his shoes, then picked up where their previous discussion had left off. "You can't be serious about buying this land."

"I might be. Mr. Stein called today. We discussed several areas of opportunity in and around the county. There's a very good chance that I will acquire property for the corporation. In fact, his suggestion came more in the form of an executive mandate."

"Before you could build anything larger than an out-house on this land, it would take millions to get it ready."

"We've got millions."

Her flippancy annoyed the hell out of him. "Well, since you've got all the answers, why bring me along?"

"Protection."

Angrily, he regarded her for a moment, then threw the transmission into reverse, stretched his arm across the back of the seat, swiveled his head around, and guided the truck back to the intersection with the highway. Against the fingertips of his outstretched hand he could feel Jade's hair. It was damp and soft, and it made him mad that he noticed. He wanted to grip handfuls of it and rub it against his face. The falling rain had cooled the windows. They were beginning to fog up. He could smell Jade's perfume in the still, sultry air.

Jade's hair. Jade's perfume. He was far too aware of Jade.

Searching for something to distract him, he noticed a rural mailbox leaning precariously on a rotting post. Through the rain, Dillon read the name that had been painted on the dented metal years ago. The letters were faded, but he was still able to make them out: O. PARKER."

"I want to know what the little bitch is up to." Querulously, Ivan waved away the housekeeper who was trying to serve him a second helping of sweet potatoes. Four years earlier, Eula had retired. Her daughter had taken her place, assuming the additional responsibilities of taking care of an amputee.

"Bring me a bottle of brandy," he ordered brusquely. As she left to do his bidding, Ivan glared at Neal, who was slouching in his chair, toying with the food remaining on his plate. "Well, have you gone deaf? Say something."

Moving nothing except his eyes, Neal glanced up at his

father. "How many times do I have to say it? I don't know any more than what I've already told you."

Ivan snatched the bottle from the housekeeper and poured a hefty amount into a snifter. The maid removed Neal's plate when he signaled that he was finished. When she returned to the kitchen, they were left alone in the dining room—two people at a table that would easily seat twenty.

Neal said, "That contractor, Burke, just awarded the excavation job to an outfit out of Columbia. They're already hauling in earth-moving equipment."

"Well, they can just as well haul it right back outa here," Ivan growled as he poured himself another brandy.

He wheeled away from the table and into the den. "Get in here," he hollered through the empty rooms of the house. The interior hadn't changed beyond the modifications required to accommodate Ivan's wheelchair.

Neal entered the den behind his father, bringing a snifter of brandy with him. "You can't stop this thing by willing it to disappear, old man. You made a damn fool of yourself at that town meeting, snarling like a wounded gator. That isn't the way to go about it, Daddy."

Neal threw himself onto the leather sofa. "We've got to beat Jade at her own game. We were asleep at the switch while she was buying that land where the plant is going to be. We won't be caught napping this time."

"What've you got going?" The brandy had helped mellow Ivan's sour mood.

Besides, these days it drained his strength to be tyrannical. Since the train accident had so seriously impaired his health, Neal had assumed more responsibilities. Having avoided work before, he had been pleasantly surprised to discover that it was like a game. He always played to win—and he was a sore loser.

"I've been sniffing out everything Jade does," he told his father. "She's set up shop out there at the construction site in a portable building, right next to the trailer where that Burke fellow lives. About the only curious thing she's done is go out to the Parker place twice."

"The hell you say!"

"Twice that I know of," Neal added with a frown. "Once with Burke, then next time alone. She doesn't go to visit them, you understand, just to snoop around. The second time, she didn't even get out of her car, only drove around the perimeter of Otis's fence several times. Yesterday, she went to the courthouse and asked to see the plans."

"You're sure they were for the Parker place?"

"I'm sure. I complimented Gracie Dell Ferguson's fat ass," Neal said, referring to the courthouse clerk. "After that she was willing to tell me everything. Jade asked to see all the records on the Parker place and its surrounding property."

"I own most of the surrounding property."

"That's right, Daddy, you do. Gracie Dell pointed that out while making sure I noticed her big tits."

"Did Jade tell Gracie Dell why she was interested in looking at the plans?"

"No."

As Neal poured them each another brandy, Ivan asked, "Why do you think Jade is interested in the Parker farm?"

"I can't imagine, but I don't like it," Neal grumbled. "I want to know what she's got in mind."

"Well, she's not likely to announce it ahead of time.

And sooner or later she's bound to find out that you've been following her and asking questions."

"No problem. I found a couple of boys who are halfway smart and can keep their mouths shut. They're watching her in shifts and reporting back to me. And in the meantime," he added with a slow grin, "I'm being my charming self. I sent her flowers yesterday."

Ivan regarded his son shrewdly. "She's a better-looking woman than she was a girl."

"So it didn't escape your notice, either?" Neal laughed. "She blew into town and made a big splash, but beneath her corporate image, Jade's just a woman. They can cry equality all they want to. But when it comes right down to it, all they're really good for is what's between their legs."

"Ordinarily, I'd agree with you. But this one worries me. She hasn't forgotten what happened right before y'all graduated." Ivan stabbed his blunt finger at the space separating them. "She's out to bury us, boy. She wasn't a dim-witted child, you know. If anything, she's smarter now. She's out for blood. Our blood."

Neal's eyes glittered above the rim of his brandy snifter. "All I know is, if there's a new industry in Palmetto, it's going to belong to the Patchetts."

Ivan cackled. "That's the way I taught you to think. It does my heart good to know that some of the lessons took. Nobody's gonna come in and muscle us out."

"No, but Jade can sure as hell muck things up temporarily. For beginners, she can cause a wage war. If she offers a dime more an hour to her employees, who do you figure folks will want to work for?"

"Our employees are loyal."

"Loyal, my ass," Neal said scornfully. "This is the *new*

South, Daddy. Wake up. All that generational crap is just that—crap. If Jade promises to pay them more than we do, we'll lose them. It won't matter if their daddies and granddaddies worked for us. Damn! Every time I think about it, I wish I had my hands around her throat."

Ivan looked at Neal from beneath his brows. "Y'all probably should have gone ahead and killed her that night, then blamed it on niggers or white trash."

"Yeah. Wish I'd known then what I know now."

"She's out for revenge all right. I've gone after it enough times myself to recognize the signs." Ivan smacked his lips with disgust. "Wouldn't you know it, that chickenshit kid of Myrajane's had to up and die. Our venerable sheriff sure as hell ain't in any condition to fight this thing. So, guess who's left?"

Neal clamped his hand on his father's shoulder. "Don't worry, Daddy. We're all we need."

Jade pulled the Jeep Cherokee into the yard, which looked remarkably, and lamentably, the same as it had the last time she had seen it. The chickens were probably several generations removed from the previous ones, but they still pecked about the yard. A sow grunted from her muddy sty.

Through the kitchen window she could see Mrs. Parker wiping her hands on a cup towel and looking through the window to see who had arrived. Jade experienced an eerie sense of déjà vu. She should have come at another time of day, one not so reminiscent of that other dusk when she had made the grisly discovery in the barn. But suppertime was the only time she was certain to catch Otis in the house.

She approached the front door and knocked. With the cup towel slung over her shoulder, Mrs. Parker answered the door and peered at Jade through the loose screen, shading her eyes against the setting sun. "Can I help you?"

"Hello, Mrs. Parker. It's Jade. Jade Sperry."

Jade heard her quick intake of breath. It gave a brief rise to her bony chest. She adjusted her hand against her brow and took a closer look.

"What do you want here?"

"I'd like to come in and talk to you."

"We got nothing to say to each other."

"Please, Mrs. Parker. It's important or I wouldn't have come. Please."

Jade waited anxiously through a seemingly interminable silence, then the screen door squeaked loudly as Mrs. Parker pushed it open. She inclined her gray head; Jade stepped into the front room of the house. The upholstery on the sofa was so threadbare that, in spots, the cotton stuffing showed through. There was a stain on the headrest of the easy chair. The rug had unraveled around the edges. No improvements had been made in the room since Jade had last been in it. It was a gloomy room with dingy wallpaper, derelict furniture, a loudly ticking clock, and a framed picture of Gary in his graduation cap and gown, which he had never worn to commencement.

Since her return, Jade had visited Gary's grave. Seeing his face smiling at her now from the dimestore frame gave her a start, but strengthened her resolve. She turned back to Gary's mother, who had aged beyond the fifteen years that had passed. Her hair was thin and unkempt, and her clothes fit loosely. Beneath them, her skin sagged, covering nothing but bone.

"Where are the younger children, Mrs. Parker? What happened to them?"

Without any elaboration, she told Jade that two of the girls were married and had children. One of the boys lived in town with his wife and worked at the Patchett soybean plant; another had joined the navy; another had left home without saying where he was going. The last postcard they had received from him had been mailed in Texas.

"The baby's still here at home," she reported tiredly. "She'll graduate high school next year."

Sadly, Jade remembered all that Gary had wanted to do to pave the way for his younger brothers and sisters.

She heard a door closing in another part of the house.

"That'll be Otis," Mrs. Parker said anxiously. "He won't cotton to your being here."

"I need to see him."

Otis Parker had aged even more than his wife. He was stooped, and what hair he had left was white. The elements, along with fatigue, despair, and grief, had carved deep ravines into his face. He drew up short when he saw Jade.

"We got comp'ny, Otis." Mrs. Parker had removed the cup towel from her shoulder and was wringing it between her hands.

"Who is it?" He moved forward in his rolling, bow-legged gait and stopped a few feet from Jade, squinting at her through nearsighted eyes.

"It's Jade Sperry, Mr. Parker."

The breath left his body in a slow hiss. Jade almost expected him to deflate. Instead, he pulled himself to his full height. "I can see that now. What are you doing here?"

Jade wanted to put her arms around them. Embracing them would almost be like touching Gary again. She resisted the impulse. She had tried to share their grief at Gary's funeral and had been rebuffed. They believed, as everyone else did, that her unfaithfulness to Gary had caused his suicide.

"I'd heard you were back in town," Otis said. "What do you want with us?"

"Could we sit down?"

The couple silently consulted each other with exchanged glances. Otis turned his back and went to sit in the chair with the dark stain on the headrest. Mrs. Parker indicated the sofa to Jade, then sat down in a straight chair with a ratty cane seat.

"You said you'd heard that I was back in town," Jade began. "Do you know why?"

"Heard you was building a new plant of some kind."

"That's right." She gave them an elementary explanation. "My company is already considering several ways to diversify. In order to expand, we'll need more land. That's why I came to see you this evening, Mr. Parker." She drew a breath through her tight chest. "I want to buy your farm on behalf of GSS."

Mrs. Parker raised a hand to her lips but didn't utter a peep. Otis continued to squint at Jade. "This place? What for?"

"There are several possibilities," she replied evasively.

"Like what?"

"I'm not at liberty to discuss them, Mr. Parker. I would also ask that you keep this offer in strictest confidence." She glanced at Mrs. Parker, then back at Otis. "I hope you understand that. Absolutely no one must know."

"It don't matter. I ain't interested in selling."

"I realize that the property has been in your family for a long time, Mr. Parker. There's certainly a sentimental attachment to consider, but—"

"It ain't for sale."

Jade rolled her lips inward. She was making them remember, pushing them into painful recollection. Her presence in their home was a reminder of the son they had loved so much and lost so tragically. She was tempted to leave and alleviate their misery. Instead, she forced herself to go on.

"Would you at least grant me permission to have the property appraised by an impartial third party? It would be done with the utmost discretion and with no inconvenience to you, I promise. Once I review the appraisal, I'd appreciate an opportunity to speak with you again."

"It won't hurt nothing, will it, Otis?" Mrs. Parker asked.

Otis regarded Jade with animosity. "You hurt my boy. You broke his heart and his spirit right in two."

Jade bowed her head. "I can't explain to you what happened that spring, but you must believe that I loved Gary with all my heart. If I'd been given a choice, I never would have hurt him."

"You think buying this place is going to ease your guilty conscience?" Mr. Parker asked.

"Something like that."

"Well, neither you or that highfalutin company you work for has enough money to make up for our Gary."

"You're absolutely right, Mr. Parker. A price tag could never be placed on his life. It's just that your farm lies in the path of our progress. GSS is prepared to pay you a premium price for it."

"It ain't for sale. Not to you." He rose to his feet and left the room.

After a moment Jade reluctantly stood to go. Mrs. Parker led her to the door. "Do you think it would be all right if I have the property appraised?"

The woman cast a worried glance toward the rear of the house. "He didn't say a flat-out no, did he?"

"No, he didn't."

"Then I guess it'd be okay."

"Afterward, may I come to see you again?"

Her pursed mouth began to work with emotion. "Jade, we loved that boy. We like to never got over what he done to hisself."

"Neither have I."

"It almost kilt Otis, too." She wiped her nose on the cup towel. "He's proud, you know, the way men are. Me, I figure we got something coming for all the grief we suffered over Gary. Somebody ought to pay for what happened."

Jade reached out and pressed her arm. "Thank you. I'll be in touch soon. And please remember not to say anything to anyone about this."

Chapter 22

———◆———

"Say, Mom?"

"Say, what?"

Graham looked up from the *Sports Illustrated* he was thumbing through. He was stretched out on the floor of their living room, lying on his stomach. "That sounded funny coming from you. Mostly black guys say that to one another."

"I met a man once—a white man—who began most of his sentences with 'say,' and it annoyed me so much I sent him to jail."

Graham rolled to his back, then sat up. "No kiddin'?"

"No kidding."

His dark hair was tousled, his eyes bright. Unabashedly, Jade took a moment to adore him. Since his and Cathy's arrival in Palmetto the week before, Jade couldn't seem to look at him enough. She had missed him terribly during their six-week separation. It was the longest stretch of time they had ever spent apart, and she hadn't enjoyed it.

"If you don't believe me," she said, "ask Mr. Burke the next time you see him. He knows better than I that the man belonged in jail."

"Mr. Burke's so cool."

"Cool?"

Jade tried to apply the slang adjective to the man. He worked incessantly and took every delay—such as inclement weather or malfunctioning equipment—as a personal affront. He elevated conscientiousness to the degree of fanaticism. Building the plant had become his crusade. He was almost as obsessive about it as she.

"I guess you could call him cool." She deliberately kept her tone noncommittal.

Dillon had no vices that she knew of. He had never been drunk or hung over in her presence. If he saw women, he saw them away from the trailer. To her knowledge, he had never brought a woman to the construction site.

"When I first met him, I thought he was sorta mean," Graham told her.

"Mean?"

"He doesn't smile a lot, does he?"

"No, I guess he doesn't," she said thoughtfully. On the few occasions she had seen him smile, it had been a self-derisive expression.

"And the first day you took me out to the site, he yelled at me when I climbed up on the bulldozer."

In the brief time he'd been in Palmetto, Graham had talked her into taking him to the site three times. He was fascinated with it. Now she wondered if it was Dillon and not the excavation that attracted him.

"I'm glad Dillon yelled at you. You had no business playing around that machinery. It could be dangerous."

"That's what Mr. Burke said, too. He told me that people who flirt with getting hurt like that have shit for brains."

"Graham!"

"He said it, Mom, not me. I'm just telling you."

"What other quaint expressions have you picked up from Mr. Burke?"

He grinned. "I think he likes me now, but he totally lost it when Loner and me got up on that gravel heap."

"Loner?"

"His dog. That's what Mr. Burke calls him. Anyway, I was just scaling it like a regular hill when Mr. Burke came running out of his trailer yelling at me to get the hell down from there—that's what he said, Mom. Then he took my arm and kinda shook me and asked me didn't I have a lick of sense and didn't I know that kids smother in gravel heaps all the time.

"I told him I wasn't a kid. He said, 'You aren't grown, either. And while you're around here, you'll do as I say.' He was scary, 'cause when he talks all quiet and mean like that, you can't see his lips move under his mustache, you know?"

"Yes, I know." She'd seen Dillon lose his temper. Like Graham, she had caught herself watching his mustache and his lips for signs of movement.

"He didn't hurt you, did he?"

"Hell no. I mean, heck no. Later he apologized for grabbing my arm. He said when he saw me and Loner up on the gravel, he was scared shitless it would swallow us whole." She frowned at his language. Again Graham grinned up at her guilelessly. It was fun to be saying words he was ordinarily forbidden to use. "He's gotta grip that would break bone."

His strength had never been in doubt. On more than one occasion Jade had paused at the window of her portable office to gaze at him while he was at work and unaware that anyone was watching. His stride was long and sure as he moved about, overseeing the excavation. Even at a distance, she could pick him out from the other workers because he always wore a white hard hat and aviator sunglasses . . . and there was his mustache, of course.

". . . if I could. Can I?"

"I'm sorry, Graham. Can you do what?"

He rolled his eyes the way teenagers do when their parents demonstrate incredible stupidity. "Can I ride my bike out to the site? I know the way."

"But it's several miles."

"Please, Mom."

"It sounds like some big-stakes negotiating is going on here," Cathy said. She entered the room carrying a tray of cookies and drinks. There was a glass of milk for Graham and coffee for Jade and her. "You'll need sustenance to carry on."

In the brief time she'd been there, Cathy had already exercised her knack for making a house into a home. Jade hadn't realized how vital Cathy was to her until she'd had to do without her for six weeks. She did all the shopping, cooked all their meals, and managed the house. That's what she wanted to do, and she was excellent at it. Without someone to fuss over, Cathy would consider her life meaningless.

She set the tray on the coffee table and took a seat beside Jade on the sofa. "What topic are we debating tonight?"

Around his first, oven-fresh chocolate chip cookie, Graham explained. "Mr. Burke said I could come out to the site anytime I want. What's wrong with riding my bike out there, Mom?"

"In the first place, it's too far to go on a bicycle. Second, the construction site isn't a playground. You could get in the way of the workers or you could get hurt. Finally, you should be making friends your own age."

"I've already met several boys in the neighborhood."

She hoped he would develop some friendships over the summer, which would make enrolling in school easier next fall. Being with boys his own age would be a much healthier pastime than hanging out with her reclusive general contractor.

"Mr. Burke has better things to do than entertain you."

"But he said I could, Mom. You don't want me to have any fun," he grumbled.

Cathy, ever the diplomat, said, "Maybe I could ask Mr. Burke to dinner one night soon."

"Gee. That'd be neat," Graham said, smiling again.

"I'm not so sure," Jade said hastily.

"Why not, Mom?"

"Unless he goes out, he eats alone in that trailer night after night," Cathy argued gently. "I'm sure he would appreciate a home-cooked meal."

"If he wants to live like a hermit, I think we should honor his privacy."

That was a feeble excuse. Even if their expressions hadn't told her so, she would have known it. The truth was that she and Dillon were together a great deal each day. He was so competent that she found herself asking for his opinion or advice on a number of decisions. They were friendly, but strictly professional in their treatment of each other, and that's the way it would have to stay.

"You still haven't said whether I could ride my bike out there," Graham reminded her. "Please, Mom. Palmetto's not like New York. Nothing bad happens here."

Unsteadily, Jade returned her cup and saucer to the tray.

Cathy quickly interceded. "Give her a day or two to think about it, Graham. Since you've demolished that plate of cookies, you can help me clean up the kitchen. Take the tray in, please. I'll be there in a minute. Now scoot."

Graham reluctantly came to his feet and carried the tray from the room. Once he was out of earshot, Cathy covered Jade's hands which were tightly clenched on her knees. "He didn't know any better than to say something like that, Jade."

"Of course he didn't. Until I was gang-raped, I never would have believed that anything bad could happen here, either."

Cathy chose her next words carefully. "I know you've never wanted Graham to know how he was conceived."

"I haven't changed my mind."

"But what if he finds out from someone else?" Cathy asked worriedly. "What if someone comes right out and asks him which of the three men was his father?"

"The people who know about the rape aren't going to tell about it. And even they don't know that Graham was conceived that night."

"Your enemies are the most important men in town— the Patchetts and Sheriff Jolly. When they hear about Graham, they're bound to put two and two together."

"And then what? Confess to rape? Hardly."

Cathy searched her young friend's face. "Jade, I've

never interfered in your personal life. If I had, I would have had you married to Hank Arnett years ago. I've never presumed to tell you what you should do."

"Why do I feel that's about to change?"

The older woman ignored her sarcasm and, in an urgent whisper, said, "Let it go."

"Let what go?"

"I'm not stupid, Jade. You didn't whimsically select Palmetto as the site of the TexTile plant. Why would you return to a place of such unpleasant memories if not to get revenge?"

She squeezed Jade's hands tighter. "Your achievements should be revenge enough. You've overcome every obstacle put in your path. You've got Graham, and he loves you dearly. What more do you need? Let it go."

"I can't, Cathy." She didn't even attempt to deny Cathy's charge. "I've waited years for this. I won't back down now."

"I'm afraid for you. This thing is consumptive. It might destroy you before you can destroy them."

"I don't want to destroy them. If I had, I would have killed them fifteen years ago. I thought about it." She shook her head. "But killing them would have been the easy way out. No, I want them to lose something that they cherish, the way I lost my innocence and the boy I loved. I want to see them stripped of their dreams just as I was stripped of mine.

"More than that, I want Gary's death avenged. They killed him, Cathy, just as surely as if they had put a gun to his head and pulled the trigger. I won't rest until they've paid dearly for his life."

Her tone softened, became wistful. "He was such an idealist. We dreamed of someday dethroning the Patchetts, to stop their economic tyranny over Palmetto. They prey on victims who have no wealth, no strength or influence, just as I was fifteen years ago. They're lawless and unconscionable, and they'll continue to hurt people and suppress this town until somebody stops them." Her expression hardened again with resolve. "I worked for fifteen years toward having this opportunity. I can't squander it."

Cathy said nothing for a moment, then lifted imploring eyes to Jade. "Tell Graham what happened to you. If these men are as villainous as you say, they'll fight back. They could try and get to you through him. Tell him, Jade, before someone else does."

She recognized the wisdom in what Cathy was telling her, but she could also recall Velta laying the responsibility of her father's suicide on her. If she told Graham about the rape, he might wrongly assume the blame for his conception. She refused to burden him with a guilt that would last a lifetime.

"No, Cathy. He must never know."

The question of whether Graham had permission to bicycle to and from the construction site was temporarily shelved when Dillon went out of town to interview several concrete contractors.

"He asked me to make sure that Loner had food and water while he was gone," she told Graham that evening when she returned home. "There's no point in you even asking to ride your bike out there. We'll discuss it again when Mr. Burke comes back."

Graham was crestfallen. "When will that be, a hundred years?"

"Two weeks, he said."

"A hundred years," he mouthed as he walked away dejectedly.

He wasn't pleased by the turn of events, but secretly Jade was. Cathy's caution couldn't be dismissed lightly. She had been so single-minded about her plans that she had failed to consider the kind of countermoves the Patchetts and Hutch might make. Since the town meeting, they had kept a low profile. That alone was suspicious. No doubt they were up to something. Until she knew what it was, she couldn't relax her guard for a moment. She didn't want Graham roaming freely about town.

Despite Dillon's absence, work at the site continued. He had appointed the excavator as temporary overseer. Because Dillon's standards were so high, Jade trusted the man to do the job correctly, but she felt safer and more confident when Dillon was within reach.

The site had almost become a tourist spot, drawing curious onlookers by the hundreds. Rarely a day passed when Jade didn't grant an interview to a media reporter. Lola Garrison, a freelance features reporter from Charleston, spent almost an entire day with her. She was writing an article about the TexTile plant for the Sunday supplement, which was circulated by several major newspapers throughout the South.

Spring was gradually becoming summer. The days grew longer. One evening Jade decided to work overtime after the excavation crews had turned off their machinery and left for the day. She became so involved in what she was doing that she lost track of time and wasn't roused until Loner began to bark outside.

A little trill of gladness shimmied up through her midsection. Dillon was back, she thought. But the tread on the steps outside wasn't heavy enough, and Loner wasn't barking his glad bark of welcome. The door to the trailer swung open.

"Hello, Jade."

"Donna Dee!" She was at once shocked to see her old friend and relieved that her visitor wasn't someone menacing.

Loner was still on the threshold, barking furiously. "Down, boy," Jade told him. She rounded the desk and crossed the room to close the door. Turning, she faced Donna Dee.

"You look good, Jade." Her smile was tinged with bitterness and envy. "But then you always did."

"Thank you."

"Don't worry. I don't expect you to return the compliment. You'd be lying."

That left Jade with nothing to say. The years hadn't been kind to Donna Dee, who had never been pretty in any case. Her appeal had always lain in her animated personality. But today she didn't even have that. Her wry sense of humor had turned to rancor.

"Why did you come to see me, Donna Dee?"

"Can I sit down?"

Jade nodded toward a chair, then returned to her desk. Donna Dee sat down, primly tugging the hem of her skirt over her knees, revealing her nervousness. There wasn't a modest bone in Donna Dee's body. She didn't care whether her knees were covered. Something else was causing her jitters. Perhaps guilt.

"I went to your house," she said. "They said you were working late."

"They?"

"The older woman and the boy...Graham?"

"Yes, Graham."

Donna Dee glanced away. Jade noted that she was clutching the strap of her handbag with both hands, as though fearing a purse snatcher. "I, uh, I didn't know you had a son until a few days ago."

"He's been in New York, finishing his school term. How did you hear about him?"

"You know how gossip travels around here."

"Yes, I do. All too well."

Donna Dee ducked her head and hooked a strand of hair behind her ear. "He's a good-looking boy, Jade."

"Thank you."

"He looks like you."

"And my father."

"Yeah, I remember the pictures you had of him." Her fingers worked along the stitching in the leather strap of her handbag. "How old is...is Graham?"

"Fourteen."

The two women stared at each other across the room, across the years of bitterness. Donna Dee broke the strained silence. "You're going to make me ask, aren't you?"

"Ask what?"

"Was he conceived that night?"

"You mean the night I was raped?" Jade suddenly stood up. "That should give you and Hutch something titillating to discuss over dinner tonight."

Donna Dee stood also. "Hutch and I won't be having dinner together. We won't even be talking to each other tonight. Hutch is in intensive care in a hospital in Savannah, Jade. He's dying!"

Her words echoed off the walls. For a moment the two

women glared at each other, then Donna Dee collapsed into her chair again and held her forehead in her hand. "He's dying."

Just as Fritz had been, Hutch was a figurehead behind a badge. He was the Patchetts' hand puppet. Before Jade's return, it had been nothing except a theory. Her first day in Palmetto, she had tested it. She deliberately broke the speed limit and was stopped by a patrolman.

When he tried to give her a ticket, she demurred. "Mr. Patchett won't like it when he hears about this. I'm a friend of his. He told me that if I ever got a speeding ticket, not to worry about it. All he has to do is call the sheriff and he'll fix it, he said. Why put everybody to so much trouble? It would be pointless, wouldn't it?" Assuming a role she detested, she removed her sunglasses and dazzled the deputy with a smile.

"Well, I'm glad you told me, little lady." He slipped the citation book back into his pocket. "Sheriff Jolly would have chewed my ass good if I had offended a friend of Mr. Patchett's. Are we talking Neal or the old man?"

"Take your pick," she said, starting her car.

"I don't reco'nize you. What'd you say your name was?"

"I didn't," she said, and drove away, feeling smug for proving her guess right.

Now she felt numb. She wouldn't have the pleasure of exposing Hutch as a corrupt coward who didn't fear damnation as much as he feared Ivan and Neal Patchett's ridicule.

"I didn't know, Donna Dee," she said. "I'm sorry to hear it."

Donna Dee snorted scornfully. "Yeah, I'll bet. If Hutch dies, that'll be two down and one to go, won't it?"

"Careful. That's as good as conceding that what the three of them have in common is raping me."

"They're the three you *accused*." She regarded Jade curiously. "Ivan is as good as dead too, you know. He'll never fully recover from that accident. Neal was in bad shape for a while. At first everybody thought he'd been emasculated. Wouldn't it have been a hoot if the superstud of Palmetto couldn't get it up anymore? Turns out, that was a nasty rumor. Plenty of women swear he's as hard and horny as ever."

"I'm really not interested."

Donna Dee continued as though Jade hadn't spoken. "Fritz and Lamar are dead. Ivan's crippled. Hutch is dying. God has almost evened up the score for you, Jade. You must be living right."

"I'm not responsible for any of their misfortunes. And no matter what you think, Donna Dee, I don't wish Hutch were dead."

"You're not going to cry at his funeral, though, are you?"

"No. I cried all my tears at Gary's funeral."

Donna Dee took a swift breath and said defensively, "Hutch didn't have anything to do with that. Neal told Gary, not Hutch."

"Told Gary what?"

"That you were pregnant and went to Georgie for help."

The bit of information, so offhandedly revealed, paralyzed Jade. Though she remained motionless, her mind spun crazily. Her blood rushed through her veins at an alarming rate.

"Neal told Gary that I went to get an abortion?" Her voice was nothing more than a dry rasp. The question that had haunted her for years had finally been answered.

Donna Dee didn't realize that she had put the missing puzzle piece in place, but she had.

Jade had craved to know what had prompted Gary to suicide. Now she knew. He had been told she was pregnant, thereby making her not only unfaithful to him but a liar.

It was inconsequential how Neal had found out she was pregnant—Patrice Watley had probably told him. He had wasted no time in telling Gary. Then, having had his faith in her completely destroyed, Gary had killed himself. There seemed no limit to Neal's treachery.

Jade clasped her hands together at her waist. "You'd better go, Donna Dee."

"You didn't get an abortion that day, did you?"

"I'm asking you to go."

"Your son is that same baby, isn't he? Listen to me, Jade." She inhaled deeply, as though bracing herself. "About a year ago, Hutch got to feeling bad all the time. For as long as he could, he disregarded the symptoms. You know how stubborn men can be about things like that. They never want to admit that they're anything less than Superman.

"So," she continued, "we didn't find out what was wrong until he had renal failure. He was diagnosed with a rare kidney disease. Since then, he's been on dialysis. Nobody in town knows. We've kept it a secret so he wouldn't lose his job. But even that isn't important now."

She took a tissue from her purse and blotted her eyes. "Anyway, his kidneys are shot. The dialysis isn't working anymore. He's got to have a transplant to survive."

"I'm sorry for you both."

"Jade," Donna Dee said beseechingly, "the best hope Hutch has of a transplant is your son."

"What?" she gasped with disbelief.

Donna Dee left her chair and moved to within inches of Jade. "Hutch and I never had any children. We tried everything, but I never got pregnant. Dora died two years ago, so Hutch doesn't have any family left.

"Before we find a random donor, he could run out of time. Jade," she cried, reaching out to clutch Jade's arm, "if Hutch is Graham's father, Graham could be the donor Hutch needs."

Jade pulled her arm free and backed away from her as though she had a contagious disease. "Have you lost your mind? Never, Donna Dee."

"For God's sake, we're talking about a human life!"

"Yes, exactly—Gary's life. He died as a consequence of what Hutch did to me, no matter how you whitewash it for your conscience. You knew damn well I was telling the truth that day in the sheriff's office. You knew, Donna Dee! Afterward, you perpetuated the lies being told about me."

"I was eighteen fucking years old," she shouted. "I was pissed off because the guy I was crazy about lusted after my best friend and not me."

"That's hardly justification. Your petty jealousy is partially responsible for driving Gary to commit suicide."

Donna Dee covered her ears with her hands, but Jade pulled them down.

"I wouldn't sacrifice one drop of my son's blood on the outside chance that it would save Hutch's life."

"You're a self-righteous, self-important bitch," Donna Dee said scathingly. "You always were."

"The most important thing in the world to me now is my son. *My* son, Donna Dee. He belongs to no one but me. And no one is going to touch him."

Donna Dee's glare was so blatantly full of hatred

that, had Jade's resolve not been so strong, it might have quelled her. Donna Dee turned her back, opened the door, and stalked out. Jade hastily locked the door behind her, then lunged for the telephone.

Cathy answered on the second ring. "Cathy, is Graham there?"

"Of course. He's sitting right here eating his supper. You told us to go ahead without you."

"Yes, yes, I'm glad you did." Her knees were trembling. She sank into the chair behind her desk. "Listen, Cathy, I'd rather Graham not go outside again this evening. Not even to ride his bike on the street, or to skateboard or shoot baskets."

"We planned to watch a movie on HBO after supper."

"Good. That's fine."

"What's wrong?"

"Nothing."

"Does this have anything to do with Mrs. Jolly stopping by earlier?"

"Yes, but I'd rather you not say anything about it to Graham."

She sensed Cathy's disapproval through the ensuing silence. "He wants to say hi."

"Put him on."

"Hey, Mom, when're you coming home?"

"Soon. Wait up for me."

"What the—"

Dillon swerved to avoid hitting the dog. Loner had darted out from the ditch along the highway and ran across the road directly in the pickup's path. Dillon slammed on his brakes, laying rubber for several yards.

"You stupid mutt!" he shouted through the window.

Hearing the familiar voice, Loner skidded to a halt on the pavement. He cocked his head and looked at the pickup, then charged toward it in a frenzy of glee. Dillon opened the drivers-side door. Loner leaped into his lap, licking his face and thumping the steering wheel with his wagging tail.

"Dumb dog, get off me. Jesus, you stink. When's the last time you had a bath?" He shoved Loner off his lap and dropped the car into gear again. Once they were under way, he cast the animal a sidelong glance. Loner was giving him a lovesick look. His tongue was lolling from one side of his mouth. He was panting hard.

"I've told you a thousand times not to love me, but you just don't listen, do you?"

Dillon admitted that it was nice to be welcomed home after a twelve-day absence, even if the only one to have missed him was a mongrel with no more brains than to run across the road in front of a two-ton pickup. In spite of himself, he'd grown attached to the dog. He watched for him when he wasn't lurking around the trailer and worried about him until he showed up again.

He scratched the animal behind his left ear. "Where were you off to? Or were you on your way home? Were you out to see a lady?" Loner stopped panting and raised his eyebrows. "Oh yeah? Did you get any?" Loner whined. Ruefully, Dillon said, "I know the feeling."

He draped is left wrist over the steering wheel and continued patting Loner with his right hand. At this time of night there was little traffic. It was mindless driving, which was good, because Dillon's mind wasn't on driving.

He had missed her.

He had cut his trip two days short. Unnecessarily, he had driven for six hours to get home tonight when tomorrow by noon would have done just as well. And since when had he started thinking of this place—or *any* place—as home?

Since there was someone here he was eager to see.

That had scared the hell out of him—scared him so badly that he had almost talked himself into abandoning the TexTile pickup in Knoxville and simply disappearing again. He hadn't wrestled with the notion for long, however.

"For one thing," he said to the attentive Loner, "walking away from problems like that is a cowardly way to deal with them."

What purpose had it served for him to drop out of society when Debra died? It had temporarily anesthetized him, enabling him to continue living when he had been absolutely indifferent to life. Following his discovery of the bodies, his only reason for living was to give Haskell Scanlan pain. Having done that, he hadn't cared if he ever drew another breath.

But some motivating factor had kept him alive. Like a computer chip, something minute but active, buried deep inside his consciousness, had seen to it that he went on living. Now, he knew why. TexTile. He was meant to build this plant. He believed that with every fiber of his being.

"So, I've got to complete it. I've got to prove to myself that I can stick it out to the bitter end. Understand?" Loner whined and dropped his head onto Dillon's thigh. "Yeah, I know. Life's a bitch."

He hadn't wanted to grow attached to the dog, yet here he was with a lump in his throat because the stupid mutt was glad to have him home. He hadn't wanted to like the boy, either, but Graham was exactly the kind of kid he would have wanted Charlie to be. He was inquisitive, bright, friendly, and was just mischievous enough to keep him from being a nerd.

"How's Graham been doing?" he asked Loner. "Seen him around much? Maybe next time I go out of town for any length of time, I'll ask him to give you your weekly bath." Loner flopped his tail from one side of his rump to the other in half-hearted approval of the idea. He wasn't crazy about baths. "I could offer to give him a few bucks. Boys his age always need spending money."

Before he left, Jade had apologized for Graham's hanging around the site. She thought the boy had made a nuisance of himself by getting in Dillon's way and asking questions. Actually, he was flattered whenever Graham tagged along beside him. His questions and observations were sometimes humorous, other times astute. In spite of himself, he looked forward to seeing Graham again.

He had avoided thinking about it during the six-hour drive, but now, when he was only a few minutes away from his destination, he felt compelled to acknowledge the real reason for his rush to get back: he was eager to see Jade.

He had a lot to report, of course. And he was sure there was a lot she would need to fill him in on. Things that had happened while he was away would have to be discussed.

But was business the only reason he wanted to see her? He hoped to God it was, because any other reason was disloyal to Debra and just plain stupid. He should have picked up a woman while he was out of town. If he had taken a warm, willing woman to bed, maybe he wouldn't be so edgy. Maybe he wouldn't be looking so forward to seeing Jade. Maybe his cock wouldn't be hard with just the memory of how she had looked standing against a rising thunderstorm.

He wheeled the pickup into the gravel track leading to his trailer. Loner, sensing that he was home, stood up in the seat and shook himself from nose to tail. Dillon chuckled, but his laughter broke off when he saw the light on inside the portable building and Jade's Cherokee parked out front.

"What the hell is she doing out here at this time of night?"

He parked the pickup and got out. Loner slipped past him and headed for his water dish. Dillon tried the door of the office. It was locked.

"Jade?" He removed his key from his jeans pocket and inserted it into the lock. The door swung open silently.

Her head lay on top of her desk; she was asleep. Dillon tiptoed forward. "Jade?"

She didn't stir. Her head was pillowed on her extended arm. His eyes were drawn down to her hand. She had very slender fingers. Her hand was delicate and, in repose, fragile-looking. Her hair was a riot of wavy disarray, spilling across her arm and the paperwork she had fallen asleep over. It was inky black, the perfect complement to her fair complexion.

There was a faint blush on the cheek that was turned up. Her eyebrow was as smooth and glossy as one painted onto a china doll. She was deeply asleep. She breathed through slightly parted lips.

Dillon's desire to touch her was a visceral ache.

He debated with himself on what he should do. She wouldn't welcome being found in such a vulnerable position. It would be awkward for them both and might affect their working relationship, which he didn't want to jeopardize under any circumstances. She obviously wasn't in any discomfort.

All things considered, it would be best to leave her as she was. If she woke up and noticed that he was back, she could come to his trailer and initiate a conversation if she wanted to. Otherwise, they would see each other first thing in the morning. He saw no reason for the lamp to be shining full on her face, however, and leaned across the desk to switch it off.

The instant the office went dark, she woke up.

"No!" She shot out of her chair, nearly knocking heads with him.

"Jade, it's me."

"Don't touch me." She fumbled with the items strewn across her desk.

"What are you doing?"

"If you touch me, I'll kill you."

Dillon, bewildered by her violent reaction, looked down at her outstretched hands and saw the cold glint of metal. "Jade," he said calmly, "it's me, Dillon." He reached for the lamp switch.

"No!" She made a jabbing motion toward his belly with the letter opener.

"Christ."

She was obviously still asleep, or so disoriented that she didn't realize what she was doing. Before one or both of them got hurt, he lunged across the desk and grabbed her hands. The telephone crashed to the floor. Paperwork scattered like autumn leaves in a high wind. Jade screamed. They fought for control of the letter opener. She fell against the wall behind her, knocking a calendar off its hook.

He twisted her hands, but she wouldn't release her grip on the letter opener. Even though she seemed to be imbued with superhuman strength, he knew he must be hurting her. He would apologize later. First, he had to keep her from ripping a hole in his gut.

He finally got a firm grip on both her wrists and swung them up above her head. He slammed his body into hers, pinning her between himself and the wall. She slung her head wildly from side to side.

"You'll have to kill me first."

"Jade."

"I won't let you. You'll have to kill me."

"Jade!"

It was as though he had entered her nightmare and slapped her awake. She ceased struggling instantly. Her head became still. Her breasts rose and fell drastically against his chest.

"Who is it?"

He could feel her rapid breath on his face. "It's Dillon."

"Dillon?"

"That's right."

"Dillon?"

"Yes."

Exhausted, he bent his head over hers, resting it on her forehead while he sucked in drafts of air. He released her wrists. When he did, her arms fell lifelessly to her sides.

"Are you okay?" he asked hoarsely.

She nodded. He stepped away from her and clicked on the lamp. The letter opener still in her hand had a serrated blade. It could have been deadly.

"Jesus," he swore. "What the hell were you trying to do with that damn thing?"

Jade dropped the letter opener onto the desk and simultaneously collapsed into her chair. "Protect myself."

She was pale, trembling, and breathless, but otherwise seemed no worse for wear. Seeing that she was all right, Dillon allowed himself to get mad. "You damn near gutted me."

Jade propped her elbow on her desk and pushed a handful of hair out of her face. "You shouldn't have sneaked up on me."

"I didn't sneak. I made a hell of a racket outside. I called your name twice."

"Why didn't you wake me up?"

"I didn't want to startle you."

"Oh, so you just leaned over me like you were going to smother me."

He let loose a string of curses.

"What are you doing here anyway? What time is it?" she asked, apparently still confused from being awakened so abruptly.

"Not that late," he replied. "Just after eleven."

"Oh, lord." She picked the telephone off the floor. While she placed a call to her house, Dillon stood at the edge of her desk, glaring down at her. "I'm glad you arrived when you did," she said as she replaced the receiver. "Cathy was worried, but said she hated to call and interrupt me while I was working."

"What the hell were you thinking of to stay out here by yourself after dark?" he asked angrily. "You're lucky it was me who came through that door."

"The door was locked."

"As though that would stop anybody who wanted in badly enough."

"Well, nothing tragic happened, so let's just forget it, shall we?"

That belittling tone of hers never failed to set his teeth on edge. As she came around her desk, he blocked her path. "We'll forget it when I say it's time to forget it. It's not safe for a woman to be out here alone, miles from town, after dark. Don't do it again."

"May I remind you that you're not in a position of authority over me?"

"Dammit, forget our positions. This has nothing to do with work. Besides, the only time you pull rank on me is when you know you're wrong."

Her eyes blazed up at him. "If it had been anybody but you, Loner would have barked to alert me of danger."

Dillon lowered his head closer to hers. "Is that right?"

"That's right."

"Well, for your information, Loner wasn't here," he said softly. "He was out looking to get laid. If he had gotten lucky, he probably wouldn't have been back before daylight."

Irritated and embarrassed, she glanced away. "I appreciate your concern for my safety."

"Don't flatter yourself. I'm not all that concerned. I'm just trying to talk a little common sense into somebody who obviously has shit for brains."

Her head came back around swiftly. "I'm glad you used that particular turn of phrase. It reminds me to tell you not to use foul language in front of my son."

"Have you been eavesdropping on my conversations with Graham?"

"Certainly not. He quotes you. He thinks you're bloody marvelous."

That gave him a warm rush of pleasure. "Really?"

"Really. So watch what you say around him."

"I haven't said anything he doesn't hear on cable TV, and probably in his classroom at school."

"That's beside the point, isn't it?"

"No. It's precisely the point. Unless you want Graham to be a pantywaist, cut him some slack, let him say a few dirty words. He's around women too much. The time he spends out here with the men is good for him."

"Which brings me to another matter. Don't encourage him to ride his bicycle out here."

"I didn't."

"He said you did."

"I didn't."

"You've never talked to him about riding his bike out here?"

"Sure, the subject came up. I said it was something for you to decide."

"Well, since I'm his mother, thank you very much."

He knew then that he was going to kiss her again. It was folly of the highest caliber, but he was going to do it anyway, and, once he made up his mind to, he didn't think anything could have stopped him.

He slid his fingers into her hair and tilted her head back, then lowered his mouth to hers. In her surprise, her breath rushed out of her mouth. He felt it against his lips, tasted it. When he did, every other thought flew right out of his head. He didn't think about the consequences of this kiss—because it was a foregone conclusion that as soon as it was over, she was going to fire him. He didn't think about Debra. He didn't think at all. He merely responded to the wonderfully erotic stimuli that kissing Jade transmitted to him.

The tip of his tongue flicked across her lips, then he pressed it into her mouth. She was stunned; he could tell. Her body became as inflexible as a flagpole and she stopped breathing. He didn't let her nonparticipation deter him, however. He exercised the technique he had mastered years ago and slowly made love to her mouth. His tongue dipped into it, then withdrew, again and again, until her breathing resumed and she raised her hands to clutch his arms.

"No," she whispered. "Please."

She didn't mean please stop. She meant please continue. Because, even though she had prefaced that please with a no, he sensed her excitement. It was building inside her. It generated heat that he could feel through her clothing. Her breathing was rapid and light—aroused breathing.

He cupped her head between his long fingers and tilted it farther back. He nuzzled her exposed throat and kissed the soft, fragrant pallet of skin beneath her ear.

"No, Dillon," she whimpered.

"You don't mean no."

Returning to her lips, he angled his head and kissed her deeper than before. Heat and lust concentrated in his loins. He groaned over the intensity of the ache, the potency of the pleasure. He dropped one hand to her derriere and lifted her front against his. His erection nestled in her cleft. He rubbed it against her. She moaned.

His other hand moved to her breast. It was firm, full, perfect. Her nipple responded to a stroke of his thumb. He wanted to put his mouth to it, even through her blouse, and lowered his head to do so.

"No!"

She backed away from him so quickly that she stumbled,

lost her balance, and careened into the far wall. She folded her arms across her chest and moved her hands up and down her arms as though trying to scrub them clean. Her eyes were so round that white showed all around the alarming, electric-blue irises.

"I said no," she cried raggedly. "I told you no. No. No. Don't you understand? No."

Flabbergasted, Dillon took a step toward her. "Jade, I—"

"Don't touch me. Don't." Her voice rose to a hysterical pitch, and she thrust a hand out in front of her to stave him off.

He raised his hands in a sign of surrender. "Okay, okay, I won't touch you. I swear."

He had never been in a situation like this before. Women sometimes put up token resistance to be coy, but none had ever gone hysterical on him. She wasn't faking it, either. If he had thought it was an act, he would have been furious. It wasn't an act. Without a doubt, she was genuinely terrified of him.

"You don't have to be afraid of me, Jade," he said gently. "I won't force you to do anything."

"I can't."

"I see that now."

"I *can't*," she repeated.

"It's cool, all right? Now, please stop looking at me like I'm Jack the Ripper. I'm not going to hurt you."

Gradually her panic subsided. She stopped rubbing her hands up and down her arms, but kept them crossed over her chest. Her eyes lost that trapped, wild animal alarm, but they were evasive. She smoothed her hand over the breast he had caressed. That very feminine, self-protective gesture made him feel as vile as a child molester.

Still avoiding his eyes, she hastily gathered up her purse and keys. "I'd better get home or Cathy will start worrying again."

"Jade, what—"

She shook her head brusquely, eliminating any plans he might have to probe for a reason behind her bizarre behavior.

She left the building at a near run and climbed into her Cherokee. Dillon stood in the doorway, staring after her with perplexity. He watched until the darkness absorbed the red glow of her taillights.

Chapter 23

———◆◆◆———

The idea that George Stein had discussed with Jade on the first of May involved building a GSS corporate annex somewhere in the vicinity of the TexTile plant. It would accommodate not only the upper-echelon executives of that facility but those affiliated with GSS's shipping, petroleum, and diverse other industries located in the Southeast. In the month since then, he had called her almost daily, asking for a report on land acquisition. She had stalled him by saying that she was being very choosy. Recently, he had hinted that if the job was too much for her to handle alone, perhaps he should send someone to assist her.

She recognized the intimidating bluff for what it was, but knew that she couldn't stall him forever. The annex was an enticing prospect, one that she wanted to be an integral part of...but all in good time. Unfortunately, once Mr. Stein conceived an idea, he wanted to see work in progress immediately.

The morning following Dillon's return, Jade decided to

approach Otis Parker again. As unobtrusively as possible, she had had his farm appraised, along with several other tracts of land in and around Palmetto.

She arrived at the farm early, just as Otis was climbing onto his tractor, about to leave for the fields. "I won't take but a minute of your time, Mr. Parker," she said as she approached him.

"If you come about me selling the place, you're wasting your time."

"Please hear me out." She waited while he reluctantly stepped to the ground. After a moment, she continued. "I find it hard to believe that you and Mrs. Parker wouldn't like living the rest of your lives in luxury. You could buy a beautiful place in town and retire. You wouldn't have to work another day of your life unless you wanted to. Think of all you could do for your children and grandchildren."

He looked at her resentfully. "That all sounds real attractive, all right. But if I ever did decide to sell, it wouldn't be to you."

"What do you mean?"

He whipped a faded, red shop towel from the hip pocket of his overalls and pretended to tinker with the tractor. "I don't owe you any explanations."

"Mr. Parker, I asked you not to discuss my interest in your land with anyone."

"I didn't. But you, better'n most, ought to know how things is in a small town. Word gets out. That appraiser feller you hired was out here for two days straight. He made some other folks curious."

Hastily, she zipped open her attaché. "Here is what GSS is offering for your property, including the house."

She handed him the legally prepared contract and

pointed to the sum at the bottom of the page. He blinked his poor eyesight into focus, then his narrow jaw went slack.

"Five hun'erd thousand dollars? Are you shittin' me?"

"No, Mr. Parker, I'm not. All you have to do is meet me at the title office this afternoon and sign the contract."

"I dunno," he said, shaking his head.

"I can assure you that no one else will offer this much on the property, Mr. Parker. It's far above the appraisal."

He regarded her suspiciously for a moment, then shook his head. "Well, I ain't going to do nothing rash. Like I told you, I ain't even decided on selling."

Turning his back on her, he climbed onto the tractor again and started the motor. After clapping a straw hat on his head, he steered the tractor out of the yard. Jade laid the contract on the porch and anchored it down with a rock. As she turned to leave, she heard the screen door open and looked up to see Mrs. Parker.

"Good morning."

"I've heard folks say that you've got a boy." Mrs. Parker said the words in a rush, as though it was very difficult for her to say them.

"That's right. His name is Graham."

"I's just wondering if, you know, he might be my Gary's child?"

Sorrow settled over Jade like a shroud. The desperate hope she saw in the tired, homely face was heartbreaking. She was tempted to lie and claim that Gary had been Graham's father, but ultimately that would only be doing a disservice to the Parkers and to Graham.

"No, he isn't, Mrs. Parker," she said sadly. "But I've wished from the day I learned I was pregnant that he was."

Without another word the gaunt woman slipped back into the house. The screen door slapped closed.

In a matter of minutes Jade reached the intersection with the highway. Just as she did, a candy-apple-red El Dorado sped passed.

Headed toward the construction site, she was so lost in thought about the Parkers that she didn't notice the El Dorado again until it was almost even with her. Apparently it had made a U-turn and was following her. Neal Patchett was at the wheel.

Smiling, he signaled for her to pull over.

"Go to hell."

Still smiling, he speeded up enough to give his car the advantage of a few yards before cutting his wheels sharply, almost swerving into Jade's Cherokee. Reflexively she stomped on the brake pedal. Neal parked sideways in front of her, so that the two cars formed a T on the narrow highway.

Jade flung open her door and got out. "What the hell do you think you're doing?"

"I asked you nice to pull over." His tone, his swagger, his ingratiating grin were all too familiar as he moved toward her.

Ironically, they were almost at the same spot where he had kidnapped her from Donna Dee's car fifteen years earlier. "And as usual, if you don't get your way, you impose it."

He made a courtly bow from his waist. "Guilty."

"If you wanted to see me, you should have made an appointment."

"Well now, I've tried, haven't I? Didn't you get any of those messages I left on your answering machine?"

"I got them. I ignored them."

"And haven't you hung up on me every time I've called? I never even got a thank-you note for the flowers I sent, welcoming you back to town."

"I threw them away the moment they were delivered."

He *tsk*ed her. "Jade, Jade, you went up North and got rude. You must've picked up a bunch of bad habits from all those Yankees up there. What happened to the sweet girl we all used to know and love?"

"She got gang-raped."

He winced, but it was a rehearsed reaction. "I see you're still carrying a grudge. Better watch that, Jade. Bitterness will make you old before your time, put lines in your face. Besides, what's the point? Lamar's dead and buried. Hutch is as good as. Me—I'm coming to you as an old friend, offering a peace pipe, hoping you'll forget our little misunderstanding."

To reduce her rape and Gary's suicide to a little misunderstanding was grotesque. It took every ounce of willpower she possessed not to claw the complacent smile off his face. "You're coming to me as a man running scared, Neal. My company is a threat to the feudalistic economy around here. You stand to lose your ruling power, and you know it. Better yet, *I* know it."

"Don't count us Patchetts out yet, Jade."

"I never have. Only this time you're not going to win."

She got back into her car and shut the door. He bent down and stuck his head in the open window. "Are you sure about that?"

"I'm going to make damn sure."

His eyelids lowered to half-mast. "You know, Jade, I couldn't believe my ears when I heard you had a son, seeing that you don't even have a husband. So I moseyed over to your house the other day, and lo and behold, there he was—a teenage boy, shooting basketballs in the driveway just like I used to do."

She couldn't conceal her panic. Seeing it, Neal continued in that same soft, unruffled tone. "He's a good-looking kid, Jade. Reminds me of myself when I was that age." He leaned in closer. "I was just wondering if maybe Georgie didn't take a baby out of you that day we watched you go into her house."

"We?"

"Why, Gary and me. We went to buy some moonshine from her. Damned if we weren't shocked to see you tiptoeing up her sidewalk with your fifty dollars clutched in your tight little fist."

"You didn't go there to buy moonshine. Patrice Watley told you I would be there. You took Gary so he would see me."

"He went plumb crazy," he said with a soft laugh.

She was shaking uncontrollably and so enraged that she could barely speak. "I thought that killing you was better than you deserved. I was wrong. I should have killed you fifteen years ago."

He snickered with unconcern. "Know what I think, Jade? I think you came out of Georgie's house with your fifty dollars still in your hand and a baby in your belly." He reached into the window and twined a strand of her hair around his fingertip. "I think I put that baby there. I think your boy is mine. And what we Patchetts consider ours, we take."

She jerked her head back at the same instant she dropped the gear shift into reverse. The car lurched backward, almost tearing Neal's arm off before he got it out of the open window. Jade shoved the car into drive and depressed the accelerator. The Cherokee shot forward, missing the rear end of his late-model El Dorado by a hair. Jade's fingers flexed around the steering wheel. She gritted her teeth to keep from screaming. *Damn them!* Why was it that the Patchetts were endowed with the power to terrorize her?

Fear and suspicion were still gnawing at her when she arrived at the site and parked in front of her portable office. Inside, the building was already stuffy. Agitated and afraid, she switched on the air-conditioner and removed her jacket. As she was hanging it on a coat tree, the door behind her opened.

Dillon's silhouette was large and stark against the bright morning sunlight. "Good morning," she said.

"Morning."

It was difficult to look at him after what had transpired the night before. She quickly diverted her attention to making coffee. Her hands were still shaking from what Neal had said. She was clumsy and inefficient, scattering coffee grounds everywhere. "I didn't have a chance to ask you last night about your trip. How was it?"

"It was productive, I think."

"I wasn't looking for you to get back before Thursday."

"I got around to seeing everybody on my list faster than I expected."

"Did you award the contract?"

"I wanted to discuss the main contenders with you first."

"Good. We'll do that as soon as the coffee's ready."

"Then I still work here?"

Jade turned to him suddenly. Although he was dressed

in his customary workclothes, he hadn't moved inside. He was poised on the threshold as though waiting for permission to enter. "Of course you still work here. And please close the door. You're letting out the cool air."

He moved inside and shut the door. "After what happened last night, I wasn't sure I still had a job. I thought you might send me packing this morning."

Sometimes she wished he would wear more than a tank top. She especially wished so now. It was hard to look at his exposed chest, but even harder to meet his intense eyes. "Firing you wouldn't be fair, would it? Over something as silly as a mere kiss?"

She deliberately minimized the kiss's significance because that was the only swift, safe, and sane way to approach this situation—in other words, she was copping out. If she didn't dismiss its importance, she must take him to task. In doing so, she would be forced to grapple with her own ambiguities about it. That, she wasn't prepared to do.

His kiss had rocked her, yes. It had terrified her, certainly. But coupled with these reactions she had come to regard as normal for herself, there was an additional confusion arising from a deep-seated curiosity over what would have happened if she hadn't stopped him.

Through a sleepless night, she had played mind games with herself: What would the outcome have been if her no's hadn't been adamant enough to quell his desire? No matter how she posed this hypothetical question to herself, the answer was always the same. His caresses would have become more urgent. Shortly, clothes would have become an impediment, and eventually he would have expected her to receive into herself that which had made a hard impression on her lower abdomen. He would know her intimately. She would know him, his strength, his power, his essence. The very thought of it made her tremulous inside and out, and not strictly from revulsion and fear. That was the source of her confusion. Why wasn't she outraged? Why wasn't she repulsed?

Hank's attempts to woo her, once he understood her reluctance to be wooed, had been soft and sweet. There had been nothing soft in the way Dillon's mouth had seized command of hers, nothing sweet in the hungry probing of his tongue. She hadn't been kissed like that since Gary. If she was baldly honest, she would have to admit that she hadn't been kissed like that ever.

Her reaction to Dillon's aggression was conditioned. She had responded in a fashion symptomatic of her psychological problem. Yet, she hadn't responded with her usual speed and inflexibility. She had granted him time and space in which to maneuver. Why? Because, in spite of his aggressiveness, his embrace had made her tingle in places she had believed were immune to sexual stimulation. Her heart had pounded not only with fear but with a peculiar excitement that, because of its strangeness, was equally as frightening. Her unprecedented reaction to it was as disturbing as the kiss itself.

That's why she wasn't equipped to deal with it right now. Her encounter with Neal, his veiled threats, had left her feeling frightened and vulnerable. Cathy had predicted that they would attack her through Graham. She vowed to redouble her efforts to keep him away from them.

Her most pressing problem, however, was reestablishing a working relationship with Dillon. That must be dealt with immediately, for the good of the project.

Temporarily shelving her concern for Graham, she said, "Sit down, Dillon. Tell me about the concrete contractors you have in mind for the job."

He took a seat while she poured their coffee. Knowing by now that he drank his black, she handed him a steaming mug, then moved behind her desk and sat down.

"I've narrowed it down to three bids," he said, passing her a folder he had carried in with him. "They're in no particular order."

She glanced through the three bids Dillon had received, then returned to the first one and began to read more thoroughly. He fidgeted in his chair. She knew he was about to speak before he uttered a single sound.

"I feel like I should apologize to you, Jade, but I'm not sure why or what for."

"No apology is necessary."

"I can tell you're upset."

"I'm upset, but it has nothing to do with you."

She kept her eyes on the sheets before her but retained very little of what she read. Her concentration kept drifting to the memory of how his mustache had felt against her mouth.

"You set me straight on that once, about kissing you, I mean."

"I remember that conversation."

"That time I kissed you in the limo . . . well, I want you to know that that was something entirely different from last night. Last night—"

"I didn't ask for an explanation."

"Nevertheless, I don't want you to think that I've read anything into your friendliness."

"I don't think that."

"You haven't put out any sexy signals."

"That's good to know."

"I didn't plan on kissing you, Jade. It was spontaneous."

"I understand."

"If you had told me sooner that you didn't like it—"

"I never said I didn't like it."

Only after she heard her own words did she realize what she had admitted. Their eyes connected, soundlessly but jarringly. She drew in a swift breath. It was no armor against the intensity of his gaze.

"Then you did like it?" he asked gruffly.

"No. I mean..." She lowered her gaze again. "What I actually said, Dillon, was that I can't...can't do that."

"Can't kiss a business associate?"

"Can't kiss anybody."

She heard him set his coffee mug on the edge of her desk. His clothing brushed against the cushion of his chair as he scooted forward. "You can't kiss *anybody*?"

"That's right."

"Why?"

"That's my business."

"And now it's mine," he said, raising his voice.

Bravely, she flung up her head and glared at him, then wished she hadn't. His forearms were propped on the edge of her desk, and he was leaning forward slightly. The summer sun had brought out light streaks in his hair. His bare arms, his wide chest, his face with its mustache and steady hazel eyes, all exuded a masculinity that both fascinated and repelled her just as his kiss had.

"The subject is closed," she said huskily.

"For now, maybe."

She glanced down to the work on her desk and cleared

her throat. "I'd like to discuss these bids so that you can make a decision."

"All right," he said slowly.

He had agreed, but, for the duration of their meeting, he continued to gaze at her in that steady, unflinching way that made her uncomfortably warm. He did everything with that same damned intensity—work, stare . . . and kiss.

"Goddammit, I'm getting sick of this shit."

Ivan wasn't referring to his disability or the wheelchair, although he slammed his fist down on its armrest. He was provoked by the contract lying on the stumps of his thighs, the contract that Neal had weaseled from Mrs. Parker.

"Who in his right mind would pay half a million dollars for that sorry parcel of land?"

"It looks like I'll have to," Neal said grimly.

"What in blazes could she want it for?"

"Maybe nothing more than to put a railroad trunk through. According to the papers, the plant will be shipping goods overseas out of Port Royal. Whatever she wants it for, it's bad news for us."

Neal stared down at the contract, his brow furrowed. "That's probably only Jade's first offer. GSS has got money coming out its ass. She'll keep upping the ante until Otis gives in."

"Pour me a drink," Ivan growled.

Neal poured a stiff bourbon for himself, too. He had put up a good front for Jade earlier that morning. Actually, she had hit the nail on the head. For the first time in his life, his confidence was taking a beating.

Jade wasn't as easily maneuvered as he and Ivan had

fooled themselves into thinking. She had patently ignored his phone calls. She claimed to have thrown away the roses he sent her. She had spread a communitywide fever of interest in the new plant. He had a sick feeling in his gut that she was going to get the best of them.

His daddy was old and crippled. His voice still carried, but did people really listen to him anymore? How much clout could Ivan wield when a new industry moved in? Ivan had been known to manipulate people by bartering with coveted jobs. Before too long, he might have to beg people to work for him.

Neal surveyed his surroundings. The Aubusson rugs, the Spode china, the Waterford crystal—all were heirlooms from his mother's family, all were priceless. He enjoyed having the biggest, fanciest house in the county. He liked driving a new car every year. He like being Neal Patchett and what that name meant in this town. Goddammit, he didn't want things to change at this stage of his life.

He glanced at his father, who sat hunched in his wheelchair, and realized that their future couldn't be trusted to an old amputee. His daddy wasn't up to fighting this battle, but he had coached his son on how to fight dirty. It was time Neal flexed his own muscles.

"Here's what I'm going to do, old man. I'm going to the bank and sign a note for five hundred thousand dollars."

Ivan glanced at him sharply. "Using what for collateral?"

"An acre or two here, an acre or two there. I'll scrape together enough deeds to cover the note."

"I don't like selling off land."

"You've never liked my ideas about diversifying, either. So now we're stuck with one factory that's about to be overshadowed by a whole new industry. If you had let me expand and update, do some of the things I wanted to do, we wouldn't be in this fix," Neal said angrily. "So shut up and listen for a change."

Ivan scowled but remained silent.

Neal said, "Jade has shown an interest in several properties, but the Parker farm is by far the largest, and therefore the most important to her. That's what we'll go after. We've got to get our hands on Otis's property."

"The bank might not loan you that much."

"They will if I tell them that it's only short-term. All I have to do is secure the Parker property. Then Miss Astorbutt will have to come to me flashing a contract with the GSS logo on it. And you can bet your sweet ass that when she does, the price of that property will have inflated overnight. Not only the Parkers' land, but all the acreage we own surrounding it.

"If she's willing to offer half a million, she's willing to offer more. She'll buy from us, I'll pay off the bank note, and all it'll cost me is the interest. In the meantime, I'll have made a substantial profit."

"What'll you tell the bank you need the money for?"

"I'll make up something. I don't want word of this spread all over town. I want this to shock Jade like a bite on the ass."

Neal had plans on how to use the profit he would make, plans he didn't want to discuss with his father until this other mess had blown over. He hoped Ivan would agree to updating and expanding their own business. They'd been quarreling over this issue for years. Ivan stubbornly clung to tradition and poo-pooed modern technology. Maybe this scare would change his mind. Neal had been operating the business since the train accident, though Ivan still remained the figure of authority. It was time everybody, including his old man, started regarding him as boss.

He tossed back the remainder of his drink. "You want me to bring you back a girl for tonight, Daddy?"

Ivan's eyes twinkled. "That redhead you gave me for my birthday present had a mouth like a Hoover."

"I'll see if she's still in town."

"Naw, not tonight. I've got too much on my mind to have my brains sucked out." He stroked his jaw ruminatively. "I keep thinking we've overlooked something. What about Otis? What'll you tell him?"

"Since y'all go back so far, I'll let you deal with Otis."

Ivan cackled. "He's dumber than the dirt he farms. I'll remind him how good I've been to him all these years. I'll say if he sells his place to anybody, it ought to be to a 'friend.'" He paused, thinking. "Maybe you'd better ask the bank for six hundred thousand. It wouldn't hurt to sweeten the pot. That Sperry bitch can be mighty persuasive."

"Good idea."

Neal made to leave, but Ivan detained him. "Show me the boy's picture again."

Ivan had been as shocked as Neal to hear that Jade had a teenage son. Neal had taken a Polaroid snapshot of Graham and brought it back to show Ivan. Once again, he passed the photo to his father, who had studied it for hours at a time.

Neal said, "I drove by their house again this morning and saw him mowing the grass. He's the right age."

"You told me she went to Georgie."

"She did, but she came out with a baby."

"You don't know that. And Georgie's dead. We can't ask her."

"I confronted Jade with it today. She didn't deny it.

Even if she had, I know I'm right. I busted her cherry. She wasn't pregnant by Gary Parker."

"Hell, son," Ivan said, leaning forward, almost salivating, brandishing the photograph. "Think what it would mean to us if this boy is yours."

"I don't have to *think*. I know he's mine." Neal's expression was sly and menacing. "I want him, Daddy."

"Three of you had her that night," Ivan remarked with a frown. "He could belong to Hutch, too. Or even Lamar."

"He doesn't even look like them!"

"He doesn't look like you either!" Ivan shouted back. "He's the spitting image of her. Playing devil's advocate, what makes you so goddamned sure he's yours?"

"He's mine."

"You want to believe it so bad you can taste it, don't you, boy?" Ivan said with a nasty laugh. " 'Cause you know he's the only heir you'll ever have."

Neal passed the back of his hand across his damp upper lip. The accident that had robbed Ivan of his legs had robbed Neal of his ability to reproduce. The freight train had pulverized the front third of their car. Neal had been trapped in the wreckage for hours before a rescue team was able to cut through the mangled metal and free him. The blood supply to his testicles had been suspended for such a long period of time that it had resulted in irreversible sterility. He didn't like to think about it.

Thank God he hadn't been left impotent, too. He would have killed himself if that had happened. But every time the subject of an heir came up, he got queasy. From the cradle, he'd been told that the one thing required of him was to produce another Patchett male. It was expected. It was the only thing that really mattered.

He clapped Ivan on the back. "You leave everything to me, Daddy. That's my son, and I'm going to claim him. First we've got to get his mama groveling on her knees."

On his way into town, Neal hummed beneath his breath. Now that he had a specific plan, he was feeling better. It was galling that Jade still spurned him as though he were white trash. Long ago she had rejected him in favor of Gary Parker. She still looked at him like he was something you'd track in from a barnyard. He couldn't tolerate any woman thinking she had gotten the best of him. Before he was finished with her, Jade Sperry would rue the day she'd chosen him to be her adversary.

Jade wheeled her car into the driveway. Graham was out on the front lawn, practicing his moves with a soccer ball. "Hey, Mom."

"Hi."

"Watch." He maneuvered the ball across the yard. When he was only a few feet away from her, he kicked the ball hard, straight into the trunk of a pine tree. "That's a score!" he shouted, raising his fists above his head in a sign of victory.

"Easy to do without any opposition."

He shoved several locks of sweaty, black curls off his forehead. "Huh?"

"Try it again with me acting as goalie."

"Okay!" He retrieved his ball and carried it back to the far side of the yard.

Jade kicked off her high heels and assumed a challenging stance in front of the tree. "Whenever you're ready."

Instead of taking a direct route as he had before, Graham weaved his way across the yard, adroitly maneuvering the ball with fancy footwork. Jade stood ready in front of the "goal," but he pulled her off center with a tricky maneuver, and before she could recover he kicked the ball into the tree trunk.

"Point!" he cried.

Baring her teeth, Jade lunged forward, tackling him, and following him down into the grass.

"Foul! Foul!"

Jade tickled his ribs. But he surprised her by rolling to his side and throwing her off. She sat up, panting. "When did you learn to do that? Only a few months ago I could hold you down for an hour."

"I'm growing."

She looked at him with maternal pride. "You certainly are."

"How much do you weigh, Mom?"

"How indelicate!"

"No, really. How much?"

"About a hundred twelve pounds."

"I already outweigh you!"

"What in the world are you two doing?" Cathy was watching them from the veranda.

"Playing soccer. I lost," Jade said ruefully. Graham bounded to his feet and helped pull her up.

"There's a telephone call for you," Cathy said. "Should I tell them to hang on until half-time?"

"Very funny," Jade remarked as she trudged up the steps.

Cathy laughed. "I'll pour you a Coke."

"Thanks," Jade said over her shoulder as she padded in stocking feet toward the telephone in the hall. "Hello?"

"Miss, uh, Jade?"

"Yes."

"This is Otis Parker."

It had been over a week since she had left the contract at his house. She had resisted the temptation to call him and was very pleased that he had finally phoned her. She responded with feigned equanimity. "Hello, Mr. Parker."

"Some feller answered the phone when I called the number on the card you left. He gave me this number."

"That would have been Mr. Burke. I hope this call means that you've decided to accept my offer."

"No, not quite. I'm gonna think on it awhile longer."

She folded both hands around the telephone receiver and nodded a distracted thank-you to Graham when he delivered her cold drink.

"Mr. Parker, I'm prepared to increase my offer." She had to proceed with caution, especially since she didn't know for certain why he was stalling. "What would you say to an offer of seven hundred fifty thousand?"

He covered the mouthpiece. Jade could hear snatches of a muffled conversation. He was conferring with someone. Mrs. Parker? Was he asking her opinion, her advice? Or was he being coached by a third party?

He returned to the line. "To offer that much, I'd say you want the property real bad."

"I do."

"What for?"

"I'm not at liberty to disclose that."

"Hmm. Well, I—"

"Before you give me your answer...I'd also be willing to give you eighteen months to vacate. In other words, GSS would own the property as soon as the deed was transferred, but we wouldn't assume occupancy for a year and a half. That would give your family ample time to relocate. You wouldn't be obligated to take that amount of time, but you would have the option."

Jade sipped her Coke while another muffled conversation ensued. Her fingers were almost as cold as the frosted glass.

When Mr. Parker came back on the line, he said, "I'll have to call you back."

"When?"

"When I've made up my mind."

"Mr. Parker, if another party is—"

"That's all I'm saying tonight. G'bye."

For a long moment after she hung up, she stared at the telephone receiver, wishing she had said more, wishing she had said things differently. So much was riding on her handling this situation with kid gloves. Not only was her pride at stake, but her future with GSS.

Otis Parker hung up the telephone and turned to his guests.

"Well, Otis, what will you tell her when you call her back?" Ivan peered at him from beneath his brows.

Otis scratched his head and looked uncomfortably toward his wife, who was sitting silent and rigid on the sofa. "I don't rightly know what to do, Ivan. She's offering seven hun'erd and fifty thousand and giving me over a year to move out. You can't hardly beat a deal like that."

"We can and we will." Neal's jaw appeared carved in granite, his eyes as brittle as glass. Throughout the meeting with the Parkers, he had declined to sit down. After carrying Ivan in and depositing him in the easy chair with the greasy headrest, he had stood, negligently leaning against the wall, appearing to be more at ease than he was.

It had been a hell of a week. He wanted this deal consummated, the sooner the better. He didn't like being in hock up to his eyebrows. But he'd gone this far, so he'd just as well go the distance. If it meant mortgaging a few luxuries like the boat and the beach house on Hilton Head, he'd do it. He gave his father an imperceptible nod.

"Give us a few weeks to match her offer," Ivan said, turning back to Otis. "You owe me that after all the times I've extended you credit." Then Ivan did what he did best. He employed subtle fear tactics. "I don't mind telling you, Otis, that I'm disappointed in you. The first time Jade broached the subject of buying this place, you should've come and told me. I wouldn't have found out if I hadn't had spies on the lookout for my interests. I thought they were lying the first time they told me you were involved in that Sperry gal's scheme to ruin me."

"I ain't in on no scheme, Ivan."

"Well, it sure as hell looks like that to me. There's my offer still lying untouched on the table. And here I am, figuring we were friends, figuring I'd promote that son of yours who's working for me. Yes, sir, I was about to promote him to a foreman's job and give him a big raise, just on the basis of our friendship. Figured he could use the extra money with another baby coming." He snorted, leaving the Parkers to fill in what had been left unsaid.

Neal picked up his cue. "You ready to go, Daddy?"

"I reckon I am, since it looks like no deal is going to be struck tonight." Ivan motioned for Neal to come and get him. "I'm tired of this dilly-dallying around, Otis. I'm ready for you to make up your mind about this, you hear?"

Forlornly, Otis nodded.

Neal gathered Ivan into his arms and lifted him out of

the chair. Otis ambled toward the door and held it open for them. As they went through, Neal said, "I can't believe you'd do business with Jade after Gary hung himself on account of her. If you sell this place to her, he'll roll over in his grave."

Mrs. Parker made a small, injured sound. Neal shot each of them a contemptuous look, then carried his father across the creaky porch and strapped him into the front seat of the El Dorado.

As they pulled away from the house, Ivan said, "Good work. Putting in that last dig just might make the difference."

"We can't count on that, though."

"What do you mean?"

"Money's a better motivator than sentiment. Instead of matching Jade's offer, we should come back with a better one."

"In hell's name why?"

"She's waiting for him to call her with his answer, right? We could get the jump on her, bowl the old fool over and get his name on the dotted line before he has a chance to recover his wits. This game could go on indefinitely. With the resources she's got behind her, she can keep upping her bid till doomsday. And there must be a lot riding on this acquisition or she wouldn't have increased her offer by so much so soon."

"Do whatever it takes, boy," Ivan grumbled, absently rubbing the center of his chest. "I'm not going to get a good night's sleep until that bitch is out of my life."

Chapter 24

———◆◆◆———

"Do you think I could play professional soccer, Mr. Burke?"

"I told you to call me Dillon."

"I know, but it feels weird."

"Call me Dillon. That was a good move you made with that knight, Graham. In answer to your question, yes, I think you can make it to the pros, if you want it badly enough."

"That's what my mom says, too. She says I can do anything I want to if I want to bad enough."

From the hallway where she stood unseen, Jade smiled.

"Smart lady, your mom."

"Uh-huh. Did you see her picture in the Sunday magazine?"

"Sure did. That was some write-up. You should be proud of her."

"I am." Graham's enthusiasm gradually dimmed. "But she's still being uncool about me riding my bike out to the site."

"She's got her reasons."

"They're dumb."

"Not to a mother who cares about her kid."

Maybe Dillon's coming to dinner hadn't been such a bad idea after all, Jade thought as she listened to the conversation that was running concurrently with their chess game. Cathy had continued to harp on inviting Dillon for dinner, so she had asked him that afternoon. She had made it sound spontaneous and casual, saying something like, "Why don't you come over for supper tonight? Graham's been wanting to play chess with you."

He had hesitated for several seconds before accepting. "Sure. I'll be there as soon as I clean up."

"Fine. See you later." Her attitude had been light and carefree, reducing any significance he might place upon the invitation.

Dinner had been a convivial affair. They treated one another like old family friends. As they joked and bantered, it was hard to believe that, only a few weeks ago, his mouth had plundered hers with passion, that his hand had caressed her breast, that his body had ground against hers in sexual excitement.

Nor would Jade have ever guessed that so many days later, she would recall that embrace with such stark clarity, or that the recollections would induce the same ambivalent and foreign responses in her as the actual kiss had.

"What are you doing out here in the hall?"

She jumped guilty when Cathy came up behind her and caught her eavesdropping. Whispering, she explained, "They were deep into male bonding, and I didn't want to interrupt."

Cathy gave her an arch look that said she knew better and preceded Jade into the living room, where the chess board had been set up on the coffee table. "There's more peach cobbler, Dillon, whenever you want another helping."

"Thanks, Cathy, but no. Dinner was delicious."

"Thank you."

"Mom, Dillon said that maybe this fall, me and him could go to a Clemson football game."

"We'll see."

Graham was preparing to demand a firmer commitment from her when the doorbell rang. "I'll get it." He shot to his feet. "One of my friends is bringing over his new Nintendo cartridge. Dillon, if you want me to, I'll teach you how to play."

Dillon made that slanted expression with his mouth that passed for a smile. "Not knowing how to play Kid Icarus makes me feel real old and very stupid."

"No more than I," Jade told him with a soft laugh. "I still haven't developed the knack of handling a joy stick."

A glint of mischief appeared in his eyes. "I've heard that all it takes is practice."

Jade welcomed Graham's shout from the front door.

"Mo-om! It's that lady again." Jade left her chair and moved toward the hall, drawing up short when Graham led Donna Dee into the living room. "She came here once before, looking for you," Graham said.

Donna Dee's eyes landed briefly on Dillon before finding Jade. "I probably should have called first, but...can I see you for a minute?"

Jade had made her position clear during their last conversation. She didn't want a repeat performance, especially in front of Cathy, Graham, and their guest. "Let's go out on the veranda."

Once they had cleared the front door, Jade turned to

Donna Dee and said, "You should have called. I could have told you not to waste your time by coming here again."

Donna Dee dropped all pretense of civilities. "Don't get snotty with me, Jade. I saw the spread on you in the Sunday supplement last weekend. You're a big shot now. The way that Garrison broad wrote about you, you'd think you're the best thing that's ever happened to the low country. But wild horses couldn't have dragged me to your front parlor if you weren't my last hope."

"For what?"

"Hutch. He's gotten worse. His condition is critical. If a kidney donor isn't found within the next few days, I'm going to lose him."

Jade lowered her gaze to the painted floorboards of the porch. "I'm sorry, Donna Dee, but I can't help you."

"You've got to! Graham is the only hope he's got."

"You don't know that." Jade kept her voice low, but it was taut with anger. "I resent your placing full responsibility for Hutch's life on my son's shoulders."

"Not on his—on yours. How can you let a man die without doing something to help him?"

"Not just any man, Donna Dee. A man who raped me. If Hutch were on fire, I would throw water on him, but you're asking a lot more than that. I wouldn't even put Graham through the necessary testing." She shook her head adamantly. "No. Absolutely not."

"Even if Hutch is Graham's father?"

"Shh! He'll hear you. Lower your voice."

"What are you going to tell your son when he wants to know about his father? Are you going to say that you let his daddy die because you're out for revenge?"

"Be quiet, for heaven's sake."

"For *your* sake, don't you mean? You don't want Graham to know that you're as good as a killer. Do you think he'll love you if he ever finds out that you let his father die without lifting a hand to help him?"

"What the hell is all the shouting about?"

Jade spun around. Dillon was looking at them through the screen door. "Where's Graham?" she asked, fearful that he, too, had overheard Donna Dee's vituperative words.

"Cathy hustled him upstairs." He stepped through the screen door and joined them on the porch. "What's going on?"

"I came to plead for my husband's life," Donna Dee said to him. "Jade can save him if only she would."

"That's not true, Donna Dee. You don't know anything for certain."

"This very minute, Hutch is lying in an ICU," Donna Dee explained to Dillon. "He's going to die unless Jade lets their son donate a kidney to him. She refuses because she doesn't want the boy to know his father."

Dillon's eyes swung to Jade. They were inquisitive and penetrating. Mutely, she shook her head. "Okay," he said, his gaze moving back to Donna Dee. "You've said what you came to say. Goodbye."

Haughtily, Donna Dee looked up at him. His expression remained intractable. Her bravado faltered. To Jade she said, "If your son finds out about this, he'll never forgive you. I hope he winds up hating you." She left the veranda, hastened down the sidewalk, and got into her car. Just as she pulled away from the curb, Graham came barreling through the door with Cathy close on his heels. "Mom, what were y'all yelling about?"

"Nothing, Graham. It doesn't concern you," she replied, avoiding the hard stare Dillon had fixed on her.

"This is the second time she's come here, so it must be important. Tell me what she wants with you."

"It's a private matter, Graham."

"You can tell me."

"No, I can't, and I don't want to argue about it! Now drop it!"

Her raised, chastening voice embarrassed him in front of his hero, Dillon. "You never tell me anything," he shouted. "You treat me like a damn kid." He rushed back into the house and ran upstairs.

Cathy appeared ready to intervene, but wisely refrained. "I'll be in my room if you need me."

Once she had gone back inside, Dillon spoke. "Want me to talk to Graham?"

Jade turned abruptly and glared up at him, channeling her anger toward him because he was a convenient scapegoat. "No, thank you," she said crisply. "You got quite an earful tonight, didn't you? I'm ordering you to forget everything you heard."

He grabbed her by the shoulders and yanked her forward against him. "Fat chance." After that succinct statement, he released her as swiftly as he had taken hold of her. Over his retreating shoulder he said, "You know where to find me if I can do anything for Graham. Good night."

He didn't need this crap.

Such was Dillon's mood as he wheeled his own battered pickup to the door of the trailer and turned off the engine. Apparently Loner was on another canine excursion. He wasn't there to greet him. It was just as well,

Dillon acknowledged as he let himself in. He wasn't fit company, even for a dog.

Inside, the trailer was as hot and steamy as a pressure cooker. He switched on the air-conditioning unit and stood in front of the icy blast of air as he peeled off his shirt and unfastened his jeans. He lay his forearms flat against the wall above the air conditioner and rested his forehead on them. The air blew against his damp skin and stirred the pelt of hair on his torso.

For the life of him, he couldn't understand Jade. Every time he thought he had her figured out, he was thrown another curve ball—like tonight. He never would have predicted that a woman would show up at Jade's house after supper, claiming Jade's son for her ailing husband.

She had mentioned Hutch. There had been a story in the local newspaper over the weekend about Palmetto's sheriff, Hutch Jolly, being in a Savannah hospital awaiting a kidney transplant. Unless it was a crazy coincidence and Palmetto had two men named Hutch waiting for a kidney donor, Hutch Jolly was Graham's father. Graham was obviously unaware of that, and Jade intended to keep him in the dark.

Had Jade known about Jolly's illness before she moved back? Was she dangling Graham in front of the critically ill man like a carrot? If Jolly was Graham's father, where did that leave the Patchetts? How did they figure into it? Jolly's wife hated Jade, too, but not for the expected reason. Ordinarily, the wife would want to deny her husband's paternity of an illegitimate child.

Experience had taught him that nothing was ordinary where Jade Sperry was concerned.

Evidently, she needed help. Yet, when he had offered

it, she threw up that icy armor of hers and flatly refused. What kind of fool would reject an offer of help when it was so desperately needed?

Dillon shoved his fingers up through his hair. "Christ."

He recognized Jade's foolishness because he had been guilty of it himself. At Debra and Charlie's funeral, he had been downright rude to the Newberrys and all their friends. He had spurned every sincere expression of sorrow and rebuffed every offer of help, because being with people whom Debra had known and loved was too painful for him. He had shut them out, believing that he might find numbness in solitude.

Only after accepting this job had he contacted the Newberrys. He had written them a letter, apologizing for the seven years of silence and advising them of his whereabouts. He had been able to write down Debra's name without feeling as if it were being carved into his heart with a razor blade. The Newberrys had written him back, expressing their joy over hearing from him and extending an open invitation for him to visit them in Atlanta.

He was now able to remember Debra alive—loving and laughing—instead of envisioning her lying dead with their son in her arms. In spite of his dogged attempts to cling to his misery, he had healed.

He adjusted the thermostat on the window unit and went into his bedroom. He removed his boots, stepped out of his jeans and underwear, and slid naked between the sheets of his bed. He stacked his hands beneath his head and stared at the ceiling. Just as he had been seven years ago, Jade was reluctant to accept help because her problem was something she couldn't bear to confront.

"But what?" Dillon didn't realize he had spoken out

loud until he heard the sound of his own voice. *"What?"* What had made her so afraid of trusting others, of her own sexuality?

Until he met Jade, he had thought the word *frigid* was a catch-all phrase to describe coy bimbos. The ingenues in B-movies were called frigid before they put out for the smooth-talking male lead. It was the antonym of *nymphomaniac,* a word with numerous applications but no real definition. Unfortunately, it perfectly described Jade Sperry. She was terrified of a man's touch.

Had Hutch Jolly robbed Jade of her right to gratifying sexuality? If so, Dillon hated the bastard, sight unseen. Jade was intelligent, savvy, and beautiful, but she had a scary secret locked away in the closet of her mind. It would continue to haunt her until someone exorcised it.

"Don't even think it," he muttered into the darkness. *You only work for her,* he reminded himself. *You're not her shrink or her lover or even a would-be lover.*

But Dillon lay awake for hours, thinking about opening Jade's heart and banishing her fears.

The sleeping body in the ICU bed was a human effigy being kept alive by machines devised to prolong a life no longer worth living.

Jade gazed down at her former classmate, her rapist. Hutch had never been handsome, but he looked pitifully ugly now. The bones of his large face were grotesquely pronounced, his cheeks sunken. His pallor clashed with his rusty-red hair. He had always been a strong, robust athlete; now, oxygen was being pumped into his nostrils. Medical technology was performing for him the functions his body no longer could.

While his vital signs were being electronically monitored and recorded, while he was struggling for life, the two attending nurses discussed the stifling heat outside and the Civil War epic starring Mel Gibson that was being filmed on location nearby.

"Only two or three minutes, Ms. Sperry," one said as they withdrew.

"Yes. Thank you."

She must have struggled subconsciously with the decision all night, because the knowledge that she would drive to Savannah and see Hutch had awakened her that morning. It wasn't that she doubted the severity of his condition. She certainly hadn't changed her mind about having Graham tested as an organ donor. She simply felt compelled to come and confront Hutch, for what would probably be the last time.

She had talked her way into the ICU. Luckily Donna Dee hadn't been there to dispute her claim that she was a relative who had come all the way from New York City to say goodbye to Cousin Hutch.

She was glad she had come. Hate required energy. Sometimes her hatred for the three men who had caused Gary's suicide was so consumptive, it left her replete. After today, she would have more energy, because it was hard to work up hatred for the man in the bed.

Suddenly he stirred and opened his eyes. It took a moment for him to focus on Jade, and even longer for it to register with him who she was. When it did, his dry, chalky lips parted, and he rasped her name in disbelief.

"Hello, Hutch."

"Jesus. Am I dead?"

She shook her head.

He attempted to wet his lips, but his tongue looked pasty. "Donna Dee told me you were back."

"It's been a long time."

He gazed at her for a moment. "From what I can see, you look terrific, Jade. Exactly the same."

"Thank you."

There was an awkward pause. Finally Hutch said. "Donna Dee said you've got a son."

"That's right."

"A teenager."

"He'll be fifteen his next birthday."

He squeezed his eyes shut and grimaced as though in pain. When he opened his eyes again, he had no trouble focusing on her face above him. "Is he mine?"

"How would I know, Hutch, when three of you raped me?" He groaned like a man in spiritual torment. "He's mine," she stressed. "I don't want to know who his father was."

"I can't blame you, I guess. I'd just like to die knowing."

"That's not going to happen if you live for another fifty years."

He wheezed a mirthless laugh. "I don't reckon that'll be the case."

"Ms. Sperry, I must ask you to leave now."

Jade signaled to the nurse that she understood. Quietly she said, "Goodbye, Hutch."

"Jade?" He raised one needle-bruised arm to detain her. "Donna Dee got this harebrained notion. She was going to ask your son to donate a kidney to me."

"She's come to me twice."

Again he looked pained. "I told her not to. Hell, I'd rather die than involve that boy. If he is my son, I wouldn't put him through an ordeal like that. Don't let her talk you into it. Don't let her bother the boy."

His vehemence surprised her. The tears that filled his eyes were incongruous with his masculine face. He swallowed convulsively several times. "If he is my son, I never want him to know about me...about what I did to you." Tears rolled down his gaunt cheeks. "I wish to hell I could undo it, but I can't. All I can say is, I'm sorry, Jade."

"It's not that easy, Hutch."

"I don't expect you to forgive me. I don't even want your pity. I just want you to know that our lives were never the same after that night.

"My daddy knew he'd done wrong by you and never got over it. We didn't talk about it—I just know. Lamar was sure as hell punished. That train got even with Ivan and Neal for you."

"Neal?"

"He's sterile. Can't have kids. Nobody is supposed to know. Even Donna Dee doesn't know. Neal told me by accident one night when he was drunk." He took a moment to garner breath and strength. "What I'm saying, Jade, is that we all suffered for it."

"You may have suffered, but Gary died."

He nodded remorsefully. "Yeah, I gotta die with that on my conscience, too." He blinked more tears out of his eyes. "I never planned on hurting you like I did, Jade. For all of it, I'm damn sorry."

They exchanged a long stare.

It was broken when Donna Dee burst into the ICU, looking flushed and breathless. She stumbled to a halt when she saw Jade at her husband's bedside. "If you came to gloat, you're out of luck," she said defiantly. "Hutch has got a donor."

She rushed to the opposite side of Hutch's bed and raised his pale hand to her chest, cradling it. "A twenty-year-old male had an accident on his motorcycle just before dawn this morning." She smiled down at him through glad tears. "The tissues are a pretty good match, so your doctor has given the go-ahead. They'll be in shortly to start prepping you for surgery. Oh, Hutch," she whispered, bending down to plant a kiss on his forehead.

He seemed too overcome by the news to speak.

Donna Dee straightened up and glared at Jade. "We won't be needing your son after all." Her beady eyes glowed maliciously. "And I'm so very glad. I'll never have to thank you for saving my husband's life."

Dillon had stayed up half the night trying to make sense of the few facts he knew. When he finally went to sleep, his dreams were more disturbing than consciousness—and decidedly more erotic. At daybreak, he decided he could postpone his Saturday errands and chores and drive to Savannah instead.

He was after more than just a change of scenery. He was on a quest for information. If he couldn't get it from Jade, perhaps he would tap Donna Dee Jolly for it.

Technically, Jade's personal life was none of his business. If he continued probing into it, she was apt to fire him. But he had reached the point where he was willing to take that chance. Whether he liked it or not, he was already involved with Jade, even if it was only a one-sided relationship.

He had arrived at the hospital by the time Jade

emerged from the ICU. Upon seeing him in the corridor, she showed her displeasure. "What are you doing here?"

Her face looked pale beneath the overhead fluorescent glare. There were violet crescents beneath her eyes, but they only enhanced their size and vibrant color. She had on a short, straight, stone-washed denim skirt, a white linen shirt, a red leather belt, and red sandals. She looked outstanding.

"I could ask you the same question," he said. "After what I overheard last night, I figured this was the last place you'd be today."

"I have a reason to be here. You have none."

"Consider me a curious bystander." Noticing the flurry of activity going on around the ICU, Dillon looked beyond Jade's shoulder. The corridor was suddenly full of medical personnel, all rushing around. "What's going on?"

"Hutch has a donor."

His gut knotted. "Not—"

"No, not Graham. An accident victim."

She glanced back at the ICU, then turned and headed toward the exit. Dillon fell into step beside her. "Is Hutch Jolly Graham's father?"

Without faltering, she maintained her brisk stride. "I don't know."

"Oh, for Christ's sake." Irritably, he stepped in front of her to block her path. "Is he or isn't he?"

"Why don't you stay out of my personal life? Your morbid fascination with it really puts me off."

"What's Mrs. Jolly to you?"

Supremely annoyed, she held her breath for a moment before releasing it with a sigh of resignation. "Donna Dee and I were best friends."

"Until when, Jade? When did you stop being her friend? When Hutch fathered your baby? Were they already married at the time?"

"Of course not! How dare..." She compressed her lips to keep herself from saying more.

He could tell that the question had really pissed her off. It was time to fall back and punt. Taking her arm, he guided her toward the exit. In a mollifying tone he said, "If you'd be honest and up front with me, I wouldn't have to pry."

"This is none of your business."

"I think it is."

"Why?"

Again he stopped to face her. So much for punting. He backed her into the nearest wall and whispered fiercely, "Because I want to know why you freeze up every time I touch you. Damn you, Jade, you've made me want to touch you. But I can't stand for you to look at me like you're the human sacrifice and I've got fresh blood on my hands."

"I don't want to hear this."

"You may not want to hear it, but that's the way it is, and you damn well know it. You can tell by the way I've kissed you that I want to sleep with you."

"Don't. Don't say any more."

"Jade—"

"Mark this down," she said with emphasis. "There can never be anything intimate between us."

"Because you sign my paycheck?"

Anger flickered briefly in the desolate blue eyes. "That, too. But mainly because of things you don't know."

"What things, Jade? That's what I'm trying to find out. Tell me what *things*."

She shook her head. For the time being, her stubbornness appeared impenetrable. Swearing beneath his breath, Dillon stepped aside and let her precede him to the exit.

It was midafternoon by the time Jade reached the outskirts of Palmetto. She noticed in her rearview mirror that Dillon was still following her. He hadn't let more than one car get between them at any point during the trip from Savannah. He took the cutoff right behind her.

The winding country road was banked on either side by dense forests. It eventually came to a dead end at an abandoned plantation house. The For Sale sign had been there so long it was nearly obscured by the tall grass growing around its stake. The elements had faded the lettering. The house itself was architecturally impressive, though it had fallen into disrepair. Paint was peeling off the Corinthian columns. Window shutters were loose or missing altogether. A portion of the roof had been ripped off by the last hurricane to move ashore.

The surrounding live oak trees had escaped damage, however. From their branches, trailing moss hung motionless in the humid heat, unless it was relieved by a breath of coastal breeze. Birds twittered among the stately pines and drank at a lichen-covered stonework fountain. Crepe myrtles were so burdened with ruffled fuchsia blossoms that the branches bobbed like the heads of old maids stealing naps.

Jade got out of her Cherokee. "Nice place," Dillon remarked drolly as he alighted from his pickup.

"Isn't it wonderful? I'm thinking of buying it."

Undaunted by his lack of enthusiasm, Jade moved toward the house and carefully picked her way up the steps to the veranda. It wrapped around three sides of the house. Her footsteps echoed hollowly as she walked along it, peering into window casements. Those that still had glass were grimy with salt spray. The beach was only half a mile away.

"You can't be serious," Dillon said, moving up onto the veranda with her.

"I am."

"Isn't it a little large for the three of you?"

"It's not for us. I want to buy it for GSS."

He gave a harsh laugh. "First a piss-poor farm and now a derelict Tara. I hope George Stein didn't give you carte blanche with the company checkbook."

Taking no offense, she left the veranda and ventured to the eastern side of the house, where once there had been a formal flower garden. The crushed seashell paths were now choked with weeds and, in the flower beds, wild grass grew where carefully cultivated plants once had.

On the far side of the garden there was another live oak. A swing hung suspended from one of its branches. The ropes attaching it to the tree were bigger around than her wrists. The knots beneath the plank seat were larger than her knees. Gingerly, she sat down in the seat and gave the swing a desultory push with the toe of her sandal.

Tilting her head back, she closed her eyes and let the dappled sunlight spill across her face. She breathed deeply of the sultry air, which was heavily scented with honeysuckle and gardenia.

"You've been here before."

She opened her eyes. Dillon, standing with both hands in the rear pockets of his jeans, was watching her. His hazel eyes looked more green than usual, reflecting the verdant branches of the tree.

"Several times. I wasn't kidding when I said I want to buy it. I'd like for this to be a company playground, sort of a corporate bed-and-breakfast facility."

"I thought you were scouting out property for an annex."

"This would be in addition to that. Think how wonderful it would be to entertain clients and upper-echelon executives here. I picked up a floor plan from the realtor and sent it to Hank." Dillon had met Hank in New York. They had conferred on the TexTile plant.

"I told him I'd like for the house to be modernized without compromising on the Southern grace and charm. If we get the foreign markets we hope to, we could bring their reps here for formal dinners. Maybe transport them by horse-drawn buggies and serve them mint juleps on the veranda. They'd eat it up."

He moved behind her, placed his hands above hers on the ropes, and began pushing the swing, not too vigorously, but enough to let the wind sift through her hair.

"Have you bounced this brainstorm off ol' George yet?"

"Not yet. I want Hank to do some watercolor sketches first."

"You and Hank seem to be pretty thick."

"We've been friends since college."

"Hmm."

She ignored the speculation in his voice. "I also asked Hank to design a beach house in the nature of a gazebo, where we could hold company parties, picnics, and receptions. We could lease it to other groups when it wasn't in use. That would defer some of the maintenance costs."

"George'll like that. And maybe while you've got those

foreign executives sitting on the veranda sipping mint juleps, darkies could sing spirituals from the slave quarters."

She lowered her foot and plowed a yard-long furrow in the ground before the swing came to a stop. She had to angle her head far back in order to look him in the eye. The crown of her head came close to touching his belly.

"You're patronizing me."

He didn't move, although conversation would have been much easier if he had let go of the ropes and stepped around the swing to face her. "That's right."

"Thank you for admitting it, at least."

"You're welcome."

"I guess I got carried away. Do you think I'm crazy?"

"I think you're...intriguing," he admitted after pausing to search for the right word. "In fact, Jade, you confound the hell out of me."

His voice sounded too intense for comfort. She tried to make light of what he had said and divert the topic to him. "You're a fairly puzzling character yourself."

His mustache spread wider over his smile. "Me?"

"Uh-huh. For a bachelor living alone, you don't go out much."

"No mystery there. My demanding boss doesn't leave much time for the pursuit of pleasure."

"You don't see women."

He arched one of his eyebrows. "Are you keeping track?"

"I just had you pegged as a man who would frequently need female companionship."

"You mean sex."

"Yes, sex," she repeated uneasily.

Suddenly, the still afternoon had become more torpid

than before. Even the insects had ceased their droning buzz. The air was too muggy to inhale. Jade became aware of her clothing, and every place that it clung damply to her skin. Her hair felt heavy and hot against her neck. A butter-colored sun beat down on the earth, which released its heat in rising shimmers. It was like being in a perfumed sauna—only they weren't naked.

She became very conscious of how close behind her Dillon was standing, how near her shoulders were to his hips. Mere inches separated their hands on the ropes. His scent mingled with myriad others, but she could distinguish it.

"What I was going to say," she said breathlessly, "is that your lack of an active social life must have something to do with losing your wife and child."

His mustache resettled into place. He lowered his hands and moved away from the swing, keeping his broad back to her. "How'd you know about that?"

"I knew days after I met you in L.A."

"Leave it to you to check out everything," he said tightly, spinning around to confront her.

"TexTile was vitally important to me. I couldn't afford to make any bad choices. I checked you out as thoroughly as I could."

Angrily he stared down at her for several moments, then his shoulders gradually relaxed. "I guess it doesn't matter one way or another that you know."

"What happened?" she asked gently.

"Why ask? You already know."

"Only the basic facts."

He plucked a twig from the tree and twirled it between his fingers. "We were living in Tallahassee. I was working for this slimy son of a bitch who assigned me a job out of town. I commuted home only on weekends. Debra hated the arrangement. I hated it even worse. At the time, we had no choice.

"She was getting depressed, so we planned a special weekend. I got home on a cold, wet Friday night. She had planned a big evening for us." His voice became monotonal as he walked Jade through the house and told her what he had discovered on the bed in the master bedroom.

"They looked so perfect," he rasped. "There was no mess, no blood, no..." He made a gesture of misapprehension. "I thought they were asleep."

"What did you do?"

His eyes turned cold. "For one thing, I beat the shit out of the man who had kept me away from my family."

"Good."

"Then I stayed drunk for several months, shut myself off from everything, even the 'companionship' you mentioned before. Once I resumed, I nailed any woman who said yes. Fat, skinny, ugly, pretty, old, young. It didn't matter, you know?" Jade shook her head. "Well, maybe you have to be a man to understand that."

"Maybe."

"Anyway, I moved around a lot, stayed a loner until you offered me this job." He speared her with his eyes. "This is the first time in seven years I've got something to live for. I owe you thanks for that, Jade."

"You don't owe me anything except hard work for the money I pay you. So far I haven't been disappointed."

He dropped the twig to the ground and dusted off his hands. "I should have been at home with them."

"Why? So you could die in your sleep, too? Would that have made things better?"

"I should have checked the furnace."

"And she shouldn't have turned it on before it was checked."

"Don't be argumentative."

"Then don't talk crazy, Dillon. It was a tragic accident; no one's to blame. You can't go through your life trying to atone for something that wasn't your fault." She gazed at him for a moment. "Hearing you talk about it explains a lot. I knew the TexTile job was important to you. I didn't realize until now how much."

"I look on it as a second chance. I don't want to blow it." He slid down the trunk of the tree until he was sitting on his heels. "So now you know what motivates me. What about you?"

"A fantastic salary. Position and respect in a man's world."

"Hmm. With all that going for you, why'd you come back to Palmetto?"

"Because GSS needed the community and the community needed this plant. As observant as you are, it can't have escaped your notice how depressed the economy is. Some of the people living around here still don't have indoor plumbing. They subsist on whatever food they can grow.

"TexTile is going to employ hundreds of people. Before we are even operational, I'm going to organize workshops and classes to teach necessary skills. Those who are hired will be paid a percentage of their salary even while they're in training. The plant will have daycare facilities so that more than one parent can work. There will be—"

"That's bullshit, Jade."

Her mouth went slack with astonishment. "What?"

"I said that's bullshit. It all sounds terrific. On the sur-face, you're drenched in altruism," he said, coming to his feet. "But if I dug deep enough, I'd find the real reason you want to build your plant here, and it isn't compassion for the poor and economically oppressed."

Straddling her legs with his, he gripped the ropes of the swing and stood in front of her, talking down into her upturned face.

"It has something to do with your former best friend and the sheriff she's married to, who might or might not be Graham's father. Mixed up in there somewhere are the Patchetts. There's no love lost between you and the big-wigs of this town."

"It's getting late. I've got to go."

She stood up, even though it meant making heart-stopping contact with the front of his body. She ducked beneath one of his arms and almost made good her escape before he caught her hand and brought her around.

"Not good enough, Jade."

"The reasons I gave you for wanting to build the plant here are genuine."

"I don't doubt that."

"Then why can't you just accept it and leave it alone?"

"Because it doesn't jive. Someone who oozes that much compassion for her fellow man would offer a needed kidney."

"No one is cutting Graham open and removing his kidney."

"Right—especially if the recipient is married to your former best friend and *might* be your son's father." He took a step closer. "Did Jolly dump you for Donna Dee when you were pregnant and still in love with him?"

"I hated him."

"Now we're getting somewhere. Why?"

"Leave me alone, Dillon."

"Not until I understand what's going on."

"You're not supposed to understand."

"Why do you flinch every time a man comes near you?"

"I don't flinch."

"The hell you don't," he said softly. "You nearly fainted a few seconds ago when your breasts came up against me. And the expression on your face when you discovered I'm hard defied description."

"I didn't notice."

"You're lying. Is Hutch Jolly the man who made you frigid?"

"I'm not frigid."

"No? Could have fooled me."

"Maybe I just don't find you attractive."

He linked his fingers at the back of her neck beneath her hair where her skin was dewy from the heat. "That's another lie, Jade." Ducking his head, he whisked his mustache across her lips. "You said yourself you liked my kiss."

"I don't."

"Liar."

He touched the corner of her lips with his tongue. It was thrilling, terrifying. His teasing caress made her hot and dizzy. She curled her hands into the front of his shirt, feeling the solid muscles beneath the cloth. His size and strength overwhelmed her; he could hurt her. He felt and smelled masculine. His maleness both seduced and repelled. She fought its appeal and her terror of it.

"Don't do this, Dillon," she begged against his seeking lips. "I can't replace her. No woman can."

His head snapped back. "What did you say?"

"I won't be one of those women you 'nail' in grief for your wife."

"Is that what you think you are, just another soft, wet route to forgetfulness?"

"It's possible, isn't it?"

He muttered an expletive. "Listen, if that's all I wanted, I could have a naked woman in my bed by nightfall."

"But would she also have a teenage son?"

"Oh, I get it," he said tightly. "Graham is supposed to be a replacement for the son I lost."

"You've certainly made overtures to get close to him."

His fury was as palpable as the heat. It shimmied through his body and into hers. He gave her a crude once-over, stopping at her breasts and at the tops of her thighs, before lifting his gaze back to her face. "You don't give yourself enough credit, Jade. Whether or not you had Graham, I'd still want to fuck you."

He turned and strode toward his parked pickup. Jade, now angry in her own right, charged after him. She caught up as he was climbing into the driver's seat. "If you persist in saying things like that to me, I'll have no choice except to dismiss you."

"Go ahead," he said with a belligerent jerk of his chin.

He was probably only calling her bluff to scare her, but it worked. The thought of his walking off the project now was sobering. Where would she find a contractor as good? What excuse would she give George Stein, who had nothing but glowing things to say about Dillon?

She tried another tack. "I'm still convinced that you're the best man for this job, Dillon."

"Thanks."

"Don't you see that it wouldn't be smart for us to become lovers even if...if I could."

"I never claimed it was smart."

"It would permanently alter our good working relationship. Neither of us wants that, do we?"

"No."

"TexTile is too important to both of us. We can't let personal conflicts interfere with our work."

"If you say so."

"Then, you see my point?"

"I see your point."

"And I have your word that you won't pursue this any further?"

"No way."

Until then, he had avoided looking directly at her. When he fixed his eyes on her, she felt their impact like a soft blow to the abdomen. Then he slid on his opaque sunglasses, and she couldn't see his eyes at all.

Chapter 25

———◆———

Son of a bitch." Graham kicked the flat tire of his bicycle. "Damnshitfuckscrew."

He luxuriated in saying all the words he heard from the construction workers—sometimes even from Dillon when Dillon didn't know he was around. If his mother caught him talking like that, she would ground him for a week at least. However, there was no one around now to hear him, so he let fly with another round of vulgarities.

He had finally won his mother's consent to ride his bike to and from the site, if he called her before leaving and didn't make any unscheduled stops along the way. He had made the trip only a few times when a spell of bad weather had set in. It had rained for a week. By the time the weather cleared, he had come down with a stomach virus that had him vomiting for one whole day, then lying listlessly in bed the next.

For several days following his illness, his mother had curtailed any vigorous activity. "If that was the summer flu, you could have a relapse."

"But, Mom, I feel great now."

There'd been no swaying her. So, this was the first day in almost two weeks that he'd been granted permission to visit the construction site, and now his tire had gone flat.

Graham looked down at it balefully. If he rode on it, he'd ruin it. He should roll his bike back home, but that would nix getting to visit the site today. If he rolled it to the site, he wouldn't make it by the expected time, and his mother would have a cow.

Any way he looked at it, he was screwed.

A car sped past him, sending up a cloud of dust. Despite the recent rains, the following days had been so hot that the ground was dry again. Graham waved the dust out of his face, then shot the driver the finger.

Immediately, the brake lights of the car flashed on. "Oh, hell," Graham whispered fearfully. To his further mortification, the car began backing up. "Oh, shit." He licked the dust off his dry lips and wiped his perspiring palms on the seat of his shorts.

The candy-apple-red El Dorado rolled to a stop beside him. The tinted passenger window was lowered electronically. "Hey, boy."

Graham gulped down a wad of nervous spit. "Hi."

"Unless I'm mistaken, you shot me the bird."

Graham's knees turned to jelly. He had to pee real bad. "Yes, sir."

"How come?"

"I, uh, I nearly choked on the dust you raised." Then, not wanting to be a total wimp, he added, "I think you were speeding."

The driver laughed. "Hell, boy, I'm always speeding. I've got places to go and people to see." He nodded toward the bike. "Looks to me like you're in trouble."

"My tire went flat."

"Where were you headed?"

"Out where they're building the TexTile plant."

"Hmm." The driver tipped down his sunglasses and peered at Graham over the frames. "That's in the opposite direction from where I'm going, but I reckon I could give you a lift out there."

"Oh, no thanks. I'll—"

"Your bike'll fit in the trunk."

"Thanks anyway, sir, but I don't think I'd better."

"You're Jade's boy, aren't you?"

Graham was momentarily taken aback. "Yes, sir. How'd you know?"

"What's your name again?"

"Graham."

"That's right, Graham. Well, Graham, me and your mama have known each other since grade school. Maybe she's mentioned me—Neal Patchett?"

The name was vaguely familiar. Graham was sure his mother had talked about some people named Patchett. "Does she know your father, too?"

"That's right," Neal replied with a wide grin. "His name's Ivan. Did you know that a freight train chopped off his legs clean as a whistle?"

As with most boys his age, Graham was fascinated by gore. "Jeez. No kiddin'?"

"That's a fact. Right here above his knees. It was a real mess." He depressed a button in the glove compartment and the lid of the trunk popped open. "Put your bike in there and climb in. I'll be more'n pleased to give you a lift."

Graham had been forbidden to accept rides from strangers, but he knew who this man was, and his mother knew him, too. If he didn't ride with him, he'd be stuck out on the road and still uncertain about what he should do. All things considered, it was his best option.

He rolled his bicycle to the rear of the car and lifted it into the trunk. He had to rearrange the fishing gear and two shotguns stowed there, but was finally able to fit his bike inside and close the lid.

The luxurious leather interior of the car made him self-conscious of his dusty sneakers. His sweaty, bare legs stuck to the seat. But after being out in the hot sun, it felt good.

"All set?"

"Yes, sir."

"Cut out that 'sir' shit, okay? Just call me Neal."

"Thanks."

Neal asked him how he was liking Palmetto. Graham answered all his questions politely. They had gone almost a mile before he said uneasily, "Mr. Patchett, we need to turn around. The site's the other way."

"Hell, I know that. But I thought we'd get your flat fixed while we're at it. I know this mechanic who'll do it for free. While we're waiting, we'll have a cold drink. Doesn't that sound good?"

"I guess so."

A drink did sound good. He was parched. He might be a few minutes late getting to his mother's office, but consoled himself with the thought that it couldn't take much longer to have the flat fixed than it would have taken him to ride the rest of the way on his bike. As soon as they left the garage, he'd tell Mr. Patchett to step on it. The slick Cadillac would get them to the site in no time, a hell of a lot faster than he could pedal it.

"I'll call my mom from the garage and tell her I'm running late," he said with a sudden burst of inspiration.

"Sure, if you think it's necessary." Neal glanced across at him. "Does she still go out to the Parker place every now and then?"

"Where?"

"The Parker farm."

"I don't know."

"Oh. I've seen her out there and thought she might have mentioned it."

"I know she's buying property for her company," Graham offered, trying to be helpful.

"She's a regular go-getter, isn't she?"

Taking that as a compliment, Graham responded with a happy smile. "She sure is."

When they reached the garage, a man in greasy overalls sauntered out to greet them. He smiled at Mr. Patchett, revealing three snuff-stained teeth. While he fixed the flat, he invited them to wait inside the office, where it was cool.

Graham followed Neal into the cluttered office. It was only marginally cooler than outside and reeked of an overflowing ashtray, axle grease, and motor oil. Graham would have found it unpleasant if he hadn't been stupefied by the glowingly naked girl on the wall calendar. He hadn't realized that nipples could be that big and red, or pubic hair that lush and dark.

"There's the phone if you want to call your mother."

Graham wasn't actually doing anything wrong, but he felt too iniquitous to speak to his mother right then. Besides, he didn't want Neal Patchett, who was supercool, to think he was a geek.

"Naw. It's cool."

Neal kissed his fingers and patted the calendar girl's round behind. "She's something, isn't she? When I was your age, I used to come here just so I could ogle the calendars. Later, I bought my rubbers here. Quicker than the drugstore, you know. There's a vending machine in the bathroom yonder if you ever need some in a hurry."

Speechless, Graham tore his eyes away from the calendar to gape at Neal.

"You know what rubbers are, don't you, boy?"

Graham nodded stupidly, then cleared his throat and his vision, and said, "Hell, yes, I know what rubbers are."

"I figured you must. How old are you anyhow?"

It was flattering that Mr. Patchett talked to him as one man to another. Proudly, he stated, "I'll be fifteen my next birthday."

"And when's that?"

"November twenty-seventh."

Neal gazed at him for a moment, then broke into a wide smile. "Around Thanksgiving."

"It's on Thanksgiving every seven years."

"Imagine that. Well, what'll you have to drink?" He opened a cold-drink machine, the likes of which Graham had never seen before. It was a chest of refrigerated air. The bottles stood in rows formed by a metal grid.

Neal banged on the drawer of the cash register, and it flew open. He scooped out a handful of coins. Graham stared down at the money, then nervously glanced through the window. "Won't he mind?"

"He owes my daddy too many favors to mind. Don't worry about it. What'll you have to drink?"

Graham looked for something familiar among the rows of bottle caps. "Do they have Dr. Pepper?"

"Dr. Pepper? Doesn't look like it. Grapette, Orange Nehi, Big Red, and Chocolate Soldier."

"Chocolate Soldier? What's that?"

"Are you telling me that you've reached the ripe old age of fourteen without ever drinking a Chocolate Soldier?"

Neal's incredulity made Graham feel gauche, yet self-defensive. "In New York we drank egg cremes. You buy them from street vendors."

Neal pushed two quarters into the money slot. "Egg creme? Now if that doesn't sound like something a Yankee would drink, I'll pay for lying."

The Chocolate Soldier was delicious. Mr. Patchett offered to treat him to another, but he declined. He was worried about the time. "How much longer do you think it'll be before the flat is fixed?"

"Looks like he's finishing up now." Neal opened the door for him and they moved into the service bay.

Graham was relieved that they would soon be on their way. "I'm supposed to be there by now. If I'm late, my mom gets mad."

"Well," Neal drawled, "you know how women are. They get their panties in a wad over the least little thing." Companionably, he clapped Graham on the shoulder.

"Stop giving me the same tired excuses you give your other clients." Jade smiled into the telephone receiver. "When will you have something to show me?"

"You should know better than to pressure an artist," Hank Arnett said. "Pressure stifles creativity."

"*When?* I don't want to take the proposal to our friend George until I can bowl him over with your drawings."

Jade's plans to buy the plantation house for GSS were

still in place. Hours had been spent on long-distance phone calls to Hank. He had liked the idea from the outset, but said he couldn't commit himself until he saw pictures of what he had to work with. Jade had made arrangements with the realtor to get inside the house. The Polaroids she had taken were currently with Hank. He claimed to be toying with some ideas. She was impatient to see them.

"In all modesty, a few of my watercolors would be a persuasive bonus," he conceded. "As you know, George is crazy about my stuff."

"So get off your duff and do them."

"Give me two more weeks."

"Ten days."

"You nag worse than Deidre," he complained.

"Your wife is no less than an angel. Speaking of which, how are my twin goddaughters?"

Dillon came into her office just as she was hanging up the telephone. "You look happy."

"I was talking to Hank."

"Does he always make you smile like that?" he asked sourly.

"Sometimes."

He harrumphed sarcastically. He'd been in a foul mood ever since the torrential rains, which had turned the construction site into a hazardous quagmire. Dillon had finally relented and called a stop to the excavation until the weather cooperated and the ground dried out.

The delay had created an understandable glitch in his schedule. He was the only one who considered that unacceptable and was now driving himself and everyone else to the limit to make up for the lost time. He smiled even less frequently than before. Today, his disposition was especially truculent.

There was a wedge-shaped sweat stain on the front of his tank top. His boots and jeans were dusty. He had left his hard hat outside, but not his sunglasses. He was twirling them by the stem. Rather than looking like an idle, relaxed gesture, it conveyed pent-up frustration. His lips were firmly clamped beneath his mustache.

He hadn't touched her since that day at the deserted plantation house. Their conversations were kept strictly to business. Nevertheless, what he had said before they parted company was still very much on Jade's mind. If she doubted the resolution behind his, "No way," all she had to do was look into his eyes now.

"Did you want to see me about something in particular, Dillon?"

"Yeah, dinner."

"Excuse me?"

"Dinner. Let's have dinner."

"Fine. I'll call Cathy. I'm sure she won't mind setting an extra place."

"That's not what I'm talking about." He approached her desk. "Let's go to dinner together. You and I alone."

"You mean like a date?"

"Exactly like a date."

"When?"

"Soon."

"Why?"

"Why not?"

Their eyes made sizzling contact.

Jade raised a hand to her throat and fiddled with the broach she had pinned there. He planted his fists, knuckles down, on the edge of her desk and leaned across it. "Well?" he asked crossly. "Is there something wrong with us having dinner together? Or don't you like it if the man is the one who's buying?"

She took affront at that. There was a distinct chill in her voice when she said, "I'll check with Cathy and see which night would be best for her to stay with Graham. Then I'll—" She broke off and stood up suddenly. "Dillon, is Graham here yet?"

"I don't think so."

"You haven't seen him?"

"Not today. Not since he got sick, in fact. Were you expecting him?"

She rounded her desk and rushed to the door of the trailer, throwing it open. Loner was dozing in the shade on the step. He raised his head and regarded her indifferently. If Graham were around, no matter how hot it was, Loner would be tagging after him, not napping in the shade. She scanned the immediate area but saw no sign of Graham or his bicycle.

"What time is it?" She was surrounded by clocks and was wearing a wristwatch; her question was reflexive.

"Going on five. Why?"

Sidestepping Dillon, she returned to her desk and picked up the telephone. "It's been over an hour since Graham called me," she said as she punched out her home phone number. "He should be here by now."

"Maybe he didn't leave right after he called."

She shook her head. "He was chomping at the bit to get here before the crew knocked off for the day . . . . Hi, Cathy. Is Graham there?" Hearing the dreaded answer, her fingers tightened around the telephone cord. "Yes, I know he called, but he's not here yet."

"What did she say?" Dillon asked when Jade hung up.

"Exactly what I was afraid she would say. He left as soon as he called. Cathy was standing right there. She waved him off. She's leaving now on her way here to see if she spots him along the way."

"Maybe one of his friends waylaid him."

"He's conscientious. He knew I was expecting him. He would be here...unless something has happened to him."

Dillon caught her by the shoulders as she dashed toward the door again. "Jade, he's fourteen years old. Boys that age are easily distracted and lose track of time. Graham can take care of himself. Don't panic."

"He's too afraid that this privilege will be revoked to waste time getting here. Something's happened to him." She worked her shoulders out of his grasp and left the portable building. She had no specific plan in mind. She was propelled by adrenaline to act, to move, to locate Graham immediately.

"Where are you going?"

"To look for him." She climbed into her Cherokee.

"You can't go chasing around aimlessly," he argued. "If he shows up, how will we know where to find you?"

"Let's worry about finding him first."

As she was reaching to close the door, she spotted the El Dorado turning in off the highway. Recognizing it instantly, she sprang from her car.

Before Neal had even come to a full stop, Jade had her hand on the passenger door, pulling it open. "Graham!" Her knees almost buckled with relief. She drew him out of the leather seat and wrapped her arms around him. Loner ran in crazy circles around them, barking gleefully until Dillon ordered him to settle down.

"Mom, you're smothering me," Graham muttered with adolescent embarrassment.

Holding his shoulders between her hands, she thrust him at arm's length away from her. "Where have you been?"

"My bike had a flat on the way. Mr. Patchett picked me up and took me to the garage to get it fixed, then we came straight here."

She cast a murderous glance toward Neal, who was smiling at her from across the roof of his car. "You should have called me from the garage, Graham."

"I didn't think about it," he mumbled.

"Where's your bike now?" Dillon asked him.

"It's in my trunk." Neal moved to the rear of his car and used his key to open the trunk. Loner was sniffing at him suspiciously.

Dillon pulled the bike out and said a terse, "Thanks."

"Don't thank him," Jade spat out viciously, almost too angry to speak.

"Mom, he gave me a ride."

She wanted to shake Graham very hard for jumping to Neal's defense. To keep herself from doing that, she held her arms rigidly at her sides and dug her nails into her palms until they hurt. "You know better than to accept a ride from a stranger, Graham."

"But he's not a stranger. You know him. And he knows you. I thought it would be all right."

"You thought wrong!"

"Jade."

"Shut up, Dillon. This is my affair. I'll handle it."

"Well, you're doing a damn poor job of it."

Cathy prevented any further discussion when she sped

up in her car. She hastily alighted. "You had your mother and me scared out of our wits, Graham Sperry. Where have you been?"

Jade said, "He'll tell you all about it on your way home."

"Home?" Graham wailed. "I have to go home?"

Jade gave him a hard look that squashed any further argument. Even Cathy didn't dare pose another question. She threw her arm across Graham's shoulders and walked him to her car.

As soon as they were on their way, Jade rounded on Neal. "I ought to have you arrested."

"You threatened that once before, but chickened out, remember? When are you going to learn, Jade, that if you take me on, you can't possibly win?"

"Stay away from my son. If you harm him, I'll kill you."

"Harm him?" Neal asked silkily. "Why would I harm my own flesh and blood?"

"What the hell are you talking about?" Dillon demanded, taking a threatening step toward Neal. Sensing his master's shift in mood, Loner began to growl.

Neal wasn't intimidated by either. "I'm that boy's daddy. Didn't Jade tell you?"

"That's not true!" she shouted.

"Should I call the sheriff's office or handle him myself?" Dillon asked her.

Neal taunted, "Yeah, Jade. What do you want him to do? Do you want him to stick around and hear all the sordid details of our long-ago romance? If he's the one keeping your snatch damp these days, I'm sure he'd be interested."

"You lousy son of a bitch." Dillon was ready to throw a punch, but Jade stepped between the two of them.

"No, Dillon. That's what he wants you to do. I've seen it happen before. Leave me alone with him."

"Like hell," Dillon snarled, still straining to get his hands on Neal.

"Please, don't argue with me."

His eyes roved over her face as though he couldn't comprehend her at all. Then, cursing, he stomped into her portable office and slammed the door behind him.

"Call off this stupid animal," Neal said.

Loner was still skulking around him, growling. She called him down. "Say what you have to say, Neal."

He reached out and stroked her cheek before she was able to swat away his hand, then grinned when she did. "You're not scared that I'll harm that boy of yours. You're scared that I'll claim him, or better yet, that he'll claim me."

Neal was sterile. The Patchetts' thinking was dynastic. In that startling, terrifying moment, Jade realized how significant Graham's existence was to them. They would try to make him one of them. Hiding her fear, she said, "There isn't even a remote possibility of that happening."

"No? He liked me, Jade. Ask him."

"I don't doubt that you charmed him. Boys his age are easily attracted to wickedness."

He gave a short laugh. "Why don't you make it easy on us all? If you would only say the word, I'd do right by you and offer you marriage, like I should have fifteen years ago. We could be one, big, happy family, living in the family home—three generations of Patchett men and the house's new mistress."

"Stay away from my son," she said in a sinister monotone. "I'm warning you, Neal."

"Jade," he cooed, "you know better than anyone that,

in Palmetto, the only warning worth shit is one that comes from a Patchett."

He stepped closer to her and closed his hand around her jaw. "Let me give you one. Don't fight me. I'm going to have my son with or without you." He smiled at her meaningfully. "I'd just as soon it be a package deal." Then he winked. "You had me once, and it wasn't all that bad, was it?"

She yanked her head out of his grasp and backed away from him.

"That's all for now," he said, his smile still in place. "I'm late for an appointment."

After blowing her a kiss, he got into his El Dorado and drove away. Jade maintained her fearless posture until he was out of sight, then she slumped against the exterior wall of the temporary building. Dillon barged through the door.

His face was as fierce, dark, and angry as a fallen angel's. "Okay, I've been nice. I've been patient. But I'm up to here with this crap. I want to know what the hell is going on and why. You aren't leaving here until I do."

Chapter 26

Taking her hand, he pulled her up the steps behind him. He locked the door, took the telephone off the hook, and pointed her toward the short sofa. "Sit down."

"I've still got work to do, Dillon."

"You're shot for the day. Anyway, I don't care what was on your agenda, we're going to have a chat. Now, sit down."

She dropped down onto the sofa, covering her face with her hands, capitulating more from emotional distress than blind obedience.

"Can I get you something to drink?"

She shook her head. Dillon drew up a metal folding chair, placed it only inches beyond her knees and straddled it backward, propping his arms on the back of it. "Okay, let's have it."

"Have what?"

"Jesus," he swore irritably. "Are we going to play more guessing games?"

"This is your game, not mine. I want to go home."

"A minute ago you wanted to work."

"Stop bullying me!"

"Then start talking."

"What do you want to know?"

"For starters you can explain why two men are claiming Graham as their son."

"Either would have a lot to gain if Graham was his child. Hutch would get a kidney. And Neal would have an heir." When Dillon raised his eyebrows inquisitively, she added, "He's sterile as a result of the accident that took off Ivan's legs."

Dillon digested that, but he was dissatisfied with her explanation. "It still doesn't make sense, Jade. Men don't ordinarily leap forward claiming paternity. Usually it's the other way around."

"Their circumstances are unusual."

"Did you sleep with both of them?"

"No."

"So their claims to Graham are totally unfounded?"

She said nothing.

"Who is his father, Jade?"

"I don't know!"

"Then you *did* sleep with both of them."

"No!"

"Goddammit," he shouted, "come clean with me."

"They raped me!"

The words echoed loudly off the walls of the small room.

They reverberated inside Dillon's skull as he stared at Jade, shocked speechless. Once again she covered her face with her hands.

"They raped me," she repeated softly. "They raped me."

Dillon shoved all ten fingers through his hair and held

it off his face for several moments. When he lowered his hands, he rubbed his palms up and down his thighs. He had wanted to know. He had hounded her to tell him. But he hadn't counted on this.

He had expected to hear the confessions of a reformed wayward teenage girl, or of a shy introvert who had sought attention by being easy, or of a rebel out to torment strict parents. He hadn't expected rape.

"When, Jade?"

"In February of my senior year in high school. It was the day I learned that Gary and I had received full academic scholarships to the university."

"Gary?" Hell, just when he thought he knew all the players in this drama, she introduced another one.

"Gary Parker," she said. "We were high-school sweethearts, but much more than that. We were going to get married and, together, change the world."

In a quiet, faraway voice, she told him about their relationship. "We had such great expectations for the future. I loved him very much."

"Could he be Graham's father?"

She looked toward the window, which was, by now, a square patch of lavender twilight. "No. I was a virgin when they raped me."

"Christ. And the two of them got away with it?"

Her eyes came back to him. "Actually there were three. The third was Lamar Griffith. He was a shy, sensitive boy, but he went along to save face with Neal."

"Does he still live in Palmetto?"

She told him about Lamar's fate. After a lengthy pause, Dillon said, "I take it, it was Neal's idea."

"Oh yes," she replied fiercely. "He was their ring leader.

If it hadn't been for him, it would never have happened. But Hutch and Lamar could have stopped it. Instead they raped me too, then left me there."

"Left you?"

"Donna Dee was driving me out to Gary's house so I could tell him about our scholarships. On the way there, we ran out of gas."

Dillon listened as she recalled that dreary afternoon. She didn't spare a single detail. Through the years, her recollections had remained crystal clear.

"When they first drove away with me, I was mad. I began to get afraid when Neal didn't take the turnoff to Gary's house. Instead, he drove to a channel where they had been fishing earlier. He ordered everybody out of the car. I argued, but he dragged me out."

"And the other two went along like dumb sheep?"

"It's hard to imagine how much control Neal had over them. They would do anything he said. He passed out cans of beer. I refused to drink any. When they were finished, I asked if we could go. Neal said, 'Not yet.' I asked him why. And he said..." She faltered. Her eyes dropped to her lap. "He said, 'Because before we go, the three of us are going to fuck you.'"

Dillon folded his hands together and, propping his elbows on the back of the chair, covered his mouth with his double fist. He closed his eyes, wishing that he had never used that crudity with her, wishing with all his might that he had smashed Neal Patchett's complacent mug when he had the chance.

"I didn't doubt for an instant that he meant it." Jade's voice sounded hollow. Dillon knew she wasn't there with him; she was back on that cold, rainy, February night.

"I turned and ran, but Neal reached out and grabbed a handful of my hair. It hurt. I cried out, and tears came to my eyes. I raised my hands to try to work his hand out of my hair, but I couldn't. While my arms were raised, he put his other arm around my waist and pushed me to the ground. It was cold and wet." She grimaced. "It smelled bad—like dead fish.

"Hutch shouted, 'Neal, what the hell do you think you're doing?' And Neal replied, 'Exactly what I told her we were going to do. Shut up and help me. Hold her arms.'

"I was screaming and crying and saying no, no. I couldn't see anyone except Neal. I struck at him until Hutch dropped down behind my head and got hold of my wrists. He pinned them to the ground above my head. Neal was bending over me, telling me to shut up. He slapped me several times.

"Lamar said, 'Jesus, Neal, have you gone nuts?' Neal glanced over his shoulder and said, 'Make yourself useful and stop acting like a pussy. We're not going to hurt her.' Lamar hung back. I couldn't see him, but I heard him say, 'She's crying.' Neal got really angry then. He said, 'Do you want a piece of this or not? If not, get the fuck out of my sight.'

"Neal had been lying on top of me. He pushed my thighs apart and dug one knee into the muscle on the inside of my thigh. I screamed. He slapped me again. I tried to kick. That's when Lamar took hold of my ankles. I couldn't move. I began pleading with them not to do it.

"'Shut her up,' Neal said. 'I can't stand that whining, female bullshit.' Hutch took both my wrists in one hand and covered my mouth with the other. I tilted my head back and tried to plead with Hutch for help with my eyes, but he wasn't looking into my face. He was watching what Neal was doing."

Dillon didn't move a muscle. He said nothing. For a moment, Jade fiddled with the buckle on her wristwatch. It was so quiet in the room, he could hear it ticking.

"Neal ripped open my blouse. My bra fastened in the front. He unhooked it and laid it open. I remember...I remember being so embarrassed for being exposed that way. I squeezed my eyes shut. I bit my tongue until I tasted blood. He said, 'Isn't that a pretty sight? Jade Sperry's tits.'"

She hiccuped a dry sob. "I thought I would die. I wanted to die. The mortification of it...Neal, whom I hated..." She cupped her mouth with her hand as though she were about to be sick, but she continued, her speech muffled by her hand. "He put his hands on me. He squeezed and pinched and pulled at me. It was awful and painful and debasing. Then he leaned over and sucked hard on my left nipple. So hard it hurt."

Dillon shot from his chair. Palms out, he shoved his hands into the rear pockets of his worn jeans and prowled the room as though looking for an easy exit. The violence inside him was frightening in its intensity. He wanted to hit something, smash it, destroy it. Obviously, Jade didn't notice his reaction. Her horrifying account continued.

"Neal was laughing when he came up on his knees and unzipped his pants. He shoved them down and took his penis in his hand. He said, 'Nice, isn't it, Jade? Bet your cunt can't wait.' Apparently Hutch began to get worried. He said, 'Neal, come on, you've had your fun. Let her go now.' 'Go?' Neal said. 'Hell, no, I'm just getting to the fun part.'

"Neal pushed my skirt up. I rolled my hips from side to side, trying to stop him from taking off my pantyhose. He was in such a hurry, Lamar had to help him. Then Neal…"

Dillon had been standing at the window, gazing out sightlessly at the darkening sky. When she stopped speaking, he glanced over his shoulder at her. Her head was bowed over one hand; she was massaging her temples.

Dillon went back to his chair, turned it around, and sat down facing her. He didn't say anything and somehow resisted the impulse to touch her. His presence alone seemed to reassure her. He took heart in that. She lowered her hand from her face and moistened her lips.

"Neal spat into his hand and rubbed the saliva over himself. He said, 'I'll bet you're good at sucking cock. Don't you suck Parker's? I ought to make you do this for me.'" She closed her eyes, as though blessedly thankful. "He didn't," she said gruffly.

"It wasn't easy, but he got inside me. I think he was surprised that I was a virgin because he looked into my face and laughed. He leaned over and whispered, 'Well, glory be. I'm going to get your cherry after all,' like that was an inside joke between us. Then he…" She bowed her head lower. "He…he pushed hard and hurt me really bad."

The halogen security lights outside switched on automatically. Some of their blue-white light came though the windows, but for the most part the office was filled with deep shadows and the sibilant sound of her voice.

"I thought it would go on forever. Afterward, I realized that it didn't take him long at all to climax. As he pulled away, he smeared semen on my stomach. He looked up at Hutch and grinned. 'I've greased the skids for you.'

"They switched places. When Hutch removed his hand from my mouth, I tried to scream again, but I didn't have the energy. I barely managed to lift one arm. As Hutch bent over me, I scratched his face. He cursed me and put his hand to his cheek. It came away with blood on his fingers. That made him angry. He grunted, 'Hold her hands, Neal.' Neal took my hands and held them on either side of my head.

"Hutch was the only one who kissed me. At first I thought that was all he was going to do. His weight nearly smothered me, and he kept poking his tongue deep into my mouth. It made me retch. I was screaming my outrage on the inside, but the only noise I made sounded like a mewling kitten.

"I heard Neal laughing behind me. 'Will you get on with it, Hutch? Jesus! You're making me horny all over again. Even Lamar's getting a stiff one.' Lamar giggled nervously.

"I did scream when Hutch shoved himself into me. He was twice as rough as Neal. I knew he was tearing me on the inside and making me bleed. I could feel it."

"Those bastards," Dillon hissed. In barely controlled rage, he was thumping his fists against his thighs.

"When Hutch climaxed, he arched his back and made this horrible, braying sound. I remember him pulling his lips away from his teeth. He looked so ugly, repulsive. Then he collapsed on top of me. I couldn't breathe, but I felt his hot breath on my neck. It smelled like beer and made me nauseated, but I was afraid that if I gave in to it and vomited, I would drown in it. So I managed to keep it down.

"Lamar went last. By then I didn't have the strength to

fight. I thought Lamar might cry when he looked down at me. His hands were at his fly, but he hesitated. Neal said, 'What's the matter? Let's see you do your stuff.' 'I don't know if I should, Neal.' Lamar's voice was shaky and uncertain. That was characteristic of him.

"Since Hutch had proven himself, he was feeling frisky. 'Hell, we might have known the little faggot would chicken out.' 'I'm not a faggot,' Lamar shouted. I suppose that even then he was struggling with his sexual ambiguities. He must have realized that he either had to perform or be the brunt of their ridicule, so he . . . performed.

"When he pulled down his pants, the other two applauded his erection. I know it was Lamar's first time. He didn't know where to . . . He kept ramming into me. It hurt, because I was bruised and sore. Once he got inside, he thrust at me frantically and quickly, like a rutting animal. Sweat popped out on his face. Neal kept cracking jokes and making fun of Lamar's 'technique.' Finally he climaxed.

"He was laughing with relief when he pulled away from me, but the moment he looked into my face, his smile collapsed. I think Lamar realized the extent of what they had done. His eyes silently apologized. But I didn't forgive him then or when I saw him years later."

"When was that?" Dillon asked.

She briefly told him about Mitch Hearon's funeral and Lamar's unexpected appearance. "I don't forgive him— any of them—to this day."

After an extended silence, she raised her head. "Will you pass me a Kleenex, please?" Dillon located a box of tissues on the edge of her desk. He reached for it and handed it to her. "Thank you."

She didn't use the tissue to blot her eyes, because, throughout the entire recital, she hadn't shed a single tear. She used it to wipe the perspiration off her palms.

"Did they leave you out there, Jade?"

"Yes." She laughed bitterly. "Like a cruel cliché, Neal smoked a cigarette before they left. I remember smelling the sulfur of the match and the burning tobacco. I had rolled myself into a tight ball. At that point, I was numb. I don't remember feeling pain so much as numbness.

"They discussed what to do with me, and decided that I was resourceful enough to find my way back into town. Lamar asked, 'What are we going to say if somebody finds out what happened?' Neal said, 'Who's going to tell? You?' 'Hell no.' 'Then what are you worried about?'

"Hutch asked what they would do if I told. Neal simply laughed. He said I wouldn't tell because I wouldn't want my 'lover boy,' meaning Gary, to know about it. He said I had asked for it, that I'd been flirting with all of them.

"Of course Hutch and Lamar agreed with him, chiefly because they knew that's what he wanted them to do, but also to justify to themselves what they had done.

"I don't believe that Neal has any remorse or feels any guilt. He's amoral. He has no conscience. He wanted to teach me a lesson for loving Gary instead of him, and he wanted vengeance on Gary for outsmarting him in a silly fight. He saw a way to do both with one act. Because his name is Patchett, he considered it his right."

"You should have gone to the authorities immediately."

Again, she laughed without humor. "Dillon, you don't know me very well, do you? As soon as I could move, I crawled to the highway. I didn't care if I died afterward, so long as I lived long enough to see them punished."

She recounted her visit to the hospital and all that had happened the following day in Sheriff Jolly's office. Dillon was incredulous. "So a gang rape was swept under the rug and forgotten?"

"Until now."

"Here, fifteen years later, you've come back with a vengeance. You want to make them pay for raping you."

"Not just for that."

"You mean there's more?"

"Gary."

"Oh, right. I forgot." Gently, he said, "Boyfriends often have a tough time dealing with something like that, Jade."

"Gary certainly did. Especially when Neal and the others painted me as a scarlet woman. Neal couldn't leave it alone. He taunted Gary with innuendoes until he couldn't take it anymore."

When she told him what Gary had done after seeing her at Georgie's house, Dillon was stunned. He plowed his fingers through his hair again and searched for something to say. He thought better of saying what had first occurred to him: that Gary should have had more faith in the woman he loved. She wouldn't welcome hearing that.

"I couldn't stay in Palmetto after Gary's suicide. But I swore that one day I would come back, and that when I did, *I* would be in control."

"You've already constipated Ivan and Neal. They see the handwriting on the wall. They know what a new industry will mean to them."

"They've got a lot to answer for. I'm not the only one they've hurt over the years."

"Did you know before you came back that Hutch was sick?"

"No. I planned on exposing the corruption in his sheriff's department."

"Is it corrupt?"

"I would bet my last nickel on it. He covers the Patchetts' tracks just like his father did."

"The point is moot, anyway, isn't it?"

"I suppose so."

Early indications were that Hutch's kidney transplant had been successful. His doctors were being conservative until the threat of infection abated, but their initial prognosis was good. Organ rejection was being combatted with drugs. Reportedly, he hadn't suffered any negative side effects. Even so, it was doubtful that he could ever hold public office again.

"What about Donna Dee? She's as much to blame as any of them."

"She's always loved Hutch. If I had exposed his corruption, she would have suffered disgrace along with him. As it turned out, she had to come to me, begging for his life, just as I begged her to tell the truth in Sheriff Jolly's office.

"That's not why I refused to consider Graham as a donor, but now she knows what it feels like to be desperate—abandoned by your last hope."

"Does Lamar have a family here?"

"A mother. To my knowledge, she never knew about the rape."

"Any form of revenge would be ineffective then, wouldn't it?"

"Except that Graham might be her one and only grandchild."

"You honestly don't know which of them fathered him?"

"No."

"Graham doesn't know about—"

"No! And I don't want him to know."

"Surely he's asked where he came from, who his father was."

"I diminished his importance. Graham accepts the fact that I'm his only parent."

Dillon frowned doubtfully. "For the present, maybe. But what about tomorrow, and the day after that? The older he gets, the better the odds that he'll demand to know who sired him."

"If that time comes, I can honestly tell him that I don't know."

"There are ways of detecting it. Genetic fingerprinting, it's called."

"I don't want to know. It makes no difference. He's mine. Mine," she stressed, her voice cracking. "If I had known about Hutch's illness, and Neal's sterility, I might have considered keeping Graham in New York. I never guessed that he would be a pivotal factor in their lives. It frightens me, Dillon. You think I overreacted this afternoon, but I know the kind of treachery that Neal and his father are capable of."

Her fear was obvious. Instinctively Dillon reached for her. Just as instinctively, she recoiled. "Dammit, I wish I didn't represent such a threat to you. I'd like to hold you." The darkness seemed to intensify the huskiness of his voice. "Just hold you, Jade. That's all."

After several moments, she whispered, "I don't think I would mind if you held me."

"I would never hurt you," he said as he eased himself out of his chair and onto the sofa beside her. "Never."

"I believe that."

He placed his arms around her and leaned back, carrying her with him until they were settled against the cushions of the sofa. The intimacy of the position alarmed her. She clutched his biceps. "It's okay," he murmured. "It's okay. I'll let you go anytime you say. Do you want me to? Tell me."

After a tense hesitation, she shook her head and relaxed against him. Apparently the brevity of his tank top didn't offend her. She laid her head on his chest. Her hair slid across his skin, causing him almost to groan out loud with pleasure. Her hand remained trustingly on his arm.

"Jade?"

"Hmm?"

"Since that night, you've been unable to make love?"

"Unable and unwilling."

"Unwilling to even try?"

"I have tried. With Hank."

"Hank Arnett?" Jealousy stung him.

"He was in love with me. I knew it, but didn't want him to be. I didn't want to hurt him, either. I kept telling him it was no use, that I couldn't change. I urged him not to place false hopes in my recovery. Hank's got a real stubborn streak. He wouldn't listen."

"Obviously he was finally convinced."

"Not for years. I wanted to return his affection, so I started seeing a psychologist. Eventually I was able to kiss him without freaking."

"Did you enjoy kissing him?"

"As much as I'm able to."

Dillon's jealousy was somewhat mollified. She hadn't qualified it when she had told him she liked his kisses.

"About that time, Mitch died," she continued. "Lamar showed up at his funeral. Seeing him again brought back all the horror. I finally told Hank that I couldn't have a sexual relationship with any man. It was impossible."

"Did you tell him why?"

"No. And because I didn't, he got angry and stayed away for months. One day he came back, and we've been good friends ever since. He finally accepted it."

Dillon didn't want to champion Hank's cause by saying that he was a swell fellow and that she should have given him more of a chance. Hank was in New York; Dillon was here with her, holding her.

"Why did you tell me about the rape, Jade?" When she raised her head and looked at him, he knew he had no reason to feel jealous of Hank or anybody else.

"You wouldn't accept the way I am without an explanation."

"And?"

"And because... because it was important to me that you understand *why* I am the way I am."

To keep from kissing her, he tucked her head beneath his chin. "What happened to you was a crime. It was spiteful, and mean, and violent. It had nothing to do with sex."

"I know that, Dillon."

"Sexual intimacy between two people who care about each other—"

"Is something altogether different," she stated, finishing his sentence for him. "Don't you think the psychologist reiterated that until I was sick to death of hearing it? No, I didn't subliminally blame myself. Yes, I was as angry with the sexist legal system as I was with the men. No, I do not believe that all men are barbarians. No, I do not feel any leanings toward lesbianism. No, I do not want to see all men castrated."

"That's a relief."

She tilted her head up again, and, when they made eye contact, she began to laugh. He joined in. They laughed for several minutes, and it was cathartic, because neither could cry. Their laughter made them weak. They clung to each other for support.

Then they seemed to stop laughing at precisely the same instant. One second, they were rollicking with it. The next, they were staring deeply into each other's eyes, breathless and tense.

Dillon's chest felt tight. His eyes dropped to her mouth. He watched her lips move. "Dillon?"

He closed his eyes quickly. "Christ, I want to kiss you. I want to make love to you for the first time in your life. I want to show you what it really is, what it can be. I want you to make love to me."

When he reopened his eyes, hers were startled, her lips tremulous. He was tempted to lift her mouth against his and find out why she was gazing at him with that particular expression. He hoped it was because he had aroused her—not repelled her.

He stroked her hair. He longed to soothe away the timorous quavering of her lips with soft kisses and massage the worry line from between her brows. He wanted the catchiness in her breath to come from passion, not apprehension. He wanted to give her the gift of sexual discovery, of which she'd been robbed.

But if he didn't do it right, it was liable to be irreversibly damaging. So he eased her away from him, stood up, then helped her to her feet. Ruefully he said, "Some other time."

*   *   *

The house was dark. Dillon, who had insisted on following her home, didn't drive away until she was safely inside. Cathy had left her a note on the kitchen table explaining that she had gone to bed early with a headache. There was a casserole in the refrigerator, the note said. All Jade had to do was warm it up in the microwave. She decided she wasn't hungry enough to bother. After securing the house for the night, she went upstairs.

Light shone beneath Graham's bedroom door. She knocked, then pushed it open. He was lying in bed, watching TV with what appeared to be little interest. "May I come in?"

"It's your house."

Ignoring that crack, she moved to the foot of his bed and sat down. "I get the hint. You're mad at me."

He battled over whether to continue sulking or to vent his anger. The latter won. "Wouldn't you be mad at me if I had embarrassed you half to death? Jeez, Mom, you treated me like a kid in front of Dillon and Mr. Patchett."

"What I did might have appeared unreasonable to you, Graham, but I was extremely upset."

"You had a total cow over nothing! I wasn't even that late getting there."

"That wasn't entirely it. I was upset because you were with Neal."

"Why? He was nice. And you know him, so what's the big deal?"

"The big deal is that I know him all too well. He is *not* nice."

"He seemed to be," he muttered belligerently.

"I'm sure he did. He oozes charm, but he's rotten to the

core, Graham. You'll have to take my word on this. Stay away from him. He can be dangerous." He made a scoffing sound. "I mean it. The next time he comes near you, I want to know about it immediately."

Swathed in teenage obstinacy, he studied her for a moment. "You've changed, Mom."

"Changed?"

"Ever since we moved here, you're uptight all the time."

"I've got an enormous job to do, Graham. In addition to the TexTile plant, I'm acquiring property for the parent company, doing all the—"

"Are you trying to buy land from some people named Parker?"

Jade looked at her son with surprise. "How did you know that?"

"Mr. Patchett mentioned it today."

Jade had heard nothing from Otis Parker since their last conversation by telephone. She had vacillated between calling to pressure him and giving him time to consider her offer. Graham had confirmed her suspicions—the Patchetts were on to her.

Dragging her thoughts back to Graham's, she said, "You know how busy I am. I've got a lot of important matters on my mind. You're old enough to understand that."

"But you had lots of work to do when we were in New York, too. You didn't get all bent out of shape over it. What's happened?"

She reached up and combed back his hair with her fingers. "If I've seemed high-strung lately, it's because I want to do well on this project. And because I want you to be happy here. You are, aren't you? You like the house?"

"Sure it's great, only..."

"Only what?"

"I've got all that explaining to do to my new friends."

"Explaining?"

"About why I haven't got a dad, and about Cathy not really being related to us. You know, all that shit I always have to explain." He picked at a loose cuticle. "I know you've always told me we were a special family. Unique." He raised sad blue eyes to hers. "I don't want to be special, Mom. I'm tired of being unique. I wish we were normal, like everybody else."

"There's no such thing as normal, Graham."

"Well, most people are more normal than we are."

As big as he was, she pulled him into her arms and pressed his troubled face against her throat. "Sometimes things happen in our lives that we have no control over. We have to make the best life possible with what we're given to work with.

"I wish with all my heart that you had enjoyed a 'normal' family life. It didn't work out that way. I'm sorry. I've done the best I could. I'm still doing what I believe is best," she added, thinking about Cathy and Dillon's advice that she tell Graham about the rape. She couldn't. Her son was having a difficult enough time adjusting to a new home and burgeoning maturity without afflicting him with her tragedy.

"I know you are, Mom. Forget I mentioned it." He pulled away and gave her a faint smile.

"I apologize for embarrassing you today in front of Dillon, and I promise not to do it again."

"Were you with him tonight?"

"Yes. Why?"

"Just wondering."

"What?" she asked on a laugh. "You're grinning like a opossum."

"I think Dillon likes you, that's all."

"Of course he likes me. We couldn't work so well together if he didn't like me."

"Come on, Mom. You know what I mean."

"We're friends."

"Uh-huh." He smiled with an air of superiority. "Do you think I'll be as tall as he is when I finish growing?" He glanced toward the framed photograph on his bureau. "How tall was Grandpa Sperry?"

On his thirteenth birthday, Jade had officially given him his grandfather's Medal of Honor and the picture she had always treasured. From the time he was still small enough to sit in her lap, she had told Graham the story of her father's valor in the Korean conflict. She had never told him his grandfather's death was a suicide.

"He was six feet two inches, I believe."

"So I'll be at least that tall."

"Probably." She leaned forward and kissed his forehead. "Just don't be in such a hurry to get there, okay? Good night."

"G'night. Mom?"

"Hmm?" She turned at the door and looked back at him.

"Was my dad tall?"

Thinking of her three attackers, she answered huskily, "Above average."

Graham nodded with satisfaction, then reached up to switch off the lamp above his bed. "G'night."

Chapter 27

———◆◆◆———

Jade was working at her desk when Neal came in, unannounced, without even knocking. Loner hadn't alerted her that anyone was outside. Graham was fishing in a nearby creek and had taken the dog with him for company.

Neal smiled at her as though they had parted on the best of terms. "Hi, Jade."

"What are you doing here?"

"I brought my daddy to see you."

"About what?"

"I wouldn't want to spoil his surprise."

Any surprise the Patchetts had cooked up would be nasty. "I don't want to see him."

"You don't have a choice."

He used a folding chair to prop open the door of the portable building before stepping outside. When he returned, he was carrying Ivan in his arms. He deposited him on the sofa. Jade stood stiffly beside her desk. Neal took the chair away from the door and sat down. Confident and cocky, he rested his ankle on his opposite knee.

"What do you want to see me about?" she asked Ivan.

"No inquiries after my health?" he mocked. "No pleasantries? No shooting the breeze first?"

"No." She folded her arms across her midriff—a gesture of impatience. "If you've got something to say, say it. If not, leave."

"That's not the way I deal with folks."

"That's the way I deal with you."

He fondled the smooth, arced handle of his cane. "I've seen pictures of your boy. He's a real good-lookin' kid."

She remembered Ivan's trait of staring people down from beneath his heavy eyebrows. He was using that method of intimidation on her now. It was hard to maintain a facade of indifference, especially since he was speaking of Graham. His evil personality was heightened by his physical deformity.

Keeping her tone cool and level, she replied, "I think he is."

"He favors you. At least from a distance. I'd like to see him up close."

Her heart was hammering, but she kept her expression impassive and said nothing.

"Why don't you sit down, Jade?" Neal suggested.

"I'd rather stand."

"Suit yourself." Ivan's speckled, veined hand disappeared into his suit jacket and removed an envelope from the breast pocket. He extended it toward Jade. She gazed at it suspiciously.

"What is that?"

"Open it and find out, why don't you?"

Jade reached for the envelope, opened the flap, and took out a property deed. She quickly scanned the page, then focused on the important lines that bore the signatures of the parties involved in the transfer of ownership.

"Otis Parker," she whispered. The starch in her posture went limp.

"That's right." Ivan licked his chops, reminding her of a carnivore that had just devoured its prey. "We own his land now. The deal was finalized yesterday."

Trancelike, Jade returned to her desk chair and sat down. She smoothed out the folded pages of the deed. A notary public had sealed it. It was indisputably official. No wonder Otis had been avoiding her. He hadn't responded to the messages she had left with Mrs. Parker, who always sounded flustered when she called. Jade had driven out to see them, but no one had answered her knock, even though she knew they were at home.

In a gruff voice she asked, "How much did you give him?"

"One million dollars."

"One million?"

"That's right."

Neal, leaning back in his chair, said, "We extended Otis the same courtesy you did. He doesn't have to vacate for two years if he doesn't want to. That'll give him time to bring in two years' crops. Not that he'll be needing the revenue now," he added on a chuckle.

"How . . . how did you raise that much capital?"

He winked at her. "I liquidated some assets, mortgaged others, and took out a short-term loan. When you sit on the board of the local bank, you can swing deals like this." He assumed a sympathetic expression. "See, Jade, you've still got a lot to learn about how good ol' Southern boys conduct their business."

"You came to town, wagging your ass around like you

was somebody." Ivan grinned at her evilly. "Those New York bastards you represent are pussycats compared to me." He thwacked himself on the chest.

Anxiously, Jade moistened her lips. "What are the terms of the payout?"

Neal glanced at his father and laughed. "Do you think we were born yesterday, Jade? We left you no room to maneuver. We closed the deal with a cashier's check for the full amount. Otis nearly peed in his overalls when I handed him that check."

Jade managed to keep her features composed. She carefully refolded the deed and replaced it in the envelope, then laid it on the corner of her desk.

"Congratulations."

As though the meeting were concluded, she picked up her pen and resumed what she had been doing when Neal came in.

"Well?"

Jade looked up at Neal, an inquiring smile on her lips. "Well?"

"Don't you have anything to say?"

"About what?"

"God *damn!*" Ivan roared. "About the land. What do you think?"

"You want it. We've got it," Neal said, spreading his hands wide. "You can forget sucking up to Otis. He's out of the picture. I have what that highfalutin company of yours is after. From now on, you're dealing with me."

She laid down her pen and folded her hands beneath her chin. "You're mistaken. My company isn't interested in acquiring the property that formerly belonged to the Parkers and now belongs to you." She smiled sweetly.

Ivan laughed. "Aw, hell, she's playing coy to lower the price."

"Not at all, Mr. Patchett. I'm most sincere. I have absolutely no interest in buying that land. Now, if you'll please excuse me—"

Neal shot to his feet. "You lying bitch! I know damn good and well you want that property. Ever since you got to town, you've been crawling all over it, measuring it, having it appraised. Don't try and deny it. I've had you followed."

"Yes, I thought you would," she calmly stated. "In fact, I counted on it."

Ivan's lungs wheezed when he struggled to pull in oxygen. "God damn you." He glared at her malevolently. His evil soul had an odor. He smelled foul. "You cheating little cunt. You conned—"

"Shut up!" Neal barked to his father. He covered the distance to Jade's desk in two long strides, reached across it and manacled her biceps, hauling her to her feet. He spoke between clenched teeth. "You mean you never wanted the Parker place?"

"That's right. I only wanted *you* to want it."

"She played us like a couple of fools," Ivan snarled. "We spent one million dollars on a pile of pig shit."

She swung her head toward the older man and looked at him through smoldering blue eyes. "Small compensation for Gary's life, wouldn't you say?"

Neal pulled her from behind the desk and shook her hard. "You've ruined us."

"Just like you ruined Gary and me."

He backhanded her across the mouth. She cried out. The door was flung open so suddenly that it created a vacuum inside the building. Dillon's stance and fierce expression belonged to the god of thunder, but he was lethally soft-spoken. "You're going to regret that."

He charged across the room, grabbed Neal by the neck, and slung him into the wall. Ivan struck Dillon across the backs of his knees with his cane. He yelled in pained surprise, spun around, and snatched the cane from Ivan. At first Jade was afraid he would use it to crack the old man's skull. Instead, he stepped on one end of it and lifted the other, snapping it in two like a twig.

He tossed aside the two pieces and responded to Jade's frantic shout as Neal lunged at him from behind. Neal had always relied on others to do his fighting for him. Dillon, on the other hand, had learned to street-fight in order to survive. He moved with precision and swiftness, catching Neal in the gut with his elbow, then slugging him in the face, crunching cartilage, splitting skin.

Neal reeled backward, crashed into the wall, then slid to the floor. Dillon stood over him, breathing heavily. "Get the hell out of here and take that miserable old son of a bitch with you. Or stay, and give me the honor and privilege of stamping the hell out of you."

Neal tried to lick the blood off his chin, but it trickled from his swelling nose and dripped onto his shirt. Mustering what dignity he could, he struggled to stand up. After the blows Dillon had delivered, it wasn't easy for him to lift and carry Ivan.

Jade followed them out the door, knowing that the moment she had waited fifteen years for had finally arrived. The Patchetts were defeated and humiliated.

Neal strapped Ivan into the passenger seat of his El Dorado. Jade was standing in front of the polished chrome grille when he came around the hood. She slapped the deed into his palm. "I hope you never have another day's peace for as long as you live."

He crumpled the deed in his fist. "You're going to be sorry for this. Damned sorry."

Painfully, he got behind the wheel. Jade shaded her eyes against the sun and watched them drive away. She didn't even cough on the cloud of dust the squealing tires left in their wake.

Her knees folded and she plopped down where she was. At her sides, she dug her hands into the earth. "I did it. I did it."

Dillon squatted beside her. "Are you hurt?"

"No. I feel wonderful." She smiled at him. His face was streaked with dirt and sweat. There was a red band across his forehead where his hard hat had been. His sunglasses had left crescent impressions on his cheeks beneath his eyes, which radiated concern. "Thank you, Dillon."

"I saw his car and got here as soon as I could." He gently touched her lip. It was puffy but wasn't bleeding. "Not quite soon enough."

"It doesn't even hurt." She looked after the speeding car, the dissipating cloud of dust. "I did it," she whispered again.

"What?"

She told him about the coup she had pulled off. "I was so afraid they wouldn't fall for it, that they would guess my interest in the Parkers' farm was a con."

"What if they hadn't taken the bait?"

"Mitch left me a legacy. I didn't even know about it until his will was read. If this had backfired, I would have used it to buy the Parkers' land myself."

He shook his head with chagrin. "You dragged me out there, had me marking off yardage like a damn fool, and it was all for show?"

"I'll admit that I used you. I apologize."

"After what the Patchetts did to you," he said, giving a slight shake of his head, "you don't have to explain your motives or your methods."

"This was my vendetta. I didn't want to involve you or anyone else more than I had to." Again she gazed into the distance. The day was warm and muggy, although summer was waning. Change was imminent.

"Gary hated being poor," she said wistfully. "He hated it for himself, and he hated it for his family. He used to say that one day he was going to come back to Palmetto and dump a million dollars in his daddy's lap." She turned back to Dillon, her expression radiant. Reaching out, she gripped his bare biceps. "Dillon, I did it for him."

Spanning her waist with his hands, he stood up, lifting her with him. He broke a rare, bona fide grin beneath his mustache. "I think this calls for a celebration."

When the housekeeper peered into the den and asked Mr. Ivan and Mr. Neal when they would be wanting their supper, Neal threw a crystal decanter at her. She ducked out of its way in the nick of time and had the common sense not to bother them again.

The room reeked of the brandy dripping off the wainscoting onto the rug, but both were too besotted with all they had drunk to notice the fumes.

"The bitch," Neal muttered as he splashed more liquor into his glass. "The hell of it is, she wasn't even that good. She was a lousy virgin." He made a broad gesture, waving his glass of liquor and sloshing it over his hand. "That's what all this is for, you know. For that time Hutch and Lamar and me had our fun with her. How the hell did we know that she'd take it so hard or that her boyfriend would hang hisself over it?"

"Sit down and shut up," Ivan growled from his wheelchair. His head was sitting low on his shoulders, as though his neck were being swallowed by his body. His eyes were pinpoints of malicious light beneath his glowering brows. "You're drunk."

"I've got every reason to be." Neal weaved his way across the room to his father's chair and loomed over him. "In case you've forgotten, Daddy, we no longer have a pot to piss in. Among other things, we used next year's estimated profit for collateral on that loan."

"And who's brilliant idea was that?"

"It was supposed to work," Neal said defensively.

"Well, it didn't!"

The pattern had been set when he was a boy. Neal was cocksure and arrogant until he got into trouble, then he turned to his father to get him out. "Whad're we gonna use for money, Daddy?" he whined. "How're we gonna pay our employees? The plant'll have to shut down."

Ivan looked at Neal with patent disgust. "Why in hell are you worrying about that? Soon we won't have any employees, because they'll all be working over at Tex-Tile for Jade Sperry. Patchett Soybean Factory will be history."

Neal's battered face twitched with emotional upset. "Don't say that, Daddy."

"That's what she planned on doing all along. She wanted to shut us down, ruin us." Ivan stared at a target on the far wall as though the force of his stare could obliterate it. "And that's exactly what she's done."

Neal fell onto the sofa and dug his fingertips into the sockets of his dark eyes. "I don't know how to be poor. I don't want to be poor."

"Stop that goddamn whining!"

"Well, what do you care what happens, old man? I'm the one who'll be left alive to shovel through this shit. The doctor says your heart and lungs aren't worth crap. You're gonna die soon anyway."

"I don't need a doctor to tell me that." He didn't look near death. His eyes shone with a fiendish light. "But one thing is for damn certain. I ain't going to die without settling this score once and for all. That Sperry girl ain't going to get away with this. Not completely. Let her have her small victory—in exchange for something else much more important."

Sobering instantly, Neal set his drink on the coffee table. "Her son."

"That's right, boy. The Patchetts might be wounded, but we're not dead. First thing tomorrow, you're going to make a phone call and extend an invitation . . . to Myrajane Griffith."

Dillon was manning the patio grill. "Good-looking fish," he remarked to Graham, who was assisting.

"Thanks," he replied, smiling proudly. "Every time I go to that spot in the channel, I catch at least one."

"How's school?"

He had been enrolled in Palmetto High School for two weeks, and so far everything was going well. He told Dillon so. "I hope I make the soccer team. Tryouts are next week."

"No sweat." Dillon flipped over a fish filet. "Do you miss New York?"

"Not really. I kinda like living in a small town. Do you?"

Before answering, Dillon glanced toward the house. Graham followed his gaze. They could see his mom through the kitchen window. "Yeah, I like it here," Dillon said, bringing his attention back to the grill.

"What'll you do when the plant is finished? Will you stay here or go somewhere else?" Since the subject had come up, Graham welcomed the opportunity to ask Dillon about his future. It would be great if Dillon's future somehow coincided with his.

"The plant is a long way from being finished," Dillon said. "Years. After that, I'm not sure what I'll do. I don't plan that far ahead."

"How come?"

"I found out that it didn't do any good."

Jade poked her head through the back door. "Everything else is ready. We're waiting on you menfolks."

"Not anymore. The fish is ready," Dillon called back. "Graham, turn off the gas, please."

"Sure." His mother's interruption had come at an inopportune time. Dillon's last statement puzzled him because it contradicted his mother's belief that one should set specific goals and work toward them no matter what setbacks arose. He would also have liked some guarantee that Dillon would be around for a long time yet.

"Be sure the knob is shut all the way off," Dillon cautioned him.

"I will."

Dillon dished up the fish filets and carried the platter through the back door, which Jade was holding open for him. Graham watched as she bent down and sniffed the grilled fish, licking her lips in anticipation. Dillon said something that made her laugh.

Suddenly feeling buoyant again, Graham carefully turned off the gas and followed them indoors. He always liked having Dillon to dinner, but tonight there was a party atmosphere in the house. He wasn't sure what they were celebrating and didn't care. All that mattered was that his mom seemed more relaxed than she had been since leaving New York. Maybe she was taking to heart what he had told her a few weeks ago about being too uptight. Tonight she was plumb bouncy.

She had changed clothes when she came in from work and now had on an outfit made of some soft, floaty, white material. Friends told him all the time that his mom was hot-looking, and it was true. As they sat down to dinner, she looked exceptionally pretty.

He was asked to say grace and mumbled a hasty prayer of thanksgiving. As they were filling their plates, he asked, "Can we play Pictionary after dinner? Dillon and me'll be partners again like before."

"Not on your life!" Jade exclaimed. She clutched her knife and hammered the handle on the table. "You two cheated last time."

"I wouldn't go so far as to call their hand signals cheating," Cathy said diplomatically.

"It was cheating," Jade said adamantly.

"I take exception to that. Take it back."

Dillon reached across the corner of the table and slid his hand beneath her hair, squeezing her neck. Reflexively, she raised her shoulder and tilted her head to one side, trapping his hand between her cheek and shoulder.

There was an instantaneous change in her expression, Graham noticed. She couldn't have looked more stunned if Dillon had gotten up on the table and started dancing naked. Her head popped up, and she turned to him.

"I take it back."

Her voice sounded funny, too, like she had just swallowed a shot of straight whiskey. Her cheeks turned red, and she was breathing like she'd been doing calisthenics. They continued looking at each other long after Dillon slowly removed his hand from her neck. When they finally broke their stare, Dillon began buttering his corn on the cob. His mom seemed at a loss. She stared down at her plate and fiddled with her silverware like she'd never seen any before and wasn't sure how to handle it.

Graham smiled to himself. If his mom and Dillon didn't want to have sex, then he didn't know shit from Shinola.

"I still can't get over it. Every time I remember it, I want to pinch myself to make sure it really happened." Jade turned to Dillon, who was seated with her in the porch swing she had recently installed. "It did, didn't it? This isn't a dream?"

"Undoubtedly a dream for the Parkers. More like a nightmare for the Patchetts. You've got them running scared."

"Oh, I'm real scary, all right," she said, laughing.

"You can be. You scared me spitless that night you got me out of jail."

"Me? You were the one with the heavy beard and dark scowl."

"But you had control of the situation. I hadn't had a

grasp on my life since Debra died. Your cool competence intimidated me. Why do you think I behaved like a macho pig?"

"I thought it was an outgrowth of your charming personality."

Smiling wryly, he shook his head. "Stark fear."

Jade gazed out across her front yard. Through the dense branches of the trees, moonlight cast patterned shadows on the grass. Crickets chirped. The breeze smelled faintly of seawater.

"I wish my mother knew about what I did today." There was no bitterness in her voice, only wishful thinking.

"I've never heard you mention your parents. What happened to them?"

"You'll wish you never asked." Jade spent the next half-hour telling him about her awkward relationship with her mother. She told him about her father's suicide and how differently it had impacted the two women. He was dismayed to hear that Velta had held Jade partially responsible for the rape.

"You're wrong," he told her when she concluded with Velta's desertion. "I'm glad I know. I'm also glad I never had an opportunity to meet your mother."

"All my life, I wanted her to love me. She never did. She was unhappy when I came along, and it never got any better."

"Truth be known, she was probably jealous of you, Jade. And even though she wouldn't admit it, you probably had her grudging respect."

"Maybe you settle for respect when you're thirty. But not when you're three, or thirteen. Or even eighteen. I never could be what she wanted me to be."

"What was that?"

"A simpering Southern belle who would make a good marriage—and in Palmetto that meant nabbing Neal Patchett."

Dillon swore.

"My goals went so far beyond hers, she couldn't even see them, much less understand them."

"Well, wherever she is, she's bound to know she was wrong, Jade. She probably regrets what she did."

"I wish I could see her and talk to her. I don't want an apology. I'd just like for her to see how Graham and I fared. I'd like to know if she finally found something or someone who would make her happy."

"You sound as if you've forgiven her."

Jade pondered the word *forgive* and decided that it didn't apply. Her mother belonged in another lifetime. Velta no longer had the power or authority to hurt her. "I'd only like her to know that I have accomplished what I set out to do. Whether she's regretful or whether I've forgiven her is immaterial. That belongs in the past. After today, I want to look forward, not back."

Dillon left the swing and moved to the railing that enclosed the veranda. Without them noticing, it had grown late. Behind them the house was quiet. Cathy and Graham had already retired. Dillon seemed to be in no hurry to leave. He braced his hands on the railing and leaned forward from the waist.

"I've been thinking about the past a lot lately."

"About anything in particular?"

"Yeah. I've come to the same conclusion as you. It's time to let it go. Move forward."

He turned and braced his hips on the railing, facing her. "All my life I've been operating under the theory that if an individual is good enough, that if he works hard enough, that if he doesn't rock the cosmic boat, he'll be rewarded. Things will go right for him.

"The flip side of this philosophy is that if he screws up, he pays dearly. Bad things happen to him. Lately, I've begun thinking this theory is wrong."

She felt his eyes touching her out of the silvery darkness. "You're talking about your wife and son."

"Yes."

"When an accident like that happens, Dillon, isn't it human nature for us to search for an explanation? And isn't it also customary that—because we have to blame something—we blame ourselves?"

"But I made a science of it. It started when my folks got killed. I remember worrying myself sick over what I had done to get God so pissed off at me. That was before child counselors knew to tell kids that when things go wrong, it isn't their fault."

He turned up one of his palms and examined the calluses at the base of his fingers. "If you start thinking that way when you're a kid, it carries over into adolescence and adulthood. I was constantly juggling to keep good deeds in balance with mistakes so I wouldn't get out of favor with fate. If I did something *wrong,* I waited for the hammer to fall."

He turned his head, giving her his profile. "When Debra and Charlie died, I figured I'd fucked up real bad." He laughed self-deprecatingly. "It's the height of conceit to believe that you control other people's destinies, isn't it?

"But for all these years I've taken the blame for their deaths. I figured it was retribution for something I had done or had failed to do."

Jade crossed the veranda to stand near him at the railing, but she didn't interrupt. He shook his head with chagrin. "The bottom line is that shit happens, just like the bumper sticker says. Shit happens. Tragedies befall good people. Fortune smiles on pond scum." His eyes connected with hers. "I can't tell you how good if feels to be out from under that burden of guilt."

"Debra and Charlie were victims of misfortune, Dillon. And so were you."

"Thanks for helping me to see that." He raised his hands to either side of her head, letting her adjust to the idea that he was about to touch her. Then the backs of his fingers swept dark tendrils of hair away from her cheeks. "You're beautiful, Jade."

She became very still and quiet on the inside. Because she wasn't experiencing the clamorous alarm she usually did when a man touched her, she didn't want to do anything—not even blink, swallow, or breathe—that would set off her clanging terror.

Instead of concentrating on herself and her reactions, she tried directing all her attention to Dillon. What did he see when he looked at her with those intense gray-green eyes? Did her hair feel silky against his fingertips? Was he subject to the same breathless anticipation as she?

Anticipation for what? she wondered.

It was a jarringly disruptive thought, so she impatiently shoved it aside. She would take this one heartbeat at a time, and, for right now, she didn't want anything disturbed.

He extended his right arm at shoulder level, bracing himself against the support column behind her. Trapped between it and him, she felt a flurry of panic. When he spoke her name, however, his deep, calm voice was reassuring.

"Jade?"

"Hmm?"

"I'm about to do something you've told me repeatedly not to do."

Her stomach rose and fell weightlessly. She felt his breath, warm and dewy, on her face. She kept her eyes open for as long as she could, before they closed involuntarily. His mustache tickled her upper lip. He flicked the center of her lips with the very tip of his tongue, so lightly that, at first, she thought she had imagined it.

"I'm going to taste you now, Jade."

Tilting his head, he aligned his lips with hers. Shockingly, her lips parted receptively. He made a low, wanting sound and pressed his tongue into her mouth. He applied a safe and nonaggressive amount of pressure to her lips and a delicious suction to her mouth. His tongue moved inside it, but it didn't feel invasive.

The dark heat of the night descended over her along with the deep mystery of his kiss. Feeling lightheaded, she reflexively reached for support. Her hand curled around his arm, which was still supporting him against the column. He sighed her name and relaxed his elbow, which brought him close enough for their clothes to touch.

Tentatively, he placed his other hand at her waist. His lips nuzzled and nibbled hers. He brushed them with his mustache. He gently drew her lower lip between his teeth. He ducked his head and kissed her neck.

She gave a little gasp. "I'm afraid."

"Of me?"

"Of this."

"Don't be."

Jade closed her eyes and tried not to think.

Dillon waited. "Is it all right?" He raised his head and looked into her face. "Jade?"

She flatted her hand on her quickening chest. "I can't breathe."

One corner of his mustache tilted up. "Is that a good sign or a bad one?"

"I'm not sure."

"I'll take it as a good one."

"Okay."

"Relax." He eased her back until she came up against the column. "Breathe deep."

Like a child, she did as she was told. Eyes closed, she drew in calming drafts of air. When she opened her eyes, Dillon's face was bending close to hers, and she became breathless all over again. "I feel so foolish."

"You shouldn't. You've got a woman's worst nightmare to overcome."

"I want to overcome it." The words tumbled out. "I really want to, Dillon."

"Good. That's good," he said thickly. "We'll work on it. What I have in mind is a long weekend spent alone together. No strings. No expectations. Just isolation from everything familiar so we can relax. What do you say?"

"No."

He dropped his hands and stepped away from her. His expression was a mix of anger and frustration. "Then I can't go on kissing you, Jade. Because sooner or later I'm going to lose my head. My cock will start doing my thinking for me, and I'll end up making you afraid of me. I won't have that."

He turned away from her and jogged down the steps. She caught up with him before he reached his pickup. "Dillon, you don't understand."

"I do. I swear I do. It's just…" He raked his hand through his hair. "Christ, I can't take anymore."

She grabbed his sleeve. "No. I mean, you don't understand what I was trying to tell you. I don't want to wait for a long weekend. I want to try tonight." Nervously wetting her lips, she looked up at him imploringly. "Now, Dillon."

Chapter 28

———◆———

W here are we going?" Jade asked. "I mean, I know where we're going, but why?"

"Wait and see."

The headlights illuminated the tunnel of trees that eventually came to a dead end at the plantation house Jade had recently purchased for GSS. Except for the deepest shadows beneath heavy foliage, the yard was bathed with moonlight. The house looked white and stately, faring better than it did in harsh daylight.

Dillon smiled secretively as he took a flashlight out of the glove box. "Come on. It's all right. The owner is a personal friend of mine."

Together they made their way across the deep yard and up the front steps. The ancient planks creaked beneath his weight. "I need to fix those before somebody gets hurt," he remarked as he fished a key out of his jeans pocket.

"Where did you get a key?"

"If you don't stop asking questions, you'll spoil the surprise."

"What surprise?"

"That's another question."

The musty smell peculiar to vacant houses greeted them as he pushed open the front door and ushered Jade into the wide vestibule. He switched on the flashlight and swept it across the Italian tile floor.

"This is quite a showplace."

Jade hugged her elbows. "I like it much better in the daytime. This is spooky."

She was confused and vaguely disappointed. When they had left her house, she had assumed he would take her directly to his trailer. Staying at her house had been out of the question. Even if they could sneak him past Cathy and Graham, she would feel awkward, knowing that they were in nearby rooms. She didn't need anything contributing to her inhibitions tonight.

Given time to think about this, she might lose her nerve. This rambling old house, which had stood empty for years, was hardly putting her at ease. She was also a trifle miffed over the delay. Was his ardor that easily cooled?

"Take my hand and watch your step."

She gave him her hand. He started upstairs, surprising her by avoiding the steps that were damaged and could have been hazardous. "You've been here before?"

"Uh-huh."

"Without me?"

"Uh-huh."

"When?"

"Careful, there's an exposed rusty nail."

When they reached the landing, Dillon turned right, sweeping the hallway with the flashlight. The doors to all the rooms stood open, except one at the end of the hall. It was to that door that Dillon led her. He looked at her expectantly before turning the porcelain knob and swinging the door open.

Jade crossed the threshold and stepped into the room. Unlike the rest of the house, this room had been cleaned. There were no cobwebs in the corners of the tall ceiling or clinging to the crystal teardrops of the overhead chandelier. The finish on the hardwood floor was dull, but it had been swept free of dust and debris.

There was one piece of furniture in the room—a brass bed. Jade had admired it during her first visit to the house, although it had appeared hopelessly tarnished. Now, it shone in the beam of Dillon's flashlight. In the Victorian style, the tall headboard was elaborate with swirls and curls. Pillows in fresh white linens were piled against it. There were fresh sheets and a comforter covering the mattress. Mosquito netting had been suspended from the ceiling to drape the bed.

Dumbfounded, Jade stood gazing at it all while Dillon moved to the marble fireplace and lit the candles that had been arranged on the hearth. Then he went around the room lighting dozens of other candles, until the pale moiré walls shimmered in the soft light and the brass bed beneath the gauze gleamed incandescently. When the last candle had been lit, he blew out the match and tossed it into the fireplace, then turned to face Jade. He looked sheepish and apprehensive.

"Well, what do you think?"

She raised her hands at her sides and opened her mouth to speak, but no words came out.

"I don't have a lot to do most nights," he said. "Ever

since you swung the deal on this house, I've been coming here after hours, doing odd jobs."

He directed an uneasy glance toward the bed. "It might seem presumptuous, I know. But I knew how much you liked this place. So I thought that if you ever…that if we…Hell." He ran his hand around the back of his neck and shoved the other one into the waistband of his jeans.

"Look, I couldn't take you to that damned trailer, okay? That's about the least romantic setting imaginable and… and I thought you needed, deserved, to be romanced." He muttered a string of curses. "I sound like a jerk, right? Well, I feel like a goddamn fool. The most romantic thing I've done for any woman, since Debra died, is ask her her name first." He blew out a breath of pure disgust. "This probably wasn't a good idea after all. You can back out if you want to."

Mutely Jade shook her head.

"I won't be mad, I swear," he said. "Say you want to call it quits, and we'll call it quits."

She approached him. "I'm beginning to think you're the one who's scared, Dillon."

"I am. I'm scared you might back out." Gruffly he added, "I don't want you to."

"I'll probably be a miserable flop."

Candlelight was reflected in his intense stare. "That's not possible."

Self-consciously, she averted her gaze to the bed. "The room is lovely. Really. It was a thoughtful—and romantic—gesture."

"Thanks."

She brought her head back around and smiled shyly. "I'm glad it's going to be with you, Dillon."

He reached for her hand and clasped it. His thumb followed the bumpy ridge of her knuckles. "So am I. But why *is* it me?"

Her lashes swept down to obscure her eyes. "I'm still not sure I can go through with it, but...you're the first man that ever made me wish I could. For the first time, I think it's worth taking the risk."

Raising her hand to his lips, he kissed the back of it. "At any point along the way, all you have to say is stop, and I'll stop. I'll probably curse. I might even cry," he said with a half-smile. "But I'll stop."

She didn't want him to stop what he was doing with her hand. He held it against his lips as he spoke, his breath leaving moist patches on her skin. He turned it slightly and, as he opened her fingers, sank his teeth into the plump base of her thumb.

Closing his eyes, he kissed the center of her palm, burying his mouth in the heart of it. His lips were warm and earnest, his tongue playful and erotic. He guided her index finger up to his mustache. He explored it from one curving end to the other with her fingertip, riding the rim of his upper lip.

Lightly, he scraped his teeth against her index finger. It tickled—on her finger and in her lower belly. He took turns with each of her fingers, nibbling the flesh, stroking the skin with his tongue.

Jade derived almost as much pleasure watching him as she did from feeling what he was doing. Candlelight picked up the lighter strands of his hair. Dark, stubby eyelashes lay against his cheekbones, which were faintly traced with squint lines. His mouth, with his fuller lower lip beneath the wide mustache, looked unmitigatedly sexy.

Looking at it made her tummy feel like a cat, stretching with animalistic pleasure after a long sleep.

He kissed the inside of her wrist, then worked his way up to the bend of her elbow. She felt the damp sweep of his tongue and the slick surface of his teeth as he drew her skin against them. The side of his head bumped against her breast, and Jade feared the dreaded panic had returned. But slowly, from the center of her breast, her body told her this was good and right.

"They're supposed to get hard."

She didn't realize she had breathed the words aloud until Dillon's head came up. "What?"

"Nothing."

"What did you say?"

"I said...said that they're supposed to get hard."

"What are?"

"My nipples."

He lowered his eyes to them. "Are they?"

She nodded. "When you rubbed your head against me."

"Did it feel good?"

"Yes."

"Have I done anything so far that you didn't like?"

"Yes."

"What?"

"You stopped to chat."

He chuckled softly. "See? I'm slipping back into my old ways. I'm expecting something to go wrong when I want like hell for everything to go right."

As though this were a slow routine that they enacted every night, he raised her arms and laid them on his shoulders. Clasping her loosely around the waist, he drew her closer, until their bodies made contact. As he adjusted them together, Jade couldn't conceal her astonishment.

"Your nipples aren't all that get hard, Jade," he reminded her in a rough whisper. Pressing his forehead against hers, he continued in the same, urgent tone. "It's only flesh. It's me, and you're not afraid of me, are you?"

He waited for her to answer. She finally shook her head, rolling her forehead from side to side against his.

"Please don't be afraid of me."

"I'm not."

"Then kiss me." He angled his head back and looked down at her. "Kiss me, Jade."

"I have."

"No, I've kissed you. There's a difference."

She wanted to prove to him that she wouldn't chicken out. More important, she needed to prove it to herself. She slid her fingers up through his hair, drawing his head down as she simultaneously went up on tiptoe. She pressed her mouth against his.

His response was lukewarm at best, and that piqued her. "It would help if you kissed back."

"You're not kissing me. We're touching lips. That doesn't count."

Her fear of intimacy warred with her determination to defeat it. On tiptoes again, she tested the line between his firm lips with the tip of her tongue. It gave way, and suddenly she was skimming the inner lining of his mouth with her tongue, rubbing against his, tasting Dillon. She drew his head down farther. His mouth closed upon hers.

Something wonderfully sexy happened. They both felt it. Making a hungry sound, he crossed his arms at the small of her back, bending her against his middle.

Because Jade still felt that she was in control, she allowed it. In fact, she welcomed the solid heat of his body.

For the first time in fifteen years, she let her senses run wildly ungoverned. She relished the feel and taste of his mouth. The texture of his hair and skin were new and exciting pleasures to her fingertips. Her ears enjoyed the yearning sounds that issued from his throat with a sexy vibration. His strength didn't frighten her. It felt good where her softness cushioned and complemented it. Explosive sensations erupted at every point where they touched.

The kisses continued. As her desire mounted, she thrust her tongue deeper into his mouth. He responded in kind until each kiss was an act of love, a carnal exchange.

Finally, out of breath, Jade tore her mouth free and leaned against him weakly. "Dillon, can we please sit down?"

"Let's lie down."

She pushed away from him.

His eyes were lambent, intent, but his voice was reassuringly low. "Okay?"

The thought of lying down with him made her heart strike loud and hard against her ribs. Apprehensively, she glanced toward the bed.

He touched her cheek with the back of his fingers and drew her head back around. "Side by side, Jade. I won't lie on top of you."

She moistened her lips. They tasted like Dillon— wonderfully like Dillon. "All right. Side by side." Nodding in agreement, he stepped away from her and began unbuttoning his shirt. "I'm not ready to take off my clothes yet," she said quickly.

"That's fine."

Apparently her choice didn't alter his. He peeled off his shirt and dropped it to the floor. He wasn't wearing a belt. The waistband of his old jeans was so bleached out, the threads were almost completely white. It curled outward, away from his body, creating a tantalizing gap between it and his flat, hair-spattered abdomen. Parting the mosquito netting, he dropped to the side of the bed and tugged off his boots one at a time, then removed his socks.

He stretched out on his back, his tanned skin looking dark against the white sheets and mound of pillows. He extended his hand to her through the part in the netting. With trepidation, she lowered herself to his side. She slipped out of her sandals, but that was the only concession she made before closing the mosquito net.

Without his shirt, he seemed more threateningly male, and his raw masculinity began to overwhelm her. The dizzy euphoria that their kisses had created began to dissipate. The giddy sparks twinkled out one by one, like the embers from a dying firework. She felt the blackness of fear descending on her. Apparently Dillon sensed it, too.

He said softly, "I'm made out of the same tissue as you are, Jade. It's just shaped differently."

She glanced at his wide, hairy chest, the drastic dip that his abdomen took beneath his ribcage, the mystery of his navel, and the evident bulge in his crotch. "Quite."

With his index fingertip, he touched one corner of her anxious frown. "It's not that bad, is it?"

"It's not bad at all," she replied huskily. "I like the way you look. I have since I first saw you through the binoculars."

He frowned with puzzlement. "Binoculars?" From the tip of his thumb to the tip of his little finger, he could almost span the width of her back. He rubbed his hand up and down her spine.

"Remember in L.A., when I recruited you, I told you I had been watching your work for several days. I watched you through binoculars from my hotel room across the street. Several times I thought you sensed me watching you. You seemed to look right at me." Her blue eyes found his and held. "You took my breath."

His hand stopped moving on her back and burned like a brand through the thin cloth of her blouse.

"I didn't know how to respond to the way you made me feel," she confessed in a throaty voice.

"What about now?"

"I still don't know how to respond."

"Find out."

"How?"

"Touch me. The promise still holds," he added. "I won't touch back. Not if you don't want me to."

Warily she regarded his bare chest. "I would rather just kiss some more, if that's all right."

His smile was only a little strained. "I can stand that, I think." He reached to pull her down to his level, but she bristled. His hands relaxed on her arms. "If we're going to kiss, we've got to get our mouths on the same level. Lie down, Jade."

After several tense moments, she stiffly lay down. He cupped her face between his hands and drew it toward his. Their mouths came together in another deep, wet kiss. It was soft, sensual, sexy. Provocatively, his tongue moved in and out of her mouth. Before long, the kiss wasn't enough. She wanted more.

It was easier to touch him when she wasn't looking

him in the eye. Timidly, she laid her hand on his chest. He grunted with surprise and pleasure, but didn't release her mouth from his thorough kiss.

His skin was warm. His chest hair felt springy and alive against her palm. His nipple was raised and firm. She could feel it in the center of her hand. For several minutes she couldn't bring herself to move. But his kisses were potent, pulling from her all her anxiety and imbuing her with a restless curiosity and desire.

She moved her fingertips a fraction. More hard muscle. More hair. Her thumb glanced his nipple. He sucked in a quick breath and held it. Jade's hand froze where it was.

"I didn't mean to scare you," he rasped. "Don't stop."

"I didn't expect you to feel so—"

"So what, Jade?"

"So...nice."

Laughing softly, he buried his face in her hair and hugged her close. He rolled her on top of him. The shift in positions was so sudden and unexpected that Jade didn't have time to prepare for the shock of lying between his thighs. Frozen, she stared down into his face.

"If you don't like it, we can change it," he said solemnly.

After analyzing it, she realized that she was experiencing arousal, not fear. It had been years since she had necked with Gary Parker. Because it had been so long since she had felt like this, she almost hadn't recognized it for what it was.

Yet the adolescent petting they had done couldn't compare to this. Gary had been a boy. Dillon was unquestionably a man and she was no longer a girl. She had been a woman for years, but Dillon was the first man to make her aware of her womanliness. It was a heady, exhilarating awakening.

His erection nestled in the vee of her thighs. Warmth radiated from that point of contact to every other part of her body. Her femininity felt feverish. It pulsed with the sweet swelling of arousal. She was aching, and it was delicious.

"I like it, but I don't know what to do," she said on an anguished whisper.

"Do whatever you want to, Jade. This isn't a test. I'm not grading you. You can't pass or fail. Anything you do is right."

She lowered her lips to his for another kiss. He held her head steady between his hands while his mouth engaged hers in an orgy of kissing that left them gasping. She threw back her head to draw a breath; he seized the moment and nuzzled her throat. He raised one hand to the first button on her blouse.

"What . . . ? No."

Keeping his hand where it was, he said, "This is part of it, Jade."

"I know, but—"

"I want to see you. Let me touch you." Their eyes remained locked. Finally he said, "Okay. If you don't want me to."

"No, wait." She hesitated only a moment longer before walking her hands backward over his chest and stomach. Sitting back on her heels between his thighs, she drew Dillon into a sitting position and guided his hand toward her chest. "Don't hurt me."

"Never. I never would. I want to show you how good it can feel to be touched."

She nodded assent and released his hand. He undid the first button and moved to the second. His movements were unhurried. When he was finished with the buttons, he eased the hem of her blouse from the waistband of her skirt. Then, reaching inside the loose blouse, he bracketed her ribcage.

"Can I touch your breast, Jade?"

His hands felt cool against her skin. They were callused and rough, but his touch was gentle.

"Yes."

He cupped her left breast. "Tell me if I hurt you. Tell me when to stop."

"I'm not afraid you'll hurt me. I'm afraid I'll be unable to stand it. I'm afraid it'll make me remember, and the memory will ruin it."

"Don't think about anything but now. Concentrate on the sensations." He kneaded her gently through her brassiere. He lightly rubbed his knuckles across her nipple. It drew taut. Involuntarily, she made a small purring sound.

"I'd like to unfasten your bra."

She nodded.

Reaching behind her, he undid the hook, then slipped his hand into the loose cup and took her breast in his hand. She gasped his name.

"Do you want me to stop?"

Soundlessly, she shook her head.

His hand moved over her breast experimentally. It defined and reshaped. She bit her lip when his caress finally focused on her nipple. It was hard and distended even before he began fondling it. "Jesus, you're perfect, Jade." He continued to sweep his thumb across the rigid tip, barely touching it, eliciting chills and heat waves.

Jade, made weak by his caresses, bowed her head forward and rested it on his shoulder. She put her arms around him. Her nails sank into the supple flesh of his back.

"Jade, I want to put my mouth on you. Here." He pressed her nipple. "Can I do that?"

She gave her consent with a small movement of her head against his shoulder.

He parted her blouse and worked down the cups of her bra. She felt the night air from the open window on her exposed skin. It felt cool against her flushed breasts. His first kiss was soft, tender, affectionate. His lips flirted with her skin. His tongue teased. He brushed the raised tip of her breast with his mustache until she thought she would go mad from the unbearable pleasure.

Then his lips drew her in and surrounded her with the hot, sweet, sucking motions of his mouth. Each gentle tug plucked corresponding chords of response deep within her womb. They were glorious, mind-boggling, compelling. Reflexively, she came up to a kneeling position, making herself more accessible. Dillon cradled her breast between his hands as though he drank from a life-giving chalice. When he withdrew his mouth, he nuzzled her with his nose and rubbed his hard cheek against her, before taking her into his mouth again.

Her clothing kept getting in his way, and it aggravated her as much as it did him. "If I slide your blouse off your shoulders, will you pull your arms out of the sleeves?" he asked hoarsely. "Please, Jade."

She nodded.

He peeled her blouse from her shoulders and guided her arms out of the sleeves. Suddenly losing her nerve, she clasped her bra against her breasts. They gazed deeply into each other's eyes. She noticed that a vein in Dillon's temple was visibly ticking and that his jaw was clenched.

"Are we going to stop here?"

"I . . . No, I guess not." She removed her hands, and her bra fell forward onto his lap.

"Oh, God, thank you," he said on a deep exhalation. Using both hands, he touched her hair first, the individual features of her face, then her lips, which were swollen and rosy from his many kisses. His fingers combed down her throat, chest, and the slope of her breasts. He stared at her as though she were a miracle creation.

"Show me what you want me to do, Jade."

Taking his face between her palms, she guided it to her breast and watched as his lips sank into her flesh. Her nipples grew stiff against his caressing tongue. His mouth gave her unbearable pleasure.

With a groan, he fell back onto the pillows, brushed her bra off his lap, and groped for the buttons of his jeans. Jade's eyes widened with alarm.

"I'm not going to do anything you don't want me to," he explained quickly. Raising his left hand behind his head, he gripped a curving tube of the headboard. "I can't do anything with one hand, right? But I've got to make room, Jade."

His right hand worked frantically to undo the stubborn buttons. When they were unfastened, he spread his fly open, exposing only a wedge of white cotton briefs. Nevertheless, the shape and dimension of his erection was evident. Jade stared at it fearfully.

True to his word, he kept one hand on the headboard, but reached up with the other to cup her cheek. "I'm hard, yes. I'm supposed to be hard. But I'm not hard because I want to violate you, or hurt you, or prove to you that I'm physically superior.

"I'm hard because you've got gorgeous blue eyes that

make me wish I could swim around in them. I'm hard because you've got terrific legs that I've been unable to keep my eyes off since the night we drove around in that damn limousine. I'm hard because your mouth is delicious and your breasts are sweet and I know you must be wet by now." He grimaced from the eroticism of his own monologue. With an effort he moaned, "I don't want to defile you, Jade. I want to make love to you."

Forming an X over her breasts, she crossed her arms and rested her hands on her shoulders. "I know that, Dillon. In my heart, I do. But in my head—"

"Stop listening to your head," he said on a near shout, which he immediately ameliorated. "What do you want to do, Jade? Listen to your heart. What is it saying?"

"It says I want to make love to you, too, but I'm afraid I'll freeze when you try to penetrate me."

He smoothed his hand over her hair. "Then I won't even try. I knew this was going to take time. I counted on going slow. We'll take it a step at a time, and won't even attempt intercourse until you're ready."

"That's not fair to you."

"I'm not suffering." She gave his lap a dubious glance. He chuckled ruefully. "Well, there's suffering and there's suffering. I'm going to sit up again, okay?"

When she was once again kneeling between his thighs, he slowly lowered her arms from her breasts. "You're so pretty," he whispered.

One kiss melded into another, until it was impossible to distinguish when one ended and another began. His hands were in constant motion. They caressed her neck, her back, her waist, her breasts. Jade was no longer timid about touching him, either. His chest was uncharted territory that she explored with inquisitive hands and curious, but cautious, lips.

"Go ahead," he murmured when her lips hovered above his nipple.

She licked it daintily and discovered how exciting that was. She was thirty-three years old, and this was the first man's body she'd had access to. It was a wonderland of new experiences for her eyes, hands, and mouth.

Frequently Dillon's lips returned to her breasts. He kissed them repeatedly. With the nimble tip of his tongue, he could make her almost delirious. She folded her arms around his head and clasped him tightly to her chest, loving the feel of his thick hair against her smooth skin and the warm, wet motion of his mouth.

Her center grew achy. The lips of her sex pouted with an influx of blood and desire. To ease the feverish ache, she instinctively arched her pelvis and ground it against him.

He swore lavishly.

She didn't realize that he had slipped his hands beneath her skirt until she felt his palms sliding up the backs of her thighs. "Is it all right, Jade?"

She could only moan incoherently.

His hands moved over her derriere, palming her, pulling her closer. Then he lowered his head and nuzzled the valley of her thighs through her skirt.

"Ohmygod." She gasped at the burst of pleasure the unexpected caress brought her. Her thighs liquefied. She clutched his shoulders tightly. He splayed one hand over her derriere and moved the other to the front panel of her panties. His fingers slipped beneath the lace and into the dense, glossy curls above her sex.

Jade didn't even think to be afraid. Rather, she released a ragged sigh and bent her head over his.

"Open your thighs a little, Jade."

He didn't poke at her. He didn't crudely probe. His fingers were gently questing, persuasively stroking, applying no more pressure than the beat of a butterfly's wings. She inched her knees farther apart.

"That's it," he whispered encouragingly. "Christ, you're wet." He nudged her breast, then turned his mouth into it. "Silky wet."

His finger slipped between the swollen flesh but didn't penetrate her. Gently, slowly, he separated the full lips to expose that most sensitive spot to the revolving strokes of his finger. By instinct, Jade began to undulate against his hand.

The candlelit room began to shrink around her. Her universe was reduced to the center of the bed, the center of her body, where Dillon was giving her more pleasure than she had ever dreamed possible. His tongue was on her nipple, flicking it as delicately as the pad of his finger was moving over her slippery clitoris.

Her tummy quickened. Her breasts heaved on each rapid breath. Heat consumed her. Shamelessly, she rode his hand. When the pressure became unbearable, when her body had become a combustion chamber, she caught his muscled shoulder between her teeth to keep from crying out as the shattering release came.

He fell back among the pillows, bringing her with him, so that she was sprawled across his chest and belly, her legs lying between his. He strummed her spine, stroked her bottom, massaged her shoulders.

Her head remained buried in the hollow of his neck.

On her descent, she breathed deeply of the scent of his sweat mingling with her perfume and his cologne. Occasionally a tiny tremor shimmied through her.

Eventually, he placed his hands on either side of her head and lifted it so he could gaze into her face. "You were something," he whispered gruffly.

She ducked her head with chagrin. "I never knew it would be so...so..."

"My words exactly." They laughed softly. They kissed softly. Then they kissed carnally, their tongues entwining. Dillon unfastened the waistband of her skirt and pushed it down her thighs. His hands slid into her panties. His rough palms closed over her derriere, drawing her up.

"I want to feel you against me, Jade. Your wet, your heat—against me. I swear my cock will stay where it is, but, hell..."

She wanted to feel him, too. Moments before she had thought that all her desire had been exhausted in one act. Instead, his kisses were already renewing the longing ache that was at once new and yet familiar.

She kicked away her garments and stretched out over him. When Dillon caressed her again, his hands touched naked flesh, and he groaned. He continued to pull her up his body until his mouth could reach her breast.

It seemed natural for her legs to part. Her knees separated to straddle his waist. He wrapped his hands around the backs of her thighs and slid them up and down in a caress that made her weak.

"Dillon, please."

She couldn't specifically name what she was begging for. But she never would have anticipated what he gave her. Grasping her hips between his hands, he drew them up as he leaned forward off the pillows. He buried his face in the glossy hair between her thighs. To keep from pitching forward, Jade gripped the rails of the headboard behind his head.

He kissed the springy, dark curls.

"Dillon—"

He slipped lower and kissed her again, his mouth open and loving. She almost swooned when she felt his tongue—separating, searching, finding, tickling, stroking—while his hands massaged the backs of her thighs just below her buttocks.

The roaring in her ears returned. Her heart rate accelerated. A rosy blush spread upward from her pubis to her taut nipples.

It was about to happen again. She wanted it. And yet...

"No." She tried to draw away from him. "Dillon, no. Stop."

Having heard the key word, he released her, but looked befuddled and anxious. "For God's sake, why?"

"I want you inside me."

She peeled back his briefs and lowered herself over the tip of his penis, which was already moist from its glistening emission.

"No, Jade, let me—"

"Let me!" she said emphatically. The first rhythmic contractions were already seizing her when she took the smooth head of his organ between the protective folds of her sex. Her body pulsed around it.

He moaned something profane and placed his hands on the tops of her thighs. He brushed his fingers through the damp cluster of curls and pressed the distended little kernel of flesh beneath their apex.

Jade called his name as her climax rocketed through her. She impaled herself on him, then collapsed on top of his chest while the spirals of sensation continued to curl through her. Dillon wrapped his arms around her slender body. He needed nothing more than penetration to make him come.

The walls of the candlelit bedroom echoed soft cries of gladness, whimpers of gratification, and, eventually, sighs of repletion.

Chapter 29

————•————

The mood in the hospital room was sepulchral.

The doctor standing at the foot of the bed no longer kept his pessimism concealed. Looking first at his patient, then at the patient's wife, he said, "I'm sorry. We've done all we can."

For several moments after he left, neither said anything. Finally, Hutch turned his head on the pillow. He reached for Donna Dee's hand. "Well, I guess that's that."

"No." Her small, pointed face screwed up as she struggled to hold back tears. "That new antirejection drug might work."

"You heard what he said, Donna Dee."

"He said it was experimental and that he's not very optimistic. I heard every word. That doesn't mean I believe it. I refuse to believe it."

"You always have had a knack for refusing to believe what you don't want to." Wearily, Hutch closed his eyes.

"What's that supposed to mean?" He lay there, saying nothing. She gave his hand a tug. "Hutch?"

He opened his eyes, though the effort obviously taxed his diminishing strength. His voice was faint. "You never wanted to believe what really happened with Jade."

"Jade?"

"We raped her, Donna Dee. Just like she said."

She tried to pull her hand away, but he gripped it with surprising tenacity for a dying man. Donna Dee was frantic to change the subject. "You've got more important things to worry about than something that happened fifteen years ago, Hutch."

"I've got an eternity in hell to worry about. I raped her. And helped prod Gary Parker into killing himself."

"Hutch, that doctor has depressed you. You're talking crazy. Now hush!"

"Stop lying to yourself, Donna Dee!" he wheezed. "I'm guilty as sin. We all are."

"Jade provoked you into it, Hutch. I know she did."

He released a longsuffering sigh. "You know better than that."

"Maybe she didn't do anything outright, but—"

"My daddy told me the day after it happened that I'd be real sorry before it was over with. He was right." Hutch turned his eyes up toward the ceiling. "I'm glad of one thing. I'm glad it's not Jade's boy's kidney that I'm rejecting."

"Why do you say that?" she asked resentfully.

"Because if he is my son—and I like to think he is—I wouldn't have wanted him to give up anything for me. Jade was right to tell you no when you asked her. None of us has a claim to her son. None of us is good enough."

Donna Dee felt a stab of envy and jealousy that only Jade's name could evoke. She clutched her husband's hand. "Why'd you do it, Hutch? Did Neal goad you into it? Was it just one of those crazy situations that got out of hand?"

"Yeah, Donna Dee," he mumbled dispassionately. "It was just one of those crazy situations that got out of hand."

She could forgive him for rape easier than she could forgive him for desiring Jade. "There was no other reason you ... you took her?"

Hutch hesitated, then softly replied, "No, there was no other reason."

But Donna Dee didn't believe the denial any more than she believed his forced smile.

A ray of sunlight fell across Dillon's face. Sunlight didn't filter into the windows of his bedroom in the trailer, so for a moment he wasn't sure where he was or why he was feeling so damn good.

He opened one eye, saw the gauzy mosquito netting, and suddenly remembered why he should be feeling like the prince of the world today. He had freed Jade of her demons.

Wearing only a complacent smile and a night's growth of stubble, he rolled to his other side, eager to pull her sweet body against his for another round of exorcism.

The other side of the bed was empty.

Alarmed, he threw off the sheet and flung back the netting. He called her name, but it echoed off the walls of the empty house. He stumbled to the window. There were no curtains or drapes, only a screen. He searched the yard, anxiety making his chest feel tight.

When he spotted her, he expelled a deep breath of relief, then leaned against the window casing to enjoy the view. She was dressed, but her feet were bare. The sunlight painted iridescent stripes on her tousled hair. Cupping his hands around his mouth, he called out to her.

She looked up toward the second-story window. "Good morning." Her shining smile rivaled the new sun. She had pinched up several gathers in her skirt to form a bowl with the fabric. She had filled it with peaches. "Peaches fresh off the tree for breakfast. I've already had one. They're delicious."

"Not as delicious as you," Dillon said to himself. The first stirring of arousal tweaked his loins. Turning back into the room, he located his jeans at the foot of the bed and hastily pulled them on. He didn't bother buttoning the fly before jogging down the hallway. He leaped over the stairs that needed repairs and burst through the front door at a run.

The yard was empty.

"Damn!"

Suddenly, it struck him where he would find her. He ran through the formal garden. Sure enough, on the other side of it, he found her sitting in the swing beneath the live oak.

He was out of breath by the time he reached her—more from excitement than exertion. He placed his hands on the ropes supporting the swing and leaned down to kiss her for the first time since daylight.

Her lips were moist with peach juice, and, though only their mouths were touching, it was a potent kiss. When he lifted his lips from hers, he looked down at her through eyes that were drowsy with lust. She had knotted her shirt tails at her waist, but, to his delight, hadn't bothered buttoning it. From his vantage point, he could see the enticing cleft between her breasts.

"I like your outfit, Ms. Sperry."

Contradicting the formal address, he slid his hand into her shirt and covered her sun-warmed breast. She always reported for work looking like a woman of the world, a female executive on her way up. Even in casual clothes, she emanated a professional air.

This barefoot, shiny-faced, disheveled Jade was a real turnon, although this morning it wasn't taking much to turn him on.

She leaned her head against his forearm and sighed pleasurably over his bold caress. "I couldn't find my underwear."

"It'll turn up. Right now, I like you the way you are."

Her cheeks turned the same color as the ripe peaches lying in her lap. He laughed, and it felt odd . . . and good. It was as though he had lost a hundred pounds overnight. He felt that light, that free. He was happy. And, he realized, he was madly in love.

The estate was an unworldly setting. The empty old house was private and romantic, their island of seclusion. The birds seemed to have slept late. Even industrious squirrels were taking a day off. The air was sultry and still. It was a hazy, lazy morning when everything that lived and breathed intimated sex. He wished he could stop the clock for about a hundred years and spend every minute of it making love to Jade.

"Get up and let me sit down."

"Then where will I sit?" she asked saucily.

"In my lap."

The idea must have appealed to her because she got up to let him have the swing, then sat down in his lap. "Peach? One of the last of the season."

He bit into the peach she held to his mouth. The sweet, fragrant juice oozed out of it, running over her hand, down his chin and dripping onto his bare chest.

"Good?" she asked.

"Mm-hmm." He curved his arm around her neck, tilted her head back, and kissed her with unapologetic carnality. When it ended, he sighed, "Very good." He guided her hand up to her own mouth. She took a bite of the peach. He forced her to take another one, then another, until her mouth was full and juice was streaming over her chin and down her throat.

Dillon watched it trickle onto her chest before lowering his head and licking it up. He untied the knot at her waist and parted her blouse, baring her breasts to the sunlight and his own seeking lips.

Forgetting about the peach in her hand, she folded her arms around his neck and leaned back, offering her throat and breasts to him. He kissed his way up to her lips. When their mouths fused, he growled with animal arousal.

He turned her to face him and guided her legs to rest on his hips. As they kissed, her body squirmed against his, making him crazy.

Against his mustache, she murmured, "Would you think I was forward if—"

"No, not at all."

Her hand disappeared beneath her skirt, which was bunched around her waist. When her fingertips brushed him, he moaned. When her hand cupped his testicles, he muttered a mix of prayers and curses. And when she lifted his cock out of his jeans, he kissed her hard. She guided it into her body, and took all of it, slowly sheathing every hard inch.

Dillon nudged the ground with his heel and the swing moved forward, driving him even higher into her. The pleasure was immense. Then the swing arced back and Jade was pressed down on him. He wrapped his arms around her and held her close.

"Don't let me hurt you," he whispered.

"It doesn't hurt. But I can feel more of you than last night."

"I'm in deeper."

"Yes. Yes."

The swing continued to rock. Each time it started to slow down or stop altogether, Dillon would give them a gentle push. He was ready to come before she was, but he held back. Dipping his head low, he whisked his tongue across her nipple, then rapidly fanned it until he felt her body begin to close around his like a velvet fist. She gave a series of choppy, breathy cries as her body milked from his a long climax.

They clung to each other, damp with sweat and sticky with sex and peach juice. After a slumberous time, he raised his head and gazed into her face. He brushed damp tendrils of hair off her dewy cheeks. "I woke up this morning," he began softly, "and before I even realized where I was, I wondered why I felt so good."

"I feel good, too, Dillon. I can never thank you for—"

He laid his finger against her lips. "The pleasure was all mine."

"Not *all* yours."

"It was some great sex, Jade. But it was more than that." He clasped his hands behind her head. "I liked having you asleep next to me."

"I liked that part, too," she said mistily. "Very much.

It's the first time I've ever slept with a man. I didn't know that it could feel so safe. No wonder people make such a big deal over it."

"No wonder." He grinned and pulled her against his chest.

She laid her head on his shoulder. "Dillon?"

"Hmm?"

"Last night, just as I was about to, you know, for the first time..." she said haltingly.

"Yes?"

"You said, 'No, Jade.' Why did you say no?"

"I was going to put on a condom first."

"Oh. I didn't even think about that."

"Well, you should have, but since you didn't, let me reassure you that there's no need for you to panic. The worst that could happen is that you could get pregnant."

She raised her head and looked at him. "I'd never strap you with a baby."

His eyes delved into hers. "I can't think of anything nicer."

On a catchy little breath, she asked, "Are you saying you love me?"

"That's what I'm saying."

"I love you, too, Dillon. I love you, too." She softly kissed his lips before returning her head to his shoulder.

The only sounds they could hear were those of their matched heartbeats and the squeak of old rope. They stayed in the swing long after it had coasted to a full stop.

Myrajane Griffith parked her gray Ford sedan in the semicircular driveway in front of Ivan Patchett's house. Neal's invitation to brunch had come like a bolt out of the blue. Myrajane had retired two years ago. Since then, she hadn't seen or heard from the Patchetts. She had often thought it tacky of them to present her with her gold pin, shake her hand, and then forget her entirely after working for them for thirty-five years.

Of course it was Lamar's fault that folks shunned her. Who wanted to be friends with the mother of a man who had died in disgrace in a condemned, heathen city? Not that she believed a word of what folks said about her son. Lamar had *not* been a pervert. He had *not* engaged in the unspeakable aberrations people said he had. He had died of pneumonia and a rare form of skin cancer.

To this day, she refused to believe his monstrous death-bed confessions. He had made admissions that weren't true because his mind had been distorted by painkilling drugs and the brainwashing of a medical staff on a witch hunt. Everyone in San Francisco was so terrified of AIDS that anybody who got sick was believed to have it.

Obviously the Patchetts didn't believe the lies any more than she did, or they never would have invited her into their home. As she gazed at the impressive facade of the house she had always envied, she pulled on a pair of white cotton gloves. Her hands were damp with perspiration caused by nervous excitement.

Whatever could Ivan want to see her about? Neal had hinted that it was important and urgent. It really didn't matter to her what was on Ivan's mind. She was flattered to be summoned.

Her floral voile dress was perfect for the morning appointment. It was several seasons old, but it was a quality garment. Her daddy had always said that it was better to own a single quality item than a dozen that were substandard. Whenever Myrajane went downtown, she was appalled by how women dressed nowadays. They didn't seem to care what they wore. You couldn't tell quality folk from trash because they all dressed badly.

Propriety and modesty were things of the past—just like the Cowan dynasty, just like the family estate. It had recently sold, she had heard. The rumor was that the bank was glad to unload it. When she heard about it, she had cried bitter tears.

Sadly, some things were irretrievable. She would never live in her family's house again, but, to her dying day, she was going to cling to the gracious traditions of the past, such as never wearing slacks in public and never appearing at a social gathering without gloves and a handkerchief. On her way up the veranda steps, she adjusted her wide-brimmed straw hat, which would be appropriate until five o'clock in the afternoon. It was never going to be said of the Cowans that they didn't know how to conduct themselves with dignity and decorum. As the last living one, Myrajane took it as her personal responsibility to uphold the reputation of her maiden name.

When Ivan's housekeeper answered the door, his guest handed her an engraved calling card. "I'm Myrajane Cowan Griffith. Mr. Patchett is expecting me."

When they arrived at her house, Jade asked Dillon to come in with her. "I'm a mess," he protested. "I haven't shaved, and the hairs on my chest are stuck together with peach juice."

"You're no messier than I am. Please. I'd like to cook your breakfast."

"I didn't even buy you dinner first."

"What do you mean 'first'?"

He laughed at the blue glare she shot him. "I'll come in for coffee—one quick cup."

With their arms looped around each other's waists, they ambled toward the front door. "How do you know Graham and Cathy aren't waiting inside for me with loaded shotguns?"

"They'll be happy about us," she said, smiling up at him.

"How do you know?"

"Because I'm happy." Jade went in ahead of Dillon and almost collided with Cathy, who was rushing out. "Good morning."

"Thank heaven you're home," the older woman said breathlessly. "I just woke up and found a note from Graham. He took off on his bike to meet Dillon and you at Dillon's trailer."

Jade ignored the inquisitive inflection at the end of Cathy's sentence. "He knows better than to leave the house without permission, even on a Saturday," she exclaimed indignantly. "I'll have to ground him for a week."

Dillon laid his hands on her shoulders and turned her around to face him. "Maybe he was worried about you. Did you think of that? It was irresponsible of us not to call. If Graham's on his way to the site, I'll catch up with him on my way out there."

"I thought you were staying for coffee."

"That was before."

"But—"

"Why don't I go on ahead and rendezvous with Graham. When you and Cathy are dressed, you can meet us at my trailer. I'll treat everybody to pecan pancakes at the Waffle Shack."

"That sounds wonderful." Jade couldn't keep from smiling. Nor could she remain angry at Graham. This morning, animosity just wasn't possible. "Cathy?"

"I'm all for it."

"Good," Dillon said. "See you in a little while." He placed his finger beneath Jade's chin and tilted her head back for a soft kiss. Dreamily Jade watched him cross the lawn and climb into his pickup. He waved as he drove away. When she turned around, Cathy was watching her shrewdly.

"I'm surprised," she said. "I didn't expect him to be someone like Dillon."

"'Him'?"

"The man who released you. I would have expected someone from the other end of the macho spectrum, someone not quite so physical."

"Dillon's very sensitive."

Affectionately, Cathy touched Jade's tangled hair. "He would have to be to overcome your fear."

"Since his wife and child died, he's been grappling with his own dragon. I've been as good for him as he's been for me. That's the best thing about it."

With a skeptical eye, Cathy took in her deshabille. "You're sure that's the *best* thing?"

Jade laughed out loud, a throaty, sexy laugh that would have been foreign to her yesterday. God, it was great finally to be a full-fledged member of the human race. No longer alienated by fear and repression, she was now in on all the grown-up jokes.

Cathy must have read the answers to her myriad questions in Jade's shining eyes. Her own glistened with tears. "You look positively radiant, Jade."

"I'm happier than I've ever been," she said without qualification.

They never made it to the Waffle Shack that morning. Jade and Cathy arrived at the construction site within forty minutes of Dillon's departure from their house. Loner circled the Cherokee, barking, glad to see them. As they were trying to calm him down, Dillon emerged from his trailer.

Jade's heart skipped a few beats at the first sight of her lover after their brief separation. *Lover.* The word was a strange addition to her vocabulary. She repeated it several times in her mind, trying to accustom herself to its sound and implications. Pride and possessiveness bloomed inside her chest. Joy bubbled from a wellspring of new-found love.

Then he said, "Graham's not here, Jade."

Her ebullience fizzled. "He's not here?"

"Oh, dear God," Cathy murmured. "This is my fault. I shouldn't have overslept."

"Boys wander off. I'm sure he's fine."

Jade could tell by the furrow between Dillon's brows that his words carried little conviction. "Where could he be?"

"I don't know. I took his normal route on my way out here and didn't see him anywhere along the way. I was expecting him to be here when I arrived. He wasn't. Loner's food bowl was empty, so I don't think Graham's been here at all. The first thing he does when he gets here is feed the dog whether he needs to be fed or not. I drove to the other side of the site, where they've been surveying, but there was no sign of him."

Jade hugged her elbows, although the sun was well up by now and the day was much too warm for her to have chills. "Maybe he went fishing," she said hopefully.

"Maybe. I was on my way to check his favorite spot on the channel when y'all drove in." He squeezed her upper arm reassuringly. "Stay put. I'll be back in five minutes." He drove away in the company pickup.

"Let's go into your office to wait," Cathy suggested.

Jade allowed herself to be led into the portable building, but after they got inside she couldn't sit still. She paced in front of the windows, glancing out every few seconds in the hope of seeing Dillon returning with Graham.

"Could his note to you have been forged? Do you think it was written under duress?"

"Of course not," Cathy said. "Graham slipped the note under my bedroom door and left an open box of PopTarts on the kitchen table. I think he was on his way out here to see Dillon and you, just as his note said."

"Then where is he?"

"He got distracted and stopped somewhere."

"He's not supposed to stop unless he has permission to."

"Children sometimes forget. Sometimes they flagrantly disobey."

"Not this time," Jade said stubbornly. "Besides, Graham isn't a child." A new thought struck her. "Do you think he was upset because I stayed out all night with Dillon?"

"I seriously doubt it. Graham fell in love with him long before you realized you had." Jade cast her a sharp glance. "What surprises you, Jade? That Graham loves the man, or that you love him? Or are you surprised that I knew what was happening between Dillon and you before either of you were aware of it yourselves?

"It was obvious from the day I met him how Dillon felt about you, and equally as obvious that you were falling in love with him. As perceptive as he is, don't you think Graham would have seen the signs, too? He's crazy about Dillon. I'm certain he's delighted that you finally got together."

Jade was distracted by a noise outside. "He's back." She ran out the door just as the telephone rang. "Cathy, get that, will you?"

Graham wasn't in the truck. "I didn't see him anywhere," Dillon told her. "I drove along the banks of the channel. There was no sign of him or his bike." Jade crammed her fist against her lips. He drew her into his arms. "Don't panic. He's somewhere, and we'll find him."

"Jade," Cathy called from the open doorway. "The telephone is for you."

"Take a message."

"It's Neal Patchett."

Chapter 30

———◆———

Dillon drove with only one consideration—speed. "Those sons of bitches. What did they do, snatch him off the side of the road?"

"I don't know. Neal didn't say." Jade's eyes were fixed on the road. "All he said was that Graham and Myrajane Griffith were at his house having a conversation he thought would interest me."

"Myrajane is . . . ?"

"Lamar Griffith's mother."

Dillon reached across the seat and tightly squeezed her hand. "They can't hurt you anymore, Jade."

"They've got my son."

"They wouldn't dare lay a finger on him."

"Maybe not physically. But they've got their ways, believe me. You don't know them like I do."

No sooner had Neal delivered his chilling message than she had dropped the office telephone. She quickly removed something from the small safe beneath her desk before running for the door.

"I'm going with you," Dillon had said. "Cathy, lock up the office, please. Take Jade's car home and wait for us there. We'll call when we can." Dillon intercepted Jade at her Cherokee and guided her toward his pickup.

"This is my problem, Dillon. My fight. I'll handle it."

"Not without me. So stop wasting time and get in."

Now, she was glad he had come along. His was a strong, reassuring presence. Besides, he drove more aggressively than she would have had the strength or presence of mind for.

They arrived at the Patchetts' estate in record time. Jade bolted from the pickup the instant it came to a stop. She raced up the steps and across the veranda. Dillon was right behind her as she barreled through the front door.

"Graham!"

Her shout echoed off the walls and tall ceilings.

"He's in here."

The scene in the formal front parlor looked as deceptively innocent as a stage setting. There was a steaming silver tea service on a low table, along with biscuits and jam, a fresh fruit compote, and a serving platter of paperthin slices of baked ham. No one was eating.

Myrajane Griffith was seated in a wingback chair, her floral dress clashing with the patterned upholstery. Her rouge had been applied with a heavy hand, making two vibrant coins of color on her wrinkled, pale face. A pair of white gloves lay in her lap. She was wearing a ridiculous hat... and a murderous glare aimed at Jade.

Ivan, sitting in his wheelchair, looked like a shapeless mass held together by ill-fitting clothes. His smile was sly and malicious. His sunken eyes looked like windows into hell.

Despite his swollen nose and bruised chin, Neal appeared as well groomed and unruffled as ever. He had on gray linen slacks and a pink oxford shirt. He was standing in front of the marble fireplace, one elbow negligently propped on the carved mantel. He was swirling the contents of a highball glass, which looked to be a Bloody Mary.

Jade took in all this at a glance, then focused on her son, who was seated alone in a chair. She rushed toward him. "Graham, are you all right?"

He sprang from the chair, circled it, and placed it between them. His hands alternately flexed and gripped the backrest, which had dogwood blossoms carved into the wood. "Get away from me. I hate you."

Jade drew up short. "Graham! What are you saying?"

"You let him die. I could have helped him, but you wouldn't let me, so he died."

"Who?"

"Hutch," Neal informed her. "He's no longer with us."

Jade was momentarily stunned. Donna Dee sprang to mind, and she felt a pang of sympathy for her. "Hutch is dead?"

"Donna Dee called us with the bad news late last night."

"You killed him!" Graham shouted.

"Don't speak to your mother in that tone of voice," Dillon said sharply.

"You, you, shut up," Graham sputtered. He was doing his best not to shed the unmanly tears standing in his eyes. "She's a whore, and now you know it, too. She probably screwed you all night."

"That's enough!" Dillon barked.

"Like a jerk, I was hoping you'd get married. This morning, I was coming to tell you that it was all right with me, but now you won't 'cause you know my mother's a slut!"

Jade said, "Graham, listen to me, I—"

"No. You're the worst person I know. You let a man who might've been my dad die. I could have donated a kidney to him, but you didn't even tell me."

"What would have been the point? He might not have been your father."

"That's what makes you a whore." He pointed to Ivan and Neal. "They told me my dad could have been three men. They told me that you did it with all of them. Two of them are dead now, and I never even got to know them on account of you. This old lady could be my grandma, only you don't even want me to know her, either."

"No, I didn't want you to know your father."

"Why?" he shouted.

"Because he did something evil."

"Evil?" he hiccuped. "I don't believe you."

"It's true."

"You're a liar. You never would tell me about my dad because you were ashamed. I'll never believe you again. Never."

Yesterday, she had thought her enemies were defeated, but they had sprung back with a vengeance. They were clever enough to have attacked her where she was most vulnerable—Graham.

She could see the fear, confusion, and anguish in his young face. His whole world had collapsed around him, and his image of her had been shattered by malicious lies. If she didn't get him back immediately, she could very well lose him forever.

Only the truth could get him back.

"What they told you is true, Graham. Any one of three men could be your father. Because the three of them raped me. I got you when I was raped by three men."

He drew a ragged breath through his parted lips.

"I never wanted you to know because I didn't want you to impose that stigma on yourself. I didn't want you to blame yourself for something that was none of your fault. It was *their* sin, Graham. Theirs. Not mine, and certainly not yours."

She took a step forward and appealed to him. "I wouldn't tell you now except I'm afraid that if I don't, I'll lose your love and trust permanently. You've got to believe me, Graham. These three men took away my virginity and my youth. They robbed me of my first, beautiful love, a boy named Gary Parker, who killed himself over what they did. Your grandmother deserted us because of what happened."

She stretched out her hand. "I can't let them take you, too, Graham. They've twisted the facts to make me look bad, but I wasn't the bad one. Neither are you. I love you. I know you love me. And because you love me, you've got to believe that what I'm telling you is the truth."

He glanced at the Patchetts suspiciously, then locked gazes with Jade again. "You were raped?"

"That's right. When I was eighteen. And the only good thing to come out of it was you."

He hesitated for only an instant before hastily knocking aside the chair and lunging toward her. She clasped him to her tightly, holding him as though she would never let him go.

"He stopped me on the road. He told me you'd be here, Mom. He said I was supposed to come with him."

"I know how persuasive he can be."

"I'm sorry I said those things about you. I didn't mean them."

"I know you didn't." Over his shoulder, she regarded Neal with repugnance. "We love each other, and nothing is ever going to change that. Ever."

Dillon placed an arm around the two of them. "Let's get the hell out of here." As one, they turned toward the arched opening.

"Not so fast," Neal said. "We're not finished here. We've got a lot to discuss with Jade that doesn't involve you, Burke."

Jade spoke up before Dillon had a chance. "I've got nothing to discuss with you, except a possible kidnapping charge."

"You can't kidnap your own child," Neal said.

"What does he mean, Mom?"

"I'll bet you'd like to meet your real daddy," Ivan said to Graham. "Wouldn't you like that? To get to know your daddy and your grandpa?"

"Stop it," Jade shouted. "Haven't you done enough damage for one day?"

Graham's eyes drew a bead on Neal. "You were the other one, weren't you? Did you rape my mother?"

"So she says," he replied smoothly. "But you'd just as well learn now how females lie, son."

"Don't call me that."

"It's not the way she says it was, Graham. Was it, Jade?" he asked, giving her a wink.

"You're despicable." Jade took Graham by the hand and turned to leave, but Myrajane stunned them all by coming to her feet and speaking for the first time.

Pointing a long, meatless finger at Graham, she said, "He's a Cowan! I see my daddy in him. That's Lamar's son, and I want him."

"Well, you can't have him." Jade divided her glance between Ivan and Neal. "Why did you bring her into this? Only to make things worse?"

Ivan said, "If he's Lamar's boy, Myrajane has every right to him, just like we do if he's Neal's."

As she moved across the room toward them, Myrajane's eyes glowed with fanatical fervor. "He's my flesh and blood. He's a Cowan. He's one of us." Looking at Jade, she hissed, "How dare you keep this child from me all these years? How dare you let me think all my kin were gone."

"She freaking nuts." Dillon nudged Jade's elbow. "Let's go."

"It won't do you any good to leave with the boy," Ivan said. "It won't do you any good to hide him, either. We plan on taking this thing to court if we have to."

"For what purpose?"

"Custody."

Jade looked at them incredulously. "No court in the country would even hear your case."

"But think of the stink it would raise," Ivan said with his nasty cackle. "You don't want that kind of scandal, do you? I don't think that Yankee Jew company you work for would like having the newspapers filled with stories about you and the three high-school classmates you gang-banged." Myrajane gasped at the crudity, but no one paid her any attention.

"Or was it four classmates, Daddy?" Neal asked tauntingly. "Don't forget Gary."

"You shut up about my mother!" Before Jade or Dillon could stop him, Graham charged toward Neal, fists poised for a fight. Dillon yanked him back.

"I get first crack at him," Dillon muttered.

Jade stepped in front of them. "Both of you, go outside."

Graham was struggling to get free of Dillon so he could reach Neal. Dillon looked ready to kill him himself. "And leave you alone with them? Like hell, Jade."

She laid her hand on his arm. "Please. Wait outside. I've got to do this alone."

"Mom, don't send me out," Graham protested.

"Graham, I must. Please."

Dillon deliberated while searching her face. "Please," she whispered urgently. At last he relented and pushed Graham toward the archway. Graham didn't like it, but Dillon didn't take any guff. Before they went out, Dillon turned and aimed a threatening finger at Neal. "If you lay a hand on her, I'll kill you. Nothing would give me greater pleasure."

When Jade heard the front door close behind them, she turned back to the room. This was the most important confrontation of her life. She prayed to God she had the courage to play it well.

Don't ever be afraid, Jade.

"This will never go to court," she said to Neal in a steady, confident voice. "You've got no claim on my son."

"He could be my son, too."

"You'll never know."

"DNA fingerprinting."

"Which I'll never submit Graham to. Any claim you make on him will be tantamount to a confession of rape."

"My son never raped anybody!" Myrajane shrieked.

Jade turned to her. "He did, Mrs. Griffith. When you came to Mitch Hearon's funeral, Lamar apologized to me for it." Looking back at Neal, she said, "So take your case to court if you want to. That's what I'll testify—that my pregnancy was the result of a gang rape instigated by you."

"Nobody in hell would believe that."

"Maybe not, but as your father said, it would certainly cause a stink."

"For you."

"And you. Do you remember a woman named Lola Garrison?"

"Who the hell is she?" Neal asked querulously.

"She remembers you quite well, Neal. She was scheduled to be a bridesmaid at your wedding, which never took place because of your accident. Just before you left the rehearsal dinner for your bachelor party, you had carnal knowledge of her in the restaurant powder room. Remember her now?"

"Vaguely. So what?"

"Ms. Garrison is a freelance journalist. Several weeks ago she spent a day interviewing me for an article in the Sunday supplement."

"I saw it," he said with affected boredom. "Again, so what?"

"She mentioned in passing that the only people she knew in Palmetto were named Patchett. She told me the circumstances under which you had met and called you a 'slimy, sorry son of a bitch' that she would love to get the goods on.

"It seems that after your intended broke the engagement, you spitefully flaunted having had her maid of honor, virtually right under her nose. Your confession ruined a friendship."

"Friendship my ass," he scoffed. "Lola, or whatever the hell her name is, went down on me. What kind of friend was she?"

"I wasn't referring to the friendship between the two girls, but between their fathers. The men were business partners. The rift proved to be a costly one for Ms. Garrison's father. He never recovered—either financially or emotionally. She holds you personally responsible for his decline. I'm sure she would love to hear my story about the night at the channel."

There was a moment of taut silence, finally broken by Ivan. "I'm tired of jacking around with you," he said. "If you want to have a mudslinging contest in the newspapers, fine. We'll have one. While this gal is writing about blow jobs in public bathrooms, we'll accuse you of fraud."

"Fraud?"

Neal picked up for his father. "You drove up the price of the Parker property with no intention of buying it."

"Prove it, Neal," she challenged. "Otis Parker will testify that I put down a ten-thousand-dollar deposit on the sale of the property. So how are you going to prove that I didn't intend to buy it?"

"I just gave him a million bucks," Ivan shouted. "Otis will testify that his balls are sweet peas if I ask him to."

"Except that the deposit was placed in an escrow account. There will be records. If you have in mind to tamper with them as you did with the medical evidence following the rape, don't bother. The account was in my New York bank."

Father and son exchanged anxious glances. They looked

like two men holding on to a life raft that had a slow leak. What little they had to cling to was slowly slipping out of their grasp. Jade could smell their fear. It was sweet.

"Financially, you're ruined," she told them. "In a few months your plant will close down for lack of operating capital. You won't be able to intimidate people with the threat of firing them, because TexTile will provide jobs with better working conditions and far better pay. I'll campaign for an honest man to take over Hutch's sheriff's office. Your days as dictator of Palmetto are over, Ivan."

She looked at Neal. "You don't have the power to hurt people anymore. Your charm was exhausted a long time ago. I never thought you had any."

He moved like a striking snake and caught her arm in a bone-crushing grip. "I can still claim the kid. That would give you plenty of misery."

She worked her arm free, flinging him off. "I say again, the only way you can claim Graham is to plead guilty to a rape charge."

Neal snickered. "Whatever the statute of limitations is, it must have expired by now."

"In which case, I would file a civil suit against you. And I would, if you pushed me to it, no matter what scandal it might raise. You see, Neal, I didn't believe it was possible to send you to prison for what you did, simply because I didn't want to expose Graham to the truth. Now that you've forced me to reveal it to him, that's no longer a deterrent. Go near him once more," she threatened coldly, "and you go to jail for rape."

"It would be your word against mine," he sneered. "You could never prove it."

Jade opened her handbag and withdrew a videotape.

She held it up to them. "This has been in my safe ever since I came back to Palmetto. There's a copy of it in a safe deposit box here in Palmetto and another in a bank in New York, which only my attorney has access to. It's painful to watch. I hope I'll never have to use it, but don't think for a minute that I won't if you force me to."

Neal applauded drolly. "Good act, Jade. I'm shaking in my shoes with anticipation. What's on the tape?"

"Lamar."

Myrajane gave a soft, injured cry.

"He recorded it a few days before he died. At Lamar's request, his companion sent it to me after his death. It's self-explanatory, but, to paraphrase, he's full of remorse for what he, along with Hutch and you, did to me. He confesses to his crime—your crime, Neal.

"As a dying man, he begs my forgiveness and fears for his immortal soul. He claims that night haunted him for the remainder of his life. It's extremely effective. No one who sees it could doubt that he's telling the truth."

She set the videotape on the coffee table and turned to Myrajane. "What they've done to you today is characteristically reprehensible. They used you. You need never have known about this.

"But even though you do, you won't lay claim to Graham because you didn't even love the son you had, Mrs. Griffith. You made Lamar weak and timid and easily manipulated, just as he was on the night Neal suggested that they take turns raping me. That's why I don't feel bad for buying your family's estate for my company. It will be fully restored and occupied, but not by a Cowan."

Myrajane's wizened face was puckered up like a drawstring purse. "Breeding tells," she said waspishly.

"I pray not, Mrs. Griffith. Not in my son's case anyway," Jade said softly.

Turning her back to the woman, she regarded Ivan, who sat wheezing in his wheelchair, his dignity and power as ravaged as his body. She dismissed him as unworthy of comment, which was the greatest insult she could hand him.

Looking at Neal, she said, "Claim my son and you'll go to prison, Neal. Mess with me again, and I'll file a civil suit against you for what you did to me, and to Gary. Your crime will finally come to light and you'll be punished for it. I advise you to cut your losses now.

"When I came back to Palmetto, I planned on sending you to prison, and I could have. With this tape, I could have. But in the last few months I've realized that there are other things more important than punishing you... and far more rewarding. I have a new life, a new love, and my son. They are at the center of my world now, not vengeance. From here on, I want to look ahead, not back.

"For fifteen years, my life has been focused on you." She said the last word with a contemptuous smirk. "You're not worth another second's thought. You're finished, and that's enough. It's over."

"The hell it is. I'm not afraid of your threats. You don't scare me, bitch."

"Oh yes I do, Neal," she calmly replied. "I'm your worst nightmare—someone who has absolutely no fear of you."

She took one last look at them, then turned and walked from the room. She moved down the hallway of the house, where the first signs of decay and decline were subtle, but undeniably there. The Patchetts had seen their day.

And Jade had had hers.

As she emerged from the house, she smiled at Dillon and Graham, who were impatiently waiting for her beside the pickup. Graham ran to her, obviously concerned. Knowing the truth hadn't affected his love for her. Now that the facts of his conception had been brought to light, she was relieved of the burdensome secret.

"Mom, what happened?"

"I told them that if they bothered you again, they would be sorry."

"That's all?" he asked, somewhat disappointed.

"Essentially."

He looked at her with consternation. "You should've told me about it."

"Perhaps I should have, Graham."

"Didn't you think I'd understand?"

"It wasn't that. I was trying to protect you. I didn't want you to think any less of yourself because of what your father did—whoever he was."

"Dillon says I'm my own person. I don't need to know which one of them fathered me."

"You're Graham Sperry," she said emotionally, touching his cheek. "That's all the certainty I need."

"Me, too."

"And just so you'll know, I went to see Hutch before he died. Rather than asking you to be an organ donor, he refused even to consider it. You shouldn't feel any guilt over that."

He glanced toward the house. "Those Patchetts...I wish you had let Dillon and me beat them up."

Smiling, she hugged him and looked at Dillon over his shoulder. "I appreciate the offer."

Dillon leaned forward and softly kissed her mouth. "You're one hell of a woman."

"As of last night...thanks to you."

His wide mustache curved into a smile. "Let's go home."

They rode with the windows rolled down, along the highway that was flat and narrow, bordered by live oaks bearded with moss and tall pines that pointed toward heaven.

"You know what my father used to say to me, Graham?"

"Grandpa Sperry?"

"Uh-huh. He used to say, 'Don't ever be afraid, Jade.' I thought he was talking about dying. Today, it occurred to me that he meant something else. He was telling me not to be afraid to live. Dying is easy when you compare it to living. Mama couldn't stand her life, so she ran away from it. Daddy didn't have the courage to live at all. I do."

With youthful resilience and restlessness, Graham was fiddling with the dials on the radio, not really listening.

Dillon, however, had heard and understood every word. He reached across the seat and swept the tear off her cheek. It was the first tear she had shed in fifteen years. She kissed it from his thumb and rested her cheek in his palm.

When they arrived at her house, she told Graham, "Tell Cathy that everything is all right and that we'll be back in time for dinner."

"Where are you going?"

"Dillon and I have an errand to run."

"Where to? I want to go."

"You're not invited."

"You just want to be by yourselves so you can kiss and stuff."

"Out!"

Graham, giving Dillon a man-to-man grin, climbed out. Dillon said, "Set up the chess board. We'll play after supper." Graham smiled and dashed toward the house. "He came through it unscathed, Jade."

"Yes. Thank God," she whispered.

"Maybe. Mostly thanks to you."

She waited until Graham had cleared the front door before turning to Dillon. "I want you to take me there." He didn't need to ask where she wanted to go, only how to get there. She gave him directions.

As the landscape slipped past, she realized how little she resembled the naïve girl who had driven the same road with her best friend on a cold February evening. Nor was she any longer the determined woman who had deftly navigated the business world like a halfback running full out on the gridiron. She had already scored and no longer had to prove herself.

The two facets of Jade Sperry were merging into one. Like the ingredients of a bouillabaisse, the separate elements of her personality were simmering together. It was an odd mixture, unique in texture and flavor, one she was gradually acquiring a taste for.

After years of driving herself toward one goal, she was back where she had begun. The townsfolk who remembered her no longer regarded her as the girl who had left cloaked in scandal. They treated her with the respect befitting what she was today. Those who had never known her regarded her as a heroine who was doing great things for their community.

All that Jade had convinced herself she hated, she was surprised to find was actually dear to her—like low-country cooking and small-town life, like summer air that was too heavy to inhale and soft breezes that were redolent with intoxicating floral perfumes and the seminal scent of seawater.

The region couldn't be blamed for the few bad people it had bred. Businesswoman, mother, friend, lover—whatever else she was, she was a woman of the South. Her heart beat in rhythm to its ponderous pace.

The tire tracks leading off the highway were overgrown. No one had been there in a long time. Jade liked to think no one had been there since that night. The banks of the channel looked different in the daylight. The soft slapping sound of the water wasn't sinister. There were no frightening shadows or furtive movements in the darkness.

Dillon patiently stood nearby while Jade wandered around, remembering... forgetting. At last she came to stand in front of him.

"Make love to me, Dillon."

"Here?"

"Yes."

"Why?"

"I don't want to remember this place for the rest of my life as the scene of the rape. Whenever I do, all the degradation and anger comes back. I want to remember it while it's warm, and the sun is shining, and I'm with the man I love."

He pushed his fingers up into her hair. "I want you to love me. But are you sure it's me you love, and not what I did for you?"

"I started loving you when I thought I could never express it. And if I never could have, I still would have loved you." She laid her hands on his cheeks. "I love *you*. The love-making is a bonus."

Sighing her name, he pulled her against him. His arms went around her, strong and embracing. Their mouths came together in a passionate exchange of physical desire and soul-bursting love. They undressed each other, dropping articles of clothing into the grass. Their hands rediscovered and aroused. He lifted her breasts to his mouth and left their centers raised and flushed. She fondled the warm heaviness of his sex.

Jade lay down in the grass and pulled him down beside her. "This way."

He knelt between her thighs and gradually lowered himself on top of her. "If you don't like it, tell me to stop," he whispered.

"Love me, Dillon."

He entered slowly, sinking into her by measured degrees. He made each stroke an individual act of love, almost withdrawing before burying himself inside her again. Each time he filled her was so thrilling, she began raising her hips to meet his slow thrusts. He escalated the tempo. Instinctively, Jade repositioned her legs. Her hands smoothed over his back to his buttocks and drew him closer, tighter, deeper.

When they climaxed, Jade arched her back and neck, exposing them to his lips and his hoarsely whispered vows of love and commitment.

She drew his beloved face into the hollow of her neck. Stroking his hair, she looked through cleansing tears into the sun and felt its warm rays on her smile.

About the Author

Sandra Brown is the author of sixty-three *New York Times* bestsellers, including most recently *Mean Streak*, *Deadline*, *Low Pressure*, *Lethal*, *Rainwater*, and *Tough Customer*. There are over 80 million copies of her books in print worldwide, and her work has been translated into thirty-four languages. In 2008, the International Thriller Writers Association named Brown its Thriller Master, the organization's highest honor. She has served as president of Mystery Writers of America and holds an honorary doctorate of humane letters from Texas Christian University. She lives in Texas.

#1 *New York Times* bestselling author Sandra Brown delivers a heart-pounding story of survival that turns the age-old question "Does the end justify the means?" on its head.

Please see the next page for a preview of

Mean Streak

Emory hurt all over. It hurt even to breathe.

The foggy air felt full of something invisible but sharp, like ice crystals or glass shards. She was underdressed. The raw cold stung her face where the skin was exposed. It made her eyes water, requiring her to blink constantly to keep the tears from blurring her vision and obscuring her path.

A stitch had developed in her side. It clawed continually, grabbed viciously. The stress fracture in her right foot was sending shooting pains up into her shin.

But owning the pain, running through it, overcoming it, was a matter of self-will and discipline. She'd been told she possessed both. In abundance. To a fault. But this was what all the difficult training was for. She could do this. She had to.

Push on, Emory. Place one foot in front of the other. Eat up the distance one yard at a time.

How much farther to go?

God, please not much farther.

Refueled by determination and fear of failure, she picked up her pace.

Then, from the deep shadows of the encroaching woods came a rustling sound, followed by a shift of air directly behind her. Her heart clutched with a foreboding of disaster to which she had no time to react before sky-rockets of pain exploded inside her skull.

Does it hurt this much?" Dr. Emory Charbonneau pointed to a drawing of a child's face contorted with pain, large teardrops dripping from the eyes. "Or like this?" She pointed to another in the series of caricatures, where a frowning face illustrated moderate discomfort.

The three-year-old girl pointed to the worst of the two.

"I'm sorry, sweetie." Emory inserted the otoscope into her right ear. The child began to scream. As gently as possible, and talking to her soothingly, Emory examined her ears. "Both are badly infected," she reported to the girl's frazzled mother.

"She's been crying since she got up this morning. This is the second earache this season. I couldn't get in to see you with the last one, so I took her to an emergency center. The doctor there prescribed meds, she got over it, now it's back."

"Chronic infections can cause hearing loss. They should be avoided, not just treated when they occur. You might consider taking her to a pediatric ENT."

"I've tried. None are accepting new patients."

"I can get her in with one of the best." It wasn't a misplaced boast. Emory was confident that any one of several colleagues would take a patient that she referred. "Let's give this infection six weeks to heal up completely, then I'll set her up with an appointment. For now, I'll give her an antibiotic along with an antihistamine to clear up the fluid behind the eardrums. You can give her a children's analgesic for the pain, but as soon as the meds kick in, that should decrease.

"Don't push food on her, but keep her hydrated. If she's not better in a few days, or if her fever spikes, call the number on this card. I'm going away for the weekend, but another doctor is covering for me. I doubt you'll have an emergency, but if you do, you'll be in excellent hands until I get back."

"Thank you, Dr. Charbonneau."

She gave the mother a sympathetic smile. "A sick child is no fun for anybody. Try to get some rest yourself."

"I hope you're going someplace fun for the weekend."

"I'm doing a twenty-mile run."

"That sounds like torture."

She smiled. "That's the point."

Outside the examination room, Emory filled out the prescription form and finished her notes in the patient file. As she handed it over to the office assistant who checked out patients, the young woman said, "That was your last of the day."

"Yes, and I'm on my way out."

"Did you notify the hospital?"

She nodded. "And the answering service. I'm officially signed out for the weekend. Are Drs. Butler and James with patients?"

"They are. And both have several in the waiting room."

"I hoped to see them before I left, but I won't bother them."

"Dr. Butler left you a note."

She passed her a sheet from a monogrammed notepad. *Break a leg. Or is that what you say to a marathon runner?* Emory smiled as she folded the note and put it in her lab coat pocket.

The receptionist said, "Dr. James asked me to tell you to watch out for bears."

Emory laughed. "Do their patients know they're a couple of clowns? Tell them I said good-bye."

"Will do. Have a good run."

"Thanks. See you Monday."

"Oh, I almost forgot. Your husband called and said he was leaving work and would be at home to see you off."

"Emory?"

"In here." As Jeff walked into the bedroom she zipped up her duffel bag and, with a motion that was intentionally defiant, pulled it off the bed and slid the strap onto her shoulder.

"You got my message? I didn't want you to leave before I got here to say good-bye."

"I want to get ahead of Friday afternoon traffic."

"Good idea." He looked at her for a moment, then said, "You're still mad."

"Aren't you?"

"I'd be lying if I said I wasn't."

Last night's argument was still fresh. Words shouted in anger and resentment seemed to be reverberating off the bedroom walls even now, hours after they'd gone to bed, lying back to back, each nursing hostility that had been simmering for months and had finally come to a boil.

He said, "Do I at least get points for wanting to see you off?"

"That depends."

"On?"

"On whether or not you're hoping to talk me out of going." He sighed and looked away, and she said, "That's what I thought."

"Emory—"

"You should have stayed and finished out your day at the office. Because I'm going, Jeff. In fact, even if I hadn't planned this distance run for tomorrow, I'd still want to take some time for myself. A night spent away from each other will give us a chance to cool off. If the run wears me out, I may stay up there tomorrow night, too."

"One night or two won't change my mind. This compulsion of yours—"

"This is where we started last night. I'm not going to rehash the quarrel now."

Her training schedule for an upcoming marathon had been the subject that sparked the argument, but she feared that more substantive issues had been the underlying basis for it. The marathon wasn't their problem; the marriage was.

Which is why she wanted so badly to get away and think. "I wrote down the name of the motel where I'll be tonight." As they walked past the kitchen bar, she tipped her head down toward the sheet of paper lying on it.

"Call me when you get there. I'll want to know you made it safely."

"All right." She slid on her sunglasses and opened the back door. "Good-bye."

"Emory?"

Poised on the threshold, she turned. He leaned down and brushed his lips across hers. "Be careful."

"Jeff? Hi. I made it."

The two-hour drive from Atlanta had left Emory tired, but most of the fatigue was due to stress, not the drive itself. The traffic on northbound Interstate 85 had thinned out considerably about an hour outside the city, when she took the cutoff highway that angled northwest. She'd arrived at her destination before dusk, which had made navigating the unfamiliar town a bit easier. She was already tucked into bed at the motel, but tension still claimed the space between her shoulder blades.

Not wanting to exacerbate it, she'd considered not calling Jeff. Last night's quarrel had been a skirmish. She sensed a much larger fight in their future. Along every step of the way, she wanted to fight fairly, not peevishly.

Besides, if the shoe had been on the other foot, if he had left on a road trip and didn't call as promised, she would have been worried about his safety.

"Are you already in bed?" he asked.

"About to turn out the light. I want to get an early start in the morning."

"How's the motel?"

"Modest, but clean."

"I get worried when clean is an itemized amenity." He paused as though waiting for her to chuckle. When she didn't, he asked how the drive had been.

"All right."

"The weather?"

They were reduced to discussing the weather? "Cold.

But I planned on that. Once I get started, I'll warm up fast enough."

"I still think it's crazy."

"I've mapped out the course, Jeff. I'll be fine. Furthermore, I look forward to it."

It was much colder than she had anticipated.

She realized that the moment she stepped out of her car. Of course the overlook was at a much higher elevation than the town of Drakeland where she'd spent the night. The sun was up, but it was obscured by clouds that shrouded the mountain peaks.

A twenty-mile run up here would be a challenge.

As she went through her stretching routine, she assessed the conditions. Although cold, it was a perfect day for running. There was negligible wind. In the surrounding forest, only the uppermost branches of the trees were stirred by the breeze.

Her breath formed a plume of vapor that fogged up her sunglasses, so she pulled the funnel neck of her running jacket up over her mouth and nose as she consulted her map one final time.

The parking lot accommodated tourists who came for the nearby overlook. It also served as the hub for numerous hiking trails that radiated from it like the spokes of a wheel before branching off into winding paths that crisscrossed the crest of the mountain. The names of the particular trails were printed on arrow-shaped signposts.

She located the trail she'd chosen after carefully reviewing the map of the national park and researching it further online. She welcomed a challenge, but she wasn't foolhardy. If she wasn't certain she could make it to her turnaround point and back, she wouldn't be attempting it. Rather than being daunted by the inhospitable terrain, she was eager to take it on.

She locked her duffel bag in the trunk of her car and buckled on her fanny pack. Then she adjusted her headband, zeroed the timer on her wristwatch, pulled on her gloves, and set out.

VISIT US ONLINE AT

WWW.HACHETTEBOOKGROUP.COM

FEATURES:

OPENBOOK BROWSE AND
SEARCH EXCERPTS

•

AUDIOBOOK EXCERPTS AND PODCASTS

•

AUTHOR ARTICLES AND INTERVIEWS

•

BESTSELLER AND PUBLISHING
GROUP NEWS

•

SIGN UP FOR E-NEWSLETTERS

•

AUTHOR APPEARANCES AND TOUR
INFORMATION

•

SOCIAL MEDIA FEEDS AND WIDGETS

•

DOWNLOAD FREE APPS